Marcelle Bernst
worked as a jour
azine, the *Guard*
Mirror before wr
on nuns. She no
band, writer Er
Lili is her third novel.

By the same author

Sadie
Salka

Nuns (non-fiction)

MARCELLE BERNSTEIN

Lili

GRAFTON BOOKS

A Division of the Collins Publishing Group

LONDON GLASGOW
TORONTO SYDNEY AUCKLAND

Grafton Books
A Division of the Collins Publishing Group
8 Grafton Street, London W1X 3LA

Published by Grafton Books 1989

First published in Great Britain by
Victor Gollancz Ltd 1988

Copyright © Marcelle Bernstein 1988

ISBN 0-586-20516-0

Printed and bound in Great Britain by
Collins, Glasgow

Set in Century Schoolbook

For Charlotte

Chapter 1

They had known for two long days that something
was wrong. Even in the nursery, right at the top of
the tall house in Sloane Square, they could hear
hurried footsteps on the floors below, the muffled
click of doors and always the whispers. When Nanny
took them out for their walk there was a strange
smell near their parents' bedroom that made them
feel giddy. Once the door of the study was open and
before they were hurried past, they glimpsed in the
half-light of the drawn blinds their father's figure
slumped in sleep across the table, a bottle and a
glass beside him. Samuel da Costa was a doctor, a
man of the most precise and regular habits: his two
little daughters had never seen him other than
benign and authoritative, in control of their lives
and his own. They were too small to understand but
they knew the exhausted and hopeless man in the
darkened room frightened them. Beatrice, at seven
the older by eighteen months, did not change her
expression, only began to hum under her breath and
held her sister's hand more tightly, dragging a little
behind her. Lilith's face crumpled in dismay and
tears welled in her dark eyes and the nurse knelt to
comfort her. But Lilith would not be comforted, and
pressed to the woman's familiar, white-aproned
bosom, she called wildly for her mother.

That was on the first day, in the morning. No one
had referred to the incident again. Dr da Costa
appeared briefly several times to kiss them good-
night or to give them a quick word. He seemed quite

himself again and Beatrice smiled composedly at him. Only Lilith saw the way his eyelid flickered at one corner and sensed the nervous strain so tightly checked, and though she controlled herself in his presence ('Be good for your papa now,' the nurse had warned them), she flung herself on the floor when he had gone and refused to be coaxed by the promise of her favourite seed cake for tea.

On the second day the children were wakened before dawn by the sound of someone sobbing. Their nurse came in and lit the gas and by its light sat with them, joking about the flat metal curlers in her sparse hair and telling them the housemaid had toothache and was to visit the dentist that day. Lilith asked Dorcas when she served their breakfast which tooth hurt, and the girl looked bewildered and then, prompted by a look from the nurse, said she was better now, thanks be. The rest of the morning was strange, too, for the children were taken to visit Aunt Florence, who stroked Beatrice's hair and called them poor little mites, so that after a while Lilith took Beatrice by the hand and led her firmly to a far corner to play.

It rained so hard that afternoon – although it was early in May – that they could not go for their walk, and Dorcas came up to light a fire for them against the damp chill. They stared out of their window, inhaling the heavy scent of wet lilacs in the garden below them, a perfume that somehow made Lilith feel solemn and sad at the same time. They watched people hurrying by on the glossy pavements, the women grasping their hats tightly and lifting their skirts out of puddles, the men hung about with packages and umbrellas. When they got bored with inventing stories for these people – or rather, when Lilith grew bored, for she told the stories while

Beatrice listened – the nurse got down their favourite toy, the one their parents had given them last year as a Chanukah gift, for the children's festival.

It was a lilliputian garden with lawns of green velvet and gnarled apple trees carved from wood, brilliant paper leaves glued to the branches, hung with fruit of scarlet wax. Beatrice wouldn't touch the apples, they looked to her like drops of blood, but she loved the flowerbeds with their green wax stalks and jewelled flower heads, and the dovecote full of china birds with tails like fans. She was playing with the birds, singing one of her nonsense songs, while Lilith walked a tiny wooden lady across the velvet lawn. The two children had shut themselves off from the unhappiness that hung in the air all round them, had made themselves safe in the familiar, diminutive setting.

And then their father came into the room, and put his arms around them both, and told them their mother had died. For a long, bleak minute Lilith stared at the garden. It was all exactly as it had been before her father had shattered their little world. The grass was still as green, the flowers as bright. With a wail she buried her face in her father's shoulder and sobbed as if her heart would break.

Beside her, Beatrice stood very still. Her expression did not change, her face remained calm and sweet, her blue gaze fixed upon the white china dove in her hand. But she had stopped singing.

She never spoke again. And the only person who ever heard the soft humming, the only sound left to her, was Lilith.

Chapter 2

Lilith loved Beatrice more than anyone else on earth. She loved the feel of fairy-pale hair when she brushed it for her sister in the evenings, and the cool touch of her hand. For hour after hour, in the happy time when their mother was alive, she would listen to Beatrice singing. Her favourite – the one she sang at night as she was going to sleep – was a fragment only, endlessly repeated until it had a mesmeric quality. 'Cuckoo! Cherry-tree! Catch a bird and give him to me.' Sometimes the words were Hebrew: 'Adon olam asher malach . . .' Others were pure nonsense: 'Zumba, zumba, zim zim zim', and the tune to which she sang changed according to her mood, though it always had a foreign lilt that made Lilith think of hot sunlight. Beatrice had a voice pure and high as a dormouse: sometimes she sang so softly Lilith could hardly hear and caught the funny little words like caresses on her skin.

Lilith's perceptions of the world were rarely mental. They were physical. The feel of rain on her hair, or sun on her bare arms, the prickle of groomed grass on the soles of her feet when she disobeyed the adults and slipped off her shoes and stockings to run barefoot in the dusky garden. She was intensely aware of the sensations that living brought her and relished them like a greedy child with some delicacy; the very anticipation of the texture of chiffon velvet or moleskin, silk marocain or mousseline taffeta were enough to make her fingers tingle with pleasure, and after they had been sent to bed she would urge Beatrice to creep downstairs to savour her mother's dresses hanging in the wardrobe. Lilith was not yet six that rainy May day when Beatrice was struck dumb, and for years afterwards her strongest memory of Bella was the softness of those clothes with their smoky scent of sandalwood, the little whalebones she could feel round her mother's waist and collar when she sat on her knee. Her father's clothes, when she ran to him to be hugged, were harsh against her face and the woollen suitings scratched, the starched shirtfronts were unyielding. His smell was different, too, the bayrum he used on his hair contrasting with the Lysol she could always detect on his hands, even when he had not been in the surgery for a day.

Lilith lived through her senses, and it was this single factor which more than any other determined her relationship with her sister. Because Beatrice said so little, they might have ceased to communicate, had words ever been their medium. But since the beginning, words had not mattered, and long before their mother died the two little girls were inseparable. Bella used to find them curled together at night and firmly disentangle them, putting each into her own bed, but in the morning there they would be once more, sleeping like kittens, limbs entwined. They always walked hand in hand, even inside the house, Lilith leading Beatrice, for the older child was shy, reluctant always to enter a room first, slow to speak even to those she knew well. She had a watchful, wary quality, like a little creature that knows itself to be easy prey, and the more assertive and decisive Lilith became, the more Beatrice stood gratefully in her wake.

The two of them amused their father (who called Beatrice 'my little shadow') and worried their mother, who tried by every means she knew to make her elder daughter more assured. She told her how pretty she was, how everyone loved her, how much they admired her. It made not one iota of difference to Beatrice, who simply gazed at her from beneath the cloud of silvery hair, as if the words were not meant for her. But it confirmed what little Lilith already knew: that Beatrice was, of the two of them, the more favoured. She felt already that Beatrice was special, apart, and her mother's words were no more than a confirmation that her sister's moon-tint hair and pale skin were perfection and she dismissed her own gleaming brown curls and vivid dark eyes as ordinary and pedestrian. The two children would be brought downstairs at tea-time when their mother had guests, wearing white dresses edged with lace, to be given lumps of sugar soaked in cream and fussed over. And always it was Beatrice who was the centre of attention, turning on the enchanted watchers a limpid blue look from eyes set wide apart in a face of such porcelain purity that no one noticed how that perfect mouth smiled, smiled but did not speak. And the smaller child beside her, always holding her hand, her thick hair curling absurdly all over her head, her pudgy little waist wide beneath its satin sash, merited affectionate looks but not the adoration that was accorded Beatrice.

Beatrice's flawless features were invariably, irrespective of the circumstances, composed. Lilith in contrast revealed everything instantly, emotions passing across her mobile face with transparent openness. Her body, too, reflected her feelings. In play she used exuberantly large movements. Rebuked, her shoulders hunched and she grew angular in a moment, with spiky little elbows and needle-sharp knees. But she never behaved like that with Beatrice, about whom she was always fiercely protective, as though their roles were reversed and she the elder sibling. She ran her sister's life for her, telling her what to put on each day, what she liked to eat, when she was tired.

The pattern had developed even before their mother's death, for Bella da Costa had been ailing for years. She had become anxious about Beatrice, their first child, before she was a year old. She had seen a change come over the baby in the space of a few days, had noted fearfully how she ceased to give smiling recognition to familiar faces, would no longer look into her mother's eyes but turned her head away. She would lie for hours staring intently at the sides of her crib. She never smiled, never crowed or shouted. She moved her limbs as all babies do, but without any vigour. At first Samuel had dismissed his wife's worries, assuring her that Beatrice was delicate, but Bella had known better. She struggled to teach the little girl her first words, but she never received the longed-for response. Beatrice listened, and clearly understood, yet she gave nothing back.

On the last day of 1887 their second child had been born. Where her sister was silvery, this new daughter had locks of almost black hair and opened great dark eyes which caused the midwife to suck in her breath sharply: in thirty years she had delivered enough babies to know that for the first weeks every child's eyes were blue. She shook her head and held her tongue. There must be bad blood somewhere. But Bella and Samuel were enchanted with this odd little creature and named her Lilith. Of the night.

At first their happiness over Lilith overlaid any

13

anxiety Bella felt for Beatrice. The child was developing some speech, but that only served to increase her mother's worries. Beatrice would find a word that evidently pleased her – 'glove' was one, another was 'Plaintain', the name of the elderly man who looked after the garden – and repeat them to herself endlessly, perhaps for hours at a time. She always insisted on referring to herself as 'you'. She could not grasp the concept of the pronoun 'I'. And when she had reached the age of five and still her eyes were cool and clear and unconcerned as a lovely animal's, Bella lost all hope. Even Samuel, a distinguished physician, could do nothing for his wife. She suffered from lassitude and loss of appetite. She could not sleep at night and was frequently feverish. Because the cause was in her mind and not her body, she grew slowly worse.

In the disturbed days that followed his wife's death, Dr da Costa scarcely noticed that his elder daughter had ceased to speak, for she had said little enough before. Lilith recognized the change but took it with the easy acceptance of childhood. When her father did become aware of Beatrice's apparently self-enforced silence, he at first assumed it to be her way of showing grief: certainly she had neither cried nor expressed any violent emotion at any time, so much so that at first he had wondered whether she understood what had happened. When the days had become weeks and then months, when all attempts and pleas to make her speak had failed to produce a sound, he employed a diction teacher, who struggled in vain daily for two months without managing to coax a word out of the child, and in the end told Dr da Costa that in his view the case was hopeless.

Only then did Dr da Costa tell himself that the deeper the sorrow, the less voice it has. He was able finally to accept that his exquisite Beatrice had become, to all intents and purposes, a mute.

This made no difference at all to Lilith. She and Beatrice had become indivisible after their mother's death, and had she lived, Bella would have seen how Lilith began to develop a strong personality and a vivacity, as if in compensation for Beatrice's quiescent state. As she had since babyhood, the younger child chattered endlessly, telling Beatrice everything in monologues which neither expected nor received an answer. Strangers meeting them were charmed by the closeness, not realizing that Beatrice, for all her ravishing prettiness, was flawed: that the perfect body was a lie. Alone, the elder girl would have had no existence: she became Lilith's shadow, her reflections, the echo of her voice. And now only Lilith ever heard the sole sound Beatrice made, the soft and tuneless humming which was all that remained of the nonsense songs.

Samuel da Costa, observing with love and pain, saw her closed face and aloof, averted gaze; noted with a pang the odd repetitive flick flick flick of her fingers and the obsessions with the precise manner in which food had to be placed before her, and the same few clothes had always to be worn. Very rarely she would react with excessive fury if change was forced upon her – a new dress, for example, a winter coat she had not seen before – and then she would become violently agitated. She would flail her arms wildly, her mouth open in despair, twisting from his attempts to hold and reassure her, never uttering a sound. That seemed to him to make it so much worse, that terrible mute misery she went through, it tore him to see it, so that it was all he could do to summon his skill to calm her. He would catch hold of her hands, and speak softly, trying to get through

15

to that dark place where it hurt her, knowing that the meaning of the words mattered less than the sound of them.

It was almost always Lilith who dealt best with these disturbances. Her father tried to keep her away at first, not wanting to expose so young a child to her sister's inexplicable anguish, but summoned one day to the nursery he found that Lilith – then just seven years old – had coped where the nurse could not, had taken Beatrice into a dark corner and pushed her down into a crouching position, and had then wrapped her arms round her sister, her cheek against Beatrice's back, holding her tight. Dr da Costa, watching from the doorway, saw that Lilith was rocking gently forwards and back, and heard the crooning voice she was using – the voice her mother had used to assuage childish pains. 'There, there, bay-*bee*, there, there, bay-*bee* . . .' on and on, until Beatrice softened in her embrace and became still and passive.

That night, as he had so many other times, Dr da Costa re-read the pages in which he had painstakingly noted Beatrice's symptoms, but even his knowledge gave him no clue as to their cause. In vain he had consulted his colleagues and read all the new theories. He had followed up every course that suggested itself to no avail.

In the end, it was the children who knew best.

The Sloane Square house was tall, of reddish brick with narrow Gothic windows, decorated with the heads of curious gargoyles. It had been chosen for Dr da Costa's practice rather than his or his wife's preference, for it served both the moneyed area running towards Knightsbridge and the working class cottages which sprawled down to the river and

Fulham. Behind the square were new buildings, courts of flats, built to house the poor in decent conditions. Dr da Costa believed good health should be within the reach of all, and he as willingly answered a call to the coal-heaver's child suffering from convulsions as to the sickbed of the local magistrate. The poorer the patient, the less he charged (frequently asking nothing at all), and if his wealthy clientele suspected they were supporting his philanthropy, he was so good a doctor they kept their thoughts to themselves rather than offend him.

It was his philanthropy which prevented Samuel da Costa from ever being a wealthy man despite his skills, and it was another reason for the Sloane Square house: it had been cheap. Bella Caro had it as part of her dowry, and the couple were always promising themselves they would remodel the house to make it less dark, but they never did: there were always too many demands on their income to allow it. So all the narrow passages with their brown dados remained, and inconvenient corners with unexpected steps. In the fashion of the time – they were married in 1883 – the tall windows were hung with dark velvet, like the doorways and the fireplaces. Ferns and ivy and pampas grass flourished amidst bronzes and Oriental pots, and everywhere there were books: in glass-fronted cases, standing slightly askew in a wheeled table, the top covered with a piece of damask, heaped on occasional chairs, upon sofas and even, despite Bella's efforts, on the floor.

Their two little girls relished the clutter of objects, furniture and pictures. Lilith, especially, spent hours staring at the stuffed humming birds under their great glass dome in the dining room, run her fingers along the furry velvet bobbles which edged the runner on the mantelpiece, rubbing her cheek gently against the flanks of the bronze lion crouched in the hallway.

Beatrice and Lilith used the corridors and hallways to play, although active games were discouraged by their nurse in deference after their mother's death. For a month and more they were restrained, then gradually Lilith's high spirits asserted themselves and Samuel da Costa, in his study or his consulting room, realized how much he had missed the scamperings and shrieks from above. But as always it was Lilith's voice he heard, urging her sister on, and he listened in vain for Beatrice to reply, or laugh. The child was showing no signs of improvement and in his rare moments of leisure he grew increasingly anxious about her.

One afternoon, after a particularly tiring visit to a young man suffering from pleurisy, he came home earlier than usual. It was some time before five, and the afternoon sun slanted over the garden and lit the far corners of the rooms. Dr da Costa went upstairs to wash his hands and face. Coming out of his bedroom on slippered feet he caught sight of Beatrice at the far end of the hallway.

Something in her movements arrested his attention and he focused on her more carefully, experiencing the customary little drag of the heart he always felt for her.

Beatrice was dancing. Very slowly, her face serene as ever, she moved forward and back, her arms held above her head, pirouetting gravely in the sunlight that shafted through the stained glass window above her head. The rich, subdued colours of the formalized flowers lit up her hair and skin so that she gleamed like some fragile treasure.

Dr da Costa held his breath, almost unable to accept the evidence of his eyes: just for a moment he let himself believe that this child somehow had been restored, made whole . . . and then his vision accustomed itself to the sunlight and he saw that behind her, Lilith was dancing in the shadows, and it became obvious that Beatrice was simply imitating her steps, the way she held her arms and hands. (Copied in turn, though he did not know this, from the porcelain ballerina in her dress of gilt who twirled endlessly on top of an old German musical box in the nursery.)

The ache of disappointment was dispelled when he became aware that the odd little melody he could hear was the humming of the two children: Schubert, was it? He could tell that Beatrice was not moving in time to this music, but no matter. She was trying to do so, making the endeavour, and that was enough. It had not occurred to him that music might be the key to unlock her curious little mind, that dancing could be the way to reach out to her.

Within two days, he had engaged a dancing teacher.

Madame Cotin was an Englishwoman, though she would never admit to this. A lifetime of dancing allowed her to deceive herself that she had not been born in Harwich after all, but had spent her childhood in a Russian town and been accepted at the age of eleven into the Imperial Ballet School of St Petersburg: she had accordingly changed her name from Edith Hart to Olga (the only Russian name she knew) Hartski, and assumed with the name an accent that owed a good deal to her imagination. Her career had been modest – she had danced with the Drury Lane Theatre as a young girl, gone on to Paris and Brussels. There she had met her husband, a flautist, and eventually moved with him to London. She had not danced for years and like many once-athletic people her body had collapsed softly in upon itself and had to be constrained by rigid corseting. She always wore black satin, the carved jet buttons on her bodice looking to the children like beady little eyes, and the smooth sheen of her clothes was matched by the glossy bun of dyed hair. She was a born teacher, tireless and disciplined, and her affection for her pupils was matched by her ambition for them: she longed to discover a little Taglioni, or a Fanny Elssler.

At first, warned by Dr da Costa of the difficulties they had had in teaching Beatrice anything, she merely sat down at the upright piano and played simple pieces, and watched how Beatrice listened: she noted that the nervous fingers moved more quietly to slow music, and the blue eyes became dreamy. Before the long mirror Dr da Costa had installed for her, she showed Beatrice how to stand, fingertips touching lightly, feet in first position.

'Now,' she said. 'You try. Like this, you see?' She coaxed the child's reluctant limbs into the right position. Disinterested, Beatrice let her hands fall.

'No, dear. Try again. Like this – and *so*.' Again, Beatrice was docile but unresponsive as a rag doll. Madame Cotin watched her face, then said, 'We'll see if Lilith can manage this, shall we?' She turned to the younger child, only to find that Lilith had not waited to be shown a second time, but was already standing with the balls of her feet turned out, heels touching and forming a single line, her back straight, watching the teacher with expectant eyes. After a moment, Beatrice imitated her, clumsy but recognizably achieving the effect.

'Verrry good,' said Madame Cotin, rolling her r's

with vigour. 'Now spread your arms like this' – she demonstrated, palms horizontal – 'and place your feet apart. There you have the second position.' She waited for a moment. As before, Beatrice waited for Lilith to demonstrate for her, then assumed the pose in imitation of her sister.

By the end of half an hour Lilith had taken all five of the positions that are to dancing what scales are to the musician. Madame Cotin saw with interest that she quite naturally perfected her weight so that it was equally distributed, as though she was balanced by an invisible vertical line. Behind her, Beatrice had managed an approximation of her movements, though she looked by contrast ungainly.

'Would you like to make for me a little dance?' The teacher had asked Beatrice, but it was Lilith who replied, breathless, 'Oh, *please*.' The teacher nodded and seated herself at the piano. She started to play a wistful fragment of tune from the ballet *Coppelia*. At first she played slowly, nodding to herself with satisfaction as she saw Lilith respond to the sounds, her simple movements keeping time with the music. Then she played a little faster, and still Lilith's timing was exact. She stopped playing.

'Do you know this music, Lilith? Have you heard it before?' The child shook her head, leaving the teacher pondering the way in which her new pupil had given the odd impression that she was leading the melody on.

The little girl began to look forward to her dancing lessons. Twice a week Madame Cotin arrived at the house, and her appearance never failed to please Lilith: she liked the pretty band of fine lace the teacher pinned round her glossy hair to hold it flat, and the comfortable English slippers she always wore, with ribbon sewn to the velvet sides to hold the low heels in place as she demonstrated dance movements.

She now made a practice of showing Lilith the steps she wanted. Sometimes Beatrice would copy them easily, at other times she would try and then, discouraged, lose interest. But always Lilith would urge, 'Come on, Bee, do this, like me,' and do the steps again and again, until the older girl would finally manage to achieve them. It was an endless task, for Beatrice had no apparent memory, and with each lesson they seemed to start afresh as though the previous session had never taken place.

Sometimes, Madame Cotin would feel they were in fact making progress. Beatrice would take the steps more swiftly, with greater ease and sureness as though her body – if not her mind – was familiar with the routines. And then there would be a day when she could see that the girl inhabited a world all her own, when she would refuse even to attempt to dance, but crouch huddled, her limbs uncomfortably twisted, motionless for an hour or more. Only Lilith, she learned, could bring Beatrice out of one of these frightening catatonic episodes, and she would fan herself nervously with a sheet of music as she watched little Lilith holding her sister, crouched behind her – Beatrice could not bear at such times to see anyone's eyes – rocking her, rocking her, 'There, there, bay-*bee*, there, there, bay-*bee* . . .' until at last the stiff limbs would relax in response to that crooning voice, and Beatrice would roll over on the floor, limp and exhausted.

These occasional regressions upset the dancing teacher, but she did her best to hide it. Dr da Costa had warned her to expect them, though she had not anticipated how disturbing she would find the sight

22

of the child locked into herself. She had become genuinely fond of the girls even in the short time she had been with them, and she felt a sense of failure when Beatrice slipped out of control. But her disappointments were redressed by Lilith: the child had a natural understanding of music, an instinctive feel for dancing, that was quite outstanding. In all her years as a teacher, she had never come across a child with Lilith's innate ability.

As time went by Madame Cotin had a *barre* installed in the attic room where they practised. The lessons included *développés*, as Lilith learned how to unfold her legs slowly, with control. Her legs and feet grew stronger, the Achilles tendon became pliant and flexible. Her back was supple: she could twist from the waist upwards in *épaulement* without strain, bend sideways or backwards or simply turn her shoulders with complete grace, changing the appearance of a position as the change of expression shades the human voice.

She learned how to hold her arms and hands in *ports de bras*, so that they never showed strain, the fingers gently together, thumb falling slightly in to the palm of her hand, elbows held up but never stiff, so that the line from shoulders to fingertips was pleasing. She learned the five positions of the head and how to position her body in the three main poses of *croisé, effacé* and *écarté*, describing the crossed, open and separated legs.

As Lilith progressed, Beatrice fell more and more behind her. So Madame Cotin introduced into her lessons some radical changes. She had been considering the possibility of abandoning formal teaching, and giving Beatrice lessons which would be fashioned especially for her needs, and these she developed with Lilith. Using *pas de bourrée*, little running steps which took their name from an old French dance, weight moving quickly from foot to foot, as a link, she inserted simple poses so that Beatrice was able to follow Lilith through an entire series of movements. The first half-dozen sessions with the new system showed little improvement, but then somehow she began to get the idea. Her movements were still jerky and erratic, but the noticeable gap that had formerly been present between her realization of what she had to do and her enactment of it – as though her limbs were beyond her own control – lessened.

Dr da Costa was pleased by her progress but cautiously so: he had discovered that Beatrice's development seemed to go forward one pace and back two. He went into the upper room during a lesson and watched her carefully, then recorded his observations meticulously as he had ever since he had acknowledged her mysterious ailment. Then he let fall his pen with a sigh: that Beatrice clearly had some sort of memory proved that her intellectual ability was probably near to normal. He found it harder to bear, knowing this, for it meant that she could probably comprehend her condition. Common sense and experience told him that her obdurate loss of speech was not a matter of her own choice, but dictated by something beyond her control. Even so, his heart ached for her inability to break out of her shell of silence, and for his own failure to help her do so.

He was aware it had never occurred to Lilith to pity her sister. She accepted the older girl's voice-lessness as quite natural, as she would have accepted that of a beloved cat. She could have told Samuel da Costa it did not signify lack of intelligence, for she and Beatrice communicated perfectly, though she could not have explained how they managed this.

It was Madame Cotin who described to Dr da Costa the way in which she had seen the two children 'talk' to each other. 'They use the language of the body,' she told him, 'almost like mime in ballet. I have never seen anything like it. Beatrice will do this' – dropping her head upon an upraised hand, pillowing her cheek – 'to mean she is tired. Or Lilith will do this, so' – and she fluttered her hands in front of her black satin skirt – 'and off they go into the garden. Lilith is so expressive, you must have seen this for yourself, that you can read on her face and in her carriage the meaning she wishes to convey.' She paused. 'You have in that child something quite extraordinary, you know.'

Dr da Costa, who had been musing, looked up in surprise.

'What do you mean, Madame?'

'Just what I say. She is so young yet she has an ability to make one feel emotions she herself can scarcely understand.'

Samuel da Costa said slowly, 'She has had a chequered childhood. She has seen too much for her age, been exposed to sorrows that should be foreign to a little girl. It is my fault.'

Madame Cotin shook her head. 'You misunderstand me, Doctor. I am not offering criticism. I am saying that Lilith has a rare talent, one that should be encouraged.'

He nodded, but she could tell that he was not impressed. Dancing, for him, was a pleasant accomplishment, nothing more. It was not to be taken seriously, except perhaps as a means to help develop Beatrice's mind. He was pleased that Lilith was doing well, as he was pleased when she received good reports from her governess for her lessons. He saw both as necessary groundwork for the accomplished woman he hoped she would one day become.

Madame Cotin, on the other hand, went back upstairs frowning to find Lilith jumping. She had been forbidden to do this, because the teacher did not consider she was ready yet for the muscular effort involved. Now, standing unnoticed for a moment in the doorway, she watched Lilith start with a series of *demi-pliés*, the small jumps where the impetus is from the feet. She began to jump higher, seemingly inexhaustible, and the astonished Madame Cotin saw the ease with which she controlled her body, so that she seemed literally to hover in the air as though she would never come down, before sinking back into a *demi-plié*. Again she achieved the bouncing rise, and again, landing each time with relaxed arms and her body poised.

'I should be extremely stern with you, Lilith.' The girl started at her teacher's voice when she had thought she was alone with Beatrice. 'But I am filled with amazement. And shall I tell you why?' The girl nodded. Madame Cotin patted her shoulder. 'Because I have only ever seen a dancer do that after much hard work. You have true *ballon*, you know? Like a ball.' She made an upward gesture with both palms. 'You give me the impression you will stay always in the air.'

Lilith laughed. 'It hurts my muscles, after,' she admitted ruefully. 'I ache and ache.' She rubbed the backs of her legs. The teacher fanned herself with a flustered hand.

' You mean you have done this before? Unknown to me?'

Lilith nodded, her lower lip caught between her

teeth as it dawned on her that she had done something wrong. 'I know you said I mustn't, but sometimes when I'm dancing by myself, the music *tells* me to jump and so ... please don't be angry. It makes me feel as though the air was holding me up.'

Madame Cotin sat down very suddenly. 'Come here,' she commanded. 'Stand in front of me.' She ran a practised hand down Lilith's legs, feeling her knees. There was no sign of swelling or strain, none of the tell-tale puffiness where incorrect landing could damage the tissues. 'How old are you now, Lilith? Almost eight? We must see what we can do.'

Over the following months, Madame Cotin chose for Lilith exercises which suited her stage of development. They were not ones she would normally have given to a child of that age. She had already mastered the rudiments of *barre* work on the wooden rail fixed to the wall, the *grands pliés*, bending her legs smoothly, feet in fourth and fifth position until her thighs were parallel with the floor before she rose again to straightened legs. The *battements* – *tendu, dégagé, fondu, grappé* – strengthened instep and thigh muscles, *en cloche* with straight legs swung the working leg forward and back, high in a pendulum movement. Now Madame Cotin added *grand battement*, the 'big beating' developing control of the whole leg, the limb raised forward, backward or sideways to hip height or – in Lilith's case – higher, starting and finishing in fifth position. Within days of learning this, she was able to execute it in the centre of the room, without the *barre* to steady her.

Just after Lilith had her eighth birthday, Madame Cotin approached Dr da Costa to ask his permission for his daughter to appear in a smoking concert. His immediate response was a refusal, but when she explained that it was to raise money for the Elizabeth Garrett Anderson dispensary for women and children in the Euston Road, he promised to consider it. In the meantime, the teacher told Lilith, whose eloquently pleading gaze her father could not resist. And so at 9.30 P.M. one Thursday evening – far later than she had ever been permitted to stay up before – she was in an improvised dressing room at the Grosvenor Club in Bond Street, dressed in white tulle, her hair braided round her ears, watching admiringly as the other 'artistes' – the duettists, the harpist with her black lace mittens, the comedienne and the sleight-of-hand performer – hurried past for their entrances. After Miss Eva Osborne had sung her *Plantation Songs* and Miss Verena Cholmley had recited 'I don't want to play in your yard', Madame Cotin took Lilith's hand, and led her to the side of the small stage. Mr Arthur Deane emitted the final, robust notes of the 'Yeoman's Wedding Song', took his bows and hurried past them, wiping the sweat off his upper lip with a none-too-clean handkerchief and giving Lilith an encouraging wink.

Almost before she realized what had happened, she found herself standing in front of an audience. It was a moment she had never envisaged: she had never even been inside a theatre. The harsh footlights dazzled her eyes so that she received only a blurred impression of black and white, shot with occasional colour and the shimmer of a jewel as the wearer moved. The high room was full of dark wood and red velvet, and the potent cigar smoke rising from the auditorium stung her eyes. To her right the pianist cleared his throat and Madame Cotin whispered, '*Now*, Lilith, *now*.'

The child took a step forward. The programme

read, *Miss Lilith da Costa. Danseuse aged eight years*, but she looked even younger, and a little murmur of approval ran through the watchers as the music began. It was Madame Cotin's choice, Tchaikovsky again, and the routine was not of conventional ballet steps but the unusual simplistic poses designed for Beatrice, linked by the running steps. At the end came a rapid *enchainement*, with gliding movements that took her forward and back across the stage, and in those few moments she was lost in what she was doing, utterly absorbed, so that when she took the last pose, on tiptoe, her back arched and head thrown back, arms outstretched like a creature in flight, the sudden outbreak of applause frightened her into a realization of where she was. She threw an imploring glance to Madame Cotin in the wings, who gestured her to move forward. She did so, suddenly filled with unreasonable fear at the smiling faces in the darkness before her, the furiously clapping hands.

'Curtsey, Lilith, *curtsey*.' Madame Cotin's voice reached her faintly above the noise.

Hesitantly, she took a step to the side, and sank down in a curtsey as she had been taught, arms extended, head bent low. For a moment, the applause ceased, and then it began again more strongly than ever. Lilith stood up wondering helplessly what to do. From the side of the stage someone, a young man, held up a little bunch of carnations. She took them uncertainly. She had never been given flowers before, and in her pleasure she smelled them and held their scented heads for a moment against her cheek in a gesture at once childish and charming. The audience loved it, and clapped even harder, so that Lilith had to curtsey again. It seemed as though they would never stop.

Had she really done this, pleased these people so much? She couldn't believe it, and elation surged through her body so that she felt as though she would float like a bubble to the ceiling. In the wings, she saw Madame Cotin beckoning. With a last glance at the auditorium she fled from the stage, so that the watchers felt she had been reluctantly torn from them, and applauded even more.

Lilith had never in her life felt such excitement. Even after Madame Cotin had wiped the greasepaint from her face and removed the dark shading that had emphasized her eyes and taken her home, even after she was tucked up in bed and Nanny had turned down the gas, she lay in a trance of happiness.

'You can't imagine,' she confided to Beatrice, who as always had crept silently into bed beside her, 'you can't imagine how it felt, Bee. As if I could fly. And you know,' she turned impulsively, 'if it hadn't been for you, I might never have learned to dance.'

As she kissed Beatrice's soft cheek in a flurry of affection, the nightlight illumined her sister's smooth and shuttered face.

Chapter 3

When Beatrice was thirteen years old, and Lilith eleven, Dr da Costa's worst expectations were realized. He had begun to fear puberty would be a difficult time for his troubled elder daughter. The contours of her body changed from narrow immaturity to unmistakeably feminine curves, childhood became womanhood, and the ripening brought with it feelings and emotions too powerful for her mind to understand or control. She became increasingly disturbed, the bouts of rigidity increased and were more worryingly prolonged, so that even Lilith could not bring her out of them.

Lacking any guidelines, Dr da Costa decided to treat Beatrice as if she suffered from hysteria. Though he knew she did not spring from hysterical stock, he could at least give her tried care. He assumed that some psychic stress was involved, and ordered that after a rigid attack she should be bathed for at least half an hour in a prolonged tepid bath to soothe her. If that failed he prescribed tincture of gelsemium from the root of the yellow jasmine, in minute amounts, for it was dangerous poison, and dulled the central nervous system so that she could sleep. He directed that she kept regular hours, saw few people and ate the simplest of foods: barley broth, broiled meats and vegetables, custard puddings. The same regimen applied to Lilith, although he made it clear to her this was not necessary, but she insisted that she wanted to be with Beatrice, not treated differently in any way.

31

The result was that the two girls led, even for the times, a most secluded life. In the middle of London, they might as well have been in the depths of the country, for only rarely did even Lilith venture beyond the gates: she would not go out if Beatrice did not. It was a curious situation, and one that would not have come about had Dr da Costa not been so immersed in his work and his anxieties. As it was, Lilith learned young how to live in the world of her imagination. The Sloane Square house was a rich treasure-trove for a mind like hers. Her mother had loved the Pre-Raphaelites, and copies of their work hung even in the most unlikely corners: Holman Hunt and Millais on the stairs, Dante Gabriel Rossetti and Edward Burne-Jones in the sitting room. Each reception room boasted the dark decorative wallpapers designed by William Morris, and Lilith would gaze at them for hours, seeing in the curling fleshy shapes mythical creatures. But her favourite picture hung on the wall beside her parents' bedroom. It was a painting of Christina Rossetti's poem *Goblin Market*: Lilith would sit enthralled before it, daydreaming herself into those lamplit stalls in the bright dusk, amongst imaginary imps. At first, her father was alarmed to find her sitting there rapt, afraid that she was keeping some sort of vigil outside her dead mother's room, but he soon realized the painting was the object of her absorption and offered to put it in her bedroom. She refused, for she liked making the secret voyage down the narrow stairs from the nursery to see it.

In summer there was the garden to explore. When Bella da Costa was alive this had been beautifully kept, for she liked to give elaborate tea-parties there, where women in white took care to keep their pale skins from the sun, little boys frolicked in

sailor suits and small girls gravely held lace parasols. But that had been long ago. Now moss had
turned the trim turf to velvet and old Mr Plaintain's
rheumatics kept him from doing more than rake the
once immaculate flowerbeds where in the past he
had planted China asters and the sweet-scented
marvel of Peru, Venus's looking-glass, purple jaco-
baea, and tulips from the Levant. The roses that
had been Bella's great love were too much for him
now, and ran wild where they had been pruned and
perfect: the common Provence roses, white and red,
the Tuscan, rose de Meaux, the Bengal celestial and
Tudor and the little early crimson that Mrs da Costa
used to pick for the doctor to wear in his buttonhole.

The children did not care that green and golden
creeping Jennie had overtaken the tiger-flowers and
the gladioli brought from the Cape of Good Hope.
They did not notice that no one now picked lavender
from the sprawling bushes that sweetened the
London air, nor that beneath ivied walls deep purple
peonies drooped neglected on the stem. They hid in
the old vinery, where panes of glass were missing
and birds nested, and played hide-and-seek in the
overgrown rustic seats where clematis and honey-
suckle hung.

They were seated in one of these, out of sight
beneath the canopy of leaves, one afternoon when
their Aunt Florence, Samuel's sister, was talking in
the garden with him. Beatrice did not, apparently,
listen, and Lilith did not mean to do so, but it was
hard not to hear, for her aunt was becoming
extremely agitated. Lilith liked her aunt. She was
the wife of Nathan Hartsilver, a banker and a man
of considerable property. Where he was short and
dapper in an old-fashioned way, Florence was angular and aristocratic with hands that always fascinated Lilith, the fingers so long and tapering that

when she put them together the fingertips did not meet, but sprayed away like a bunch of pale flowers. At the thought Lilith glanced down at her own childishly plump fingers, and tried to stretch them.

She heard Aunt Florence say in her most ringing tones, 'I tell you, Samuel, you cannot bring them up like domestic pets. You don't even take them regularly to synagogue. It isn't enough that they're clothed and fed, you know. They must learn to behave properly in society.'

Her father gave a contemptuous snort. Lilith wondered who her aunt was talking about.

'Don't you make that noise to me, Samuel. You may be an excellent doctor, but it's clear you're no psychologist. Do you realize how old Lilith is now?'

Her father muttered something about supposing she was around eleven.

'Eleven? Eleven, Samuel? The girl's fourteen years of age and running wild as any savage.'

Lilith gave a gasp of surprise and glanced down at herself: her pale dress was covered with grass burrs and stained green from sitting on the ground. She put a hand up to her hair and found that her slides were slipping. Beatrice, beside her, was quite tidy, but then Bee only ever followed her around.

Aunt Florence was still speaking.

' . . . something must be done before it is too late, and I propose to do it.' In this mood she was difficult to oppose as Samuel well knew. He inquired mildly, 'And what is that, Florence? I warn you, Beatrice is not to be excited. She hates meeting strangers, as you know, and I will not have her exposed to that kind of strain. She needs quietness and certainty, and if that means staying in the safety of this house, then so be it.'

Florence laid a conciliatory hand upon his arm.

'Now, Samuel. Of course I understand about Beatrice, poor child. There's nothing to be done for her. But Lilith is another matter altogether.'

Lilith stood up suddenly, so that Beatrice, who hated sudden movements in others, drew back sharply, fingers to her lips, as though to stifle a sound she had not made. Samuel and Florence looked amazed at the untidy figure risen out of the midst of the trailing greenery like a grubby sprite. Samuel started to laugh, but Florence pursed her lips.

'You see, Samuel? This is exactly what I mean. No girl of her age should behave like this. She should be sitting drawing quietly, or engaged in needlework. Not running about like a hobble-de-hoy and,' she gave Lilith a frown, 'listening to the conversations of her elders and betters.'

'I'm sorry, Aunt Florence.' Lilith tried hard to sound sincere. 'We were just sitting there, and before I realized what you were saying . . .' She let her apology trail away.

'Well, Lilith,' asked her father, 'did you hear enough to know that your aunt wishes to make a lady of you? What do you say to that?'

Lilith smoothed her skirt and caught his smiling look.

'No,' she said. 'Thank you.'

'And may one ask why not?' her aunt asked tartly.

'Because it won't be for Bee, will it? I can't . . .' Lilith looked imploringly at them, 'I can't leave her behind, don't you see? She needs me, always.'

The two adults exchanged an expressive look, as Lilith caught Beatrice's hand and pulled her unresisting from the undergrowth. The older girl, her silver hair caught up on either side of her face, looked only at Lilith, as though the adults were not present.

'It must be tea-time,' Lilith told her. 'We must go in. Please excuse us,' she added to her aunt. 'And thank you for bothering about me. But I'm very well as I am, really.' She kissed her aunt's cheek and gave Beatrice a little push to do the same, but the older girl looked away, like a cat that does not wish to be petted.

Samuel and Florence da Costa watched the two girls walking hand in hand down the garden.

'So lovely,' said Florence, sadly. 'She's so very lovely, Samuel. Do you think there's any hope of a normal life for her?'

Samuel da Costa shook his head. 'I don't know, Florence. I don't know what's wrong with her. I've noted down every symptom, but the pages don't add up to any illness known to medicine. Or not yet, at any rate. Perhaps in years to come . . . but that will be too late for Beatrice to benefit.' He bent to pick one of the tiny crimson button roses Bella used to pin in his coat in the mornings. 'I have thought, lately, that perhaps I should seek more aid than I have in treating her. But I can't bring myself to do so. I'm afraid of what my colleagues may tell me.'

Florence said soberly, 'She would be labelled cataleptic.'

Samuel sighed. 'I don't believe her attacks are associated with epilepsy, though. It seems likely she might be diagnosed as suffering from some grave form of mental disease – that would explain the mutism.' He paused, considering. 'I am convinced she isn't, but as a trained physician I must offer more than instinct to avoid this obvious conclusion. And since I cannot do this, I must keep Beatrice out of the hands of other members of my profession, which would be delivering her into a life of misery. If she is suffering from schizophrenia – some of her mannerisms, like her repetitive words and actions, suggest this – then there is no cure, merely continued treatment.' He twirled the flower moodily between his fingers. 'Not my field, thank God. But I know enough of what goes on in mental institutions to be determined that Beatrice, come what may, shall never enter their doors.'

Florence took his arm sympathetically and said with an optimism she did not feel, 'I'm sure in time – once she is in her twenties – when she is more settled and less immature, these rigid attacks will become less frequent. She could seem like a normal person. Until one knew. We understand it is because so much of her is blank – a void – but to the casual observer she must seem like a faery creature, untouched by this world. Which is true, in a way.'

Her brother's voice was strained. 'What concerns me is that I can see it would not be impossible for Beatrice to have a dramatic influence on the lives of others. Not in the normal way, as a beautiful woman does, but precisely because she is so strange.'

'That would be something,' Florence answered.

'It would be unhealthy, and might even be dangerous. She does not seem to know what another human being is. I do not believe she cares for anyone or anything. Only Lilith is real to her.'

'There is no record in the family at all, is there, of such an occurrence? No kind of madness that we know of, no stories we have ever been told.'

'If there had been, nature would have seen to it that the strain died out. Such a child would not have married and bred children in turn. No. My lovely Beatrice is a freak. Maybe it is my fault. Maybe it was Bella's. Who knows, now? Who can say?'

He turned to Florence, who could find nothing to reply. With an abrupt gesture he pulled the crimson bud from his lapel and tossed it on the ground.

Samuel and Florence da Costa were proud of their family and with good reason. They were the aristocrats among Jews, the Hispano-Portuguese known as Sephardim – literally, 'those who came over from Spain' – and their history stretched back to the middle of the first century.

In 586 B.C.E., Nebuchadnezzar of Babylon destroyed Jerusalem. Women were ravished, and the maids in the city of Judah. Princes were hanged up by their hand, and the terrible famine that followed blackened the skin of the survivors as though by an oven. And foxes walked on the desolate mountains of Zion.

Among those who escaped was a man named Uziah. He was forty years of age, experienced enough to foresee that the recovery of his country would take more years than he had left to him. He was a healer, versed in the use of ointments and skilled with the knife, and he looked in despair at the mutilated and wasted bodies of his countrymen and knew that his arts were useless in the face of adversity such as this. There was nothing he could do but save his own family. His wife was a sturdy woman and their four daughters were old enough to survive a hazardous journey, while his son was fourteen and tall for his age: many punier boys had already been seized for slavery by the Babylonians.

Uziah and his family did not wait to pack more than drinking vessels and a few clothes while Uziah took with him the crude tools of his trade: the wooden case containing his instruments and jars of salve. They took his wife's jewels and what gold they could quickly muster, hoping these would see them through their journey.

Had Uziah anticipated that it would be six years before he and his family could stop running, six years before they could feel truly safe, six years during which their second daughter vanished, inexplicably and completely, one winter night, then it is unlikely he would have left his homeland that terrible August. During those years, they travelled to the very end of the known world. They were on a small boat passing down the Iberian peninsula when a member of the crew fell ill. Uziah told the captain he could save the man, but that he could not hope to do so under the conditions prevailing on board. So they put in at a small settlement called Tarragona where Uziah was able to procure the herbs he needed for his poultices. The sailor survived and long before he was fully recovered Uziah was inundated with requests from the townspeople to cure their ailments: their sores and sprains and sicknesses. When the boat was ready to leave, Uziah and his family stayed behind.

The warmth of the Catalonians, their harsh, vigorous, dynamic speech, appealed to Uziah and his wife. They saw the superb fruit and vegetables in the markets, the grapes and olives, the green hills and rivers surrounding the settlement, and could not believe their good fortune in finding so civilized a home. As time went by they discovered they were not the only Jews in the area. All along the coast, individually or in small groups, there were families of Jews. Uziah's son married the daughter of a rabbi, his own remaining daughters were found husbands, and many children were born to them.

Uziah and his wife were dead by the time their children moved to other centres, to Tortosa and

Elche. Only then did they become known as da Costa – of the coast. When, in 711 B.C.E., almost the whole peninsula fell like a ripe fruit into the hands of the Arab conquerors Moussa and Tariq, the da Costa family remained in Christian pockets and continued to lead peaceful and neighbourly lives.

Uziah's descendants were part of a vast upsurge of Jewish cultural activity in Spain, the great days of pride, of flourishing Talmudic colleges and centres of learning in Cordoba, in Alisana, in Granada. Rabbi Hisdai ibn Shaprut, the physician, scholar and diplomat, became the first court Jew of Muslim Spain and his palace was the centre for the first Hebrew poets of the country.

In the next century Samuel ha-Nagid, the poet, scholar and statesman, rose to become vizier to the emir of Granada, and led armies to rescue his Jewish brethren in Almeria and Sevilla.

In the second half of the eleventh century and into the twelfth Jewish settlements expanded in Northern Spain and Toledo became the main Jewish city and later a centre of European culture. Key works in Arabic and Hebrew were translated into Latin. The mathematician Juan de Sevilla – a convert to Christianity – translated medicine, philosophy and astronomy, bringing works of Plato and Aristotle to the West. A Jew called Maestro Pedro of Toledo translated the entire Qur'an in the course of one year. The Sephardim's great philosophical achievement, Maimonides' *Guide to the Perplexed*, became known through its Hebrew translation and was only later put into Latin, influencing among others the thinking of Thomas Aquinas.

By now local laws and customs in Spain – the Fueros – dictated the rights and status of Jews. These – here Spain was unique – emphasized the absolute equality of Jew and Christian. Jewish oaths were accepted, Jews were treated with complete impartiality, could choose their careers as scholars, students, religious dignitaries or – like many of Uziah's descendants – physicians or pharmacists. They could practise all crafts, own land or work as peasants. They were great lawyers, of civil as well as Talmudic law, and poets so accomplished that the conventions of the Spanish school pervaded poets in Babylonia and Egypt, North Africa and Provence. Poets in Greece, Turkey, the Yemen all wrote sacred and secular poetry in the Hispano-Arabic manner. Love and yearning for Zion, its past glories and its future, characterized these writings.

It was the golden age in Spain, and it only ended when a fanatical Berber sect from North Africa invaded and destroyed the Jewish centres in Andalusia, in Muslim Spain. So the Jews moved again, northward to Christian Spain, and new centres for Hebrew poetry were founded in Barcelona, Zaragoza, Toledo, Navarre.

In many members of the da Costa family a strong strain of melancholy manifested itself: they were sombre people, introspective and imaginative. Over the generations, some of them were intensely aware of their harrowing history, others less concerned, but always they were passionately determined that the family must survive against all odds.

In time, Uziah's descendants became valuable men, personal physicians in the courts of small rulers: one, Samuel da Costa, cured Alfonso the Wise of a skin disease and was rewarded with a fortified palace. They were to discover the borderline from such assimilation was easily crossed, for when – as frequently happened – there was an outburst of anti-Jewish feeling, their protectors urged them to accept baptism and become conversos to ensure their safety. Unwilling, they had looked at their children, balancing faith against survival. Many tears blended with the water of the baptisms they were forced to undergo. Always, in secret, they practised their own faith, and venerated the god of their fathers; they joined the many thousands of secret Jews in Spain, living at one and the same time in two different worlds. It was a hazardous enterprise, and for many of them it intensified the hereditary strain of sadness. More than one da Costa, finding he could make peace with neither his own half-forgotten Judaism nor with the inexplicable tenets of Christianity, took his own life – and in doing so, committed the most heinous act of all, for it is a *hillul Ha'Shem*, profanation of the Name, showing he did not trust in God to save him.

There was, however, another side to conversion: it opened the way to marriage with Spanish Christians. The da Costa men were highly regarded, their women handsome, and as the years went by their blood mingled with that of Castile, of Aragon, of Catalonia and Leon. They numbered among their ranks a great judge, a general, a brilliant composer, writers, distinguished thinkers and eminent mathematicians. There was even a converted Catholic theologian.

At the top of their communities were the court Jews. Every king in Spain had one, and while this gave the Jews access to the crown, it primarily served the king, for these men provided funds for him, either directly or through supervising taxes. For hundreds of years Jews were employed as tax 'farmers' not only for regular and accepted payments by the people, but for anything extra the king needed, to finance a war or pamper a queen: the

Jews were thus identified with such unjust demands and hated for them.

By the fourteenth century, these things, combined with a church which preached intolerance, made conditions for the Jews steadily worse. The Black Death – as if the Jews did not suffer its effects like everyone else – brought pogroms in its wake. In 1391 riots started in Sevilla and four thousand Jews were murdered and their property looted and burned. The violence spread and many communities were utterly destroyed. Two hundred thousand Jews converted to Christianity – among them some of Uziah's descendants who had by now become once more completely Jewish. Still others fled – some to North Africa, others towards Israel – and these families became the foundation of Sephardi Jewry outside that country.

In 1412 the Laws of Valladolid were passed – instigated, ironically enough, by a Jewish convert to Christianity – and among the edicts was one to prohibit Jews from practising medicine. Since almost all the da Costa men were physicians like their forefather Uziah, this struck at them hard, and they were forced to practise their profession, like their religion, in secret and only among their closest associates. Over the next two years, all Jews were arraigned for blasphemy and threatened with death: from all over Spain, in fear of their lives, they went to Tortosa to be baptized. It seemed the end of Spanish Jewry had come.

For seventy more years, the descendants of Uziah da Costa, among others, attempted to revive Jewish education and create a new constitution for the Jewish community, but the problems of the conversos were not easily to be solved. Though they remained faithful to their past, they were in disarray and this was made worse by the Observantine friar who suggested in the 1460s that Spain should follow the example of England in 1290 and France in 1306, and expel all their Jews: those countries, he argued, had managed well enough without them.

When the Catholic monarchs of Aragon and Castile – Ferdinand and Isabella – married, the two kingdoms became one Christian state. Isabella had as father confessor the Dominican friar Tomas de Torquemada, prior of Santa Cruz in Segovia. The Spanish Inquisition began in Sevilla in 1481, and the wave of persecution and pogroms climaxed in 1490 in the blood libel when Jews and conversos were accused of killing a Christian child to use its blood for ritual and witchcraft, though no body was ever found. Queen Isabella's trusted councillor, the Jew Abraham Senior of Segovia was implicated, and she rapidly put a stop to the insinuations, but not before a group of Jews and conversos burned for it.

At the beginning of January 1492, Ferdinand and Isabella entered Granada. It took less than two months for them to sign the order of Expulsion against the Jewish communities: a thousand years of habitation were at an end. The Expulsion order had no economic cause – indeed, it brought dereliction to whole areas at a time, for no one came to take the place of the Jews. It was purely religious, to separate the conversos from their Jewish past. For a time, the Jews sought desperately to have the order annulled, but in vain. Torquemada opposed them, Torquemada who was (it was whispered, but quietly) himself a Jew, who implemented the horrific tortures, the racking and stretching and pressing of the Inquisition upon those it sought to save.

The order of Expulsion detailed arrangements of

how guards should be hired, what routes could be taken and what the travellers might carry with them, but the Jews themselves were responsible for their own leaving. There were those who chose conversion to Christianity rather than face the hazards of an endless journey, but this time the descendants of Uziah da Costa were not amongst them. They had had enough: their livelihood had been taken from them, and even the prospect of an uncertain future was better than that loss of dignity.

The Expulsion order had taken the da Costa family, like all the other Jewish households, utterly by surprise. It seemed against all logic, that they should be forced to leave a land which had been theirs for more than a millennium, and to which they had contributed much. But it was no time for despair – the last day of July 1492 was to be their last on Spanish soil.

The head of the da Costa family, as for so many years, was named Uziah, and he too was a physician, though now forbidden to heal the Christian patients who nonetheless continued to come to his door to seek aid, careless of the penalties they might incur. He decided that the family would go to Portugal, along with many others: when the day came, and whole towns emptied of their Jewish population, the Spaniards watched them march off joyously, to the sound of timbrels, strong enough in their faith to trust that God would find them a home, as He had before.

They reached Portugal, which had already a sizeable Jewish population, and settled without much trouble. But Uziah was never happy there: he felt displaced, uncertain, unhappy, and until the day he died he mourned for Spain and the existence that was lost to him. He was, in years to come, proved

right, for the Sephardi settlers like his family, as
well as Portuguese Jewry, were expelled again. The
whole of the Mediterranean was infected by the
blight of hatred, by massacres and mass expulsions.
Some of the da Costa family chose to go East, to join
their brethren who had long lived under Islam in
Cairo, others continued onward to Iraq, where such
barbaric behaviour was unheard of, and the Jews
were not the only minority and lived in close contact
with the Muslim population.

One member of the family only, a younger son
named Samuel, decided to turn the other way. He
was barely twenty and unmarried, ambitious and
without responsibility. He went west, to Italy, where
he quickly absorbed enough of the language to be
employed by a pharmacist, whose daughter he eventually married. Their son, in turn, went to Amsterdam, where already a great Jewish centre
flourished, and the da Costa family established
themselves there.

By 1656, the time of Oliver Cromwell and the
Commonwealth, close trading links grew up
between London and the Low Countries, and many
wealthy Sephardi merchants of Spanish-Portuguese
origin left Amsterdam for the English capital. The
da Costa descendants of Samuel were still mainly
physicians and pharmacists and makers of medical
potions, and two of them, brothers, travelled to
London in 1697, the year that twelve 'Jew brokers'
were admitted to the Royal Exchange, the City's
financial establishment. The elder brother, David,
married the daughter of one of these new brokers,
and settled in the Jewish quarter in the eastern part
of the City of London, in the Aldgate ward.

There were around 25,000 Jews in England at the

beginning of the nineteenth century, and the numbers increased rapidly as fugitives from anti-Semitism in Western Europe crossed the Channel. There were almost no occupational and few residential restrictions imposed on them – whereas Jewish life elsewhere was at best obstructed and at worst impossible. But in England there was religious freedom and economic status without parallel in Europe, and a measure of social acceptance that saw wealthy and intelligent Jews in Parliament, at court, and building some of England's greatest houses.

David da Costa and his wife were prudent people who knew that hard work was, after their faith, the greatest imperative. They lived well but carefully, saving their money for the education of their sons. Only one was born to them, amidst seven daughters, and he died suddenly at the age of three. The daughters married, and the da Costa family name died out. It was almost eighty years before another da Costa arrived in England.

In 1807 the merchant Israel Henriques decided it was time for his eldest daughter to be wed. His mother had been a da Costa – one of the seven daughters of David – and had kept in touch with members of the family in Egypt. She had even, on several occasions, been visited by them. It was one of these, a well-educated and amiable Cairene, who was chosen to be the husband of Constance Henriques, and their elder son fathered Samuel and Florence.

Samuel was destined to inherit the considerable export and import empire of his father, but he was a true da Costa, and determined on medicine. In another age Florence would have been a doctor also, for she had inherited the same intelligence as her brother. But instead she married Nathan Hartsilver and expected in time to take her place as a matriarch. Only there were no children. Happy in their marriage, she and Nathan took this to be God's will and incontestable. When Bella died so tragically young, Florence was able to feel that the two motherless little girls were under her protection. She did not like to interfere too much: it was against her inclinations, and anyway Samuel was a man who kept the reins of his household in his own hands. Florence contented herself with seeing the girls at least once a week and having clothes made for them by her own dressmaker. (To avoid problems with her brother, she always gave these direct to the nursemaid, and it never occurred to Samuel to wonder that his daughters were so well dressed. Such things did not cross his mind.)

After Bella's death, Florence had been the first to notice Beatrice's disturbing silence. She, like her brother, hoped at first that it was nothing more than a manifestation of sorrow. Far sooner than he, she recognized what had happened, but when she raised the matter with Samuel, he laughed away her fears. (As, she remembered, he had tried to do for so long when Bella worried about Beatrice's development.) She knew very well why it was: accustomed to dealing always with illness, he could not bring himself to accept that in his own home were problems beyond his knowledge to treat.

Now, walking in the Sloane Square garden beside her brother, she said again, almost pleading, 'I wish you would let me take Lilith in hand. I know what she says but a child cannot be expected to see what is right for her. I really think you must put your foot down, Samuel. Tell her that if I take her about, introduce her to a few congenial people, Beatrice will not mind. She will be out of the house for a few hours at a time, that is all, and then she will be home again.' She stopped walking. 'Samuel, it would give me so much pleasure to show Lilith something of the world. You would have done so yourself, I know, if Bella had lived. I beg you, let me borrow Lilith. Let me do for her what I would have done for a child of my own.' She was absurdly conscious of the quiver in her voice. Samuel heard it too, and patted her on the back.

'You're right, my dear Florence. It would do Lilith good to become more sociable. I'll talk to her this evening.'

Lilith listened to her father and said, simply, 'Beatrice will cry.'

He looked surprised.

'Does she, then, cry? I have never heard her.' He had not thought she displayed that much emotion.

'Oh yes.' Lilith was quite matter-of-fact. 'At night, always.'

'*Always*? *Every* night?'

'Yes.'

He looked at her, stricken. 'Why did you not tell me? Does anyone know?'

She shook her head. 'It's all right, Papa. I can stop her.'

'But – why? What is wrong?' He was beside himself with anxiety. Under his roof, his own daughter was in some kind of despair and he had had no inkling of it. Lilith, as always sensitive to atmosphere, sat beside him on the brocaded seat and leaned her head against his arm. She did so without thinking, knowing instinctively that this would help her father, and he took from the light physical contact the same calming influence he might have received from an affectionate pet. He rested his cheek against the top of her head and her dark brown curls smelled of some fruit he couldn't name, and youth. She went on, 'Beatrice isn't unhappy because of any reason. There's nothing we can do about it. It's just the way she is.'

'I thought she didn't feel anything very much.'

He felt Lilith stiffen against his shoulder.

'That's a cruel thing to say. Just because she doesn't speak doesn't mean she has no feelings.'

'I have never seen her express them.'

'I know. Beatrice lives inside herself. We just see the outside, and usually that's very pretty.' She thought for a moment. 'Bee's like a flower, I suppose. Like one of Mr Plaintain's favourites. He loves her, you know. He looks at her and shakes his head and says she needs "special tendin".' Lilith imitated the old man's soft speech.

'That's what I want to talk to you about. Beatrice *does* need special tending. She needs to be kept quiet and safe, and in this house I can do that. I can protect her, and hope that she'll grow out of this difficult phase. Do you understand?' Against his shoulder, he felt her nod. 'But you need special tending, too. Your Aunt Florence says I'm neglecting you, and she's right. Yes,' he interrupted her protests, 'I know you need many things I cannot give you. More companionship. Young friends. A chance to go around and let people see what a pretty daughter I have. So for me, if not for yourself, will you do what Florence wants? It's not very much, you know. She'd like to dress you up and take you to meet some people. You'll still live with us. I'm sure Beatrice won't miss you during the day, and at night you'll be here.' He rubbed her curls with his free hand. 'Say yes, Lilith, there's my girl. I can't worry about you both, and I'll feel happier if I know you have some kind of real life.'

'Isn't this real life, then?' Her voice was muffled. Samuel da Costa didn't answer for a long time. He thought of what the house had been like before his beloved Bella had started to lose her grip on life, when her quick step hurried to meet him as he came into the house and the rooms had been bright with her flowers and the sound of her voice. Florence had always urged him to marry again, to make a proper home for his children, but he had been unable for years to contemplate such an act of betrayal against Bella's memory. By the time he had recouped himself emotionally after her death, he was immersed in work, and the routine of his life and his household had settled around him as comfortably as an old coat so that he had neither the time nor the incentive to make the effort involved in finding himself another wife. Florence still tried, though. He never dined at their Georgian house near the Marble Arch without some good-looking woman seated beside him. Sometimes he would arrange to call on them one afternoon, but the relationships did not progress much beyond that. Florence did not of course know – although she shrewdly suspected – that he had had for years a very pleasant companion in the widow of an army colleague who died during the Boer War. The lady was his own age, with an ample income and a large family of her own. He had met her originally when he called to offer his condolences in the days immediately following news of Dr Bennett's death. He had helped with the unpleasant necessities involved in bringing the body home for burial, arranging the papers and the funeral, and later settling the estate. Dulcie Bennett was exactly his own age at that time – forty-two – with soft brown hair and a perfect English complexion. She was plump even by fashionable standards, and like Samuel she was too loyal to her husband's memory to want to take another husband. But she was practical, and worldly, and she liked Samuel da Costa. It was she who, one evening when they had been taking a glass of port together, told him firmly that he must send a note home telling the staff he would be kept away all night. She and Samuel were devoted, carefully preserving their own independence and grateful for each other's affection.

Over the years it had become established that he would spend at the most two nights a week at her home – they lived a short hansom drive apart – but he was always at his own table to greet his daughters for breakfast. Both Samuel and Dulcie Bennett were perfectly content with their liaison. They were able to arrange their lives so that they had no need of concealment and their dignity did not suffer. As the years went by, and still they were happy together, it came to be something very close to marriage. Indeed, were it not for the difference in religion, they might well have married. As it was, they had a most civilized arrangement, and it certainly preserved Samuel's sanity. The only negative result was that it also preserved him from the need to forge any other emotional bonds, and his home became where he slept, and had his consulting rooms, and where his children lived. It was not the place he felt real life went on.

Now he put his arm around Lilith's shoulders, and pushed her to her feet.

'No,' he said. 'This isn't real life. You'll have to look for that, if you want to find it. Don't wait too long, or it will pass you by.'

Lilith watched him. Her eyes – he remembered

the metaphor she had used for Beatrice being like a flower – were as brown and deep as the cottage bloom his wife had so loved – what was it? heart's-ease. She eased his own heart, this vivid child, and he did not want to lose her, but he saw now that if he did not send her away, she was too affectionate to go of her own accord and he would be guilty of hampering her chances. As he had been guilty, perhaps, with Beatrice. Since it was impossible to ascertain what had caused her illness – what genetic flaw, what inherited weakness, what trick of fate – it could as well be on his side as Bella's. When he thought of Beatrice, the sombre strain of melancholy that had always been strong in the blood of the da Costas asserted itself, and he felt that he was indeed responsible for her state, the spoiler of her perfection, the canker in the rose.

All this was in his mind so that when Lilith, pushed from his side, asked, fearing to hear the answer, 'When must I go?', he replied with one word, 'Now.'

Chapter 4

Florence and Nathan Hartsilver lived in the Portman estate on the high ground at the extreme end of Oxford Street where it merged into the Edgware Road. Their house had once been part of the old mansion owned by the Dukes of Norfolk, and the long windows of the upper stories gave uninterrupted views – when the horizon was clear and bright – across Hyde Park to the outlines of the Crystal Palace and a distant glimpse of the Surrey hills. The fine reception rooms, the broad and easy staircase, were designed to accommodate large social functions, and the Hartsilvers did not waste them. Florence devoted much of her energy to charitable causes: she was a founder of the Jewish Ladies' Benevolent Loan Society to help poorer members of the community in the East End of London, in Whitechapel, Mile End and Bethnal Green, and the lavish functions held at her home provided a good proportion of these funds.

Nathan's principal interest was the bank which his father had founded. The old man had been a money dealer and trader of bills in Frankfurt, which he had left before either of his sons were born. By the time they were old enough to take over, the discounting business had become a tightly run and thriving company. Nathan and his brother were oddly alike: both short and dapper, punctilious in their dress, with sparse dark hair carefully combed forward to conceal their balding foreheads. Nathan, the younger, was the more adventurous in business:

54

it was he who was always seeking new ventures, while the older man would urge caution and waver over the smallest decision. Nathan thought of himself as an Englishman. He had received an excellent education and taken a good degree at London University but it was possible to detect, in his speech, the influence of German parentage. Not in the accent, or even the words he used, but in the shape and formation of his sentences he sounded foreign.

His wife Florence was very different. She, more than her brother Samuel, was inordinately proud of her ancestry, of her Spanish-Portuguese aristocracy, of her Sephardi lineage. In marrying Nathan, she had indeed married beneath her, for only rarely did her community ally themselves with the Ashkenazim, the Jews of East European extraction. But he had been captivated by her as no other man had ever shown signs of being, and the letters he had written her – she kept them, bound in thin satin ribbon, in the mahogany drawers of her smallest wardrobe – were imbued with poetry. Florence had been an angular girl with flat dark hair which had never lent itself to styling, and a body far too thin for fashion. When Nathan Hartsilver came home with her brother from a party at the home of a mutual friend, she had liked him immediately and the fact that he was six inches shorter than she did not seem to matter. He was almost her own age, which at that time was considered most unsuitable for marriage partners, the ideal alliance being that of a young woman with a man anything up to twenty years her senior. (That this system made for an inordinately large number of youthful widows was accepted as a matter of course.)

Like numerous da Costas, Florence had inherited the aptitude for medicine that had come from Uziah so many centuries before. But since she was a woman, this was deemed of little importance, and no one noticed that she was in fact more intelligent than her brother Samuel. All her considerable intellectual ability went into reading, which she did voraciously. Her sole possibility was marriage and she was ill-equipped for that, plain as she was, and feared she would die an old maid.

But Nathan did not find her plain, perceiving in her only beauty. He admired the line of her jaw and the smallness of her feet and her amazingly curved fingers, and he told her so, awakening in her emotions she had never expected to experience. When she looked at him she did not see a short man who wore over-elaborate waistcoats and curled his hair like his great hero Disraeli: she saw a prince among men. They became a most devoted couple, and only a child could have added to their contentment.

So when Lilith began to spend more and more time at Oxford Street, she was welcomed equally by them both. Nathan had conventional ideas and believed that a woman's place was to be a helpmeet and support to her husband. Florence believed this too, but a part of her yearned for more, for the world that lay beyond her dinner-parties and charitable functions and well-to-do circle. Because she was a practical woman she gave these feelings a positive outlet in her niece's education, and for the first time Lilith received the sort of training her mother would have given her.

She was taught household management. Although not expected to use them herself, she knew what goblets, stewpans, gridirons and other vessels should be available in a kitchen, and how to order a balanced meal for a large household. She learned how to iron fine linen, to re-pleat silk blouses, and how to check the household accounts.

When Florence was satisfied with Lilith's practical abilities, she turned to matters of the mind. Botany was added to the lessons she received, taught by a tutor engaged for the Oxford Street house, and astronomy. She was educated in natural philosophy and how to appreciate architecture. Florence herself instructed her in the preservation of health, emphasizing the need of a constant supply of pure air and a sufficiency of cheerful and innocent enjoyment.

Once or twice a week, Lilith was given lessons in water-colour painting, to refine her taste. 'Those faculties of the mind,' Florence advised her niece, 'which perceive and appreciate natural beauty, exist only in embryo until cultivated.' So Lilith and her tutor were dispatched with sketchbooks, folding easels, japanned paintboxes and green-lined parasols to Hyde Park. On their return Aunt Florence would inspect the rustic paling, the rutted footpath and the elm tree Lilith had committed to paper with intense interest and express her approval. She did not know that the composition had taken minutes only, and that for an hour and more Lilith had sat sketching in transparent gamboge, Vandyke brown and opaque vermilion tints the supple, dancing figures that her mind's eye had brought leaping through the grass.

The dancing lessons with Madame Cotin had ceased the previous year. This was partly because Beatrice had shown less and less interest in the routines she had 'learned', would merely give her sweet, enigmatic smile and ignore the beat of the music and Madame Cotin's entreaties. The lady herself was plumper than ever, and found the flights of stairs to the attic studio increasingly hard to manage though she continued to toil up them for Lilith's sake. And Lilith had not disappointed her. Week by week, she grew taller and stronger, her body responding with ever greater skill to the orders she gave it. She and Madame Cotin between them had evolved more and more exercises for Beatrice that did not use the movements of ballet, and even when Beatrice could not be persuaded to perform them, Lilith would carry them out alone, relishing the freedom of movement, finding pleasure in spring and balance, tension and release. The public performances the smoking concert had started for her tailed off as she grew older. A small child was more of a 'draw' for the public, and as she matured her father became more reluctant for her to make such appearances. At about the same time as she began to spend long days with the Hartsilvers, Madame Cotin's husband became ill and the teacher was forced to cut her lessons to one a week. Finally, they tailed off altogether, although she kept in touch with Lilith and would come occasionally to watch her dance.

For Lili did not stop dancing. On the contrary. The more time she spent away from Sloane Square, subject to the highly formalized routine of her aunt's home, the more welcome was the sight of the wooden *barre*, the white walls, the bare floor of the attic room where she could forget about constitutional monarchy and ancient mythology, where she did not have to think or decide or deliver an opinion, where she had only to exist.

For four years, until she was eighteen, Lilith danced for herself. Watched always by Beatrice – who refused to be parted from her when she was home – and no matter how tired she was at the end of each day, she would take off the new dresses of which she had to be so careful and put on the loose tunic she always wore to practise. Even without Madame Cotin's presence she would first perform the traditional exercises with which they had always started lessons together. She would begin at the *barre*, warming up slowly, loosening joints and flexing muscles with *pliés* and *battements*, *adages* and *développés*. She would do them all, gaining control, balancing, beating, her movements crisp and concise.

As time went on, and the memory of Madame Cotin's strict discipline faded, Lilith paid less and less attention to the *barre* exercises, which she had never particularly liked. To loosen her muscles she would use movements she made up for herself, lying on the floor and circling and stretching her limbs, reaching and pulling. Similar to the movements – though of course she did not know this – used by the Indian practitioners of the art of yoga.

On some evenings there would be a moment – she always thought it would never come, but it frequently did – when she recaptured her childhood ability to feel not through her mind but through her senses, through her skin.

Then she would wind up the phonograph and play one of her few recordings and music – Chopin, perhaps, or Mozart – would pour through the room, invigorating her. She would respond to the sounds without premeditation, giving herself up to the pleasure of dancing.

Almost without conscious decision, she would find she was using the special movements she and Madame Cotin had devised for Beatrice, the *pas de bourrée*, the swift little steps linked by almost Grecian poses. But dancing alone, the routines altered from the original concept. Those first movements had been put together with Beatrice's needs in mind, so they had been kept basic and simple. But as Lilith danced, alone and unrestrained, they changed. They became for her a form of expression that was entirely personal. Dancing, she shed tiredness and annoyance. As from earliest childhood, she was able physically to express subtle inflections of mood for which she had no words and the satisfaction this gave her was pleasurable and positive.

One other circumstance affected her dancing. With Madame Cotin, she and Beatrice had worn the traditional soft satin ballet slippers. But she had outworn and outgrown her last pair, and had not bothered to get any more, finding she preferred to dance barefoot. Her feet became even stronger, high-arched and muscular, and she relished the feel of the wooden floor and the sense of freedom.

Lilith danced almost unconscious of her body but at the same time aware that everything she did in this state of heightened sensitivity, to the placing of her little fingers, was exact and perfect. And every time it happened she felt it to be a small miracle. Even Beatrice, watching silently from the corner where she sat on the floor, arms clasped round her knees, would recognize it and reach out to touch her sister in unspoken admiration.

During those four years from fourteen to eighteen, Lilith's appearance changed dramatically. Where she had been inclined to plumpness, the regular routine of dancing – at a time when girls like herself took no exercise which was so physically exacting – fined down her body, making her taut and strong. She had grown tall – taller than perhaps she would have been without Madame Cotin's constant exhortations to 'Stand up. Lift yourself out of your body.'

60

She had a straight back and held her head high, and her long, thick hair was now worn in a twisted chignon at the back of her head, for Aunt Florence had let her put it up when she was seventeen. Her eyes were deeper than ever, dark and luminous with youth, glowing with vitality. Her mouth was still that of a child, pouting and triangular with soft, full lips, but the thick dark eyebrows gave her face maturity and an oddly melancholy air. She looked very much like all the da Costa family with their hidden, inherited sadness. She had also, to her great surprise, inherited hands like her Aunt Florence. The pudgy child's hands had become slender, the fingers so elongated they curved slightly backwards, so that when she put her hands together the tips did not meet. They were eloquent, more eloquent than her words, and she used them as part of her speech even though Aunt Florence considered gesticulating to be vulgar and attempted to curb the habit. But her hands frequently supplied for Lilith a phrase she could not find; she could not still them no matter how hard she tried.

And she did try, for Aunt Florence would reprimand her even in public. Gently, though, she would tap Lilith's tapering fingers when she thought the girl was using them too much, being too exaggerated. She did this once when Lilith was helping serve tea at one of her soirées, and someone had asked her a question. In replying Lilith had used her hands as usual. She took no offence when Florence stopped her, knowing that her aunt was only trying to make her behave in a more English fashion. But a woman's voice behind them said, with some asperity, 'Leave the girl alone, Florence, do. Let her wave her pretty hands around if she wants to.'

Florence laughed. 'Easy to say, Judith, but the young are like plants: they have to be trained.'

'Just because I've none of my own doesn't make me ignorant about them.' The woman who had been speaking touched Lilith's arm lightly. 'Come and talk to me, dear, when you're not busy.'

Prompted by her aunt's nod, Lilith went and dutifully sat next to Miss Mendoza and talked to her about her astronomy lessons and other subjects. She wasn't particularly interested in them, and it soon became apparent that Miss Mendoza shared her views. It was hard for Lilith to guess how old she might be. Younger than Aunt Florence, certainly, with hair concealed primly beneath her hat and long grey kid gloves to match her alpaca coat with its Irish crochet lace trimmings. She looked, Lilith decided, both rich and lonely, and when she said, rather wistfully, 'I suppose you wouldn't care to walk round and visit me one day? I live very near, just off Park Lane. I don't see many young people now, my nephews all work so hard, and I used to enjoy their company,' Lilith accepted as much out of compassion as curiosity.

When, the following afternoon, she told Florence what she proposed to do, she caught the flicker of something in her aunt's eyes – disquiet, a hesitancy. But after a moment the older woman smiled, and told her not to be late, and to mind the traffic: Park Lane was notorious for accidents caused by young men driving four-in-hand at breakneck speed.

Miss Mendoza occupied a narrow townhouse in Green Street. Lilith liked it immediately for its comfortable clutter of furniture and pictures, most of which, her hostess explained, came from her parents' home when they died. As the only spinster daughter, she had inherited all the contents.

'Not that I wanted them,' Miss Mendoza commented, touching an Isfahan rug with the tip of her shoe. 'Possessions tie you, and I didn't want to be tied. I have to look after all these things, you see, they demand my presence, as I knew they would.'

'What did you want to do?' Lilith asked politely. Miss Mendoza's expression hardened.

'I wanted to be an artist. That's all I've ever wanted. I had lessons as a child, and when I was older I begged my parents to send me to train at one of the art schools.'

'But they didn't?'

'Oh, no. They said it wasn't a suitable occupation for a girl of my rank.' She fell silent. After a moment, Lilith asked, 'And was there nothing else . . . ?' She meant, why did you not marry, but could not phrase so delicate a question. Miss Mendoza understood her well enough, though. She held out her left hand, which as always had been concealed in the folds of her skirt. Now Lilith saw that it was in fact a special pocket. Miss Mendoza was wearing severe navy that day, and her hand was encased this time in a black kid glove. Lilith glanced at it incuriously – then with a start, looked again. The glove was tiny, the hand within it clearly no larger than a young child's, and even under the black kid she could see that the fingers were twisted out of shape, bent and rigid.

'*Main en griffe*, they call it.' Miss Mendoza's tone was a mixture of aggression and bitterness. 'Claw hand. You'd think I would have become accustomed to it, after all these years, wouldn't you? It developed when I was a child. But I never have. Never.'

Lilith had consciously to prevent her own hands from curling in revulsion. She said, her voice very quiet, 'There's . . . no cure, then?'

'None. It has ruined my life. Ruined it.'

There was a silence, while Lilith looked in horrid fascination at the hand. It did look like a claw, but as she became used to it, it began to appear less dreadful. Miss Mendoza added, 'I don't talk about it to anyone. I don't know why I told you.' She put it back into the pocket of her navy dress. 'I'm sorry, Lilith. I shouldn't have spoken of it.'

Lilith said, trying to be kind but genuinely meaning it, 'But something like that – it's only little, really. Only a part of you. Could that change everything?'

Judith Mendoza got up and walked over to the window. In the sunlight Lilith saw that her companion was younger than she had realized. Her hair was drawn tightly back in an unbecoming style, but only a few silver hairs showed in the rich brown, and her skin was smooth and white.

'How can I explain to someone who looks like you what it is to be less than perfect? When I was growing up, when I was fourteen and fifteen, can you imagine the misery it caused me, this' – she banged the tiny malformed hand angrily against her thigh as though wanting to hurt it – 'this growth? I never felt confident or pretty or even normal. I told you I wanted to paint, but my parents didn't approve. And that left me with nothing to look forward to. I never for a moment imagined anyone would want to marry me. And then there was a man, a lot older than I, a widower. He was kind and I could have grown to love him, I'm sure of that.' She paused. 'Out of gratitude, if nothing else.'

'Why did you not?'

Judith Mendoza spoke abruptly. 'My parents wouldn't have it. They said it might be inherited.

That I could pass it on to a child, and that the disgrace would be theirs.'

Lilith stared at her, hearing her father once, talking to Aunt Florence, saying something very similar about Beatrice. Could Beatrice, then, never marry? And if she did not, what would become of her? She had never thought before of her sister's future, seeing her always as younger even than herself. She could not bear to think of Beatrice like this, lonely and bitter. Worse by far than Judith Mendoza, for Beatrice would have no social contacts, as this woman clearly did. Beatrice could communicate only with her. She said, suddenly desperate to share her worry, knowing that she would be understood, 'Do you know about my sister? About Beatrice?'

Judith Mendoza said carefully, 'Your aunt has told me she is ill. But that is all.' She gave an affectionate little smile. 'Florence has a great deal of pride. It does not allow anyone to know of her problems.'

So Lilith told Judith Mendoza about Beatrice: how beautiful she was, and how she used to sing her nonsense songs, and then the silence had come. She had never spoken to anyone like this before, and she scarcely realized that she could only do so now because Judith Mendoza had first revealed her own disability.

'You see,' she finished, 'Bee isn't *ill*, really. Papa says it is an illness, though he doesn't know the name of it. She's just ... different. He thinks she doesn't feel because she doesn't speak, he could hardly believe it when I told him how she wept, at night. He protects her and keeps her shut away – ' she noticed Judith Mendoza give a little grimace, as though that had happened to her also – 'and yet she's older than me. A woman, living like a little girl. He does it out of kindness, because he cares so, but I'd never thought until today, what will become of her?'

'You mean, will she be alone like me?'

Lilith, taken aback by Judith Mendoza's perception, could only nod.

'I don't know,' the older woman said gently, 'and neither does your father, what will happen to her. But whatever it is mustn't stop you living your life. You cannot be with her always. You have to leave her behind, even if it hurts to do so. I know, believe me. There are no second chances, Lilith. Not for any of us.'

Over the months Lilith visited Judith Mendoza many times. Sometimes they went out for a drive together, or strolled in Hyde Park and talked. Once or twice they visited the Royal Arcade in Old Bond Street to buy chocolates from the brightly lit and deliciously scented premises of Charbonnel et Walker, Lilith carrying home the little gift boxes with grave care, particularly the box chosen especially for Beatrice. Or they would walk down as far as Piccadilly to the emporium where Mr Fortnum and Mr Mason purveyed their high-class comestibles, to return with delicate China tea, for Miss Mendoza never allowed her staff to decide on this purchase.

One morning Lilith arrived at Judith Mendoza's house earlier than expected, and found her immersed in a copy of *The Lady*, paper and pencil beside her. She explained with a slight air of embarrassment that she was noting down ingredients for a lotion to use on her face, which required a blend of sulphate and zinc, tincture of lavender and distilled water. When Lilith asked what effect this would achieve, Judith answered shortly, 'Stops bicycle face.'

'I *beg* your pardon?'

Judith peered at her over the tops of her spectacles.

'Sit down, won't you. Now, where was I? Ah, yes. It says here that bicycling causes "a terrible malady when the face gradually settles into a hunted, drawn look, the brows become contracted, and there is a rigid appearance about the eyes"!' She glanced at Lilith, who was trying hard to stifle her laughter. '"Pull yourself together",' Judith went on, '"and make a persistent effort to relax the features"!'

'I didn't know you bicycled.'

'Certainly. Marvellous exercise. You should take it up yourself. In fact, why don't you?'

Lilith twinkled at her. 'I might acquire a bicycle face.' And added, more thoughtfully, 'Where do you ride?'

'In the park, in the early mornings. At my age, one doesn't wish to be observed, and I'm well aware that I already have a reputation for eccentricity.'

Lilith commented mildly, 'But you've been encouraging people to say that about you for years.'

Judith Mendoza looked pleased. 'I hear Florence's voice in that remark. But of course I have. Better an eccentric than a bore.' She put the magazine aside and removed her spectacles. 'As you're so early this morning, why don't you accompany me. I have to change first, though.'

When she returned to Portman House for lunch that day, Lilith announced that she planned to ask her father for a bicycle. Uncle Nathan paused in disbelief, a spoonful of consommé with lemon herb balls poised at his open mouth. But Aunt Florence was enthusiastic, and offered to outfit her niece that very day.

'I've little to do this afternoon, dear. And of course your father will agree. I'll see to that.'

They went to Stag and Mantle in Leicester Square to purchase a light all wool cloth skirt and a smart jacket ensuite, with a Tattersall cloth waistcoat to be added when the weather grew cold. Aunt Florence insisted that Lilith needed a Redfern yachting cap to add the final touch, and on their way home called in at Nathan's bootmaker.

It was a small establishment in an unfashionable district off Marylebone High Street, in a narrow street with an open garden at the far end. A barber on one side advertised with a red, blue and white barleysugar pole and on the other was a florist. Between them, the bootmaker's window with its dark surround was empty of everything but a block of wood on which were ranged a single black patent shoe with a black cloth top, a high and gleaming riding boot and a walking boot. The elderly man who hurried from the back to greet them wore a leather apron and shirtsleeves, and welcomed Aunt Florence as an old friend in a voice Lilith found thick and foreign.

When he had gone to fetch some leather to show them Aunt Florence explained quietly, 'Nathan set Mr Kreitz up in business here years ago. He and his father came from Poland with nothing. Except their skill, of course. Nathan found them in a soup kitchen in Spitalfields when he was a young man: he was taking a census for a charity of the Jewish refugees.' Aunt Florence smiled. 'He says it was the best investment he ever made. His boots last so long it's positively embarrassing.'

At that moment the old man came back, a large

piece of tan leather in his hand. He moulded it to show them how soft it was and Lilith smelled the soothing odour of leather which permeated the cramped shop. Then he knelt at her feet and removed the shoes she was wearing. He placed her foot flat on a large piece of paper and outlined it with a pencil. Then he took the foot in his hands and kneaded it, pressing the toes, feeling the heel. Lilith watched him, his head bent in concentration, the bald top of his head shining in the gaslight. Without looking at her he said, in his guttural voice, 'It is a perfect foot.'

Lilith could not repress a nervous little laugh. He looked up then, the skin at the corners of his eyes crinkling with anxiety in case she had misunderstood him.

'Please not to laugh, Miss. Feet are often so ugly, so' – he sought the word he wanted – 'so misshapen. Made lumpy by bad boots, often. You should see what I see. Corns and swollen joints – *ach*! But this little foot, so strong and hard ...' He finished his measuring and stood up. 'Once, when I was a young man, I made a pair of shoes for a great ballerina. Carlotta Grisi.' He turned to Aunt Florence, 'You remember, Mrs da Costa? They made *Giselle* for her: a lovely dancer. This young lady has a foot like hers, muscular, with a high instep. It will be a pleasure to make these boots. A pleasure.' He bowed them out ceremoniously, and the brass bell over the door chimed as he closed it behind them.

'Now,' said Aunt Florence as they rode home in the Daimler, parcels strewn about them, 'we'll write off to Jaeger for a shortsleeved vest and underbodice and a pair of knickerbockers of the same material. We don't want you catching cold.'

* * *

'You look very natty,' Florence pronounced, when Lilith paraded for her in the ensemble a week later. 'Now all we have to do it teach you to ride your machine.'

As it turned out, Lilith proved naturally adept at bicycling, and in less than an hour had mastered the technique needed for balancing on the contraption. Florence and Judith Mendoza were delighted with her progress, and she felt almost embarrassed, saying in explanation that the dancing probably helped.

'I understood that teacher of yours had stopped,' Florence said. 'Samuel was saying only the other day he regretted her going.'

'I dance by myself.' Lilith felt as if she had been caught out in some misdemeanour as her aunt's eyebrows rose.

'Isn't that a little – childish, dear? I mean, it was one thing for Beatrice, but for you . . .' Her voice trailed away doubtfully. Lilith flushed.

'I don't think so: I like it.' Before she had time to say any more Judith Mendoza flashed at Florence, 'Don't *cavil*. I'd have thought you of all people would encourage any form of self-expression.'

Florence, who did not care to be accused of frivolity, let her annoyance show.

'Self-expression is one thing. I don't want Lilith to become a dilettante. To follow an art in a desultory way is so superficial; a waste of time.'

Judith Mendoza caught Lilith's eye and shook her head slightly. Lilith kept dutifully quiet. She knew her aunt only wanted the best for her, but her attitude to dancing was much the same as her father's: a pleasant accomplishment, a means to help Beatrice. Florence had no idea how she felt each evening, going up the cramped attic stairs to the bare room and the wooden *barre*, to the music that filled her mind and commanded her body. When, later, they were briefly alone, Judith Mendoza added cautiously, for she was a woman to whom life had offered many rebuffs, and it had taught her to tread warily, 'I should so much like to see you dance. One day. When you feel like it.' And Lilith gave her a glance of gratitude that warmed her heart.

When Judith Mendoza suggested that Florence and Lilith accompany her to Richmond for a day to the home of her brother and his wife, Florence accepted eagerly. The Mendozas occupied a vast house fronting on to the Thames just behind Richmond Green, and she had long wanted to visit it. The house appeared to Lilith like a medieval castle with its round towers set over curved windows, the sweep of marble steps and the walls of ancient, many-coloured brick.

Nora Mendoza was younger than her sister-in-law, a sweet-faced wispy woman with light eyes and indeterminate hair. She showed them to rooms where they could rest from the journey. When they had recovered she took them round, explaining that Queen Elizabeth I was said to have secretly met a lover in the house, and that therefore it had romantic associations.

There must have been a dozen guests besides themselves at the informal luncheon served beneath the chestnut trees in the garden. Lilith was fascinated by one of the servants, a Chinaman in a brilliant silk jacket over baggy black trousers, a long pig-tail beneath his round hat, offering great platters of fish: trout and pike, whitebait and halibut, all served cold with aromatic sauces. She stared at him surreptitiously as she helped herself to salmon and watercress mousse: he so closely resembled the tiny carved figures of Orientals in the glass-fronted cupboards at home in Sloane Square that she half-expected him to begin – if she touched him with a gentle finger – to nod his head as they did, forward and back in endless agreement.

'Chan-Tu has been in the family's service for years.' It was Judith's voice behind her. 'My brother went to the Orient when he was a young man and brought him back as a personal attendant. He is a most reliable servant, but he continues to arouse a great deal of attention. He's in London much of the time now, with my nephew Joseph.' She looked round vaguely. 'He's here somewhere. You must meet him.'

When the meal was at last over, and only the greedy lingered over gâteau Chantilly, port wine jelly and *petits fours*, Lilith wandered away on her own through the grounds. She came to a high red-brick wall round what appeared to be a kitchen garden. At the far end of the wall a man sat at an easel, a Panama hat shielding his eyes from the sun. She walked along until she stood about five feet behind him, not liking to go any nearer, and gave a little cough so that he knew she was there. He did not turn his head. She could see that he was painting, in delicate colours, the view of heavy trees that shaded the broad tow path and the glinting water beyond. It was simple and elegant, utterly unlike her own artistic efforts.

Impulsively she exclaimed, 'That's really beautiful,' and immediately wished she had not spoken, for all he said, without raising his eyes from his occupation, was, 'No, I fear you are mistaken.'

The words were rude; she thought his tone was

not. She waited, but he made no attempt to carry on the conversation. She had assumed he was a guest also. Perhaps she was wrong. Discomfited, she walked silently back past the misty blue delphiniums to rejoin the party, and found them still sitting beneath the chestnuts, idly discussing the game of croquet someone had proposed. When she appeared, her aunt cried, 'Lilith plays, don't you, dear?' and her disclaimer went unheard as everyone began to speak at once. She felt too shy to protest, and so found herself standing on the smooth croquet ground holding a heavy mallet with a brass-bound box-wood head the shape of a dice-box, surveying with some alarm the brightly coloured croquet balls. They were playing the old-fashioned game with eight players, four to a side, and she hung back, hoping to be able to play her strokes last and copy the others, for she had no idea in what order she was supposed to put the ball through the hoops scattered apparently haphazard on the lawn. She was playing with another young woman and two men, and though she had been introduced to all of them she couldn't remember their names. They drew lots to decide which side should lead, and to her relief it was their opponents.

By the time her turn came, she had gathered that the object was for each side to be first in carrying all its balls through the hoops in order to the turning-peg at the top, and then back to the winning-peg. She was concentrating so hard that for a time she quite failed to notice that the man in the white suit with the Panama hat leading their opponents was the painter from the kitchen garden, and it was only when one of the men called ironically, 'Garden party croquet, Joseph. Shouldn't tax *you* too much,' that she realized he must be Judith's nephew. She looked at him again, with more interest, and he half-turned, feeling her glance, and smiled. Then he gave his attention back to the pink ball at his feet, and with an apparently effortless swing sent it, together with the orange ball of her partner, through the hoop of white painted iron.

'*Roquet!*' pronounced the pretty woman beside him. 'Bravo.' The man leading her own side shook his head ruefully, and watched as Joseph Mendoza moved forward and proceeded to take croquet, putting his foot on his own ball to keep it from moving, and then striking it with his mallet with such force that his opponent's ball rolled a great distance.

When Lilith's turn came, she held the mallet nervously, fingers curled round the Malacca cane shaft, and attempted to propel her yellow ball forward as she had seen the others do. She must have hit it too gently, for it merely rolled a little way, hit a bump and stopped short. The next player on the opposing side struck it with her ball and took it through the first hoop. Lilith felt herself turning pink with mortification: she would never understand this game.

After what seemed like hours, every minute of which she disliked, it was finally over. Lilith's team had been soundly beaten, thanks mainly to Joseph Mendoza's expertise. The players shook hands formally and then wandered back to join the watchers beneath the trees, where barley water was being served. Lilith was wondering what to do with the wretched mallet when it was taken from her hand and a cold glass put in its place. Her rescuer was Joseph Mendoza.

'When you've drunk that,' he said, in his quiet voice, 'I'll show you a few strokes. They'll come in useful.'

She drank the barley water eagerly and remarked, 'How odd to have ice in the middle of summer.'

'Not really. Large hunks are cut from the pond in the winter and then put in an icehouse, covered with sawdust to maintain its temperature, and used when we need it.' He spoke absently, like a man with his mind elsewhere. Trying to make polite conversation, she said, 'Did you finish your painting?'

'Oh, it was you, was it?' He turned to look at her as if seeing her for the first time. 'Yes. Or at any rate, I got far enough to know it wasn't worth the finishing.'

'I thought it was very good.'

'So I seem to recall your saying. But with the greatest respect, I submit that you are not well-placed to pass artistic comment.'

Lilith stared at him with wide eyes, wondering if he was being rude. She decided it was merely his way of speaking. 'No,' he went on, 'I know my limitations. Unfortunately, you see, I *do* know what I'm talking about when it comes to works of art. It's very inhibiting.'

Lilith recalled something Judith had said to her.

'Don't you have a gallery?' she asked, and saw his features soften into a look of gratification, as though he was pleased that she knew.

'Yes,' he said. 'Not far from Aunt Judith's, in fact. I don't sell pictures, though. I specialize in porcelain.'

'You mean – dinner services?' She felt ignorant, but he took the question seriously.

'Collector's items. Single pieces of the highest quality. Mostly English.'

Lilith nodded, watching his expression change as

he talked about his porcelain, thinking how interesting he looked. He was of medium height – no taller than herself – with dark brown hair receding slightly at the temples so that it grew in a widow's peak. Fine lines of concentration etched the corners of grey eyes. The white suit he wore emphasized the sallow tinge of his skin and he was clean-shaven but for a pencil-thin moustache. He spoke softly, almost hesitantly, but she soon realized this was an affectation, for Joseph Mendoza always knew what he was talking about. She gained the impression that he was much older than herself. At least thirty-five, she decided, and listened to him with the careful attention she would have accorded a man her father's age. When he offered to show her how to handle the mallet, she looked for somewhere to put down her glass, and found that the Chinese servant was already at her side, anticipating her need with a silver tray at the ready.

Joseph watched critically as she practised swinging the mallet at an imaginary ball, and shook his head.

'Put your weight on the forward foot. And slide your right hand further down the shaft – look, like this.' He was standing just behind her, and as he put his arm round her back to move her right hand, she straightened slightly. He had not intended any physical contact between them, for he was a man of punctilious manners. But the feel of Lilith's narrow, supple body against his own was disturbing, so that a small shock ran through him, reminding him absurdly of the time he had been taken to the great aquarium as a child and had touched, with a daring finger, the electric eel in its tank. He became very still, and stopped talking. Lilith, within his encircling arm, was concentrating on her stroke, and he registered the vulnerable nape of her neck beneath the well-brushed cluster of curls.

Neither was aware of being watched. Seated beneath the trees, sipping the tea brought by the Chinaman, Aunt Florence observed with interest young Mendoza's manner towards her niece. When Judith Mendoza joined her she indicated them with a movement of her head. The two women in the shade looked at the couple standing in the sunlight. Judith unconsciously cradled her crippled left hand in its dove-grey kid.

'Would you believe, Florence, that this possibility hadn't occurred to me until now?'

Florence gave her an affectionate look and tapped her knee reprovingly with a black lacquer lorgnette-case.

'No, dear, I wouldn't. After a friendship of twenty years, I think I know a little of your mind, and unless I'm very much mistaken you've cultivated Lilith deliberately with just such an end in view.' She unfolded her lorgnettes, holding them to her eyes beneath the brim of her hat so that she was not too obviously studying her niece and the young man. 'What's he like, your Joseph?'

Judith chose her words carefully. 'Reserved. Hard to know. Successful. A good businessman. I don't see much of him, but there seem to be many friends and he goes about a good deal. Nora and Sol have never had a moment's worry with him, I think.'

'He's good-looking. Are there women?'

Immediately she asked this, Florence knew the question was a mistake. Judith was an agreeable companion whose wit had a mordant edge she relished, though aware that it was probably Judith's deformity – and the effect it had on her life – which brought this out. Judith was a seemingly worldly woman but a spinster, and virgin, and at the tactless words a veil had come over her eyes. She said, bleakly, 'I wouldn't know, Florence. I imagine so. He is thirty-four, after all.'

There was a short silence. Then Florence said slowly, 'Lilith's very young. Not yet eighteen, I believe. But Samuel doesn't think of her future. It's a sort of self-deception on his part, to see his daughters as children still. I can understand it with Beatrice, but you have only to look at this girl to see where that attitude could lead. If she isn't taken in hand, Samuel will find he has trouble on his plate. Not that she's wild . . .' Florence corrected herself hastily, '. . . but you can see for yourself how full of life she is. She won't be satisfied with bicycling and tea-parties for much longer.'

'Do you think your brother would be in favour?'

'Oh, I'm sure he could be persuaded. And there's money, you know. Not a great deal, but Nathan and I would see that things were done in some style.'

Judith smiled at her, fully restored to good humour.

'You don't have to tell *me* that, Florence. I think we should have a word with my sister-in-law. Nora's very vague about things, she doesn't like to interfere. I feel this situation requires a little help, don't you?'

Florence Hartsilver nodded briskly, very much the committee-woman.

'I agree entirely. It would be an excellent thing for all concerned. Lilith's like my own daughter. I want to see her well settled.'

They sipped their tea. When Judith spoke again, it was cautiously, 'There's just one thing, Florence. It would be best if we didn't make too much of the matter of Beatrice. In case the family misunderstands.'

Florence set her cup carefully on its saucer. 'You think it might prevent a match? Yes, I can see that. Only of course, Lilith is not affected at all.'

Judith stuffed her kid-covered hand into its protective pocket. 'I know. But my happiness was ruined because of a defect feared to be inherited. I am determined Lilith's future must not be blighted by her sister's unknown ailment.'

Florence was startled by the vehemence in her voice; she had not realized how much Judith felt for the girl. Happy herself, she could scarcely comprehend the depths of Judith's loneliness, or her longing for the life she had been denied. She said, 'You know best. Speak to Nora and Sol, and I'll talk to my brother. And as for the young people' – she glanced across the croquet lawn to where the two figures in white still stood side by side, heads bent in concentration over the hoops and balls – 'I don't anticipate any problem there.'

Chapter 5

Joseph Mendoza would have approved his aunt's description of him. He deliberately cultivated the slightly abstracted air Lilith had noticed: he had been reserved from childhood, a watcher always, a wry observer of other people's absurdities. It was a characteristic that stemmed from his self-consciousness.

He was the only son of indulgent parents, and had been spoiled outrageously as a child. He had been given his own pony-cart when he was six years old, and by the time he was ten could speak French and German passably well, knew some Greek and Latin and had enough Hebrew to translate his portion of the Law when he came to read it in synagogue on the Saturday morning he was Barmitzvah and officially came to man's estate. The sciences did not interest him at all, mathematics he found dull and lifeless. The arts were different. He became a voracious reader, particularly of history.

Both his parents were born in Baghdad where their respective families had known each other. A few years apart they had been brought to England to settle, and the marriage – anticipated since both were in the cradle – had been an early one. Joseph was not born until the ninth year of their union, and his mother never got over her surprise, for she was in the seventh month of pregnancy before she became aware of her happy condition. A vague moth of a woman, everything about her was so lightly defined that even her husband would have been hard put to it to describe the colour of her eyes. She wore a look of faint and perpetual astonishment, which her family ascribed to the birth of a son. This was near enough the truth, for Nora Mendoza had little faith in her ability to achieve anything, least of all another human being. It was from her that Joseph had that abstracted look, and also his love of history, for Nora was obsessed by the past. It interested her far more than the present, which she found chaotic and demanding. The past was safe, ordered and contained, lodged firmly between the pages of her beloved books. Few of her friends realized how much she knew about the heritage of England, her adopted country, for she spoke of it rarely. It was a private pleasure, reading and researching, peering at the ancestral lines of long-forgotten families, collecting pictures of dead English aristocrats and their homes. She shared it only with Joseph and he delighted her by his appreciation. At first, when he was younger, it was an assumed appreciation, for he loved his mother and would have done anything to please her and win her approval. As he matured it became genuine, and he grew as absorbed as she in the minutiae of other people's lives. They would spend uncounted hours together, engrossed in books and papers and brittle old documents, in libraries and reading rooms and the Public Record Office.

When Joseph left school (he had received his education at Haberdashers' Aske's), his father was eager for him to go to university, but this met with no response. Joseph relished beautiful possessions, of which there were many in the Mendoza home, and he was knowledgeable about antique furniture and paintings. For a time, he thought that this was where his future lay, and he went to Paris for two

81

years, rented an atelier in Notre Dame des Champs and spent his not inconsiderable allowance on oils and canvas. His parents thought his work wonderful, and when he had done fifty or so paintings Solomon Mendoza obtained for him a one-man show in a London gallery of some distinction. (He never told Joseph that he paid his old friend Moritz Raphael, and had in fact bought the exhibition: he allowed his son to think his talent had earned it.) But few pictures sold, critics were unimpressed and after the initial disappointment Joseph found, by chance, his true vocation.

Moritz Raphael, who owned the Grafton Street gallery where Joseph held his exhibition, had known Solomon Mendoza for years. They had met when Mendoza married and began to buy pictures for his first home. Their sons attended the same school – though Asher Raphael was eleven years younger than Joseph – and Solomon sent many clients to the gallery, business colleagues with more money than taste. Moritz Raphael was tactful, informed and prudent, and the pictures they bought from him appreciated steadily in value, representing an investment his new clients much appreciated.

Solomon Mendoza had followed his own father into trade. The old man had been an importer but where the business had concentrated on supplying small factories with raw materials – Egyptian cotton, jute, feathers for hats, snakeskin for handbags – Solomon branched out. He built up a large and profitable business supplying retailers with exotic items from the East: Chinese lacquer screens encrusted with mother-of-pearl figures, tea services from Japan, ornaments of jade and jasper, shellwork, trinket boxes and mirror frames. He had hopes that Joseph would join him, but it became apparent that he was not interested in trade.

The exhibition at the Raphael Gallery could not by any stretch of the imagination have been called a success. Joseph was utterly downcast, for he knew in his heart he lacked the one characteristic any artist must possess; a belief in his own talent so huge it transcends any setback. He saw that no one wanted his pictures, and he was shrewd enough, even in his despondent mood, to know that he must find another way to make a living.

He was in the gallery watching dejectedly on the day the exhibition was being dismantled when an elderly man came in and bought, literally out of the packing crate, a small picture of a Parisian market.

Oscar Delal was a dapper figure sporting white spats. His bald head shone in the pale spring sunlight as he walked Joseph Mendoza down Grafton Street, talking earnestly, his hand in its butter yellow glove on the young man's arm. They spent two hours together, and by the end of the afternoon Joseph had agreed to work for him with an option to become a partner in a year's time.

The Delal gallery was less opulent than the Raphaels' establishment, but its contents were infinitely more fragile. In a room swathed in dark velvets the exhibits were all porcelain. For Joseph, walking into that place was like going home. He was immediately at ease and it took months only for him to learn almost as much as Oscar Delal had discovered in a lifetime. Five years later, Joseph had to all intents and purposes taken over the running of the gallery. He still painted, but for his own pleasure only, and when he reached thirty-three it was as though eleven years spent handling such delicate material had formed his personality.

He was a civilized man with tapering, feminine fingers which touched his porcelain – only the finest, only the most expensive – with love and reverence. He never made an abrupt movement nor uttered an expletive. He wore soft leather shoes in which he moved soundlessly upon the thick carpet of his showroom, which under his aesthetic eye had been stripped of its over-ornate velvet drapes to become cool, creamy and uncluttered. The only colour now came from the exhibits which glowed from their silk-lined glass cases, for Joseph's own clothes were always subdued, of soft greys and browns, with sometimes a touch of blue in a necktie. It was as though he, as much as the furnishings, was a foil for the *objets d'art* in his charge.

Joseph Mendoza never thought of the pieces he collected as his possessions, being conscious always that they were the children of the craftsmen who had fashioned them. And this son of Iraqui-born parents, product of a family dispersed from Spain in the fifteenth century, became an expert in Chinese porcelain and English bone china.

He loved the early Chinese porcelain, with its fragile strength and beauty, and made a study of the Chinese marks. His favourite dynasty was Yuan and he also was widely known for his collection of delicious Blanc-de-chine figurines of the Chinese immortals. He bought also the more prosaic monochrome glazes: peach-bloom, mirror-black, tea-dust. He understood the meaning of the painted symbols and was utterly absorbed in his Eight Immortals, his Lions of Fo, his Kylins, so that he felt a faint disdain for those collectors who plodded in the humdrum foothills of European wares.

Not that he despised them. He could date a piece of Derby merely by the way a painter handled the tones on a rose petal. He kept many of the charmingly anglicized versions of Continental ware, and whilst he did not care for Meissen figures by Kaendler or those modelled at Nymphenburg by Bustelli, he kept English porcelain, or soft paste pieces from factories like Bow, Chelsea and Longton Hall. He had examples of the early salt-glazed stoneware figures in pew-groups and bandsmen, and the earthenware products of potters like Astbury and Whieldon, dripping with glorious glazes.

By the time Lilith walked into his parents' garden at Richmond, Joseph was an acknowledged authority in his specialities, and was engaged in writing a book already commissioned. He was a man of the utmost formality, his manners as elegantly polished as his boots. His professional standing was so high that he numbered several members of the British royal family among his clients, as well as those of the reigning European houses. Collectors in the United States visited him twice a year to see what was on offer. He knew how high his status was, and this gave him an urbanity, an assurance that he permitted himself only in the gallery. In private, among his family and friends, he chose to appear vague, charming, amused.

He was able to slip into either personae as quickly as a man putting on a comfortable garment, as easily as an actor assuming a familiar role. Only he could not say, now, which was his true self. No one ever saw him in both settings. The one outsider who might have done so was Oscar Delal, but he was a man who had assumed so many roles during a long lifetime, he did not notice. So the only person who observed Joseph Mendoza in public and in private was the Chinese manservant his father had brought back with him from the Orient thirty years before.

Liu Chan-Tu had known Joseph from a child and loved him as tenderly as a son, but had never permitted himself to express such emotion. Only the depth of feeling in his eyes when he looked at Mr Joseph betrayed him. When his son acquired his own premises, Solomon Mendoza, well aware of his devotion, suggested he might like to enter Joseph's service rather than remain with him. Chan-Tu could have wept for joy, but he merely inclined his head and said, 'Certainly, sir, if that is your wish.' Now the sole aim of his existence was to care for Joseph, to make sure that he was comfortable and well served, that his suits and shirts were in perfect condition, his bureau drawers tidy, his every wish translated immediately into action.

Joseph occupied a charming little house in Hans Place, the perfect bachelor establishment, with a basement kitchen and a room beside it for Chan-Tu. Only one other servant was employed, a housemaid who came in each day to clean, and to whom Chan-Tu rarely spoke, though she gossiped cheerfully to him notwithstanding. The Chinese servant took care of everything: he laundered, starched and ironed. He sewed, pressed, polished and cooked. He did not care to shop at Harrods, the nearby general store on the Brompton Road, preferring to buy from the market traders in Chelsea, where he went daily in the Chinese manner, insisting on choosing each piece of fruit himself. From the butcher he would purchase fowl only after he had prodded every carcase in the shop. Meat he did not buy – Nora Mendoza sent round items chosen from the kosher butcher for Joseph, and Chan-Tu himself had not eaten meat since arriving in England as a young man, preferring stranger dishes of monkey or owl unavailable to him now.

Whenever Joseph went to stay with his parents in Richmond, Chan-Tu accompanied him, resuming his duties about their house with his customary equanimity. Joseph always suggested on these occasions that Chan-Tu take a holiday, but the man would look at him with something like horror in his eyes. He did not require so much as an afternoon off: there was nothing he wished to do that was not connected with Joseph. His rare leisure hours he spent in his room, playing solitary card games.

Liu Chan-Tu served the ladies with tea and strawberry tarts, and without appearing to do so watched his master on the croquet lawn with the lady in white. He had heard Miss Mendoza and her friend discussing them both, and knew what it augured. Until now, it had never crossed his mind that Master Joseph might marry. On more than one occasion he had assumed a bland innocence when his employer had clearly been entertaining in an intimate manner, or had returned home before breakfast in his evening clothes. But that had not happened often, and there seemed no danger of change to their way of life. But he had noticed this young woman leave the party after luncheon and seek out his employer where he sat painting beside the river wall, and felt convinced her actions were calculated. Certainly he had never before seen Master Joseph spend so much time talking to a woman. It made him uneasy.

On the croquet lawn their elongated shadows stretched before them. Lilith made another swing at Joseph's instructions with such gusto that her chiffon hat with its ostrich feather decorations fell off. She gave a giggle and before Joseph could retrieve it for her, hooked the toe of her shoe beneath the brim and kicked, so that the hat flew into the air to be caught. She stuck it on her head, uncaring, at an absurd angle, and grinned at him from beneath it.

He observed all this in some amazement. He was accustomed to the women of his family who were – apart from his vague, bookish mother – worldly and poised, interested in their pet charities, clothes, their children and their husbands' businesses. The eligible girls he met through these channels promised to become their mothers all over again, and even in youth they had an air of solidity about them, an assurance, that he found intimidating. Then there were the women whose company he occasionally sought, who wore dresses with enormous sleeves and dressed their hair à la Princesse de Galles with frizzy fringes which even he recognized as removable and switches of false hair to make 'teapot handles' on top of their heads. Their charms were obvious and without subtlety, and after a few hours he became bored with them. He did not think he had ever met anyone like the da Costa girl, with her vivid face and impulsive, almost hoydenish behaviour. He found himself asking, a little stiffly, 'Would you prefer to stop now?'

They joined their aunts, and drank tea, and spoke of the new *Twelfth Night* at Her Majesty's Theatre with Beerbohm Tree as Malvolio. Joseph took little part in the conversation, watching the ladies with his habitual remote, amused expression. When they had finished, Judith Mendoza turned to him.

'Why don't you show Lilith the glasshouses, dear? I'm sure she would be most interested.'

Politely he got to his feet.

'Of course. If you would care to.'

Lilith did not need Florence Hartsilver's imperceptible nod to prompt her.

'Oh,' she said, 'please. I'd love it,' and jumped to her feet, leaving her cake forgotten on the table in her haste. When she had gone, the two women exchanged a meaningful glance.

The glasshouses were situated behind the kitchen garden she had passed earlier. Joseph showed her the vines and early strawberries, the peaches and nectarines, the Maréchal Niel roses fanning overhead. Cucumbers and melons hung heavy in nets in a house of their own, and when they reached a glossy shrub sprawling against the red brick wall he picked for her a white flower, the matt petals just breaking out of bud, that made her think of Beatrice. Then they moved to the tropical houses, where rare orchids perched like butterflies amongst the foliage, and the air was moist and smelled of green things, of forests and rain torrents. There was the sound of water running everywhere, and Lilith thought she could hear plants growing in that rich humidity, lifting and bursting and flooding into flower. The sun still shone on the glass roof and walls, which were so beaded with drops of moisture it was hard to see in or out, and a faint steam rose from the dark soil. It was mysterious in there, as foreign as if they were not in Richmond at all, but in some dense deep jungle.

Joseph told her of plants that grew in far countries, of the talipot palm with its mast-like trunk a hundred feet high, bearing once in its long lifetime a gigantic spike of white flower that burst forth with an audible explosion; of the pandang, branched like a candelabrum, each one ending in a bunch of sword-shaped leaves guarding a treasure of blossom while snakelike roots forked downward, so the whole tree seemed supported on slender stilts. He spoke of tropical forests where hidden trees rare as gems –

ebony, rosewood, sandalwood – were entwined in creepers, choked in parasite blooms.

'Look,' he said, and led her to a corner where creepers hung from the roof, thicker than her wrist, with tentative tendrils which clung to her shoulders. He leaned down to a plant she did not know, broad, fleshy leaves the colour of limes, and very delicately touched the leaflets at the centre. After a moment, the plant reacted to his touch, and the smaller leaves began to twist and whirl. Surprised, Lilith looked up, expecting that a door had opened to let in the wind, but the air was utterly still. And now the outer, fleshy leaves had begun to close up with convulsive little shudders. Defensively, as though it were alive, the leaves drew together around Joseph's finger. Lilith gave a gasp and stepped back.

'Don't you find it fascinating?' Joseph's voice had an odd quality. 'Don't you see how beautiful it is? Imagine the sensitivity of it, closing up under my hand, protecting itself. Like a woman.'

Lilith swayed slightly. The place was so hot, there was no air at all, her forehead was sticky with sweat and her palms felt slippery. She could detect in Joseph's voice, beneath the apparently innocuous words, another meaning she did not – could not – understand. His low voice had an undertone she felt on the surface of her skin, as the plant had felt the touch of his intrusive finger, a kind of soft brutality she had never encountered before. She knew he was making a half-veiled suggestion, she was instinctively aware what he wanted of her – and to her own surprise she did not even attempt to evade him. She was mesmerized by the moment, by the shimmering heat of the hothouse, by the quivering, living plant, by this man with appraising eyes who looked at her as though she were a pretty object, as (she was sure) he looked at the items displayed in his gallery. With hypnotic intensity she watched as Joseph touched the plant again, and again it closed tremulously around his finger. *Like a woman*, he had said, *protecting itself*.

Joseph saw the effect he was producing and it amused, flattered and excited him. He was sensitive to women, and in some inexplicable way felt his sensual needs put him at their mercy. Lilith did not threaten him; he was charmed by the wild tumble of curls, the bright eyes and absorbed, childlike interest in everything around her. When they stood together on the croquet lawn, her hands under his had been small and hard and competent as a boy's. She was everything he was not: she was without artifice or affectation, she acted on instinct where he resorted to reason. She attracted him as no other woman had ever done, and for once in his life he threw caution to the winds.

So there was little need, after all, for the carefully concealed eagerness with which Nora Mendoza asked her son what he thought of the da Costa girl. When she put to him, not without nervousness, the idea that he might consider her as a prospective wife, he listened with his habitual polite and serious manner and then told her he had already arrived at the conclusion that she would suit him very well. Nor was there need for the enthusiastic eulogy to which Aunt Florence and Judith Mendoza subjected Lilith on the journey home. Something that had been sleeping was awakened in her. The humid hothouse air had allowed more than spores to take root that afternoon.

And so it was that when, a few days later, Lilith took her bicycle out early and wobbled along the grass of Hyde Park and Joseph crossed her path, ostensibly on his way to the gallery, it seemed to her no less than the hand of fate. (Though, in fact, it was the combined efforts of Florence and Judith Mendoza.) She still had not got her balance and on seeing him her equilibrium, physically and emotionally, quite deserted her, and she tumbled inelegantly off. Any other time she would have laughed and jumped up and clambered on again. Only this time she fell awkwardly, twisting her knee. Winded, she lay for a few moments on the wet grass, her body in its trim cycling outfit supple as a scarf. He looked down at her, lying there at his feet, the check Redfern cap fallen off and glossy hair spilled round her shoulders. She appeared helpless and quiet, staring up at him with those clear and candid eyes. He had no means of knowing how utterly uncharacteristic such a situation was to her. He helped her up and brushed her coat and skirt, and asked solicitously if she had hurt herself. She was so relieved after that alarming episode in the hothouse to find him kind and concerned, that she mistook the relief she felt for a different, stronger emotion and agreed, standing there in the fresh green morning, to become his wife.

Joseph escorted her back to Portman House, and they told Aunt Florence, whose excitement was mixed with embarrassment at being seen by a young man whilst still in her wrapper, even though it was so elaborate a garment he thought she was fully dressed. Lilith insisted on going home immediately to ask her father's permission. 'He'll be so surprised,' she said with satisfaction.

In fact, her father's initial response to the proposed marriage had been shock, but Lilith did not know this. It had been Florence who first put the plan to him, the evening after the visit to Richmond, and he had laughed in her face.

'Good Lord, Flo, Lilith's a child still. You women will be marrying them off in their cradles to suit your whims.'

But Florence had expected this, and it did not throw her for a moment. She said smoothly, 'You said that to me once before. The "child" is eighteen, and if you don't see it, my dear, be sure that others do.'

Samuel da Costa was still laughing, but the sound faded and he stared at her.

'Eighteen? *Eighteen*? I hadn't thought ... but then Beatrice is ...'

'Beatrice is a woman, Samuel,' Florence finished for him. 'You don't have two little girls in your house any more.' She had no need to add, *though that is what you wish to believe*, for it was in her voice. Samuel nodded. Dulcie Bennett had often told him he was blinkered when it came to his two daughters. She, who had successfully brought up four of her own, worried about the two motherless girls in Sloane Square, but her unorthodox relationship with the doctor did not permit her to interfere, though countless times she had warned him that he faced problems over their future. Now he said slowly, 'The Mendozas are a good family, of course. And you say the young man is suitable?'

'Eminently. He is the right age, and has a well-found business. There's a house, too, though probably too small for a family. That's in the future. But it's certain Lilith will want for nothing.'

He looked at her in real distress.

'And what will this do to my Beatrice? It's been bad enough with Lilith out of the house so much:

I've never known her so withdrawn. But if Lilith marries, what will she do then?'

Florence sighed. 'I don't want to sound hard, Sam. I love Beatrice as you do. But we can't hold Lilith back because of her. We can't stop her going forward.'

Samuel said heavily.

'It's in my mind to do so. For Beatrice's sake.'

'Like old Dr Barrett and that poor daughter of his? Do that, Samuel, and I'll never speak to you again. Do that, and I'll abduct Lilith myself.' Her fingers fluttered their agitation, and she had to force herself to be calm. 'How is Beatrice behaving now?'

As always when he discussed his afflicted daughter, Samuel spoke with a mixture of pain and professionalism.

'Much better, in many ways. She seems to have quietened down, and we have had only two seizures in this last year. They may die out altogether. I've been experimenting with her diet, and oddly enough this seems to have had an effect. I think perhaps she reacts badly to certain foods. Eggs, for instance, and even potatoes, seem to activate her attacks. But of course, this can only be a preventative. It doesn't represent a cure. And if she understands that Lilith is to leave her for good, then I can't anticipate the harm that will do her.'

'Maybe. But Lilith staying will do her no positive good, either. You can't sacrifice one for the other, Samuel. What would their mother have said?'

Samuel da Costa got up and pulled the curtains against the evening chill. 'I know you're right, Flo. I won't stand in Lilith's way, if this is what she wants.' He gave a wry smile. 'It's clearly what *you* want. But I tell you, I fear for the future.'

As he had promised Florence, he did not oppose

Lilith. All he did was ask her if she was sure she wanted Joseph Mendoza.

'This marriage is not of my choosing, my dear. I'm in no rush to see you leave here. Don't take this man if you aren't quite sure you want him. There are others, you know.'

Lilith had flung her arms round his neck, and he smelled that subtle scent of fruit that always came from her hair and skin. It made his heart ache, to think that another man would have all this, enjoy all this, and he would lose her. His chief concern was whether Joseph would make a good husband; time alone would tell. Florence thought well of him, and she was a sure judge of character. He must talk to the young man himself, of course, before anything further could happen, though he did not doubt everything would be settled amicably. Nor would he gainsay what Lilith wanted. God knew she had had little enough happiness. It seemed to him a woman's life was a haphazard business, directed by instinct rather than intellect, dependent upon the fortunes and foibles of some man. The least he could do was ascertain that the man was suitable. He unclasped Lilith's encircling arms.

'You haven't answered,' he reminded her.

'Oh, Pa, I do want Joseph. I know it's been ridiculously quick, but I've never met anyone like him. He's so interesting, and I like the way he talks – you will, too, you see. And there's this dear little house, and Hans Place is so near, I'll be able to come in every day ... to see Beatrice ...' Her excited voice trailed to a stop. 'I hadn't thought about Beatrice.' Like a stricken child, she had her hand to her mouth. 'It'll be dreadful for her, if I marry. She'll be left alone. I can't do that to her.'

Samuel looked at his younger daughter. He saw

the emotions passing across that vivid face, saw the regret and the love. He knew how dear she held Beatrice, knew that if he chose, he could persuade her out of the marriage. But now that the moment had come, he did not even want to try. Instead, he took her hand in his.

'Don't be a silly girl. Beatrice will be with me, after all. We'll get by without you. Just as long as it's what you want.'

She held his hand against her face. It smelled of Lysol, as always, aseptic and reassuring. Her words were muffled.

'Let me tell Beatrice myself.'

She put it off until the evening. The skies had been low all day and it had rained intermittently since dawn. It was almost dark by six o'clock although still only early in September, and the maids had been round to draw the thick velvet drapes and light the lamps.

Lilith and Beatrice were together, as usual, in the morning room. It had been their mother's favourite for it looked out on Sloane Square, and it was still cluttered with pictures and objects she had loved: the fire-screen decorated with mother-of-pearl, the lampshades of etched glass, the sprawling tea roses on the wallpaper and the draped palms, the walnut 'silver table' loaded with photographs of people the two girls no longer recognized. Here Lilith could always detect, like some faded, fragrant pot-pourri, the scent that used to linger in the wardrobes, long ago, where her mother's dresses hung.

At that thought she glanced down at Beatrice, who was sitting close beside her on a tapestry stool, her hands clasped round her knees. She was even more beautiful in the lamplight that touched her pale skin with shadows and deepened the mystery of those impenetrable blue eyes. Lilith was doing beadwork, which bored her, but she had promised Aunt Florence a purse. Beatrice enjoyed watching this, liking the sight of her sister's long fingers flickering amongst the glittering beads, humming the odd, primitive little melody that was the only sound she ever made, that only Lilith ever heard. Lilith dropped a bead and said, 'Damn' and lost interest entirely. She got up to pull back the velvet curtain with its tasselled edge, gazing out at the rain bouncing off the pavements and the last shoppers scurrying into Peter Jones, the haberdasher across the square. It was a scene unchanged since her childhood; she knew even the shadow of every lamppost, every tree. Without looking round, she opened her mouth to tell Beatrice of the dramatic change she was bringing into both their lives.

And became aware that behind her, as if in anticipation of what she was about to hear, Beatrice had stopped humming.

Chapter 6

Lilith could scarcely credit the way in which her life had so suddenly changed. In a matter of days she had passed – or so it seemed to her – from the schoolroom into society. She revelled in it, relishing the attention and the bustle. It was in her nature to leap forward, to grasp what was offered, and youth accentuated this characteristic. Everyone around her approved: Aunt Florence was ecstatic, and she was acute enough to know that Judith Mendoza was obtaining a good deal of vicarious satisfaction from seeing her matched with Joseph. Even her father, after his initial uncertainty, appeared happy with the engagement. She found it a new experience, to be able to please people by her actions and at the same time improve herself. For she felt it would be an improvement, to be married to Joseph Mendoza. He was interesting, successful, and if he also intimidated her, she welcomed his authority. Not that she saw much of him at the moment. They were both busy with preparations and perpetually surrounded by relatives or visitors. Propriety also forbade that they be alone together: after the marriage was time enough.

The only cloud on Lilith's horizon was Beatrice. They were still so close that they were able, as always, to communicate by some means other than speech. Beatrice had known, that dark evening, what Lilith had been about to say. She had jumped to her feet and crossed the room swiftly to lay her finger on Lilith's lips. Lilith had caught her hand

and started to speak, but Beatrice had pulled away, shaking her head violently, and run from the room. Late that night Lilith had woken knowing that in the room next door Beatrice was sobbing silently. In the end she had gone in, climbing into bed beside her as they had always done in childhood, and put her arms round the hunched figure beneath the blankets, stroking the fairy-pale hair sodden with tears. Gradually, the clenched body had relaxed and softened against her, and Beatrice finally slipped into an exhausted sleep. Lilith alone had lain staring into the darkness, trying to see the years that lay before the sister for whom she thought and acted, the sister she loved and had chosen to leave.

Lilith learned then that Beatrice's despair was harder to bear than her own.

When Florence and Nathan Hartsilver had asked if they could hold the engagement party at Portman House, Samuel da Costa had agreed without demur. It was to be principally a family gathering, but that only increased the flurry of preparation for Florence did nothing by halves. As the date of the engagement neared, Florence spent hours writing lists of foods and wine, scanning her post for accepted invitations. One letter in particular sent her into raptures.

Two years before, the financier Alfred de Rothschild had come to Nathan Hartsilver for help. They respected each other's acumen, although Nathan privately considered the richer man to be a hypochondriac. He was something of a fop also, but Nathan was one himself and found nothing odd in his friend's dandyish dress. Rothschild was a considerable musician, with a symphony orchestra of his own which he conducted with a baton of ivory banded with diamonds. He was also a connoisseur of prima donnas, and when Dame Nellie Melba became the darling of Covent Garden, he took it upon himself to ensure that his financial sagacity meant her income from astute investments soon outstripped her earnings from singing.

At that time, the singer lived at the Savoy Hotel during her Covent Garden season, but Alfred de Rothschild decided she should acquire a home in London. Nathan Hartsilver owned many properties in the West End, and was delighted to be of service. It was Florence, in fact, who remembered the Great Cumberland Place house which had been let to a former colonel for many years. When it fell empty, she took the singer to see it. Melba decided to buy, although insisting the entire house be remodelled in the style of the Palace of Versailles.

Florence became equally fascinated in the project, and offered to help employ skilled craftsmen from Paris, for Melba felt that only French plasterers, cabinet-makers and glass-workers could do what she wanted. A friendship grew up between the women over the two years this work took to complete, and she was a frequent guest at Portman House, though Lilith had yet to meet her.

So when Melba received her invitation to the party, and sent a note round saying that if they wished, she would sing after dinner, Florence was quite overcome.

'She never does that, Lilith, never. She wouldn't cheapen her professional standing by singing for her supper.'

'She knows the value of the notes that come from her throat,' came Nathan's voice from behind *The Times*. 'Her commercial instinct is too developed to allow her to give them away for nothing.'

100

'And she's quite right,' answered his wife swiftly. 'I would not have dreamt of asking her to sing, but for her to offer to do so ... You're a lucky girl, Lilith.'

Florence and Nathan had never hosted a more glittering occasion. The house was festooned with flowers, the balconies tented over with striped awnings. A chef was brought in, who ordered in a vast quantity of stores and arrived with a bevy of pupils. The great table was spread with a rich cloth decorated with a gold embroidered satin centrepiece and trails of smilax amongst the old silver, the bone china and the best glass.

All the Mendozas were there, headed by an unusually jovial Solomon, with Nora on his arm fluttery in mauve. Judith was spare and elegant in tête de nègre, her hand encased in matching kid, and dozens of relatives had come from Baghdad to celebrate Joseph's marriage. They spoke Ladino, Spaniolized Hebrew based on fifteenth-century Castilian sprinkled with Talmudic expressions and phrases borrowed from Arabic, Turkish and Greek. Lilith, though accustomed to hearing it spoken, could only follow it with difficulty, but that made no difference to the cousins. They embraced her warmly and admired her profusely, and handed her about amongst them, chattering and exclaiming enthusiastically over the pretty rose diamond ring Joseph had given her.

He watched all this with his customary amused air, and endured the teasing with equanimity. Lilith was proud of him: he seemed to her so sophisticated, so knowledgeable, so immaculate. When he stood beside her she experienced a proprietorial thrill mixed with amazement that this could be happening: she felt a child amidst adults, as if none of it really concerned her.

When the elaborate and lengthy meal was finally over, there was dancing in the saloon. After two sets Florence spoke briefly to the musicians, and the leader rapped his music stand for silence as she announced Dame Nellie Melba would sing. There was a murmur of excitement, for no one had foreseen this.

Melba had just returned to London after her Australian tour, and had not yet opened the Covent Garden season. She had scarcely been visible that evening, surrounded by her 'court' of friends and admirers. Now, Lilith could see that the singer, whom she supposed to be in her early forties, was dressed in scarlet gauze liberally sprinkled with minute dewdrops which made her look rather stout. She was strongly made, with dark hair held high in a Spanish comb and challenging, reddish-brown eyes. She was far from beautiful, but even before she began to sing, Lilith realized that she radiated such personality that no one in the room could take their eyes from her: even Florence's well-trained staff stood absorbed behind the guests.

She sang 'Lo, here the gentle lark', the soprano voice soaring like the bird itself. Lilith thought it sounded beautiful, but less impressive than she had expected. Then the diva gestured to the musicians who started to play the first act of *La Bohème*. Beside her, Joseph whispered, 'They say Puccini himself coached her in the role of Mimi.'

Melba was standing between the two great windows opening on to the park, her back to the wall, the light-sconces above her head emphasizing the strong bones of her face. Lilith thought, how absurd that anyone of such imposing stature should attempt to sing the part of the fragile consumptive.

When she began to sing, it became apparent that

she was making no attempt at all to impersonate the role. But how she sang it. Lilith had never before heard sounds like that: silvery, with a brilliant shivering edge cool as crystal. This large, stately person sang not with the voice of a woman, but a choirboy, sweet and sexless, piercing and pure. Lilith was conscious of the perfection of the tone, and the power of that voice, like a thread held taut between singer and listener, so that everyone in the room was linked to the figure between the open windows. At the end of the act, Melba sang the final high C and Lilith felt the hairs rise on the nape of her neck at the sound of it. The note left Melba's throat, it left her body, it came across the room like a star towards the audience, a ball of white light that touched the walls of the huge room and floated off them, and drifted out through the open windows across the waiting darkness of Hyde Park.

When it had finally faded, Lilith became aware again of the people around her, the wild applause, the shouts of enthusiasm, the excited faces. She too, cheered and clapped till her hands ached, while the figure in scarlet who had so enraptured them smiled regally and bowed like an empress.

Joseph left her side to speak to someone. Around her people gossiped about Melba, admiring words. Beneath them she caught sibilant whispers: 'In Australia, there's a rumour that she drinks heavily. Have you heard?'

'Malicious gossip,' another voice replied. 'She could never sing like that if she drank.'

Lilith looked at the two men talking, surprised at their unkindness about a woman who only a few minutes before had received such an ovation from them. She thought them unkind and ungracious, having no idea how much the public liked to tear down its gods. Just then Florence said beside her, 'Lilith, dear, come and speak to Dame Nellie. I know you want to thank her,' and pushed her through the throng to the diva's side. She offered her hand to Lilith who took it nervously, giving a small curtsey as if the singer had been a queen. She murmured, 'Thank you so much for singing tonight. You made it a most wonderful evening for Joseph and me. Your singing was perfect.'

Dame Nellie inclined her head. She was used to compliments: they were her due. She asked, 'And do you sing yourself?'

'Oh, no, I've no voice at all. But I listen to music a good deal and . . .' she paused, then added nervously, ' . . . and I dance, a little.'

The diva smiled at her.

'And I cannot dance.' She looked Lilith up and down, a swift professional glance. 'You've the shape for it. But you're marrying, after all. For a woman, a career and marriage don't go together, as I found to my cost.' Her voice grew hard. 'And I've the divorce papers to prove it.'

Florence had left them alone together, and now Lilith admitted, surprising herself, 'Listening to you tonight has made me want to dance again. Properly, I mean.'

'I like a woman with spirit.' There was approval in those assessing brown eyes. 'But it's no use having a perfect voice unless you also have brains, personality, magnetism, great willpower, health, strength and determination. I learned that long ago. And it's no different for a dancer. You must put your whole life and will into your dancing. If you're not prepared to do that, you will be wasting your time.'

Lilith nodded, her face set with concentration. Melba watched her for a moment as though about to add something, then a man appeared at her shoulder, claiming her attention. Instead, she touched Lilith's arm with the tip of the fan she carried at her wrist.

'I'll be interested to see what you make of yourself,' she said, and turned away.

Lilith moved in a dream for the rest of the evening. She had not known she was going to tell Dame Nellie about the dancing. She had not even known it was true. But she realized that almost her strongest emotion, listening to that remarkable voice, seeing the effect it had on the listeners, had been pure envy.

She remembered how she had felt on those magical evenings when she had danced at smoking concerts or charity soirées: the excitement, the extraordinary feeling that there was a cord between herself and the audience, by which she could lead them, making them feel as she wished, respond as she chose. She had felt it again, listening to Melba, only it had been the singer who held the audience in the palm of her hand, exercising her power over them – as she had been held herself, enraptured by that voice.

She remembered what the diva had said – *health, strength, determination*. Well, she had all those. In the midst of that crowded room, watched by Florence and Judith and her father, who all wished her happiness, and by Joseph, whose wife she would be in a few months' time, the realization seemed ridiculous, even to her.

Lilith knew now that she longed to dance more than anything else on earth. Just when her life was turning one way, she wanted to run, to escape, to leave behind her obligations and expectations and responsibility, to be free and unencumbered. She had no idea how to set about becoming a dancer, but her mind was filled with this one thought: she would do it, no matter what the cost.

So they started again, the evenings in the attic alone with Beatrice. After the days spent in making calls and leaving cards, opening gifts and writing letters, choosing patterns and standing patiently for fittings, Lilith escaped to change into her brief tunic and take off her shoes and stockings.

On the first of those evenings, Lilith was elated. The climb up the attic stairs, the white and waiting room, the smell of wax on the wooden floor, all added to her pleasure: she had not realized how much she had missed all this. Only when she began the exercises she was horror-struck to find that they were almost beyond her: she was like a child struggling to walk. In the months since she had abandoned dancing, her limbs had lost their flexibility, so that she had to force them into the positions she wanted. At first she experienced grey fear – had something happened to her, some strange crippling illness that made her rigid and old? Grimly she had returned to the formal ballet exercises Madame Cotin had taught, taking herself painstakingly through *pliés*, *bourrées*, *battements*, feeling with relief the tension go out of her muscles, the tautness disappear from her limbs so that eventually they obeyed her as readily as ever.

It was two weeks before she allowed herself to use the movements she had developed. Lying on her back or balanced on her side, she would stretch and subside, reach and relax, until she was as loose-limbed as a rag doll. Only then did she wind up the phonograph and start to dance.

She had chosen a piece by Debussy, and the music poured through the bare light room like water filling

106

an empty bowl. Lilith stood for a moment, arms lifted, absolutely still. Then she threw herself into the music as if seeking annihilation. She let the sound move her as it wished, she gave herself up to it entirely. And like water it bore her up, it made her light, it lifted and carried her, suspended and cradled her, until she forgot where or who she was, and became part of the music itself. And Beatrice, seated in her customary corner, watched with her faint smile, humming to herself.

And so Lilith learned that it was not a separate thing, this gift of hers, to be taken out of its box like her white tunic, shaken and put on at will. It was part of her, and she ignored it at her peril. She knew now – though she could never have put it into words, even to herself – that the events of her life would shape her dancing. It was part of her, fitting as smoothly as the silky skin, altered by her actions, affected by her experiences, called into being by her emotions.

Although she was scarcely aware of the difference, there was a quality now in her dancing that had not been there before. In the past, she had danced as a child dances, for pleasure in what she could do and delight at her own cleverness. But since the evening of the engagement, when she had noted with a pang the power Melba had apparently exerted so effortlessly over her listeners, Lilith began consciously to edit her movements. Where before she had thought only of herself – of how the movements felt, the sensation of being swept into the music – now she began to use the great mirror Madame Cotin had had put in. She watched herself with passionate absorption, striving to see how this step or that looked, trying to calculate the effect on the observer.

Only, of course, the sole observer, as always, was

Beatrice. Beautiful Beatrice, whose gentle face reflected nothing, who watched her sister's every gesture with no change in expression. In the past, it had been enough for Lilith simply to have her there; she had wanted no one else. The evening hours in that bare room had been out of time, private, hers alone.

The last weeks had changed that. She had found how pleasant it was to feel the approval of others, and like some seductive sweetmeat she craved this novel sensation. She was not given to introspection or it might have occurred to her that this was the result of childhood deprivation: had her mother lived, had her father been less preoccupied, she might always have known how pleasing people warmed her, so that she felt petted as the grey cat that sat for hours on Beatrice's lap, its claws pleasurably kneading in and out against the fabric of her dress.

Lilith wanted to be seen. She knew she was good, but knowledge was not enough. She needed proof, and the only proof was the one accorded Melba after she had sung Mimi's final high C, and the hairs had prickled on her own neck as she listened, and for a long minute there was nothing but that sound in the whole world. She could not move, not even to clap, could not speak. She, like everyone else in that room, had accorded the diva a moment of total silence. Such a moment became, in Lilith's mind, the pinnacle towards which she climbed.

Her desire for an audience was a natural one, mirroring her development as a dancer and as a woman. For too long, Lilith had lived the life of a child, sheltered and protected. She had not minded. For Beatrice's sake, because she knew her sister must be kept calm and quiet, she had consented to those endless eventless days, had gone to bed in summer while day still beat against her drawn curtains. For Beatrice's sake she had lived half a life, and then Florence had intervened. In her wake, through Judith Mendoza, had come Joseph, and the knowledge that he had chosen her, wanted her, brought change. Before Joseph she had danced without premeditation, without subtlety, without guile. But even a few weeks of his company had taught her these things. She had absorbed information swiftly, receptive as she was, and now when she stood before the great mirror in tunic and bare feet, she did not see the girl who had been there before. Instead, the reflection that swam with evening light showed her a young woman whose gestures were eloquent with new-found emotion, hesitant on some unseen threshold.

On her wedding day – 5 September, 1906 – Lilith stood before that same mirror, saying goodbye to the room where she had been so happy. She walked round slowly, touching the half-size piano, trailing a finger down the keyboard so it rippled with sound. She stared out of the high window to the rooftops opposite, where puffed-out pigeons hooted to themselves. Over the end of the piano hung a patterned shawl; it had been there for years, so long she had ceased to see it, but now she picked it up, held its softness for a moment to her cheek. Madame Cotin had worn it for warmth in the chilly room, had left it behind one afternoon and brought another. Keep it, she had told Lilith, and when the girl had finished exercising, would wrap it round her shoulders as she cooled. It had come, she told the children, from Cashmere. Somewhere near India, she had added vaguely. Lilith shook out the folds and looked at it properly. It was of a muted cream, with broad bands of dark design along each edge. She twisted it round her arm. Extraordinary that she had never noticed before how lovely it was: the rich texture, the elegant pattern. She sniffed it. It had Madame Cotin's smell, of violets, that favourite Edwardian flower. It made her think of dowagers draped in furs, violets fastened on their collars, and débutantes decorating their dresses; her mother had always had bunches of them in small silver vases in her bedroom, poking out from the powdery clutter of cut-glass bottles on her dressing table. On an impulse, she folded the shawl swiftly and put it with her tunic to take downstairs.

She almost forgot it in the end, there was so much to do that day. The ceremony was early afternoon and they had to get to the synagogue, Bevis Marks in the City, a journey of well over the hour. The wind was chilly enough for her to need a coat, said Aunt Florence, who had arrived – resplendent in electric green silk – to take command. Lilith looked at her in alarm: she had nothing suitable to put over her dress of crème faille française, for anything heavy would crush the Brussels lace decorating the front of the skirt and bodice. There was no time to fetch anything from Portland House; even with the Hartsilver Daimler it would take more than an hour to drive to Aldgate.

'You must have something? A stole?' Aunt Florence was becoming agitated. Lilith, staring round the hallway without much hope, noticed the japanned box in which she kept her dancing tunic. She had the shawl out in a moment: it was almost the colour of her dress. Aunt Florence draped it round her. It was large enough to cover her entirely, the pale cream over her shoulders, the dark pattern falling from her knees to her feet.

As they drove through London the weather worsened and by the time they reached Fleet Street the roads were slick with rain. At Bevis Marks they had to walk through a small flagged courtyard, protected by iron gates, to the door of the synagogue. The driver held a large umbrella for Dr da Costa and Lilith: ahead of her, she could see Aunt Florence hurrying in beside Nathan, her arm linked with Beatrice's.

The wind tore at her veil, which was fastened with the two large diamond pins that were a gift from Joseph's parents, threatening to rip it from her hair. She pulled the cashmere shawl higher, and draped it round her head, so that the graceful design framed her face and fell in a curve across her body. Her father grasped her arm and hurried her forward over the uneven paving flags; with the umbrella over their heads they ran up the single step and into the narrow synagogue vestibule, Lilith laughing at her father's muttered imprecations.

After all their anxiety they were early. The last guests were only just seating themselves in the high room which glowed with light from the thick wax candles in brass holders round the walls. As Lilith turned to her father, the smile fading from her face, suddenly awed by the number of guests, the garlands of white flowers hung everywhere, the solemnity of the occasion, a group of men came quickly through the far door. Among them was Joseph Mendoza.

On seeing her his father, who preceded him, stopped short and swung his son round by a shoulder. For the groom to catch sight of the bride before the ceremony did not augur well, and he was a man who believed in propitiating fate. Taken by surprise, already moving away, Joseph nonetheless glimpsed Lilith for a second before Dr da Costa stepped in front of her.

In the shadowed space of the vestibule, in the mysterious, rainy light, the figure he saw swathed in the classic cashmere draperies bore no resemblance to the woman he expected to see. Half-turned, hooded, haunting, her dark eyes gleaming against the warm tones of her skin and the subdued colours of the shawl, she might have stepped out of one of the paintings he so admired by John Singer Sargent, whose women had just this tense, tentative quality – he glanced at her hands, which she held loosely in front of her at waist height, one hand below the other, palm up in a position (though he did not recognize it as such) from classical ballet.

Even as he thought *but it's Lilith*, he remembered that her name was East Semitic. Belonging to the night. Lilith, first wife of Adam in the mythology of the ancient east. And he recalled something else, that he had never consciously associated with *his* Lilith. When he was a small child – seven, perhaps eight – his father's mother, the old lady from Baghdad, would sit for hours talking, talking, in that strange polyglot tongue that was a mixture of half-learned English and Ladino, Spaniolized Hebrew, which he only barely understood. But his lack of comprehension had only made those occasions more fascinating: his memory, jolted by the vision of his bride-to-be swathed in her shawl in the veiled light, brought back so vividly that his mouth watered, the scented taste of tiny Turkish sweets the old lady used to give him, the near-incomprehensible murmur telling so many things ... how her husband, may he rest quietly, had put four coins in the

corners of her room, inscribed with the names of
Adam and Eve, to keep the daemon Lilith away.
Lilith, who haunted the air and the wilderness and
was dangerous to children. Like himself.

Joseph Mendoza shook his head, to be free from
the web of recollection. Nonsense. It was all nonsense. He did not believe such Talmudic mumbo-
jumbo, the ancient legends which held the old Jews
in so tight a grip. But briefly, his eyes glazed with
the same look that frightened little boy had worn,
all those years before, in his grandmother's dim
room.

And Lilith, catching sight of him at just that
instant, glimpsing his face against the dark wood of
the synagogue door, half-hidden by the group of men
in morning coats and beaver hats, was taken aback
by the startled fear in his eyes, as though he had
been caught suddenly in a beam of light too strong
to bear.

Lilith and Joseph looked at each other for less
time than it took to draw breath, then both their
fathers moved to block their view, shielding them
from one another. Even in that instant, each sensed
for the first time the complexities of the other's
personality. They had not tried, during the brief
weeks of their engagement, to understand each
other. For their different reasons – Lilith because
she was young and given to action rather than
thought, Joseph because he was a self-centred man,
who knew that his family were anxious for him to
marry – they had behaved as society expected, not
as their natures dictated.

It was too late now to go back. The *Haham*, the
chief rabbi, was waiting on the *alemma*, in his black
robes with the Ark at his back. Their families were
waiting, Nora Mendoza crying already, Judith

almost beautiful with triumph at her achievement, the aunts and cousins in their braided jackets, their ribbed silk, their ostrich feathers and swansdown. Dr da Costa was waiting, Beatrice at his side mute and perfect in her dress of nun's veiling. And later, the great saloon at the Hartsilvers' home would be brilliantly lit for the wedding party, and musicians would play as loudly as they could, knowing that their efforts would be drowned by the talk and laughter as the two families and their friends celebrated the union. At the end of the evening, one of the unmarried girl cousins would be waiting patiently to launch into the carefully rehearsed recitation that would mark the end of the occasion. It was one of Lilith's favourite pieces, long and sad: 'Curlew shall not sing tonight.'

That was still to come, but it would come: there was no retreat now, nor did either of them wish it. There was, already, something that vibrated the air between them, something that drew and rejected at the same time, hinting at unthinkable nuances and dissonances.

So they married, to please other people. They married, because neither perceived the nature of the other.

114

Chapter 7

At Joseph's wish, the wedding trip was to Trouville. He knew Normandy well and even though the season would be virtually over when they arrived, the town and its environs were charming.

The Channel crossing was effected in the appalling weather they had experienced in London. The tossing and pitching did not appear to bother Joseph, who strolled on deck apparently unconcerned by the wind and rain. Lilith stayed below, made so wretched by the smells of the boat and her own internal misery that she did not care where he was. The little maid they had engaged before the wedding was so sick herself that she was the one who needed attention: Lilith spent her time consoling her. Chan-Tu was not seen at all throughout the voyage. When they reached the French coast he reappeared, bland-faced as ever. If he had travelled badly, no one would know it.

Lilith's relief as they disembarked was so great she scarcely minded the length of the drive to Trouville. When they arrived it was already dark, and her impression of the hotel was blurred by tiredness: the flight of steps, the size of their suite, the chandeliers with their noisy brilliance. Somehow she got herself undressed, for the girl was still too weak to help, somehow ate soup and sandwiches served by a tired waiter, somehow got into the narrow double bed with its plump purple velvet headboard and the carved golden Imperial eagle. It was far from comfortable, with a long bolster beneath the pillow. She wondered vaguely where Joseph was. He had excused himself earlier, saying he needed a stroll. It seemed very late. Somewhere nearby a clock struck the hour. She started to count the chimes, but long before they had ceased she was asleep.

Pale sunshine woke her, streaming through the shutters to make horizontal bars of light on the rich carpet patterned with fleur-de-lis. She buried her face in her arm, trying to recapture the dream of dancing figures in which she was enmeshed. Still half-asleep, she was aware of the warm body against her back, the even breathing. She snuggled more closely against it, a reflex movement she had made so many times before, on waking early, to find that Beatrice had crept into bed beside her in the darkness, seeking alleviation of the nameless night-time melancholy that so afflicted her. Often, Lilith would reassure her, would murmur wordless comfort almost without waking. Lying there, her own hair like a wrap around her shoulders, Lilith remembered drowsily the last time Beatrice had come weeping to her bed. The night before the wedding.

With a start, she remembered the wedding, and where she was, and that she had been a married woman for thirty-six hours and more. She became very still. It was Joseph, then, beside her, Joseph whose back she had found so pleasurably familiar against her own. Keeping her eyes shut, she examined the thought carefully.

A bell chimed steadily, the one she had heard last night, and she counted . . . four, five. Although it was so early, she could make out different sounds. A man whistled, footsteps crunched on gravel and two women started a shrill conversation, their voices rapid and unintelligible. There were other

116

sounds, too, unfamiliar ones, like the wails of unhappy children. Fully awake now, she listened more closely. No, it was birds. And beneath their cries, she could discern the susurration of a quiet sea.

Moving cautiously, she slid towards the edge of the bed and put a foot on the floor. Joseph slept on undisturbed. She padded over to the long window and opened the shutters just far enough to see out. Beyond the ironwork balcony outside their room was a wide path set with white tables and chairs facing the rising sun. A man in a waiter's apron was walking amongst them, setting up sunshades. To her left she could see a carved stone lion seated on a plinth marking the end of the hotel gardens. To her right, in the distance, rose an ornate white building, its bright flags hanging flat and windless, surrounded by small pavilions of gaily striped awning.

Best of all, the sea stretched away before her, flat and smooth after the violence of the previous day, washed clean of colour, a mirror beneath the darker sky that reached to the edge of the horizon. Beside it ran endless pale sand, swept empty and clean but for straggling ribbons of weed, the only evidence of yesterday's gales.

Lilith gave a sigh of satisfaction for the beauty of it, then remembered Joseph. Carefully she half-closed the shutters and turned back to the room, dim now to her dazzled eyes. The sun was warm on her skin, and she sat down in a patch of light on the carpet, arms round her knees, her thin silk night-dress tucked under her toes, and looked at Joseph.

He still slept, and she examined his face with the intense scrutiny of a woman who has just acquired a new and longed for coat: pleased, admiring, and yet with a touch of anxiety lest it should not suit

117

her. Had she done the right thing? Was this, after all, what she wanted?

The head on the pillow was narrow at the temples, the ears small and close. The dark brown hair was ruffled, and a fine moustache emphasized vertical creases at the corners of the precise mouth. Now that his eyes were closed, and she was not conscious of their grey and – she felt – slightly critical gaze, she saw that his lashes fanned out like a child's. He lay flat on his back, one hand clenched on his chest, his body straight and trim beneath the covers. Lilith thought that he was meticulous even in sleep.

He stirred, as though he felt her gaze, and opened his eyes. For a moment he looked at her as a stranger: not hostile, but a blank, incurious gaze. Then he smiled and rubbed his chin. The masculine, morning gesture she had often seen her father make pleased her, and she smiled back.

'Hallo.'

'You're up early, aren't you? It can't be six.'

She gave a giggle. 'It's only just turned five.'

'How long have you been sitting there?' He smiled again, and added, 'And why?'

She shrugged – not only, he noted, with her shoulders but with her whole body, and asked, simply, 'Who could stay in bed on such a morning?'

'I see.' He was looking at her properly now, and she was suddenly conscious that she was alone with a man for the first time, and wearing nothing but a thin nightdress. She wished she had thought to put on her dressing gown of flowered Delaine. But it was so pretty – until now she had always used a robe she had had for years, a childish garment of bleached cotton – that she had been reluctant to use something so delicate. Joseph said, 'Come over here.'

He patted the bed beside him. When Lilith continued to watch him steadily, without moving, he added, 'Please?'

She got up, gracefully, in one easy flowing movement that he noted with approval, and crossed the room towards him. She saw that he was looking at her body, visible beneath the clinging silk, and cupped her hands defensively over her breasts. Like shells, he thought. He was aware of the dark triangle between her legs and the mixture of feelings the sight gave him: a spasm of excitement and something else – a kind of fear, a sensation he did not like. It made him cruel, so that he wrenched her hands away with a violence that surprised him and perturbed her. He pulled her down beside him, and her hair fanned across his face. He gathered it up in one hand and held her captive. The expression in her eyes was alarmed and he shut his own.

'Sorry,' he muttered, his voice muffled by the tender skin at the base of her throat. 'Sorry.'

In response, she placed a hand over his lips, and he noticed again, as he had that first day on the croquet ground, how hard and firm and competent it was. Like a boy's. And he was relieved to find that the body against which he was pressing had the same feeling: it was rounded and feminine, but there was nothing soft about her. He thought, briefly, of other women, desired but also despised by him, who had been appealing enough in their clothes, corseted and confined, held trim and firm, but once he saw them naked his lust had evaporated, dispelled by the sight of that untrammelled flesh, that drooping and defenceless softness, like some unshelled creature on a fishmonger's slab. Joseph put his arms round Lilith, caressing her, and as she moved to fit into his embrace the muscles in her back rippled under his hands. She was tense, her breathing so

119

shallow he could hardly hear it. He thought she must be frightened, this first time, and that reassured him, made him feel protective. His arms tightened round her, and he whispered endearments.

He had never held her in his arms before, so formal had been his courtship of her, and so had never inhaled the scent of her skin and hair. If he had been asked, he would have expected her to smell as other women did, of forced flowers, perfume and powder: artificial, consciously pleasing. But from that cool, pale skin, so even in colour and texture that she seemed – it was one of the things he most liked about her – almost like one of his china figurines, came a scent that was both extraordinary and elusive, of some fragrant fruit he knew but could not name. Joseph was beginning to lose himself in the sensations of Lilith's body and his own, but vaguely he wondered where he had smelled it before. He had once, travelling in Japan, tasted the fruit of a persimmon tree, gathered for him by a child in late October. He remembered with utmost clarity that stark, snow-covered landscape, that ripe, aromatic flavour midway between apple and apricot. And he recalled the time in Portugal with his father's family, when he bought in a bazaar a golden *marmelo*, a quince at once sweet and sour, with flesh as cool and moist as that of the woman he was holding.

Lilith was still, waiting in Joseph's arms. She did not anticipate what she would think or want or feel. She had never done so, it was not in her nature. Beyond a vague wondering she had never tried to imagine what marriage to Joseph would actually be like. Her ignorance on the whole matter was far greater than even Aunt Florence imagined. She had

120

no memory of her parents together at all, and her occasional glimpses of Florence and Nathan Hartsilver embracing warmly when he returned from a short journey, had been of people so much older than herself that she could not relate to their feelings. Florence had tried, before the marriage, to talk to her, but her own self-consciousness before this young niece had made her more abrupt than ever. She had said, briskly, that no doubt 'all that bicycling' would have taken care of any physical problems and that had been that. Lilith had vaguely supposed she was referring to childbirth, though she had no idea what that had to do with a bicycle, and immediately forgotten the whole conversation. She was still almost as much of a child as Beatrice and for the same reason: her sister's mysterious ailment had touched and altered both their lives, held them both back. So there had been no young friends, no girls to whom she could talk, no young married woman who might have whispered behind her hand newly-discovered secrets; nothing to prepare her for this unimagined intimacy.

Joseph thought it was fear which made her body taut and her breathing light: in fact, it was excitement. Although ignorant of what it was he wanted of her, she liked lying in his arms, the warmth of his breath against her throat, the roughness of his chin on her shoulder, the softness of the fine brown hair. He was – after that initial roughness – touching her with a delicacy that made her skin tingle, his hands circling her back, stroking, stroking. She arched her body as a cat will, for sheer pleasure of being fondled, and clasped his warm feet with her cold ones, so that he gave a little groan.

'You're cold.'

'It was the floor. But it's a beautiful day.' She

expected that now they would get up, have breakfast, go out. But he seemed in no hurry. He moved slightly, freeing one hand, and used it to gently trace the shape of her breasts, pleased that they were so firm under his fingers, like little lemons. He turned his head to watch her face, to learn if she liked this sensation. Her eyes were wide, intent and concentrated. He saw the brown and golden lights in their depths, saw the reflection of sadness in them that he had never found in her behaviour – the inherited melancholy of her family.

He said, and his tone was not his usual light, bantering one, but another voice, deeper, 'Beautiful. You have beautiful eyes. Persian prince's eyes.' He stroked her again through the pale silk: slim arms, slender boyish thighs, the narrow curve of her waist. If he shut his eyes he might almost have been caressing a youth, a young stranger. The idea excited him, and he moved against the satiny leg beneath him, deliberately stimulating himself. When he looked at her again, Lilith was gazing at him, puzzlement in those long eyes. He murmured, 'Do you want me? Lilith?'

She caught her lower lip between her teeth, dismayed at her lack of understanding, waiting for enlightenment. He touched her again, cautiously, through the nightdress, finding to his surprise that she was ready, the thin material clinging damply to the folds of her body.

He had not expected this. The women with whom he had performed this act in the past had been – his mind veered from the thought that he had paid for their favours, if not in money, then in dinners, clothes, jewels. They had been skilled, accustomed to pleasing men, and he had always known, even as he listened to their feigned sighs of ardour, that they were flattering him. But Lilith was not like them. He had married her knowing she was free of any taint of worldliness. His aunt Judith had described the life the da Costa girls had led, the cloistered quiet of the Sloane Square house. And he had seen for himself, that day in the hothouse, the stunned, mesmerized expression on her face, like some small creature confronted with a snake. He would have been prepared to stake anything on her total innocence. And yet his tentative touch had encountered this unmistakeable response. In another woman, it would have repelled him, such moist evidence of femininity. But Lilith was different, as the golden quince had been different. This time, this time . . . He caught hold of Lilith's hard little hand and guided it to that part of himself that was growing so voluptuously against her silk thigh. Briefly, she resisted him, her hand stiff in his, and he heard her quick gasp of amazement. Then she acceded to his wishes, her fingers following his, smoothing, stroking. For one minute, two, he held her hand to guide her, sensing her reluctance. And then, as she became familiar with this smooth, warm, butting part of him, she began to like the feel of it, and caressed it of her own volition, her suddenly competent fingers spiralling, encircling, cool and disquieting.

Joseph closed his eyes, and the young stranger came back.

The second day, Joseph declared at luncheon that they should walk along the beach to the Casino, where people of fashion gathered.

'Not,' he added disparagingly, 'that there will be anyone there of consequence: it's far too late in the season.'

123

Lilith did not care. All that mattered to her was the intense satisfaction of seeing herself in one of her new dresses, an afternoon frock of chiffon poplin with a round neck and heavily embroidered bodice in a blue as pale as the sky, and a large-brimmed hat trimmed with blue roses. She would have liked an admiring comment from Joseph, but he had merely nodded politely when she presented herself in the hotel foyer, and taking up his hat and cane, led the way outside.

They followed *les planches*, the boardwalk that edged the sand, marked with flags at regular intervals. Except for a giggle of girls in short dresses and hats nearly as large as Lilith's own, the boards were almost empty. A group of young men in straw boaters like Joseph's, two elderly women arm in arm. To their left the sea glittered far out, to their right were chalets built of trelliswork, where figures wrapped in rugs sat on long chairs beneath sunshades. As they neared the Casino they could see, standing well back from the beach across the road, the imposing seaside houses of the well-to-do, elaborate edifices with turrets, towers, terraces.

When they finally reached the Casino, Lilith could have clapped for pleasure at the sight. Here the beach was thronged. Seated at small tables, men and women sipped liqueurs, or drank coffee, or merely sat in cheerful, gossiping groups exchanging scandal beneath their sunshades. Not far away she could see a row of bright little tents with pointed roofs.

'Bathing tents,' explained Joseph. 'We might try that.'

In front of the Casino, two sets of steps led up to the level of the heavily decorated white building. A couple were sitting side by side, not speaking, where great pots of green flowering plants cascaded over the painted ironwork balustrade. Lilith wanted to go and inspect the marquees of striped awning, but Joseph deflected her.

'First of all, I think, a glass of siphon.'

He left her in a folding chair while he went in search of a waiter. Lilith smoothed her new elbow-length kid gloves self-consciously, and straightened her hat. A woman's voice said, and even without looking round, she could tell the owner was smiling, 'The effect is charming.'

The speaker was the woman who had been sitting so quietly with her companion. Lilith noticed now that she wore dark grey, *décolletage* a little too revealing for elegance, hair a touch more golden than nature could have intended, greenish eyes subtly shadowed. She inclined her head in its feathery tocque.

'Valentine Audry. We're here for a month, my . . .' – there was the slightest hesitation – '. . . my husband and I. Staying just over there.' She nodded in the direction of the tiled roofs of the old town. 'And you, Madame?'

Lilith introduced herself, shyly, knowing that even as she spoke her married name, she gave herself away as newly wed. To cover her embarrassment she said, 'You must be French. But your English is excellent.'

Madame Audry laughed, displaying more of the *décolletage*.

'English, Spanish, Italian. I speak them all.'

Lilith, who had struggled unsuccessfully with French at Aunt Florence's behest, said admiringly, 'How clever.'

Madame Audry merely shrugged, a most Gallic gesture.

125

'Ah, no. I have a facility. And of course, there are ways to learn, and ways . . .' She let the sentence disappear.

By the time Joseph returned, the two women had exchanged a good deal of information. Lilith introduced her new acquaintance, and Joseph greeted her with the utmost formality. When at last the Frenchwoman rose to go, said farewell and went off with a graceful, swaying walk, Joseph said, 'I don't think you should make friends too easily. That lady, for instance, is not a suitable person for you to be talking to.'

At that moment the waiter arrived, and she was spared the need to answer, watching instead as Joseph supervised the serving of the iced drinks, fussing over the drops of moisture that beaded the glasses and threatened to mark his white suit. When he turned his attention back to her, it was to tell her that he had met an old acquaintance a few minutes before, and that they were invited to spend the following evening on his yacht. He had known Baron Gaston Dabescat, he said, for a good ten years, and the Frenchman was an excellent customer, buying good pieces both for his Paris house and the family château.

Lilith somehow expected this Dabescat to be Joseph's age, but when he welcomed them, the next night, on board his star class yacht *Griffon*, she was taken aback both by his age – he was older than her father – and his immense girth. He took her hand to guide her down the narrow ladder on to the deck, and then bowed over it, his jowls quivering, with such heavy deliberation that she wanted to laugh. She told herself *I must tell Beatrice about him* and realized she had not thought of her sister for two whole days. The social smile faded from her face and a feeling of dereliction surged through her.

She and Beatrice had never been separated. In all her eighteen years, she had not spent a night away, never ended a day without seeing her, kissing her pale cheek. And in all the rush and novelty of the wedding trip she had scarcely given Beatrice a thought. She saw the older girl as she had been when the Daimler took them away from Portman House on the long drive to Dover: standing in the protective curve of her father's arm, her eyes made bluer by the faint pink of her lids which showed she had been weeping. In her ear Joseph's voice asked, 'Are you all right? Is something the matter?' and she forced a response.

'It's just that I was thinking about Beatrice.'

'Oh, she's fine.' Joseph answered airily, with the casual indifference of an only child. She opened her mouth to protest, but stopped. What was the use? How to explain that deep current of feeling that ran between herself and Beatrice, nurturing them both, giving strength to both? Instead, she shook her head so the tears that threatened merely gave their glitter to her eyes as she was introduced to a dozen people, handed a glass of champagne, escorted to the bow to admire the coloured lights threaded over the yacht, strung in the rigging, woven up the mast.

They dined in the saloon, in the warm glow of many oil-lamps. Shallow bowls of misty blue flowers strange to her were reflected in the high polish of the woodwork, brass fittings caught the light.

Lilith looked around at the starched shirtfronts of the men, so white their faces above seemed dark-skinned by comparison, saw the jewels shimmering on the pale arms and throats of the women. Their cloying perfume mingled with the warmth of the lamps and it overpowered her, so she had no appetite for the rich food on her plate, the wine sauces on the foreign fish, the buttered vegetables. She listened to the loud laughter and the talk she could not understand. Across the table, Joseph was deep in conversation across his bored neighbour with the man by her side.

She wondered, sitting there, how she had ever imagined she could be part of his life. She felt excluded, not only by the language but by this milieu in which Joseph so clearly belonged and she did not. She felt young and gauche and uncertain: she longed to be home with her father in the shadowy Sloane Square house where she and Beatrice were safe.

Lilith put down her fork and gave a little sigh. She was seated beside their host, who had talked to her about the London theatre – a subject on which she had almost nothing to say – and had then turned to his right, to engage in conversation with a plump woman in pink. But the Baron must have been sitting at an odd angle, because his foot was touching hers. Then she became aware that this was deliberate, that he was pressing his glossy patent boot against her own satin shoe. She moved her foot away from the pressure, but he followed it, and now their knees also were touching, the whole length of his heavy calf was against her leg. Shocked by his behaviour, but too inexperienced to know what to do about it, Lilith sat like a well-brought up child while Baron Dabescat continued to talk to his neighbour.

She looked at Joseph, to try and signal to him, but he was talking earnestly. She caught the word 'Celadon' and knew that he was oblivious to everything. She pushed back her chair and stood up. No one appeared to notice. A manservant somewhere behind her pulled her chair away so that she was free to leave the circle of light round the long table, pass through the door set in the wood panelling and find her way, up a short flight of stairs, to the deck. She walked over to the brass rail and leaned on it. The *Griffon* was moored not far from the harbour, where she could see the water heaving with small craft, twinkling with bobbing lights, hear the occasional word across the still water, snatches of song, the sound of music from a harbourside café. If she looked the other way, there was nothing but the silver sea stretching out to where a dark grey line pencilled in the night sky. She must have been there ten minutes when she heard steps coming up from the cabin. She thought it would be Joseph, but the steps were too slow, and then the Baron's bulky shoulders came up into view.

Lilith glanced round, but there was no one else on the deck, not even a deckhand. With a grunt, the Frenchman got himself on to the deck and stood for a moment breathing heavily with the effort. Lilith moved fast, hurrying forward to the steps, saying, in as light a tone as she could manage, 'It's getting too cool for me. I must go back down.'

He did not reply, but caught her arm as she reached him. He gave a wheezy laugh, and linked his arm through hers, guiding her back towards the rail where they stood side by side. Lilith debated whether to pull away but told herself not to be absurd: the Baron was their host, after all. And what could happen with so many people within earshot?

Baron Dabescat let go of her and she saw that he had a large cigar in his right hand. He proceeded to smoke, staring out across the water. The silence was making her increasingly uncomfortable when he broke it with his harsh voice.

'You don't like my little party.'

It was a statement, not a question, but she said, ridiculously polite, 'Oh, no, I was too hot, that was all, so I came up here for some air. But I think now I should go down. Joseph will be wondering . . .' She took a step back, to find that the Baron had moved to block her way. She felt instant alarm, but that did not prevent her from observing how graceful his movements were for so gross a man. He was laughing again, that breathless, gasping sound.

'Your husband has noticed nothing. Only I noticed. I don't like pretty women to leave my table in the middle of a meal. Nor,' he added, 'to look so unhappy.'

'That's nothing to do with the party, I assure you.'

'I did not suppose it was. I doubt anyone could weep over *saumon fumé*.' He took another long puff of his cigar. 'I imagine you have plenty of justification for tears, albeit not culinary.'

Lilith retorted, childishly cross with this fat man, 'You know nothing at all about me. We met barely two hours ago.'

'I know more than you suppose. You are young, just married and – if I may say so – very lovely.' He paused for a moment, looking at her with a considering gaze, and she saw how shrewd his eyes were, pieces of granite in that fleshy face. 'You should be the belle of the evening,' he went on smoothly, 'yet instead I find you staring alone at a dark sea. That tells me a good deal, Madame. Would you like to hear this information?'

She shook her head. 'No. I'm going inside.' But she did not move. She was repelled by this man, but fascinated too, and despite her protestation, she wanted to hear what he would say.

Baron Dabescat levered himself from the railing, and turned to face her. He threw the barely-smoked cigar into the water: she heard the splash and small hiss as it was extinguished. He put out a stubby hand and traced the line of her cheek with a finger. His touch was soft: she had noticed when they dined how scrupulously manicured his hands were, the number of rings he wore. She was no longer frightened. She felt in control. She had suddenly recognized that he wanted something she had. She had no intention of allowing him any liberties, but the sense of power was intoxicating. This rich, worldly man, with his yacht and his château, his huge motor Joseph had pointed out to her at the quayside, the servants who scuttled at a nod of his head – that such a man should be humble with her was proof that she was a child no longer.

Lilith was not vain. She had always known that it was Beatrice, not herself, who was the beauty, that loveliness lay in pale golden hair, in calm blue eyes, not in her own tumbled dark curls or her dark glance. Even Joseph, the one time he had loved her, had kept his eyes closed, as though he did not want to look at her. But the Baron quite clearly did want to look at her. He moved nearer, on his surprisingly small, agile feet, and put a hand on the back of her neck, as though to pull her head towards him. As he moved she smelled some rich cologne and beneath it, the odour of sweat. She leaned back as far as she could, but he was stronger than she, and was forcing her closer to him: she felt absurdly fragile in his grasp, helpless. Now she was frightened. The warm bulk of his massive stomach pressed against her. She put both hands out to push him away, and felt

131

through the dinner jacket that he was wearing some sort of corset: she could make out the bones. At this, she started, ridiculously, to laugh. Even to her ears it was an ugly sound, but she had not known laughter could be so cruel until she saw his face, heard the sharp intake of breath. He said, wheezing his words, 'Forgive me, Madame. I thought I had been talking to a woman. I see that I was mistaken. I have been addressing myself to a mere child.'

Lilith turned to go. Over her shoulder she said, stung by this insult, and the more so because she knew it contained an element of truth, 'Perhaps you should have asked yourself whether I found your attentions at dinner welcome, before favouring me with any more.' Even in the darkness she could make out the angry movement of his head at this. She was already starting down the staircase to the lower deck as he replied. His voice was quiet, but the malice was unmistakeable.

'I should have thought any woman married to Joseph Mendoza would have good cause to indulge in a little harmless pleasure.'

Lilith stood stock still, starting up at the dark outline of the bulky figure.

'Whatever do you mean by that?'

The Baron shrugged his shoulders.

'If you do not know, then I cannot tell you.'

At that moment she heard Joseph's voice below her.

'Lilith! There you are – I've been looking for you.'

Filled with relief she started down towards him, hand outstretched.

'I went up for some air. Joseph, can we go back to the hotel? I'm so tired.'

Joseph hesitated, clearly anxious to stay, until the Baron's harsh voice said, 'I've tried in vain to persuade your wife to remain, Mendoza. To no avail, I'm afraid. I'll get the boat to row you back, and you can return her to the nursery.'

Lilith looked anxiously from the Baron to her husband, waiting for some response to the studied insolence of the Frenchman. In the darkness it was difficult to see Joseph clearly, as he stood in the stairwell, and she caught only the strange look on his face, that might have been anger or consternation. Whatever it was, he controlled it, thanked their host and escorted her into the summoned boat. But seated in it, watching the sailor row them with precise strokes further and further from the brilliantly illuminated yacht, Joseph told her angrily that she had spoiled the evening for him.

'I hope you realize your behaviour cost me a good sale. I would never have left a party like that so early. And the Baron is an influential man. One doesn't want to upset him.' He fumed silently for a moment, then broke out again. 'I don't know what came over you. Surely you could have managed to stay awake another hour, if only in the name of courtesy.'

He was still berating her when they reached the shore.

Chapter 8

For two days Joseph was sullen and uncommunicative. He avoided her company when he could decently do so and when he could not he was as sulky as a schoolboy, talking in monosyllables, evading her eyes. He still blamed her for what he considered to be her irrational behaviour on the yacht. Lilith was several times tempted to describe the Baron's behaviour – the fleshy thigh pressed against hers, those contemptuous words '. . . any woman married to Joseph Mendoza . . .' She desisted, partly because she did not want to hurt him, more precisely because she knew instinctively he would not believe her.

She found the whole bizarre incident hard to believe herself, however often she puzzled over it, recalling their strange dialogue, asking herself what the Baron could possibly have meant. She knew only that it subtly altered her perceptions of her husband. Until now, she had seen Joseph as he presented himself: worldly, wealthy, urbane. Yet the Baron clearly had not seen him like that. *Mendoza*, the Frenchman had called him, as if he were nothing but a tradesman.

Left by Joseph to her own devices for long periods, Lilith wandered round the hotel, or stayed in their rooms endlessly recalling the evening that had so alienated Joseph. Without him, she did not know where to go, what to do. In all her life, she had never been given freedom of movement. She had always been surrounded by people who controlled her days, demanded her presence. Her father, Aunt Florence,

134

Beatrice, even Judith Mendoza, all had in their different ways directed her own actions.

So now she was without resources, and she took refuge from her uncertainty and unhappiness in sleep. She felt utterly exhausted because she did so little. She could hardly open her eyes in the morning, she was dragged down by tiredness so that she did not want to get dressed. Joseph disappeared immediately after taking his coffee and croissants in their room, and she did not see him until it was time for luncheon. She was too proud to ask him, *what shall I do*? and so she did nothing. She slept for hours at a time, curled up in the purple velvet bed, or lay awake, staring sombrely at the day outside, repelled by the brilliance of the light and the sounds of people on holiday, thinking about her father, longing for Beatrice.

Joseph would come into their sitting room and stop short at the sight of the crumpled figure on the bed in the half-light of the room beyond, wrinkle his nose in distaste and leave as soon as he had changed.

'You cannot possibly wish to dine in public in that state,' he announced the first evening. 'I'll have something sent up.' The door was carefully shut behind him.

Perhaps, had there been sisters when he was a child, a youth, a younger man, even someone as precise and fastidious as Joseph might have become accustomed to the tempestuous emotional behaviour of very young women. As it was, he had formed his ideas of femininity around his mother, his vague, literate, absent-minded mother, who had impinged so little on his father's life. He was puzzled and irritated by the listlessness and the tears, but that was all. It did not occur to him that he could be the cause of his new wife's obvious unhappiness. Nor did it cross his mind that he could put an end to it. So he simply attempted to ignore it.

On the third afternoon, Lilith was asleep when a light tapping on the door woke her. She had been dreaming, she did not know of what, but she felt as though she had to force her way through green leaves to answer the insistent summons. She thought she said, *Yes*? but the tapping went on. Wearing only her nightdress, she padded to the door and opened it a crack. Chan-Tu stood outside, his sallow face the same height as her own. He said in his light voice which had no inflexions, 'Mister Joseph has been called to visit the local villa. Someone who wishes to discuss a big purchase with him. He does not know when he will return.'

'And that's all.'

'Yes, Mrs Mendoza. Is all.'

She sighed, leaning her cheek against the smooth paint of the door, wondering why it was she felt Chan-Tu took some satisfaction in delivering this information.

'All right. Thank you.'

'You want Doris now?'

She shook her head. 'No.'

Doris came, all the same, letting herself in quietly in case her young lady was asleep, noting with compassion the blurred features that told her Lilith had been weeping again. Doris came from a village in Kent. No one else in her family had ever been more than the twenty-odd miles to Tunbridge Wells, and she had been wild with excitement to be going to France. Trouville, to her, was exotic as Araby. She was twenty-two, with a round head accentuated by the severely parted hair and hands that were already chapped and work-worn. Her last job had been under-housemaid in a country vicarage, rising at four to light the fires and heat water. She had gone to London despite her mother's protests, determined to better herself. Even the domestic employment agency in Holborn had awed her, and she had hesitated for a long time outside Portman House, unable even to brave the servants' entrance for her interview. Mrs Hartsilver had not been impressed by her country clothes, but the young lady had clearly liked her. (She did not realize that she appealed to Lilith because she did not look in the least intimidating.) Waiting outside, she had heard the older lady telling the younger that she was sure she would not 'do', that she would be unaccustomed to dressing hair fashionably or dealing with delicate garments. But Lilith had been persistent, and had not regretted the decision. Doris had learned quickly, determined not to lose this place.

Now she was trying to take Mrs Mendoza's mind off her troubles, whatever they were, gossiping about other guests in the hotel, deliberately making her country accent broader than ever in order to amuse the silent young woman whose hair she was combing. When she had finished she said, coaxing, 'You look ever so nice. Why don't you go out for a little? 'Tis beautiful on the promenade, you wouldn't believe.'

Lilith's shoulders dropped dispiritedly.

'I don't think so.'

Doris, who had been hearing this for three days now, took no notice. She went to the wardrobe and after a moment took out a light crepon dress.

'Put this on, why don't you? 'Twill suit lovely, and keep you cool.'

Lilith refused to look.

'No, Doris. Leave it.'

Doris straightened her shoulders. She hated to

see Mrs Mendoza like this. She was too young in her ways, too sheltered. She didn't seem able to stand up for herself. Doris did not want to lose this position, she knew it would be hard to find another as good, but she had tried everything else. Now she said, her country voice suddenly sharp as a governess, 'You should be ashamed of yourself, if I may say so. Lying here moping in this nice town, with all that life outside. I never seen nothing like it.'

Lilith stared at her from those dark eyes. Doris noted with satisfaction that she at least looked angry. She went on, 'Hiding away like this, sad as a whipped puppy. I'm surprised at you, Madam. Everyone's talking, in the hotel, saying as how you must be very frail, to be in your room so much.'

Lilith bridled.

'I'm not frail. You know very well that isn't true.'

'Maybe I do and maybe I don't.' Doris struggled to hide the satisfaction on her face. 'But nothing'll convince 'em like seeing you, will it?' She held out another garment, a suit Lilith had never yet worn. 'Come on, do. Let's see how you look in this. You could go for a little walk, just for half an hour . . . you can't go on like this, 'tis a waste and a shame . . .' She went on talking, sympathizing, encouraging, while Lilith slowly got herself washed and dressed. She was still talking as she did up the last of the multitude of mother-of-pearl buttons fastening the back of Lilith's white blouse and secured the red leather belt round her waist. She stood back to admire the effect.

Lilith was dressed in fine navy serge, neat as a schoolgirl. The long skirt was cut close, the jacket curved up under her breasts like a bolero and the white sailor collar of the blouse was complemented by the straw boater with its navy and red striped ribbon. Doris repeated, and Lilith caught the wistful note in her voice, 'You look ever so nice.'

Lilith looked in the mirror, at the face of the older girl standing behind her.

'Where shall I go?'

'The Old Town's not far. Full of narrow streets and little shops: you'd like it there.'

Lilith nodded, pleased to be told what to do, and went off obediently. But once outside, she found she did not want to visit the Old Town at all. The sea was a pale turquoise today, the wind strong. There were only a handful of people in view, the women vainly clutching their veils and laces. Free of the confines of the hotel, Lilith felt restless and undecided, wild as a pony released from its stall and put to grass. Almost without thinking she started off along the boardwalk towards the Casino, the heels of her new black shoes (beautifully made by old Kindler in Marylebone) making a satisfactory clicking on the boards. The flags streamed, the warm sand was ruffled like the pelt of some huge pale creature. The wind was at her back, billowing against her skirt, filling her blouse so that if puffed around her, whipping the ribbon streamers into her eyes, making her gasp and clutch her hat and laugh out loud. And then, forgetting her new clothes and her newer status, careless of how she looked or what people would think, she started to run.

She ran like a trained athlete, even though hampered by her long skirt and the small heels of her shoes. She ran economically, her breathing steady, her boater in her hand. She ran gracefully, as a boy runs, with a long, reaching stride, not with the inturned, stumbling movements of most women. She ran with a curious, high step, lifting each foot well off the boards as though to clear some invisible object. She ran like the dancer she was.

She ran far beyond the Casino, the line of brightly coloured bathing huts, the modish couples at their gossip. She ran until she was on the other side of the promenade, and she only stopped when the boardwalk ended beneath a bridge. Quite out of breath, suddenly conscious of the curious glances she was attracting, she went up the steps on to the promenade itself and looked for one of the open cafés, where she sat down at an empty table and ordered '*Un citron pressé, s'il vous plaît,*' in the schoolroom French so painfully learned at Aunt Florence's behest. When it came, she thought nothing had ever tasted so good, the lemons tart on her tongue.

Lilith lingered over her drink for a long time, her boater on the table beside her, leaning on folded arms, lost in thought. She could not equate the tearful child in the darkened room back at the Grand Hotel with the way she felt now, acutely aware of everything about her: the passers-by and the sharp-eyed waiters, the smell of lemons and the metal chair pressed into her back, the tiny orange ladybird inching its way up her glass, the acrid smoke of the cheroot some man was smoking at a nearby table.

Lilith did not have the habit of self-appraisal, and so she did not see that salvation for her lay in action, in movement. She had just run for almost a mile with no end but the pleasure of doing so, and it had lifted her spirits and released her from depression as surely as her dancing did. She knew she felt wonderful but did not consciously recognize what had brought the change, though somewhere at the back of her mind was a faint recollection of a high stage in a room of dark wood and red velvet, where she had danced and danced until elation, surging through her body, could have floated her up to the ceiling.

She felt like that now, light and sparkling: energy poured through her, so that she glanced involuntarily at the tips of her fingers as though they were giving off sparks. Impulsively she jumped to her feet and started for the door, remembered that she had not paid and turned back, her cheeks reddening with embarrassment as she realized she had brought no money with her. Before she had time to ask herself what she should do, the waiter who had served her was there, shaking his head and smiling, holding out his palm to show that he had been paid already. Lilith held out her hands in a gesture of surprise and he, understanding, nodded over his shoulder to a table behind her. There, beneath the brim of a black hat trimmed with tulle, Madame Audry smiled and beckoned, explaining in her charmingly accented English that no, no, she had wished to pay for Lilith's drink. All she would accept in repayment was her company for an hour, if she were free?

They walked slowly along towards the harbour, past minuscule cottages bustling with activity, where fat brown-faced children gazed out, thumbs in mouths, while their mothers, in white aprons with their hair hidden under caps, scrubbed stone floors on their knees, or carried buckets of water up the cobbled, hilly streets. Madame Audry, who seemed to know the place well, told Lilith how the tiny fishing village had first attracted artists, and then, by the end of the Second Empire, became the beach à la mode.

'It's not any more, of course,' she added. 'Forty

years ago, the aristocrats decided they wanted somewhere more exclusive, and built villas along the deserted beach across the Touques. Soon Deauville will out-rival us here. Though I doubt it will be prettier than this.' She stopped, looking out at the harbour crowded with dark-sailed fishing boats. Lilith, trying not to stare at her, asked herself what it was about this woman that made Joseph declare her an unsuitable companion. She knew he had exquisite taste in porcelain – he had told her so himself – and now she wondered if it extended to people. Madame Audry seemed to her the height of elegance, with her swaying walk, her narrow waist in the tightly cinched suede belt and her eyes subtly outlined. Lilith decided that Joseph did not know what he was talking about and that he need anyway never find out. It was the first time in her life she had ever decided consciously to deceive anyone.

Later, they went back to Madame Audry's hotel room. Her hotel was far smaller than the Mendozas', situated in a sidestreet with a bar-café next door, the smell of spirits and decaying vegetables in the air. In the dark hall with its pictures of the Virgin Lilith hesitated, 'Will your husband be in?'

Madame Audry – Valentine, as she now insisted Lilith call her – smiled, and looked at the time on the watch she wore pinned to her dress.

'Alain will be playing cards and oblivious to everything else.' She was silent as they ascended in the creaking iron lift, while she inserted the key in her door and passed through, into a room filled by a double bed on which were piles of dresses, a couple of hats, a pair of gloves. Valentine started to tidy it, then gave up, drew the blinds close and flopped into a chair.

'Sit down,' she said. 'I'll get us a cool drink in a

moment. And by the way,' she added, apparently casually, 'Alain isn't my husband.'

Lilith tried not to look at the double bed. She could think of nothing to say.

'No,' went on Valentine, removing her black jacket, 'we've been together for three years now, and that's a long time. I think quite soon a little change will be called for, a little fresh air . . .' She lifted her arms over her head, clasping her hands in a graceful, impatient gesture. Lilith noticed that her silk blouse was carelessly darned under one arm. Embarrassed, she glanced away, and looked towards the dressing table set square in the window. It was a cumbersome piece of furniture, its top liberally spattered with spilled powder, with little pots of rouge, a comb with a twist of Valentine's blonde hair in it, a pair of cuff-links lying on a piece of crumpled lace and a black evening tie flung over the mirror. On the floor beside it was a bottle and two used glasses, a copy of *Le Figaro* and a single man's shoe. Valentine saw her look, reached out a foot and kicked the shoe under the bed: it was a scornful gesture, she might have been disposing of the absent Alain. She raised delicately plucked eyebrows towards Lilith: 'Have I shocked you?'

'Yes . . . no . . . I thought somehow that you were married. When I saw you together that day by the Casino.'

'Oh. And what made you think that? Beyond the fact that we were together?'

Lilith said, conscious of how childish it must sound, 'Well, you weren't talking very much.'

'And in your experience, married people don't talk to each other.'

Lilith could tell she was being laughed at, but struggled to explain.

143

'I mean, you seemed to know each other very well.'

Valentine laughed. 'We do. Indeed we do. Too well, and that's the trouble. There are no secrets any more, no surprises. And it's getting dull, dull, dull.'

Lilith asked, 'So you mean to stay together – like this . . .' a movement of her hand took in the bed, the clutter ' . . . and you don't have to? You don't want to?'

This time, Valentine really laughed, until Lilith thought she would burst into tears. Finally she wiped her eyes with the backs of her hands and shook her head.

'Lilith, how old are you? I didn't think anyone could reach the age of nearly nineteen and know so little of the world. I stay with Alain because I have to eat. I stay with him because he pays the milliner and my dressmaker. I stay with him because a woman my age cannot go around alone without appearing *déclassée*.' She looked at her hands, and on her downturned face Lilith saw a small, secretive smile. 'And then, of course, there are . . . compensations. Alain is nothing special, he's no great brain certainly, but he can be amusing. And in bed, if nowhere else, he knows what he's doing.'

Lilith winced at the crude words. She wanted to get up, get outside this stuffy room with its intimations of a personal life she could not envisage, but she could not bring herself to move. There were questions she must ask, and Valentine Audry would have the answers.

'Don't you want to marry?' Lilith had not meant to say that, she knew it was the wrong question, but Valentine merely shrugged.

'I *was* married. For five years, to a man who sold

144

Italian glass all over the Continent. In fact, I'm married to him still, but I haven't seen him for ten years, not since 1897. He walked out and left me in Bruges, and to tell the truth it was the nicest thing he ever did for me.'

Lilith stared at her, trying to understand what this woman's life was like. She said, thoughtfully, 'And then you met Monsieur Audry,' but this made Valentine smile again.

'I met several others first.' She fanned herself with a hand. 'I'll go and get a glass of wine,' she added, but made no move to do so.

'How do you . . . what about babies?' Lilith hardly knew how she managed to ask such a thing. But Valentine did not seem to mind.

'I take care there are none. There are ways.' She shot Lilith a sharp look. 'You mean you don't know them?' Lilith shook her head. 'And you want me to tell you. But surely you want children, don't you?'

Lilith stared at her in an agony of uncertainty, searching for words to express the subject on which she so desperately needed the answers this woman must have.

'I want to ask you . . . I need to know . . .' She twisted her hands together in distress while Valentine Audry watched those amazing, tapering fingers. She reached out and put her own hands over them, to still their agitation. Lilith drew a deep breath and said, more calmly, 'I don't seem to understand anything. Not anything. The Baron sneered at Joseph, but why? I don't know what he meant. And yet there is something . . . Joseph says things, he does things, that seem, that are . . .' She faltered and stopped, huddled into herself, her whole body tight and troubled.

145

Valentine Audry said, her voice as soothing as if she were talking to a troubled child.

'Tell me.'

Before Lilith left, Valentine showed her how to apply bistre to her eyes, moistening the little cake of shadow by spitting delicately into it and painting a fine line on upper and lower lids with a brush of squirrel hair.

'There,' she pronounced, bending over Lilith's upturned face. 'You look as *soignée* as one could wish.'

Lilith stared fascinated at her reflection, so unlike the pale girl who had reluctantly left her hotel room three hours before. In her place was this radiant creature, her skin like an apricot under its light bloom of powder, her glance rendered enigmatic by the bistre shadow. She had become mysterious, somehow foreign, she did not recognize herself. (Her father, had he seen her at that moment, would have declared she was the image of his mother, as she looked in a portrait he had of her, painted upon enamel when she was a young girl in Baghdad, hair bound back under an embroidered cap, dark eyes rimmed with henna.)

Valentine helped Lilith on with her jacket, solicitous as if the younger woman had been ill. 'Now, are you going to be all right? You'll remember what I told you? And come back to see me when you can – I'll wait for a message.' She kissed her on both cheeks and led the way downstairs.

Had Lilith turned back at the corner of the rue de l'Est, she would have seen Valentine Audry bend her head, mutter a few words, and cross herself.

* * *

Walking slowly back to the hotel, conscious of the way she looked, Lilith moved with a calm tranquillity. In answer to Doris's inquiries, she said merely that she had visited the harbour and stopped for a glass of lemon. When Joseph came into their suite to change for dinner she was already dressed and waiting beside the open window, pretending to read a magazine, but in fact watching the distant sea and reflecting on the conversation with Valentine Audry.

Later, sitting opposite her at the candle-lit table as they dined on *Friture de l'estuaire* and *Moules à la Crème* (for when he was on holiday, Joseph conveniently forgot his kosher rules, and Lilith was unconcerned), he was stirred by the way she looked in her narrow dress, by the straightness of her back under the cape of silver beads. His anger at her foolish behaviour on the yacht and her unreasonable tears faded, as he succumbed to the charm of her languid movements, and asked himself how it was that he had never until now noticed how the elongated eyes she turned on him were reminiscent of the painted eyes of a young Egyptian king.

He had drunk just enough – too much, perhaps – so that the marble floors of the hotel were treacherous underfoot, and as they walked later on the terrace the sound of their feet on the gravel made him think of ice crunching in the first snow of the winter when the Japanese child had offered him the persimmon. And at the thought he tightened his grip on Lilith's slim arm so that she all but cried out. She gasped, '*Joseph*. You're hurting me.'

'Am I? *Am* I?' He seemed amused, and she detected in his tone the same soft brutality she had heard in the hothouse at Richmond, when he had shown her the carnivorous plant that had closed its fleshy petals around his intrusive finger. She gave a shudder – of apprehension, of expectation – and they stared at each other. Their hotel was the last along the front, lying in secluded grounds, and the elaborately curlicued beach lamps ended here, where they stood. He had released her arm and she rubbed it with her right hand, and he thought that her eyes no longer looked so distant. And she saw a man she did not know, his cheekbones accentuated by the gaslight above his head, his face rendered unfamiliar by heavy shadow.

She gave a low laugh, a choked sound. Joseph swayed slightly and started to laugh also, only there was no amusement in his voice or face. He reached out, to take hold of her again, and instinctively she swept his hand aside with surprising force. He was standing between her and the hotel, and she spun round on her heel and darted away from him, towards the dark beach. For a moment he stood irresolute, unable to see where she had gone, and then he heard her call his name, teasing. She was still laughing – she could not stop herself – out of nervousness and something else, some other emotion she had never felt before.

He was coming after her, she could hear his footsteps on the gravel. On an impulse she bent swiftly and removed her thin shoes, wrenching them off, breaking a strap in her haste. Carrying them, she stepped on to the sand. Here in the moonlight it was pale and pocked, holding the day's warmth to itself. There was no colour anywhere, only the silver and gunmetal sea, the sky shaded subtle as the breastfeathers of a sleeping bird. It was beautiful, but Lilith scarcely saw it, for Joseph was on the sand also, treading firmly in his patent leather evening shoes, following her. She started to run.

148

For a minute or two she ran for a few steps, then slowed, then ran again, so that he would be able to catch her: she wanted to be caught. But then Joseph started to run also and glancing over her shoulder she sensed rather than saw that the man behind her was not the Joseph she knew, the Joseph of tempered tones and restrained behaviour. He had been replaced by this dark figure who seemed suddenly menacing: she could still feel that hard grip on her arm, peremptory, predatory.

Lilith was running in earnest for the second time that day, but there was no pleasure in this, no exhilaration. She was running to escape, running in mounting panic, holding up the heavily beaded skirt of her dress in both hands. She was not laughing now, she was saving her breath, conserving herself as an animal does, to make sure there is something left for the final effort.

Joseph's head had cleared and his chest was tight with tension. He was a civilized man, a city man, who took his exercise on London pavements and who was less interested in striding through the countryside than in committing it to canvas. He had never waited in a camouflaged hide for duck or pheasant, he had not ridden a horse since he was fourteen and thankfully outgrew his pony. He had never been drawn to hunt any creature, and so he quite failed to realize what he was doing. He did not acknowledge that this, too, was a chase, nor recognize the ancient excitement coursing through his blood.

He had, for the moment, forgotten that it was Lilith he was following. The slight, hurrying figure ahead of him, shoulders gleaming in the beaded cape, was the object of his desire, no more and no less. The unfamiliar surroundings, the wine he had

drunk and above all that enigmatic Eastern glance
had released all his inhibitions, broken down the
careful façade from behind which he dealt with
other people. The breath rasped in his throat as he
ran across the sand and he could feel himself sweating with unaccustomed effort, the skin prickling
under his arms and across his back as he chased
what he had always pursued and never possessed.

Despite his efforts, Lilith was getting away from
him: the distance between them was increasing.
Then she must have caught her foot on something
hidden in the sand – a stone, a piece of driftwood –
and fell, sprawling full length with a little cry. She
was still lying there when Joseph reached her, and
he stared down at her stretched supple as silk at his
feet as she had been that early morning in Hyde
Park when he asked her to marry him. Only this
time she did not remain there, helpless, but struggled to rise, scrabbling in her long, bead-weighted
dress to get to her feet.

And where that silent, smiling girl in the park
had aroused only his chivalry, so that he had picked
her up and brushed her down and asked most
solicitously for her hand, this woman on the ground
stirred other, frightening feelings within him, feelings he did not want to examine but which were
driving him relentlessly. So he shut his mind and
half-fell on to the sand beside her, dropping to his
knees and forcing her down, pinioning the backs of
her spread hands beneath his own. She turned her
head and her teeth gleamed in the darkness through
lips drawn back like a cat's in a grimace of fear and
anger. He thought she was going to scream, and
pushed his hand over her mouth. Above the gag of
his sandy fingers, her dark-rimmed eyes might have
been veiled, so little could he read their expression.

Lilith stared up at him for a long time, as if trying to make out the features of the man she knew beneath this raider's mask. Joseph bent his head and pressed his face against her neck, still holding his hand over her lips so that she choked for breath. In desperation she started to struggle, writhing beneath him, heaving and squirming, kicking vainly at his legs with her stockinged feet, determined to break free. He was amazed by her strength, by the power of those slender arms and long back: her limbs were hard against his, not pliant as they had been on that first morning in their hotel room, but unyielding as steel. He pressed her back down into the sand, and their combined struggles covered them both with the fine dust, so they had to squeeze their eyes shut against it. Sand was everywhere, in their hair, their nostrils, their ears. Joseph could feel it against his bare chest where his waistcoat and evening shirt had both been torn open, but he was too far gone to think about it: the man who a day or so before had fussed over spots of water on his white suit might never have been.

Lilith finally wrenched an arm free and got on to her knees. She jabbed back hard with an elbow and caught Joseph in his lower chest, winding him so that he gasped and sat back. Instantly she was struggling to her feet, but he caught hold of her ankles and she fell again, more heavily this time. She made no sound, nor did he: they were fighting in earnest and in silence.

But Joseph was heavier than Lilith. And for all her physical superiority, despite her trained muscles and her strong dancer's legs, he did not tire as quickly as she did, fuelled by the unaccustomed liquor and the thrill of the capture. He climbed astride her back, holding her dark hair which had long since broken free of its combs twisted between his hands, a living rope. A tether.

She lay pinioned between his legs, her body pressed into the warm sand. She could feel it shifting and trickling against her skin, between her breasts, in her hair. She whispered, 'Joseph, let me up,' but he did not answer. She said it again, more loudly, and this time he muttered, 'Be quiet.'

He was hurting her, his body was too heavy on her back, and she tried to shift away from his full weight. At her movement he tightened his grip on her hair, pulling her head up off the sand. She let out a cry but he forced his fingers under her chin so she was silenced.

'They'll hear us. Don't make such a noise.'

She twisted her head sharply.

'Good. *Good*,' and let out another cry, a real scream this time. His fingers went over her mouth again and she bit him, hard, her teeth sinking into the fleshy part of his thumb. Joseph gasped and took away his hand and she stiffened, thinking he was about to strike her. She heard his shuddering breath from the pain and then, incredibly, felt his lips on her shoulders, bare where the beaded cape had fallen away. He was kissing her, he kissed the nape of her neck under the heavy hair, her exposed ear, her shoulders again.

'*Please*.' He was breathless, half-sobbing, pleading. 'Please. Just let me . . . Just let me . . .'

Even through her panic and temper, Lilith caught his anguish: she had never heard him so distraught. She thought fleetingly of Valentine Audry, that low, knowing voice. 'There are – requests – a man will sometimes make, that Joseph could make, which you will find strange. Perhaps distasteful. If you want to keep him, it's best to comply. But you must always remember you have an alternative. Sometimes a woman is better off alone. Not many people will tell you that, Lilith.'

She became very still, rigid against Joseph's caress. Then she let out a long sigh and laid her face against her sand-crusted arm.

She could feel him alternately kissing and stroking her back, then he shifted down her body so his weight rested on the backs of her thighs. He lifted himself slightly and she wondered what he could be doing, then she felt her dress, already ruckled round her knees, being pulled higher. She started to protest, but he groaned again, 'Please, please . . . I must . . .' and she made a little sound in her throat and waited. Her dress was round her waist now, and her petticoat. She thought, ridiculously, that they would be crushed and dirty and what would she tell Doris? She tried to turn over but Joseph pushed her back on to her face.

'Stay there, stay there.'

Under her petticoat she was wearing a camisole top with narrow straps and a pair of closed thin cambric knickers that fitted closely to the knee and ended in a lace frill. Because the night was so warm and her dress straight-fitting, she had not worn a corselette: it made her no slimmer than she was already and she hated the way the bones dug into her waist in the heat. She felt Joseph sliding his hand inside her knickers at the waist, and his breathing changed. He put his left arm under her and lifted her slightly so he could pull them down, but it was difficult. He breathed in her ear, 'You do it. Do it,' and she moved, shifting her weight, reaching back with one hand to pull the fine fabric down past her knees, finally using a foot to wrest the garment from her ankles. Joseph knelt up to

153

fumble with his own clothing. He inserted a knee between her thighs, prising them apart. She was lying on her right side and he lifted her left leg on to his own, grasping her so tightly, holding her so closely against him she could scarcely breathe, and heard her own gasps in her ears as she might have heard someone else, lying beside her. She felt Joseph parting her, pressing, probing, then his bared body was butting its way into hers, too insistent, too hurried, all wrong. She gave a sob of remonstrance. *No. No, don't.* He did not stop – he was far beyond that – but he slid his right arm beneath her waist, attempting to lift her higher towards him, and muttered again, 'Help me.'

She obeyed, changing her position, trying to accommodate him so that he could guide himself into her, hearing the long-drawn-out sigh as he settled himself within the folds of her flesh. For a long time, then, there was no movement, only a waiting, a slow silence broken by their harsh breathing.

And then Joseph started to move, to draw back and push forward, slowly, with infinite caution, as though searching for something he feared to find. With each insertion, each withdrawal, Lilith held her breath. He still kept her crushed against him, his right arm round her waist, his left hand moving across the front of her body, kneading, smoothing, grasping, and his breath was hot on her hair as he laboured above her.

She lay beneath him, outwardly submissive, inwardly seething: she had grasped enough of Valentine Audry's talk to know that Joseph was not seeking to afford her any pleasure, only to further his own. She acceded out of ignorance, out of innocence. Most of all, she acceded because she thought

154

that if she did so, Joseph would love her. And Lilith
wanted to be loved.

She tried to turn her head, to see him, seeking
reassurance, but all she could make out was his
dark bulk against the sky. Joseph felt her movement, and knew that she wanted to turn and face
him. But he could not let her. As long as she was
like this – hidden, faceless, he could persuade himself that she was someone else. Someone rare and
dangerous. Someone forbidden to him. He stroked
the secret skin of her buttocks. Other women were
too rounded and voluptuous for his taste, their
amplitude disconcerted him, made him feel inadequate to cope with such abundance. But Lilith
might have been a boy; muscular and taut, her
thighs strong and smooth to his touch, her waist
narrow, her belly flat under his searching hands.
She was not like other women, he told himself, and
those rare fruits came into his mind again, the
persimmon, the golden *marmelo*, at once sour and
sweet. He thought of her Persian prince's eyes, of
young Egyptian kings, of captive cup-bearers and
catamites. This time, this time . . .

He was thrusting into her rhythmically now,
faster, frantic, frenzied. And Lilith, pinned beneath
him, pushed into the sand, did not know what it was
she felt. She hated it and yet thrilled to it – this
unthinkable, unnameable sensation, so perverse
and at the same time excruciatingly sweet. She gave
an unconscious mewl that could have been pain or
pleasure and buried her face in her outflung arm.

Lilith became very cold, though their bodies were
still linked. When she licked her lips there was the
salt taste of tears and sand gritted between her
teeth. Outlined against the dark sky she could

155

discern a darker shape that resolved itself into a pair of birds swooping so low she could hear the beating of their wings. They flew out over the sea with grieving cries which so exactly echoed her mood that for a minute she thought she had imagined them. Perhaps they were curlew. *Curlew shall not sing tonight.*

She stared out over the glimmering water and thought of their wedding, and the blessings that had been heaped upon the two of them, the hopes and the prayers. And all for this.

Joseph also heard the curlew, though for him their cries penetrated a sour semi-sleep. He did not want to wake to the bitter truth, to his own slow detumescence and the knowledge that he had not crossed any frontiers, that he was just as he had always been.

They lay on the scuffed suede sand, physically together, yet utterly separate. Impossible to say who was the more deceived.

Chapter 9

'Bee, Bee. I'm back. I'm home! *Bee*.'

Lilith whirled through the Sloane Square house, a vivid figure in her ochre travelling costume among the pampas grass and Oriental pots, the feathers on her hat quivering with her excitement. Through the shaded rooms she went, pulling back velvet curtains, bead curtains, in a flutter of impatience to see her sister. She found Dorcas in the kitchen, fat now and beaming, no longer the scrawny girl she had been when first she came into Dr da Costa's service, and hugged her, and hurried on: into her mother's sitting room, where the draped palms and etched glass, the silver table and the faded photographs were untouched, and that faint perfume misted the air. Beatrice was not there.

She was not in the dining room, with its heavy mahogany dresser bearing the blue and gold dinner service they used on high holy days. She was not in her bedroom, where – Lilith saw with an unaccustomed pang – she still kept her dolls, carefully ranged along the back of a chaise longue, each wearing her starched and ruffled frock, white stockings and kid boots, each staring at Lilith with eyes expressionless as Beatrice's own.

She flung open a window, calling her sister's name into the garden where fallen leaves raked into a pile smouldered sullenly, but there was no reply. She even tried their father's study, knocking carefully upon the door in case he should be in, peering round it as she had as a child, awed by the horsehair examination couch, the rows of stoppered bottles with their crystal contents, the pathetic skull of a child Samuel da Costa kept on top of a bookshelf, where he mistakenly thought the girls would not see it.

She found Beatrice at last in the bare white room at the top of the uncarpeted attic stairs. She was leaning against the piano, her back turned, humming to herself. Lilith opened the door so quietly Beatrice did not hear her, but continued singing the strange, evocative little melody that was hers alone, with its odd foreign lilt, its echo of the East, its Hebrew cadences. When Lilith spoke her name – softly, so as not to startle her out of whatever world it was she occupied at such times – she stopped singing but did not turn round.

Lilith said, 'Here I am. I'm home, I've brought you a present . . .'

Still nothing. And then all in a moment Beatrice whirled round and ran towards her, pushing past her, trying to get out of the room. Lilith caught her arm, 'Bee. It's me, only me. Only Lilith,' and Beatrice struggled to free herself like a desperate animal, keeping her head turned, refusing to look at her sister. But Lilith caught a glimpse of her white face and set mouth, the lids lowered submissively, the sweep of lashes; her features were as calm as ever, expressing nothing, reflecting nothing. Only for a second did her eyes involuntarily meet Lilith's, as they wrestled in the doorway, and for an instant Lilith looked into their blue depths and read an emotion she had never thought to see there.

With a gasp she let go of Beatrice's arm and stood with her back to the door. There was no key: throughout the house, because no one knew what Beatrice might do if she were ever to lock herself

158

into a room, none were ever left in doors. Lilith barred the way, panting with exertion. She said, breathlessly, 'You don't mean it. Bee, you don't mean it! You can't hate me. I haven't left you – look, I'm here, I'm back.' She reached out her arms. 'I'm here, Bee.'

Beatrice's eyes went from the door to Lilith's waiting arms. She did not look at her sister's face. Then she ran back into the room, hurled herself into the farthest, darkest corner and huddled on the ground, her back turned, her knees drawn up and her arms locked round them, head down, face hidden.

Lilith needed no words to understand what Beatrice felt, for she knew her sister better than she knew herself. She had been gone a month: twenty-eight endless days, twenty-eight dark nights. Too many to count, too many to bear. Poor lovely, lonely Beatrice.

Without a word, Lilith went over and sat on the ground behind her, putting her arms round the slender shoulders, holding her tight, holding her close. She held her face against Beatrice's back and rocked with her, rocked with her, regular as a metronome, murmuring the baby words she had always used, the incantation that brought Beatrice back from the terrifying place where her mind wandered. 'There, there, bay-*bee*, there, there, bay-*bee*.' She rocked as Beatrice's harsh irregular breathing slowed and the huddled body slowly relaxed against her and still she whispered, on and on, scarcely realizing that she was soothing herself also, drawing out the bitter feelings she harboured against her husband, feelings which had no voice, which she could never admit to anyone. 'There, there, bay-*bee*, there, there, bay-*bee*.'

By the time she loosed Beatrice and got to her feet in a single graceful movement, she could tell from the sounds in the house below that her father had come home. She urged Beatrice up, tidied her hair for her and then, hand in hand, Lilith leading, the two women went down the narrow stairs.

The house in Hans Place never felt like home to Lilith. It was Joseph's, and Joseph's it remained. He had chosen the furnishings, and they were as characteristic as the gallery, providing a subtle background for the rare and priceless items he liked to have around him. Everything was tasteful, uncluttered, elegant. In Sloane Square, Lilith thought gloomily, standing at the window and twisting the curtain of oyster velvet through her fingers, there was not a picture or an ornament which did not carry memories: the walnut furniture, the leather chairs Samuel's father had given them, the knotted silk carpet that his grandmother had sent from Baghdad to celebrate the birth of his first child. Gazing round her, Lilith saw that nothing in this cool room carried more than its own value: there was no burden of sentiment here, no threads linked to the past.

Lilith let the curtain drop with a sigh and sat down. The French carriage clock in its rosewood and floral marquetry inlaid case on the mantelpiece struck four times and as the last note faded there was a discreet knock upon the door and Chan-Tu entered, bearing a silver tray set with tea for one. She had not ordered it, she did not want it, she dared not refuse it. She thanked Chan-Tu politely as he poured the thin liquid into the translucent cup. He did not speak, but made a small obeisance, went over to the window, straightened the curtain where Lilith had creased it, and went silently away.

Lilith immediately poured the tea into the earth round one of the pendant Humility plants which hung suspended from the handsome wooden stand: she had done this so many times now that the plants were thriving as never before, causing Chan-Tu much puzzled gratification. She went back to stare out of the window, taking care this time not to touch the curtains. Hans Place was already dark, the white fronts of the houses illumined by gaslight, starlings squalling their way to the elm in the garden of number 9. Joseph would be home soon. At the thought an unconscious frown put two vertical lines between her brows.

It was hard for her to make sense of her feelings. She was devoted to her husband, she told herself, liking the picture this conjured up, unaware that she was acting a part. She certainly wished to love him, had learned the words of love he wanted to hear, learned them so well she believed they were true. Because she was kind, she was converted to loving him, for she needed to love and who better than her husband? On the surface, everything seemed so perfect, everyone was so pleased. Aunt Florence, seeing them together, told her they made a wonderful couple. At the Mendozas' Sabbath table the previous week she had caught Judith wiping a furtive tear: 'I'm so happy for you, dear.'

So why was it that every time Joseph looked at her, took her arm, kissed her cheek, spoke in affection as he often did, she felt he saw someone else, touched someone else, held another body in his arms? Even in their most intense and intimate embraces it was as though he sought a different response than hers.

161

Never did it cross her mind that he was unfaithful. She would have known, smelled another woman on his clothes, found traces on his jacket of a perfume she did not wear, a hair finer or coarser than her own. His behaviour was unfaultable, punctilious. She knew always where he was, who he was seeing. He had no secrets, no closed doors that she could find. All the same, she was aware of something between them, an invisible barrier that over the weeks and then the months affected her deeply.

Lilith longed to be loved. She craved approval, affection, she needed to feel secure. Florence Hartsilver had seen this in the little girl, then in the young woman, and had known it stemmed from her mother's death; that to the child had been seen as desertion, proof that she had not been sufficiently loveable. For many years, the mute and exclusive love Beatrice gave her had been sufficient. The silent figure hurrying in her wake, the slender warmth in her bed in the early hours and the unquestioning adoration had assuaged Lilith's need. And then the world – and Judith Mendoza – had interfered. With the best intentions they had reshaped Lilith's life for her. And now Joseph was bringing back all those childish fears again by inexplicably distancing himself from her.

Lilith was too inexperienced to see that it was her husband's inadequacies which came between them. She took him at his own assessment, believed him to be clever and sophisticated, a man of the world. Even those scathing words from Baron Dabescat on the yacht, the murmured intimacies of Valentine Audry in the shadowed hotel room, had left her unaware that what happened between her and Joseph was only a mutilated parody of the act of love. Where other newly married women acquired a sleek contentment, Lilith lost weight, and her Persian prince's eyes were shadowed and sad. She was aware that the restless hunger she felt was unappeased, but the reason was beyond her.

She knew only one way to fill the void. Suddenly decisive, she seated herself at the writing desk and took out the address of her old dancing teacher.

Madame Cotin answered before the end of the week, and the following Tuesday at ten in the morning, Lilith was on her way across London.

Behind the Covent Garden, the Drury Lane Theatre looked closed and shuttered. The ticket office was boarded up, a tattered poster announced a play that had finished the previous month, and two scruffy little boys in worn clothes played dibs in the shelter of the entrance. Lilith peered at the unpromising exterior from the taximeter cab, uncertain what to do. The driver muttered into the empty clay pipe he held clenched between his teeth. When she still did not move, he got out and held the door open for her.

'Want me to wait, 'M?'

She opened her handbag, searched for her alligator purse, paid him, thanked him, crossed the dingy cobbled street and stood watching the small boys. They were absorbed in their game, throwing up the small stones, then catching them on the backs of their grubby hands.

She said, 'Could you tell me how I get into the theatre?'

They squinted up at her, instantly suspicious. She opened her purse, took out a couple of half-pennies, spun them in the air. The boys yelped and grabbed for them, then one said ungraciously, 'Rahnd the back.'

Lilith nodded and started to walk away, hearing

the smaller boy say, mimicking her voice, 'Could you tell me 'ow I gets into the theatre?'

She walked round the theatre and finally found a half-open door. Beside it in a cubicle sat a bedizened old man. When she asked for the ballet master, he viewed her with the same suspicion as the small boys had done, but shuffled off. He was gone for a long time, while Lilith looked round at the drab brown paintwork, the stone stairs, the gas mantels on the walls. Her courage ebbed, and she was ready to turn and leave when the old man returned.

'Mr Jay will see you now . . . In there.' He held open a door, gesturing with his head which way she was to go. In trepidation, holding the small bag she had brought with her, Lilith passed into the room.

It was square and bare and colourless, clearly a room where hard work was done. The floor was of wood, there were wooden *barres* on two walls, the third held a great mirror. It was empty but for a single figure, a slight man perched heronlike on a tall stool in the middle. He did not look up as she came into the room but said briskly, 'Come. Stand,' and still without looking at her, pointed to the space before him.

Lilith walked forward and stood in front of him. He glanced at her from under thick grey eyebrows, his eyes birdbright, then returned to his papers.

'Mrs Mendoza? Madame Cotin speaks highly of you. There is a dressing room on your right. Please change and then we shall see what you can do.'

He clearly expected no answer, so she made none, but changed in the curtained cubicle into her white tunic. As always, she left her feet bare. When she pushed aside the curtain, stool and room were empty. She waited a moment then, feeling cold, started to move about. She had already spent an hour on her bedroom floor, doing her own exercises, bending and stretching, and now in this setting she did not use them again, but executed simple *pliés* with one hand on the *barre*. She was still doing this when Frederick Jay came back, and she saw that he walked with the aid of a cane. He took his stool to the side of the room, and seated himself with his back against the wall.

'There is a gramophone. You have music?'

'Yes. I'll put it on.' She had placed her record on the turntable. Now she wound the machine, adjusted the stylus and put the needle down on the disc. The familiar crackling came out, and she moved to the centre of the floor.

The music was a new piece by Ravel, *Jeux d'Eaux*, and the sound of the piano rippled through the room. Lilith had been practising this for a long time. She executed it perfectly. Smoothly she moved around, arms extended, undulating gently, floating on the stream. She forgot where she was, forgot the solitary watcher perched on his stool, forgot that the floor felt dirty under her bare feet. She danced the play of waters with a passion that disturbed the ballet master, who had never seen such movements before and knew nothing of the long hours this young woman had spent, pacing and pacing and pacing the white Trouville sands.

The music flowed and ebbed and finally died away, leaving Lilith stretched on the ground like a river creature abandoned in its wake, sinuous and spent.

She held the pose, as she always did, for one beat, two, after the music finished, and then gathered herself up and sprang to her feet. The ballet master watched her, his head on one side, tapping his teeth with a pencil. Lilith wrapped herself in the cashmere shawl she had left on the end of the *barre*, and waited.

'Well, Mrs Mendoza. You have come to me for ballet lessons.'

'Dancing lessons, yes.'

'Well, I fear you have come to the wrong man. I teach ballet, Madam. I am a purist. What you have just shown me is very pretty, no doubt. Most athletic. But it is not ballet.'

Lilith said, defensively, 'I don't claim it *is* ballet. It's my own dancing – I made it for myself. But there are movements' – she made a wide gesture with her arms – 'things I want to say through my dancing for which I don't have the vocabulary. You have such a reputation, I had hoped you would teach me . . .'

He shook his head.

'No, no, you want a mime, not the strict discipline I enforce. Look' – he sprang from the stool, apparently no longer needing the cane he affected – 'see this?' He took an *attitude*, one arm raised, the other held behind him, poised on one foot. He bent and slapped his calf with the downturned hand. 'My foot turns out, achieved *here*,' he touched his hip, 'by rotation of the hip-joint. That is the whole basis of classical technique. But you, you dance like this . . .' and he brought his feet together, pointing forward. 'You adopt natural movements. Now if you were – forgive me – rather younger, even twelve or thirteen, then I could hope to save your technique. But I fear you are too far gone. There is nothing I can do for you.'

Lilith pulled the creamy cashmere shawl further round her and listened in silence. There was no point in arguing with Frederick Jay, she could see that, no way to explain to him that to her those duck-footed positions were ugly and tortuous, quite alien to the fluid movements she wanted to achieve.

She had hoped he would be able to give her dancing the finish, the patina, she knew she lacked.

She said, quietly, 'I'm sorry to have wasted your time. I'll go elsewhere for help I need.'

Frederick Jay climbed back on his stool and glanced towards the door. For the first time, Lilith became conscious that a group of young people in practice clothes were standing there, clearly waiting for a class to begin. Having an audience, he said, in a voice that carried to where they stood, 'Take my word for it, Mrs Mendoza. These' – he sniffed to emphasize his distaste – 'these acrobatics of yours are a waste of time.' He paused, to achieve the maximum effect. 'Unless, of course,' he went on, drawling his words for the benefit of his listeners, 'you wish to join a circus.'

Lilith clutched the shawl around her, so taken aback by this unnecessary insolence that words – which never came easily – quite deserted her. She wanted to scream at him, *I'll show you. You'll see what I can do.* But all she did, in front of those many curious eyes, was to walk over to the gramophone with all the dignity she could muster, take her record, gather up her clothes and get herself out of the room. As the door swung shut behind her she leaned against a wall, shaking with the effort of controlling herself. How dare he speak to her like that? She forced herself to stand upright, to walk along the stone corridor, look for a room where she could change and get away from this horrible place, that awful man.

'Excuse me.'

A light touch on her arm. She turned, to find a woman behind her. Because her eyes had filmed with furious tears, she could only faintly make out the strong features under the severely drawn back

hair, the narrow figure in black practice clothes.
The woman put a hand under her elbow.

'Here, come to our dressing room. He's insuffer-
able, the little beast, you must take no notice. None.
He's not important, he only thinks he is.' Still
talking, she guided Lilith into an empty room, and
shut the door firmly. This room was long and
narrow, with mirrors along one wall and clothes
piled everywhere: the clutter and chaos, the spilled
face-powder and smell of women's bodies reminded
her for an instant of Valentine Audry.

'I was in the class, I heard all that rubbish about
circuses.' The woman talked on as Lilith dejectedly
sat down, moving a skirt and a pair of shoes from a
stool. 'My name is Moura, Moura Lemburg.' She
extended a thin hand and Lilith shook it. 'Lilith
Mendoza.' The oddly formal gesture in that setting
made her smile, and she immediately felt better.
She saw that Moura Lemburg was not as young as
she had first thought, but a woman in her early
thirties, with a deep voice that held traces of an
indefinable accent, odd and charming. She did not
sit, but leaned against the door with what Lilith
recognized as the studied negligence of a professional dancer.

'Look, Lilith – may I call you that? I've only a
moment, I must go back to the class. I think I can
help you – with your dancing, I mean. I'm going
home in an hour, I live nearby. Will you wait for me
and we can talk then?'

The two women walked through Covent Garden.
Moura Lemburg talked all the time, apparently
oblivious to the noise around her, the bustle and
clatter. Huge blinkered drayhorses clattered past on
the cobbles, their drivers encouraging or cursing as
the carts caught on kerbstones in the narrow streets.

Burly porters shouldered piles of boxes with evident ease, and Lilith even saw one man moving at a sedate trot with half a dozen balanced on his flat cap. The air smelled strongly of rotting vegetables, like a neglected garden, and from roadside barrows old women offered single cabbages and cauliflowers, bunches of chrysanthemums and Michaelmas daisies: 'Buy me sweet flowers, luv, buy, buy . . .' Jaunty youths in moleskin trousers whistled 'Harvest Moon' and 'Sweet Adeline' as they pulled laden trolleys, and as they turned into Russell Street Lilith was roughly pushed aside by a man in a loud checked suit. She looked up to see that she had inadvertently walked beneath a winch lowering bulging sacks to the waiting cart beneath.

Moura Lemburg merely glanced up and went on talking. By the time they had crossed the vast open square and reached Henrietta Street, Lilith had learned that the older woman was Polish-born and had come to England with her parents when she was a child. Her father had worked as a translator for a minor publishing house, and had himself written English versions of ancient Polish fairy stories. They had lived among a community of Poles, behind Charlotte Street, in a Georgian cottage facing on to a square; now only her mother stayed on, living in half the house and renting out the rest. She had been a dancer in Poland with the national ballet there, and Moura inherited her talent. At first her mother taught her, later she attended a nearby ballet school. At sixteen she answered an advertisement in *The Stage* and joined the Savoy Theatre chorus for their performances of Gilbert and Sullivan's operas. After two years she moved to a travelling dance company and spent her time in the provinces. During their run at the Coronet Theatre in Notting Hill Gate she met and soon married Cyril Lemburg. He had a post in the Foreign Office, and soon after their marriage, was posted to Denmark. They lived there for ten years, Moura occupying herself by giving private ballet lessons. When her husband contracted pneumonia and died, she came home and supported herself by dancing.

Lilith absorbed all this quietly: it sounded a hard life. They had reached the far end of Henrietta Street, and Moura stopped at a doorway, fished a key out of the battered leather valise she carried, and led the way up a long flight of stairs. The ground floor, she explained, was occupied by the publisher for whom her father had worked. She had a small flat on the top floor. It was an unlikely place, Lilith reflected, for a single woman to live, and she thought fleetingly that Aunt Florence would consider the clothes, the Russian hairstyle and the dancing, to be what she called Bohemian: it was a word that for the Hartsilvers encompassed anyone interesting, intellectual and impoverished.

The flat was three cramped rooms, a kitchen that was little more than a cupboard and a slightly larger cupboard containing a hip bath and a lavatory. It was full of steps, every room being at a different height, and Lilith noticed the pale grey paint, the brilliantly coloured rugs decorating the walls, the sofa which was almost invisible beneath its burden of shawls and cushions. The light that streamed in through the crooked windows shone on numerous small paintings, on a bronze figure poised as if for flight, and on a black and white charcoal sketch of a woman Lilith recognized as Moura, standing virtually naked beside a cane chair. Moura, pouring pale tea for them both, caught the expression on

170

Lilith's face as she looked at this, and said, seriously:

'I model sometimes, for artist friends. As you can see' – she gestured round her – 'I appreciate the supplement to my income. And I like the work.'

Lilith, disconcerted, spoke hurriedly, 'Thank you for rescuing me back there. I felt terrible.' She took a sip of her tea and said, 'Goodness.'

'It's Matte tea,' Moura explained. 'Made from herbs. All I drink.' There was a pause, then she said, 'I can help you, I think. If you would like that. I'm a good teacher. And I spent a lot of time with the Danish Ballet in Copenhagen, watching rehearsals. Their stage work is conventional, but in practice they allow a good deal of freedom. More than Jay would ever contemplate, anyway.' She stared at Lilith, her light-brown eyes intent. 'I was in the room all the time you were dancing, waiting for class. You're good. More than that: you express feelings in a way anyone can understand instantly.'

Lilith said dolefully, 'He said I was too far gone to train.'

Moura leaned forward, holding her cup between both hands, twirling it between her fingers. 'You see, Jay's part of the ballet establishment. He said he was a purist, but really he means a traditionalist: he teaches as he was taught. He's very good, one of the best, but he's too blinkered to see what you're trying to do. What you're *doing*. He believes the basic technique for a dancer must be classical. You are working on natural, freer lines, more creative and not so restricted.' As she talked, she opened a large jar of honey and dipped in a spoon, filled it and stirred it reflectively into her tea. 'Tell me about yourself. Tell me how long you've been dancing like this.'

171

So Lilith told her about Beatrice, and Madame Cotin, about the bare white room at the top of the narrow stairs and the hours she had spent working on steps for Beatrice. 'And in the end,' she said, simply, 'in the end, I was doing it for myself. It became more and more important to me, better than anything. Then, when I married, and there was no space to practise, I stopped. But without it I feel – I can't explain. Empty. If you really could teach me – and I can afford to pay you – where would we practise?' She looked around the room with a comical expression on her face.

'I don't charge as much as Jay does. I won't ruin you. And there's a room not far from here we can use for just a few shillings a month. It's over a factory, and a friend works there. The room above is empty and I practise there often.' She smiled for the first time, fine lines crinkling the corners of her eyes. 'We could start tomorrow. If you would like that.'

And so Lilith began to live two lives. One was as Joseph's wife, in Hans Place, in the oyster-coloured rooms where she wore expensive clothes and was *at home* on Tuesday afternoons, ordered meals and invited guests, went to the opera and to concerts, attended dinners and met Joseph's clients. And side by side with that she lived her other – and, she often thought, her real life – where she would travel each day to Endell Street, hurrying between high warehouse walls to the empty room above the stained-glass factory which smelled of hot metal and sulphurous fumes. Here she took off the expensive clothes and put on her white tunic, and in bare feet on the cold wooden floor she worked and sweated and worked again.

Lilith bought a large mirror which she had hung

at the far end of the room, and Moura's friend, the designer from the factory, put up a sturdy *barre* opposite, and kept their gramophone in his locked cupboard for safety.

Under Moura's eagle eye, Lilith was forced to drive herself as never before, going on until she thought her feet must surely be bleeding from her efforts. She was merciless and enthusiastic: 'You can do it, you can – that's marvellous, like that. If you hold your breath, you'll find you can jump higher – so! Now, extend that arm – reach and stretch, stretch . . .'

There were times, days, when she felt so driven she almost hated Moura, that stern, implacable face, the insistence on perfection. 'I can't do it,' she shouted, more than once. 'It's impossible. No one could do that.' 'You can, Lilith, I've seen you. When you weren't thinking about it, you did it. So do it now. Do it for me.'

And from somewhere she did summon the will-power and the strength to achieve what Moura demanded. And the reward was the incredible excitement of seeing in the glass the smooth movements, the articulate arms, the poise and balance of the body she scarcely saw as her own, but watched now as critically as Moura. The Pole proved to be the perfect teacher for her. Although Lilith was only thirteen years younger, she had lived in such seclusion in Sloane Square, been so protected in her marriage by money and position, the difference in their ages was unduly emphasized. Moura had led a very different life, had worked even before her marriage, had been widowed before she was thirty. She had longed for children and had none, and Lilith came to fill an empty space for her. The liking between the two women warmed to a deep trust.

Moura Lemburg had a quick, intuitive intelligence and understood her pupil. Without prying, she found out more and more about her, amassing a hoard of small, apparently unimportant facts that assembled themselves into a picture. She learned about the da Costa family, the numerous relatives who visited from the Lebanon and Baghdad and Portugal, speaking Ladino and wearing a fortune in jewels. She learned about the house in Sloane Square, its atmosphere dense with memories, and felt she herself saw the pale little girl with the waterfall of blonde hair who inhabited the shadows.

Moura became the first person who was able to make Lilith understand her own dancing. She put words to Lilith's instincts, explained to her why one movement worked when another did not. It was she who said, one day after the lesson had ended and the two women were sitting propped against the wall, Lilith wrapped in the cashmere shawl, Moura in an ancient hooded cape, 'You know, I realized today why you have those pauses I like so much, when you wait and miss a beat and then follow the music instead of leading it.'

Lilith shook her head. 'I don't think about it. I've just always done it, I suppose.'

'Those pauses are when you're waiting for Beatrice to catch up with you.'

Lilith had been massaging her feet. She rubbed more slowly, recognizing the perception.

'You mean, I'm always dancing with Bee? Even now?'

'I'm sure of it.'

'Do you think I should change it?'

Moura was appalled. 'Good heavens, no. It's just these things that make you different. Special. I'm technically a good dancer, but I'll never be anything

174

on a stage but *corps de ballet*, and maybe the occasional character role as I get older. It's not a question of technique. I *feel* emotions when I dance, but that's not enough. You have to make them visible to the audience in such a way that *they* feel them too: you have to make them care. You do that, you have that extra gift, Lilith. You don't know how lucky you are.'

Lilith listened to this reserved, observant woman who was fastening the laced sandals she wore summer and winter, just as she always wore flowing Grecian clothes.

She said, suddenly bleak, 'Do you know, I haven't danced in front of an audience since I was fourteen years old. Five years ago. Except for you, no one has seen me.'

Moura looked at the hunched figure opposite who seemed suddenly to have grown pinched and small in her dejection. She thought for a moment. 'You won't be ready for any kind of public appearance for many months yet. But there's no reason why you shouldn't appear privately. It would be excellent preparation. Singers and dancers nowhere near your standard perform at small functions regularly.' She put out a narrow hand and stroked the long rope of hair that hung over Lilith's shoulder. 'If you feel you must have some acknowledgement of all your hard work, there's me. I know you're going to be quite extraordinarily good. Unique.' She smiled at the gratitude that lit Lilith's face. 'But in the meantime, why don't you ask your Aunt Florence if you could appear at one of her soirées?'

Lilith said doubtfully, 'She's sure to say it would be unseemly. Married women in her circle don't do such things. Still . . .' she lifted a suddenly hopeful face to Moura, 'I could just ask, couldn't I?'

At first, the aunt was incredulous that Lilith should want to do such a thing: 'I cannot imagine, Lilith, why you should have taken up this pastime again now you are married. You know how I dislike dilettantes.' Then, when Lilith persisted, she softened. 'Well, perhaps . . .'

Mrs Hartsilver had for many years been a member of the Jewish Ladies' Society for Preventive and Rescue Work, engaged in raising money for the Jewish shelter in the East End where rest and food was offered to young women reduced by poverty to streetwalking. Before Lilith's marriage, she would never have dreamt of discussing such matters before her, but it crossed her mind that if Lilith was so anxious, a small concert might be of some financial benefit to the Society.

And so, a month later, Lilith danced in the Portman House drawing room before an audience of twenty invited guests. Accompanied only by a pianist – Aunt Florence considered a gramophone record inelegant – she performed two of the dances on which she and Moura Lemburg had been working. The audience were delighted, and Aunt Florence glowed with the praise she had received on behalf of her niece. Only two of the watchers were silent, and for very different reasons. Judith Mendoza remained in her seat for a long time after the performance was over, scarcely able to believe that it was Lilith she had been watching. When she had changed and returned to the drawing room, the elder woman observed her moving amongst the guests, smiling. When she caught her eye Lilith crossed the room to her side.

'Did you like it?'

Judith put her hand on Lilith's arm. Without

thinking, she used the left one, the claw hand in its protective sheath of suede. Both women noticed it at the same moment and Judith made to draw back, but Lilith forestalled her, placing her own hand lightly on top of the tiny, deformed one. She did not know that in thirty years, no one had ever made such a gesture. Judith said, 'You should have let me watch you before. I'd no idea, no idea at all, that you could dance like that. You're wonderful. Wonderful.'

Lilith said simply, 'I'm so glad,' and started to add something else, but she was embraced by a florid woman, pressed to an ermine bosom, and pulled away from Judith Mendoza, who did not move, sitting lost in thought, cradling her gloved hand.

Joseph also was silent, standing at the back of the room, staring with unseeing eyes at the Paul Fischer painting of a flower market that hung over the escritoire. Like Florence Hartsilver, he had been incredulous when Lilith told him she wished to dance before an audience this evening, the more so since she had never spoken to him of it before. He had raised no objections – was he not a man of the arts himself? – but then he had not known what to expect. He had not asked what dances she would perform, assuming she would entertain as his young cousins did, perhaps a Scottish dance in white dress with a tartan scarf to add authenticity or even a minuet, as he had once seen it done in period costume. His wildest imaginings would have produced no worse vision than Lilith in an ankle-length ballet frock giving a charmingly amateurish rendering of Pavlova's recent success.

Instead, she had chosen to embarrass him by appearing in a flowing garment that barely reached below her knees, and to exacerbate matters it appeared to be slit in several places; he could see her silk-covered leg almost completely exposed with her movements. And the movements themselves were unlike anything he had ever witnessed. He would not have supposed his Lilith capable of such strength and power, such beguiling sweetness. He checked himself, remembering suddenly the surprising steel of her limbs beneath him on the Trouville sands and the way she would put her arms round him when they were alone, whispering in his ear. He shook his head to dislodge the thought.

It was unseemly – worse, it was indecent – for her to be seen so by respectable men like Montefiore (he glanced behind him), Moses Ancona, Amos Henriques – though he had to admit they seemed unperturbed as they stood chatting amicably over their glasses of Muscatel. Only it was not their wives who had just made an exhibition of themselves, but his. He did not understand that what he felt was primarily jealousy. Joseph, who had so longed to be an artist himself, could clearly see that Lilith had something he would never possess: a sureness that marked out an original. Great painters had it. A line drawn on the canvas, the flourish of the signature, would hold the authority that comes from absolute certainty. He had never possessed it; at best he had achieved a formal charm. But even in the few minutes of her dance, he had to acknowledge that Lilith was her own creation.

He swung round to see Lilith standing there, docile in a demure dress of crêpe de Chine. His impulse was to grab her arm, hustle her away, but he did not do those things. Instead he smiled and congratulated her, paternal and urbane (though he felt neither). He watched her moving round the room, smiling, looking as though she was somehow on tiptoe. He found her so different from any other woman he knew, from his mother, so assertive, so self-willed, that he could not understand her at all. But he wanted her, could feel himself growing hard as he imagined those long legs wrapped around him, those slender thighs glimpsed beneath her tunic, like a Roman youth on a frieze, a neophyte . . .

Quite soon, he took her back to Hans Place.

Joseph forbade her to dance in public again. Her pleas, her sulky silences, her tears, made no difference: she was not a chorus girl, she must behave with decorum.

Lilith had never told him about the dancing lessons. No one, so far as she knew, was aware where she went each morning. She thought that Liu Chan-Tu must wonder at her regular absences, but he did not speak to her, of that or of anything else. And since Joseph, unknowing, had not forbidden her lessons, she continued to take them. For a year she went almost daily to Endell Street, to the sulphur-smelling room where Moura waited; to her other, real life.

And when she stopped, it was not of her choosing.

Chapter 10

I have something to tell you.

Lilith's voice echoed in his mind, he saw her face vivid with her suppressed secret, her long-fingered hands held out to him in a gesture of giving.

Joseph sat in the office behind the gallery, holding a Minton vase, running his fingers obsessively over the glaze like a man in a trance.

His first reaction on hearing she was with child had been disbelief, though he hoped he had kept this hidden. He knew – God help him, he knew – it could not be his. Nothing so easy, so normal as a child could come from his dry, ambiguous embraces. He had known for years he was not capable of fatherhood; he had neither the physical capacity for the begetting nor the emotional resources for the rearing. When he married Lilith, he had not even considered the possibility of children, had never discussed it with her. He was not interested in doing so, and she was too much a child herself to be concerned.

And now she told him she was carrying his baby, had pulled tight her petticoat to show her budding four-month belly in an odd mixture of excitement and anxiety. The latter emotion he could understand well enough. His favourite cousin Alice, Eliezer's girl, had borne a child only five years before, and six days later she was dead, despite all the care and the best nursing money could buy. It was a hazardous time for any woman.

She was with child, but how had it happened?

Despite all his hopes, he was as incapable as ever of finishing the act as it was meant to be finished, as it finished for every other man. Self-critical, over-controlled, he had never experienced the intense pleasure of orgasm. He was a freak, he told himself, an oddity, unable to reach that final point somewhere beyond himself. However desperately he sought it, no matter what tricks he employed, what fantasies he fabricated, he could not achieve the brief oblivion he craved, the moment of obliteration. Intercourse ended for him in a slow seepage, and he did not believe a child could be thus conceived. And yet, what other possibility was there?

Over and over the porcelain went his fingers as he tried to think clearly. Although it was English made, the vase came from the hands of Mark Louis Solon, the Sèvres-trained artist who had invented the art of pâté-sur-pâté, layer upon delicate layer of liquid porcelain which took months to complete. Joseph had wanted such a vase for a very long time. This morning it had been delivered to the gallery, but he was scarcely in a mood to appreciate it.

Six months ago he would have staked anything – and he was not a betting man – on Lilith's fidelity. But the slim snake of suspicion moved in his mind: he had known nothing of her dancing, would never have imagined her capable of that, and yet he had watched her and known very well how hard she must have worked to produce that effect. He had not cared for it at all, but he was sensitive enough to acknowledge that she had a gift. Later that night, she had told him for the first time how she had danced all through her childhood. He sighed and put down the vase.

If she could keep one secret, she could keep another. He began to list little things he had noticed but discounted, and which now clustered together like maggots in his memory: she had been so eager, that first morning in Trouville, so ready for him – was that innocence? He had told himself she loved him, had fed his own vanity on the incident. Perhaps it meant something else. Afterwards he had glanced at the bed when she was dressing, expecting to see on the white sheets traces, proof of her virginity, but there had been none. His father had told him once how in the old days the girl's mother would hang the bridal sheets from the window after the nuptial night to announce the bride's purity and the husband's prowess. Joseph winced. Maybe in their case it was just as well they had avoided so public a declaration.

They would have put out his grandmother's sheets like that in the streets of the Baghdad ghetto. (His grandmother, who as a young bride had slept with four coins in the corners of her room to keep away the daemon Lilith, haunter of the air and the wilderness, so dangerous to children. Like himself.)

Unconsciously he continued to stroke the porcelain, deriving comfort from the feel of its cool beauty. He was the expert here. This was his territory. Where his young wife was concerned he found himself increasingly at a loss, the ground constantly shifting beneath his feet, never sure where he was with her. Perhaps all women were the same, he didn't know. Couldn't tell. He had managed to distance himself from them for all his adult life. Apart from his vague, delightful mother, who carefully refrained from making any demands on him, he had not needed to come close to any other female. His domestic existence was perfectly ordered. His sexual appetites had required only occasional attention and neither he nor the women involved imagined that he would consider anything other than his own gratification.

Just at the moment – or so it seemed – when it dawned upon him that he was paying for what could not be bought, Lilith walked into the garden at Richmond, into his methodical masculine existence. He had begun his relationship with her in the unspoken expectation that she also would follow where he led, be content with such attention as he chose to pay her. He had anticipated that she would be an asset to him as his beloved porcelain was an asset, a testimonial to his excellent taste. Indeed, he had chosen her for much the same reasons as he made an expensive investment: because she was decorative and pleased him.

At first, she had perfectly filled that role. His Aunt Judith had assured him before the marriage that no expense had been spared to prepare his future wife to be a credit to him. Though the household management she had been taught was rendered unnecessary by the presence of his man-servant, who continued to run the Hans Place house, Joseph was gratified that his wife could talk knowledgeably of painting and had an appreciation of music (though he failed to divine the depth of this) and an eye for good clothes.

Even so, she never looked like all the other women in their circle. Where they were soft and plump from good living and the bearing of children – domestic cats – Lilith was like a forest creature. She never sat when she could stand, never stood when she could move. She was endlessly restless: she gave him the impression that she was always on tiptoe, poised for flight. Vitality, youth, passionate energy spilled out of her as though she was a wild thing barely tamed.

Joseph picked up the Minton vase once more. It had a French Meissen look about it, snake-handled with Cupid and Diana on a grey-green ground. He held it with the greatest care, running his fingers over the cameo figures, marvelling at their grace. But the dancing Diana might have been Lilith, and he was back with his anxieties.

He had tamed her, though. She was pregnant. Whatever his suspicions, they remained suspicions. The child was his.

His. A strange sensation fluttered somewhere deep in his guts, so foreign to him he did not recognize it for the pride it was. There would be his child, before everyone's eyes. He had done it, after all. He must not look too closely, he must not question too much. He must accept, believe, be happy.

Joseph willed himself to acknowledge the child was his, and the exquisite Minton vase shattered into irrevocable fragments between his clenched hands.

Lilith had been three months gone before it occurred to her to wonder why she felt so well. She said as much one morning at breakfast, stretching her arms above her head in the sunny window.

'Why do I feel so wonderful?'

Doris, who was the only person in the room, looked up from the stockings she was sorting and laughed.

'They say you either feel wonderful or sick as a dog the first three months. You be one of the lucky ones, seems.'

Lilith was so stunned she did not move, but stared comically at Doris, her arms still raised over her head.

The maid pushed out a hand, in a gesture she might have used to reprove a too ardent suitor.

'Go on with you, 'M. You'll be telling me next you didn't know!' She put down the stockings. 'You *did* know, didn't you, 'M?'

Lilith said in a whisper, 'You're right. I just never thought about it.'

The maid picked up the stockings again.

'Well,' she observed prosaically, 'you'll have to think about it soon, and no mistake. Your clothes won't fit, for one thing. And there's scarce room here for a babby.'

Moura Lemburg was as astonished as Lilith. The younger woman waited until they were resting after a lesson, leaning against the whitewashed walls as they always did, relaxing, talking quietly, dabbing at their armpits and their foreheads with their towels as they cooled down. Then she asked, with studied casualness, 'What happens to ballerinas when they're expecting babies?'

Moura had already answered, drily, 'They turn into mothers,' before she realized the implications. She stopped rubbing her hair and turned her head towards Lilith. 'You mean that you ...' Her face was comical in its dismay.

'I'm not going to stop dancing, though,' Lilith protested, 'It won't make any difference, not for months yet.'

Moura was less sure. 'We'll see,' she said doubtfully. 'I refuse to let you do anything that might be dangerous. You must drop all the new material we've been working on, it's far too athletic for someone in your condition.'

As time went on, Moura would not permit any of the exercises they had worked up together. Once when she arrived early at the rehearsal room, Lilith started exercising, holding on to the *barre* and lifting each leg in turn so that it was at right angles to her body. Moura arrived ten minutes later and for the first time Lilith heard her raise her voice.

'What are you *doing*? Stop that at once.'

After that, Lilith always exercised lying on the floor, on a rug she bought for the purpose, so that her back was always supported and her thigh muscles took the strain. Later still, she and Moura concentrated on arm movements. Until now, these had interested Lilith far less, and so she had not really thought about them. Forced to do so, she realized how important they were to her dancing, and how much she could improve it. She studied the line of her upraised arms, seeing for the first time how they made a frame for her body. She saw the delicate alteration in feeling wrought by a hand that drooped or was upturned to the sky.

Moura took her to the Savoy, where a small troupe of speciality dancers were appearing. They were Balinese, she said, and Lilith went along happily enough, totally unprepared for the diminutive figures in their shimmering headdresses shaped like towers. She sat in the darkened rehearsal theatre, an unconscious smile on her face, watching the temple dancers in their sarong skirts, golden bodices covering their breasts, gold bells tinkling as they moved. To one side the members of the Gamelan orchestra were seated cross-legged upon the floor, and the sounds they made upon their curious instruments were hollow and rounded. Like rain, she thought, the sudden midday downpours of equatorial countries, drops falling on the wide dark leaves of unknown plants.

To this magical music the fragile figures on stage turned and posed and stamped their belled ankles.

186

Lilith was enthralled by their expressive movements, the beauty of their arms and hands, the
tapering fingers that turned back like her own, the
infinitely touching gestures they produced with
the turn of a narrow, braceleted wrist.

The Balinese dancers were appearing for two
weeks. Joseph accompanied her once, but he did not
care for the drums and cymbals, and remained
unmoved by the extraordinary rhythmic vitality of
the music. So Lilith went back alone, again and
again, under a spell cast by the stylized movements
of those childish bodies, the softly languorous
themes played endlessly on the saron barung, a
constantly reiterated motif that hypnotized her. She
had experienced a similar trance-like state before
when she had suffered a prolonged headache. Judith
Mendoza had come to visit and had produced from
her bag a narrow bottle of ether. Lilith had shaken
her head.

'Joseph says I'm not to use it. He thinks it
unnecessary.'

Judith had shrugged.

'What does a man know of women's troubles? How
can it hurt? And it will ease your head, you'll see.'

Doubtfully, Lilith had taken the proffered bottle.
Later, alone in her room, she had inhaled so deeply
she could taste the powerful sweetness deep in her
throat. Her eyes had filled with tears of relief as the
pounding in her head subsided. Lying on her bed
she let the bottle drop from her nostrils as her head
swam with dream-like images, though she knew she
was still awake. She had seen, as she so often did in
sleep, leaping, dancing figures. And then Beatrice
had been there, sweet and silent, her hand cool on
Lilith's burning skin. Everything had slowed,

stilled, she had felt as though she were swimming through warm water.

And now this Indonesian music produced that same soft languor in her, the same opiated dreaminess. She brought a notebook with her to sketch the dancers' movements, and back in the Endell Street studio she and Moura worked to capture the undulating arms, the suppliant hands of those twelve-year-old girls. There was no way they could reproduce that Oriental orchestra, but at one of the many parties she attended with Joseph, Lilith overheard two men discussing Debussy. One of them – she recognized his name when she heard it later as the music critic of *The Times* – was talking.

'It's a commonplace of musical history,' he was saying, 'that Claude Debussy was influenced by the Gamelan at the 1889 Exposition Universelle in Paris.'

After that, Lilith begged and borrowed every piece of Debussy sheet music she could get her hands on. And she found, in the quality of the music, in the reiterations and constantly repeated motifs, the echo she wanted. In the end, she chose the overture from *Pelléas et Mélisande*, the opera he had written a few years previously. At first alone, then with Moura, she choreographed a dance based on this which incorporated many of the Balinese movements.

The work absorbed her for weeks, so that she had little time, between her sessions in Covent Garden and her life in Hans Place, to think about the coming child. Even Moura, careful as she was, became accustomed to seeing Lilith tailoring her steps to her newly-cumbersome shape and almost ceased to think about it. Then one day, as Lilith was dressing to go out with Joseph, he observed, straightening his tie in her mirror, 'I think it best if you do not accompany me tomorrow evening.' They were to hear a concert at the Alhambra in Leicester Square.

Lilith looked up from the brooch she was fastening.

'Why not? I have a ticket, don't I?'

'Indeed. But I thought I would ask my mother to accompany me, instead. It's not becoming for you to be seen publicly in the evening in your condition.'

Lilith stared at him, as if seeing for the first time the absolute decorum of his clothes, the too-fastidious mouth, the censorious eyes. She drew her black crochet silk jacket defensively round her shoulders.

'I'm very small, still. I'm sure no one will notice. And I'd like to go. Please, Joseph, I want to.'

He laid a proprietorial hand upon her shoulder.

'Better not, my dear. In fact, I think it's time to move down to Norfolk for the birth. You'll be quiet there, there isn't so much excitement.'

She said, mutinously, 'I don't want to go to Norfolk. I shan't like it there, I know.'

Joseph was flicking the shoulders of his jacket with a silver-backed brush.

'Of course you'll like it, Lilith. Don't be childish. You have spent barely a week in that house, but in time you will appreciate it as much as I do. Now then . . .' he pulled the jacket close round her throat, smoothed an imaginary crease from her skirt, '. . . you're ready. Shall we go?'

She followed him slowly to the door, trying to keep the whine out of her voice.

'I can't. I can't be away from London for months. What about Beatrice?'

'Well, and what about her? She'll be well enough, I daresay, with your father.'

189

'You don't understand: she needs me. When we went to Trouville she suffered, and that was only for four weeks. We've never been separated – Joseph, you can't ask me to leave her for so long.' She had caught the sleeve of his cashmere overcoat in her distress as a child might, trying to make him see what she so perfectly comprehended, that her sister existed entirely in the present. She remembered how it had been with the dancing, how little memory Beatrice had had even of the previous day's lesson. The past did not exist for her, and since she had no apparent capacity for imagination, there could be no future. When Lilith had gone away, she had been deserted, and her despair had been absolute. Lilith remembered how Beatrice had looked that day she found her in the attic room, her skin dull and her lips dry and cracked, as if she had been neglected. Now she said to Joseph, determination hardening her voice, 'I won't go. I won't.'

And he, anxious to get her out of the house quietly, for they were already late, and knowing that she should not be excited, said to placate her, 'Well then, she shall visit as much as you like. She can stay the whole time if that's what you want. Only come along, do.'

The village of Overstrand, just two miles beyond Cromer on the Norfolk coast, numbered only thirty houses, mostly old cobble cottages inhabited by fishermen. Some six years before, Joseph had bought two cottages and a paddock situated on a twisting road just before it began its descent to the sea. A good deal of work had been required to make them into a comfortable home for Joseph's use, but he had set his heart on a country house and nowhere would do but Norfolk: it appealed to the snob in him, and the old families of the area, the Buxtons and the Hoares, the Gurneys (the leading Quaker family of England), were known to him through the long hours he had spent as a boy when he and his mother would endlessly trace the lineage of distinguished names. All around Overstrand were numerous stately homes like Blickling Hall, the Jacobean mansion, and Houghton Hall, the largest country house in Norfolk, built by Sir Robert Walpole. There was Felbrigg, one of the most celebrated country seats, home of the Windhams, and of course, a drive away, built upon the old property of Sant Dersingham which had belonged to the Cobbes, the modern house known as Sandringham. Joseph had been invited by the royal household to supply several important pieces of porcelain for the English collection there, and his gratification made up for the inordinately long time it took for his account to be settled.

The Royals had put the seal of social approval on this area of the East Coast: Tucker's Hotel at Cromer was used to receiving foreign sovereigns, like the lovely and unfortunate Empress Elizabeth of Austria. The season lasted for around ten weeks in the summer, and during them it became difficult to find the owners of the Overstrand cottages, for they let the premises to the visitors and removed themselves to strange little makeshift dwellings or even railway carriages for the duration. The new tenants spent hours on the beach during the long days and were charmed by the stark simplicity of the homes in which they slept.

It was Joseph Mendoza's custom to occupy his house during those two and a half months, but now he and Lilith went there in April. She sat in the train watching the north-easterly wind gusting amongst sparse trees, hating the flat bleak hedge-less fields, the vast grey sky. It seemed to her as dreary as Siberia, and she longed for London and Moura's company.

For the first days she was deliberately peevish at her forced departure from the city. And then, despite herself, she began to respond to the wild sea breezes and the charm of the house. The two buildings had been made into a house that retained a basic simplicity with the cobbled walls and red bricks of the original. There were latticed windows and a paved sheltered corner where the L-shape of the completed house made a natural sitting place. Climbing plants were trained up the rough walls and in summer Joseph worked at a white painted wrought iron table, facing towards the cliffs and the sea. Behind the house, on rising ground, rose a solitary tower, part of the ancient church of St Martin. Joseph explained to her that it was of perpendicular design, built at the very end of the fourteenth century, and he told her of the oven in the tower once used to bake the Communion bread. Lilith ventured up there once to try to find the oven, wandering beneath the thick growth of ivy that roofed the nave, for only the walls and the bleached stones that had been the church floor remained, looking as smooth and swept as if still in use.

When she looked across from the rise on which the church stood, expecting to see the boundless plain they had crossed on their journey, the infinite acres planted with turnips, she found instead low rounded hills covered with bracken. In the other direction fields ran to the edge of the cliff and she wondered what would grow there, later in the year. Their own garden, increasingly unkempt, sprawled down through a wicker gate to the cliffs and one day she started out to walk to the edge. An elderly farmer stopped her, warning her that the cliffs were formed of soft rock which crumbled unexpectedly and fell into the sea. He stared at her, his face seamed and wrinkled from exposure and told her how their land was being eaten away, eaten away, repeating the words with gloomy relish. When he was a lad, he said, his parents had owned a cottage at the far end of their land – he waved a large hand towards the empty air – and had woken one morning to find their garden gone. Dropped hundreds of feet without warning, while they slept in their beds. Lilith had been about to ask him what crops he grew on his fields but forgot her question, shaken by the vision of such abrupt amputation, the little house teetering on the edge of nothingness.

After that she confined her walks to the narrow lane which ran beside the house. The Louds, it was called, a word peculiar to Norfolk, meaning a group of houses where fishing families lived in old cobbled cottages. Lilith liked to sit at her bedroom window and watch the bustle of that lane: the women and children, who reminded her of the families she had seen round the harbour at Trouville, the men in their high sea-boots and the curious jacket they wore, called a slop, in a rich red-gold. The men fished eight months of the year, and she would see them going down to their boats, built without row-locks on the old Norse pattern, the oars passing through round holes cut in the sides. Sometimes she would walk down the winding road to watch them unload hopelessly struggling crabs and lobsters in their dozens, before carrying the boats up on to the beach, the oars through the holes acting as levers.

It was all she seemed to do these days, observe other people live their lives. She felt herself to be in a strange, suspended state, waiting for something she could not quite imagine. Lilith knew little about children, she had no idea at all what was happening to her body, and the information she gleaned from Doris was heavily peppered with country lore. The result was that Lilith knew she must be careful to see only beautiful things, for Doris's sister had given birth to a simpleton after giving food to the village unfortunate. Another woman had spied a fox, and her own baby had arrived with red hair and pointed features. Yet another had been frightened during her third month and the child had been born with a deformed foot as a result.

So Doris had become very wary when Dr da Costa brought Beatrice to stay. For the first few days she watched Mrs Lilith's sister uncertainly, then her suspicions hardened into a conviction that this lovely woman was one of God's fools, for in a strange house Beatrice was more withdrawn than ever. She would not even eat with the others and Lilith would sit with her upstairs at mealtimes, leaving her father and Joseph facing each other across the long mahogany table.

It was the first time Joseph had spent more than a few hours in Beatrice's company, and he watched her with an odd expression, at once calculating and covetous. Lilith had seen him cast just such a look on a perfect piece of porcelain he did not yet own.

That she did not mind at all was a measure both of her feelings towards him and towards Beatrice. She believed she was happy with Joseph, she supposed that she loved him, having no comparison. If he was abrupt with her, she convinced herself of his tiredness; when he was withdrawn, that grave matters preoccupied him. The actress in her entered into the role in which she found herself, that of the devoted young wife.

So, consciously, she loved him. But her love for Beatrice was utterly different. She did not have to think of it, to will it into being. Beatrice was a part of her, as she had always been, since Lilith's earliest memory, smiling and secretive, subtle and sad. Her sister. Her shadow. They might have been twins, so perfect was their understanding of one another. Even now, a married woman, Lilith did not perceive herself as an individual. She was the other half of Beatrice.

Joseph's evident fascination with Beatrice did not threaten her at all: she wanted him to love her, as she did. When they went for a walk, or drove the two miles over the windy golf-links to the narrow streets and cobbled cottages of Cromer, Lilith insisted that Beatrice accompany them. Joseph would walk, in his pale summer suit, with a sister on either arm, relishing the envious looks from less fortunate men.

When Doris finally plucked up courage to ask to speak to him, and voiced her fears that in her condition Lilith should not see so much of her sister, lest Beatrice's strangeness somehow affect the unborn child, Joseph patiently explained to her – as Samuel da Costa had to him – that the elder sister was perfectly sane, but that the sorrow over her mother's death so many years before had never left her. 'So you see,' he concluded, 'we must take special care of her, Doris.' And Doris had looked at him shrewdly and seen what Lilith had not, and gone silently back to her duties.

She was not the only member of the household to notice what was going on. Chan-Tu went about his business as usual. He was well known in Overstrand

where his appearance in the narrow streets was a
signal for half a dozen small boys to follow him in
awed delight at his long silk jacket and drooping
moustaches, convinced that if they waited long
enough he would perform magic tricks for them,
like the travelling showman who passed once a year
through the village. In the house, Chan-Tu cooked
and pressed and waited at table as he did in Hans
Place, as he had done these many years for the
Mendoza family. Behind his imperturbable exterior,
behind his impassive black glance, he was in
turmoil.

The Mendozas – first Solomon, then Joseph – had
become his own family, for Liu Chan-Tu was not a
passionate man and had never considered the possibility of marriage. He told himself his circumstances
would not permit it, for where would a Chinese
manservant find a wife in London? But the truth
was, everything in his life had been directed towards
caring for Joseph, since he was a child of seven. He
loved him more, he sometimes felt, than he could
have loved his own flesh and blood, and he expressed
his emotion in the only way he had: it was there in
the sandalwood-lined drawers of Master Joseph's
bureau, in the piles of perfectly pressed garments,
in the hand-made shirts and hem-stitched handker-
chiefs, in the folded Jaeger wool socks and Turnbull
and Asser silk foulard ties. It was in the perfectly
ordered house, the speckless rooms, in the whiteness
of the linen and the gleaming marble steps.

Chan-Tu saw his love for Joseph all around him,
made real, a positive contribution to his master's
well-being. He had little time for the new young
wife, she was too much for him, with her quick
movements and her feathery laugh. He never knew
what she was about. Still, she seemed fond enough

of his master, though he privately thought Joseph could have done better, and he did occasionally wonder where she took herself off to every morning. He had gradually become accustomed to her, and reconciled to the thought that she was carrying Master Joseph's child. Like all Chinese, Chan-Tu liked children.

But he observed with sharp pain the deferential attentions Joseph paid this sister-in-law of his, this pale woman more silent even than himself, with her wide unseeing gaze. He saw how Master Joseph opened doors for her, moved chairs, brought flowers, as though she were a frail invalid.

It was Chan-Tu, not Lilith, who suffered jealousy.

In June, Samuel da Costa returned to London, for he hated to be too long from his practice. He had given in to Lilith's pleadings – as always – and had left Beatrice in her care, so that she could benefit from the country summer. The two young women spent their time in the garden, which was still being completed. When Joseph had first bought the land it had held only an ash and a sycamore tree. He had brought in trees and shrubs to shield the house from the north-easterly winds: yew and box which flourished all year round, protecting the rosery he had had planted, the long lawns, the apple and pear trees, the shady paths and herbaceous borders. There were pergolas covered with vines, hops, climbing roses, and fountains set in deep basins of blue glass in mosaic pattern, edged with sea holly and globe-thistle.

Sometimes they would walk (hand in hand as always, Lilith leading Beatrice) to the ruined church on the hill. The fields around it which had been grey and brown when Lilith first saw them were now

197

pale gold with rustling corn, speckled with poppies. Beatrice would not look at them: like the scarlet wax apples of their miniature childhood garden, she saw them as drops of blood. She seemed happier when they reached the long nave roofed only with ivy where Lilith, moving more slowly now in her seventh month of pregnancy, would dance for her on the old stones smooth as any stage.

At the beginning of July, an invitation was sent to Lilith and Joseph to attend a party given by Sir Samuel and Lady Hoare at Cliff House in Cromer. He was the MP for Norwich, and had bought from Joseph's gallery more than once. Lilith had exclaimed in delight when she opened the letter, but Joseph had shaken his head.

'I don't think, Lilith, that it's suitable for you to attend a formal social gathering.'

She stared at him in shocked surprise.

'But Joseph, this is not London. Surely, down here no one will mind?' She was nearly crying.

His tone was conciliatory. 'I'm sure if Lady Hoare had known of your condition, she would not have invited us.'

'She does know.' Lilith got up from the breakfast table and hurried across the room to pull a parcel from the long cupboard that ran beneath the window-seat. She unwrapped a toy dog made of velvet and held it up. 'Look. She made this for me herself, after we met in Cromer and I told her the news. She sent it round only last week, for the baby.'

Joseph shrugged. 'Even so, I am against the idea of your appearing before a large group of people. You might become over-excited and tired. You must conserve your strength.'

Lilith bent her head over the toy dog in her hands, to hide the ridiculous tears that were falling on to the brown velvet. She wanted to scream at him, *I'm stronger than you*! but she was conscious that Chan-Tu was in the room behind her, and dignity made her sniff, and rub the back of her hand across her cheeks in a touching gesture, and turn away to look out at the bright garden until she was in control of her features. She knew Joseph well by now, there was no point in arguing with him. Once he had made up his mind, he stuck rigidly to decisions. In matters like this, he followed rules of etiquette that had prevailed in his mother's day. Useless to point out that the baby made a bulge so slight it scarcely showed if she dressed carefully. She thought the fact of her condition must be shaming to him, proof somehow of the animal side of his nature, whereas she wanted to flaunt it before everybody in her pleasure.

Joseph looked at her straight back and sighed. He found her so difficult to handle, so very difficult. He remembered his father repeating to him – the only piece of advice he ever gave before he married Lilith – 'Be careful not to make a woman weep, for God counts her tears.' That was all very well, but he could not for the life of him see what he had done to upset her. His only care was for her health, and the child's. And, of course, for propriety. It did not occur to him that he had never told her what her pregnancy meant to him, that he was beginning to experience a new confidence in himself and his powers.

So to her back he said, 'I shall refuse for both of us. I won't go without you.'

Mollified, she finished her breakfast. And that evening, after dinner, when she had taken Beatrice to her room, she said, 'I've been thinking. You should go to the Hoares'. And if you won't take me, take Beatrice.'

Joseph looked up from his copy of *Punch*.

'Yes,' she went on. 'Please do. You would have to stay with her every minute, but it would be wonderful for her. She has only ever been out with Papa, and he does not go to parties such as this.' Her face was bright with anticipation of her sister's happiness. 'Oh, say you will.'

Joseph looked doubtful. 'I understood from your father that she became overwrought among too many people. I couldn't risk that, what would our hosts think?'

Lilith said swiftly, 'I'd thought of that. But she was perfect at our wedding, remember, and Papa thinks now that she may have reached a different stage. She certainly seems calmer and more controlled. And you could always come home early . . . do say yes.'

'Have you spoken of this to Beatrice?'

'Not yet. But if I tell her, she will do it for me.'

'Very well, then. If you can assure me she will not be an embarrassment . . .'

She caught his hand.

'I promise. And I'll make her look wonderful, you'll be proud of her.'

Lilith took Beatrice into Cromer next day. Two narrow streets of fishermen's houses converged at a corner where ramps led down the cliff to the pier. The corner shop was shaped like a piece of cheese to fit the acute angle, and the two sisters who ran it always reminded Lilith of white mice, so busy and round and pink-eyed amongst their lengths of dress material, their reels of cotton and embroidery yarns, their trimmings and buttons. She bought white silk and yards of tulle, and the sisters held up their plump little paw-hands and exclaimed that the young lady would look a perfect dream.

When Doris, with Lilith's help, had made her a filmy frock with a deep neckline, Beatrice did indeed look like a dream. She was twenty-two, and had never in her life been dressed like this. She stood in front of the pier-glass in Lilith's room while the two women pinned and fitted and fussed about her, the clouds of tulle round her shoulders making her skin more transparent than ever, and gazed at herself with her impenetrable smile.

On the day of the party, Lilith was up at eight, to finish embroidering the dozens of shell-pink rose-buds on the bodice. She spent much of the day in the garden, the dress on her lap as she worked, Beatrice beside her watching her deft movements. And all the time, she talked to Beatrice, about the evening, and how she must keep calm, and accept only one glass of white wine.

Doris, bringing them out lemon tea, watched for a few moments and then asked, in a low voice, 'Does she hear you, 'M?'

Lilith gasped with indignation. 'Of course! What do you suppose, that she is deaf?'

Embarrassed, the girl muttered, 'I only meant, to be sure, does she understand you?'

'Of course you understand, don't you, Bee?'

But the only answer was that blue gaze.

When she was dressed that evening, Lilith and Doris put up Beatrice's hair with the aid of a picture in *The Lady*, pinning in pink ribbons. Lilith took her hand and led her downstairs to Joseph waiting in his black silk dress jacket, whose expression of astonishment at Beatrice's beauty made Lilith laugh aloud.

Only when they had left in the motor and Lilith

stood alone watching them out of sight along the upper road did she let herself imagine the scene at Cliff House: the brilliantly lit rooms, the music and flowers, the dancing couples, the gallooning and glitter. Despite her apparent lack of response, she divined Beatrice's excitement: she had felt the tremors of emotion as she wove the silk rose into her sister's moon-pale hair. Turning back into the house, she felt suddenly old and tired, weighed down by her pregnancy, by Joseph's apparent indifference to her in her present state and by a sharp little fear that had begun gnawing its way into her consciousness.

Chapter 11

In September Lilith gave birth to a son, a large baby whose cries commenced the moment the midwife gave him a vigorous slap. She wrapped him quickly in a shawl and handed him to Doris, then turned back to the linen covered couch that served as a birth-bed. She was waiting for the afterbirth but it did not appear, nor had it when the doctor arrived from Cromer at dawn. It had been a busy night for him: he had just delivered another child in the village of Sidestrand. He had left hurriedly on receiving word of Mrs Mendoza's confinement, and when he saw the child safely arrived, asked the midwife to take her bicycle and go over to Mrs Risborough while he reassured himself that all was well here.

Only when she had taken off her apron and bustled away, and Doris had carried the baby into the warmed dressing room to wash, did he realize that there was another child waiting in the womb. He hastily sent down for the chloroform to be brought from his motor, and gave Lilith the mouth-piece. She, unable by now to comprehend exactly what was happening – for she had been in labour since mid-afternoon – found the pleasant giddiness and tingling the gas produced did not seem to affect her mind at all: on the contrary, she felt tremendously elated and began to sing, although she wasn't sure what words she chose. The doctor, growing increasingly concerned, listened to her breathless voice chanting such pretty nonsense: 'Cuckoo!

Cherry-tree! Catch a bird and give him to me . . .'
and waited for the words to slur and fade as she
entered the dreamy state that accompanied partial
loss of sensation.

It was a further twenty minutes before he could
deliver the second infant that lurked as if reluctant
to be born. When he saw the size of the diminutive
body he understood why neither he nor Dr da Costa
had detected its existence. Alone in the room, he
wrapped the little boy in a soft towel and looked
about for somewhere to lay him while he attended
to the mother, finally pulling out a bureau drawer
and placing the child on a folded sheet inside. When
he looked again at the pathetically small bundle the
faint, irregular heartbeat had almost ceased, though
to his surprise the baby lived for more than an hour
– just long enough for a stunned Joseph to name
him Judah, thus ensuring his safe passage through
Gehenna, that dark accursed valley where the
wicked dwell after death. Then the doctor closed the
drawer.

For more than twenty-four hours afterwards
Lilith was in the grip of fever and only vaguely
aware of what was happening. Far more real than
her room and the bed and the murmurs around her
was the terrible realization that something had been
lost, something she had to find or forfeit her reason.
Weeping bitter tears she searched her room, the
whole house, the garden. In her dream she ran to
the cliff, knowing that it was there – whatever it
was she so desperately sought – lying in the long
grass on the very edge, where she had so foolishly
left it. But as she ran, her steps shook the ground
and caused the edge of the cliff to crumble away so
that it rolled – the thing, she could not see through
the grass that stood man-high between herself and

it – rolled and fell, even while she howled her despair, to the flat beach hundreds of feet below.

Over and over, Lilith endured this dream and her sense of irredeemable loss, though the anxious watchers beside her bed saw only her extraordinary tapering fingers plucking at the sheet, and the occasional tear that slid under her closed lids. The cold compresses took effect, her fever abated, but still she appeared unconscious. Dr da Costa, who had set out from London as soon as he received Joseph's telegraph, told him that her unconsciousness was now probably self-induced, a form of defence against her unhappy experience. He and Joseph had buried Judah on the second evening. Chan-Tu had dug the grave in a quiet corner of the garden and Joseph had carried in his arms the pitifully small pink coffin made by the Overstrand carpenter. Because of the rapid burial demanded by Jewish law, no one else was present.

If the ceremonial was small, their grief was great enough. The elderly man spoke the *Hashcabáh* for his grandson: 'May God the father of mercy, who had compassion upon our fathers, that did His will, have mercy upon the soul of this child Judah; to him may the spirit of the Lord give repose in Paradise.' It was useless for him to tell Joseph that so small a baby would at best have been a sickly, backward child, that he would have had no chance of vigorous life. It was the first time this protected, careful man had had to face a death so close to himself, and he found it almost impossible to come to terms with the thought of that tiny pink coffin out there in the darkness.

On the third day, Dr da Costa took Beatrice with him into Lilith's room: he would not have brought her to Overstrand had he known about the tragedy, but Joseph's telegraph had told him only that he was needed, and Lilith's health had been so good he was unprepared for this eventuality. As it turned out, he could not have produced a better tonic.

Beatrice sat beside Lilith's bed for the whole day. She did not appear to look at her sister, but gazed out of the window at the somnolent September garden and the fields beyond blurred with flowering grasses and gossamer, the spiders' webs floating in the still air. Nor did Lilith apparently waken. But the midwife and Doris noticed that the long fingers ceased to pluck at the covers and lay still, and the tears ceased. In the afternoon Joseph found the sisters hand in hand, although Lilith was still apparently unconscious, and though he asked Beatrice whether Lilith had stirred, he did not expect an answer.

Lilith responded to the presence of Beatrice beside her, and by the evening she was awake and lucid, still holding Beatrice's hand in a tight grip. They gave her the baby, and she took him with a cry so full of passionate relief and gratitude that Joseph and her father could not look at each other. Afterwards, while they ate the first full meal Joseph had been able to face for three days, they decided they would not speak of the dead baby to Lilith, at least not for the present. Dr da Costa had conferred with the Cromer doctor, and been assured that by the time of the second birth, she had been given enough chloroform to confuse her memory. He himself had thought her barely conscious, and was convinced she could not have known what was happening to her.

'Of course,' Dr da Costa told Joseph, 'you must explain to Lilith when she is stronger. She will have to be told.'

Joseph listened but said nothing, and Samuel sighed at his son-in-law's averted head and his seeming indifference. He himself understood the nature of this tragedy: what was it they said? *It is better not to have had children than to bury them.* But he was a doctor, and in a lifetime of ministering he had seen many such things, so that he sometimes felt sorrow had thinned his bones. He wished this introspective man would weep one tear for that piteous little boy, but his composure was such he feared that even alone Joseph had never allowed himself to break.

He said, suddenly anxious, 'You *will* tell her, Joseph? She must be allowed to know what happened or she cannot mourn for the child. There is consolation, you know, in weeping.'

Joseph looked at him with a closed face that gave nothing away. 'When the time is right,' he said flatly. He might as well have said, *Don't interfere.* He had chosen to deal with this situation by ignoring it. He thought that by refusing to acknowledge the violent emotion that had swept him as he stood looking down at that second, unsuspected baby, its skin so ominously tinged with blue, it would vanish and leave him untouched. But as he had watched, his little son had opened his eyes, only for a moment, and then so briefly that Joseph had not even had time to speak, to draw the doctor's attention. Even in that second he had caught the gleam of intelligence and something else, troubled and disturbing, as though the child knew itself to be in an alien place. And then the mauve lids had drifted over those grave eyes, leaving Joseph hurt and helpless.

And however much he told himself that if they had lost one child, still they had Simeon, this did not soften his sadness. The surviving baby was beautiful, with silky dark hair covering his well-shaped head, marred only by a faint birthmark between his eyes. It was a pressure mark, Dr da Costa assured them, holding his little grandson; they called it the sign of the stork, and it would disappear by the time he was a year old. Apart from that, he was perfect. Lilith had by now recovered from that strange fever, and was fretting at being confined to her room and the upper storey: the stairs, declared Dr da Costa, were too much for a newly-delivered woman to attempt. Three more weeks she must stay in bed, drinking stout to help her suckle her baby.

When she wailed her protest he said, looking to Joseph for confirmation, 'We must have you strong for the ceremony. You will be bringing Simeon to London, and that will be a big effort for you.'

To her puzzled expression Joseph explained, 'We have to take him to the synagogue. To Bevis Marks, when he is thirty-one days old, for the *Pidyon Habben*.'

'Blessed art Thou, O Lord, our God, King of the Universe, who has sanctified us with thy commandments and commanded us to redeem the first-born son.'

Lilith heard the faint quiver in Joseph's voice as he addressed the black-robed *Haham*, the chief rabbi, who stood a little above him, waiting on the first of the carpeted steps before the wooden Ark, the massive carved cupboard which held the sacred scrolls, the five books of Moses, written by hand on rolled parchments. It was a dark afternoon, and candles glimmered in the seven-branched candelabra that hung from the ceiling, and in the ten great brass candlesticks illuminating the Ark, shining on the green marble columns and the grapes of gold-leaf.

Joseph turned to her and held out the curved silver platter. Very carefully, she placed the baby on it, tucking the creamy shawl under his head so that the metal would not strike cold. Joseph stepped forward and the *Haham* ceremoniously took the platter from him. Lilith waited for Simeon to cry but he stared up at Dr Gaster's lined and benevolent face as solemnly as though he understood.

Joseph then took out a small leather purse. Before the ceremony, he had counted out fifteen silver shillings, the equivalent, he had told her, of the biblical five shekels of the Sanctuary. Another man, portly, with deferential movements, stepped forward and Joseph handed him the purse. The Cohen received it with an inclination of the head and smiled at Lilith.

'Have you,' he asked her in a low tone, 'previously been delivered of any other child?'

She said in a small voice that surprised her, 'No.'

'Or have you miscarried another child?'

'No.'

'Then,' said the Cohen, formally addressing the congregation, 'this son is a first-born and the blessed God has commanded us to redeem him.' He stepped back so that he could see the baby in Dr Gaster's arms. 'While thou wast in thy mother's womb, thou wast subject to thy Father who is in heaven, and to thy father and mother: but at present thou art subject to me, for I am a priest, and thy father and mother wish to redeem thee, for thou art a sanctified first-born.'

Lilith swayed slightly. It was hot in the synagogue, she could smell the charcoal braziers beneath the building which gave out heat through grilles in the floor. It had been barely a month since her confinement and she still felt unlike herself, weak and frequently tearful. Nor could she shake off the images that haunted her dreams, of the crumbling cliff and the concealing grasses, so that she woke sweating and distressed, gripped by inexplicable grief. With a hand that trembled slightly she smoothed the gold velvet skirt of her suit and tried to concentrate. The Cohen was still speaking.

'And the Lord spake unto Moses saying, Sanctify unto me all the first-born, whatsoever openeth the womb among the children of Israel, both of man and of beast, it is mine.'

Although she and Joseph had read the ceremony, it sounded different spoken like this in the Bevis Marks synagogue. The words now seemed harsh and implacable. *It is mine.* She wanted to rush forward and grab Simeon, but glancing around she saw her father sitting just to the side of her, and she took a deep breath' to calm herself. The Cohen moved nearer to Joseph.

'I have received from thee these five shekels for the redemption of this thy son; and behold, he is therewith redeemed, according to the law of Moses and Israel.' He lifted the baby off the silver salver and placed him in Joseph's arms. Simeon, who had been soundless all this time, immediately burst into loud wails. A ripple of amusement went through the congregation, and Joseph hurriedly handed him to Lilith, who bore him away to a quiet ante-room to nurse him.

The room smelled stale and unused. She held Simeon close as she waited for Joseph. The baby stared up at her unwinking, then yawned and slept. He was heavy in her arms, his breathing gentle; he was safe. Sitting there, in the synagogue where little more than a year before they had been married, she told herself how lucky she was, and wondered again why she carried somewhere behind her eyes the image of a crumbling cliff.

The Mendozas spent the winter in Hans Place, though there was far less space than they needed with the baby. Had there been a nanny also, as Joseph wished, it would have been impossible. But Lilith insisted on looking after Simeon herself.

'Doris and I can manage perfectly well,' she told him, and he did not oppose her. She was in a strange mood, these days, unpredictable. And she had grown thin, accentuating the flush on her cheekbones and the size of those sombre eyes. She was more restless than ever, she never sat still, and she poured her energy into looking after Simeon. Only when Beatrice was in the house did she soften and quieten. The two sisters would remain perhaps an hour in silence, while Lilith nursed the baby and Beatrice sat nearby, although she never appeared to look at Simeon. Nor did Joseph ever hear – though it happened often – the low, mesmeric humming that Lilith loved, that was the only sound Beatrice ever made.

The child had changed their lives dramatically. For one thing, Joseph's pride in his son dictated that they exhibit him among the family. Relatives who had scarcely set eyes on him for years suddenly found themselves prevailed upon to visit Hans Place. His parents invited them regularly to Richmond, delighting in their grandchild. Florence Hartsilver could not have been more excited had the baby been her own flesh and blood, and greeted each gurgle, each sign of communication, with relief, confident that this child had not inherited Beatrice's affliction. Judith Mendoza was another frequent visitor, always bringing with her expensive and frequently unsuitable gifts which Lilith accepted gracefully, seeing them for what they were – the offerings of a lonely woman to the child she never bore.

But the family was one thing. Society, and his business acquaintances, quite another. Joseph saw himself now in the role of father, and became censorious of Lilith, critical of her behaviour. Her vitality and energy, which had so attracted him in those first days, now appeared unseemly for a married woman with a child: it was as though he expected her to transform herself overnight into a copy of his own vague and undemanding mother, giving everything, requiring nothing. Nor did he care for the way in which men were drawn to Lilith's side. Standing, as always, a little apart, he had frequently observed the sharp glances other women gave their husbands or sons as they danced attendance upon his charming wife. He knew she did nothing untoward. Not for a moment did he believe she consciously lured them – or did he? Somewhere in his mind it stayed coiled, the suspicion that perhaps after all it was not he who had fathered this baby whom now he loved.

Joseph did not rationalize these half-formed doubts, but managed to find other, more acceptable reasons to act upon them. He decided that it was entirely unsuitable for a nursing mother to go about in society. Just as he had refused to allow Lilith to the Hoares' party before her confinement, now he would not contemplate her accompanying him to any formal functions. In vain did his parents and Dr da Costa protest that he was absurdly old-fashioned.

In vain did Judith Mendoza and Florence Hartsilver attempt to make him see reason. Only Lilith said nothing. She understood Joseph well enough by now to realize that there was something more behind his stand than he professed. She recalled the moment in the dim vestibule moments before their wedding, when she had been so suddenly and strongly aware of the complex nature of the man she was marrying.

Weeks went by and still Joseph could not bring himself to speak to her of the child they had lost. And the longer he waited, the harder it became. He knew that he had to do it, he was sensitive enough to see that Lilith's gaiety and verve would suddenly be extinguished by a thought he would read first in her long eyes and then in the expressive droop of her whole body as she turned away. Samuel da Costa saw the same thing and begged him to talk to Lilith, offered to do so himself, insisted that he must. Joseph simply closed his mind to it and the doctor would not interfere between husband and wife. When he tried to explain that Lilith would remain dejected until she was told that her sorrow was real, that she must be allowed to grieve for the dead baby, Joseph's face became stiff with his own unhappiness. That little death had been a failure, and he wanted to hide it from himself as much as from others. He did not want their commiseration, their condolences. He wanted this shameful secret kept.

And it was kept, for so few people knew it. The doctor in Cromer had seen such things often before. His was a country practice of fishermen, farmers, labourers. They were practical and realistic, their lore as simple and prosaic as themselves. The strong survived, the weak went to the wall. They took away the runt of the litter to have more sustenance for those that would survive. It was kinder to let the suffering die than needlessly to prolong life.

He had himself instructed the Overstrand carpenter who made the coffin, and warned him to hold his tongue. Not that he need have taken this precaution, for the man was by nature taciturn, an elderly bachelor with no interest in talking for talk's sake. Joseph's parents had been told but Nora kept her weeping to herself as she always had, and accepted that Joseph knew best. The only other person aware of Judah's brief existence was Liu Chan-Tu, and he was as tight-lipped as his master.

Lilith lived in dread of the oppressive sadness that stalked her days, since there seemed no justification for it. So she and Joseph suffered separately and this took its toll of their life together and spoiled their happiness in the child who survived. Lilith could not make sense of her own confused feelings and Joseph would not. Nor would he offer her the physical closeness that might have assuaged her. He disliked the changes the baby had made to Lilith's slender body, and the sight of her blue-veined breasts hard with milk made him hurry from the room. She was too much for him: too fruitful, too voluptuous. Too feminine.

As he was repelled now by Lilith, so he was drawn to Beatrice, to her moonlight hair, her translucent skin, her silence. After Lilith's deep stare, her Persian prince's eyes that spoke so eloquently, Beatrice's gaze was cool and empty. She was twenty-three now and as her father had hoped, her alarming symptoms and tantrums had become more infrequent. Joseph had never witnessed one of her attacks and had almost ceased to believe in them. Her very lack of emotion appealed to him, exhausted as he was by what he considered Lilith's excessive

214

excitement and despondency. There was something in his sister-in-law's still and eerie beauty that fascinated him.

He was working on a book about the history of porcelain. He wrote at home, and one afternoon when Lilith was out, he had taken his papers into the sitting room where Beatrice had been left by her father to await Lilith's return. He had greeted the pretty figure in her dove-coloured dress, charmed as always by her delicacy, and asked – purely as a formality, for he knew she would not answer – 'May I stay and keep you company?'

To his surprise, she had glanced up as though seeing him for the first time, though the look in her eyes vanished as swiftly as it had come. He took it for assent and stayed, and talked for a while about his book, and then began to work. She sat so still he almost forgot her presence. But not entirely. He found it pleasant that she should be there, more than pleasant: he told Lilith, when at length she returned, that her sister had positively inspired him. Lilith had hugged Beatrice delightedly.

'There, you see, we both need you!'

So when Simeon was nine months old and a brilliant May promised a long summer, the Mendozas travelled down to Overstrand and took Beatrice with them. At first, Joseph hoped the change of atmosphere and strong coastal air would restore Lilith's spirits, and for the first few days she was invigorated by the novelty of informal meals and visits from neighbours bringing flowers and pots of honey. Then it became apparent that this was a false elation, and once again she succumbed to the see-saw of her emotions.

Joseph sighed and went back to his book. It was to be completed by September and he liked to be finished well ahead of time. In the past he had always worked in the small library he had arranged at the top of the house. This year the weather tempted even him outside, and the paved court in the 'L' of the house became his workroom. Every morning he would go out after breakfast, to the white painted wrought iron table where Chan-Tu had set up the umbrella and laid out his books. He would place his piles of paper in neat rows, each secured with a heavy glass weight against the wind, and settle himself with his back to the nasturtium-covered wall, facing the garden and beyond it the cliff edge and then, at last, the sea. Not that he ever really looked at the view, for his powers of concentration were admirable. He worked for three hours, until lunch time, then walked for an hour before resuming until five o'clock. He discouraged Lilith from interrupting him by simply failing to hear what she said, and anyway she preferred her walks with Simeon in his high-wheeled perambulator of woven cane.

Beatrice he did not discourage, and by the time they had been in Overstrand two weeks, she was in the habit of spending the afternoons sitting in the terrace while he wrote, apparently content to contemplate the gardens. Before they arrived the sunken Japanese water gardens had been completed and two bronze storks set one at either end, guardians of the streams and pale pools, the miniature pagodas and pathways paved with coral and amethyst, where only pink and purple flowers grew.

Perhaps it was the scale of everything that appealed to Beatrice, reminding her of the lilliputian garden of their childhood, with its velvet lawns and china doves. Every morning she would wordlessly ask Lilith to take her there, communicating her wish by a pressure of her hand, a tilt of her head, which Lilith as always divined by that instinct which for so long had made Beatrice comprehensible to her alone.

The two young women were closer than ever, despite Lilith's marriage. Or perhaps, she sometimes thought, because of it. She and Joseph no longer slept together, nor had they done so since before Simeon's birth. The baby had been the rationale both used; his nursing, his wakefulness, his teething. But that was not the real reason. Lilith was aware that in some obscure way Joseph did not like what she had become. She had seen how he made an excuse to leave the room whenever she – however discreetly – prepared to nurse the baby. On the rare occasions when he came to her room at night, and she had responded to his first cautious caresses, he had found his fingers faintly sticky from the leaking milk she could not suppress. Then he had drawn back as if she had bitten him, and not long after returned to his own room, telling her he did not want to disturb her sleep. She had looked at him sadly, and accepted his absence, and supposed that all men were the same. Though she had occasionally wondered what Valentine Audry would have said.

Because of Simeon, Lilith slept very lightly. Any sound woke her now: a creak, the incessant Norfolk wind, a rabbit's scream from the cornfields. During the long slow summer at Overstrand, she stopped many times on her way to Simeon's nursery, hearing the stifled sobbing from Beatrice's room. At first, she had done nothing, for it was so much a part of her sister, something she had always done. And then one night, moved as much perhaps by her own need for consolation as by her sister's, she had tucked Simeon back to sleep and then tiptoed into Beatrice's room, and climbed into bed with her as she had so often in the past, and put her arms round her, pressing her cheek against Beatrice's hair. Slowly Beatrice had relaxed, her slight body no longer shook with her unspoken fears, and after a while they both slept. The following week, Lilith had awoken later than usual, conscious of a feeling of happiness and well-being she had almost forgotten, of a warm shape lying snugly against her back: Beatrice. Before she had time to speak, to say to her sister, *what if Joseph comes in*?, she found she had the bed to herself again. Beatrice, paler than ever in her voluminous white cambric nightdress, had slipped silently away.

That was the day when Chan-Tu broke his unspoken promise to Joseph.

The Chinese manservant was enchanted by Simeon. Like all his race, he loved children – had Joseph not been an impish four-year-old when he first came to the Mendozas' house? – and babies to him were there to be cosseted and cuddled within an inch of their lives. This new little boy was an object of adoration for him, and he loved to watch him play, though he himself would have preferred to see the child in brighter clothes – yellow and blue – than the discreet cream and white the English favoured. But because of his role in the household – primarily that of superior butler and valet – he had little contact with Simeon. Lilith had often seen him watching her with the baby, his expression indecipherable, and so she had never realized that he longed to snatch the boy up and hold him close, to feel those round limbs and sturdy little body.

On this particular Tuesday, Doris had gone into Cromer. It was her day off, and she put on her best costume and announced her intention to walk out along the pier and eat a fish tea at one of the guest-houses. Joseph had remarked that he had anyway to go to the station there to collect a parcel of books; he would pick her up at Tucker's Hotel at six o'clock for the drive home. He did not offer to take either Lilith or Beatrice with him.

So that afternoon, Lilith was looking after Simeon, who had slept late and was full of energy. He was still not walking, but had lately begun to crawl round the floor, even impeded as he was by the skirts he, like all small boys, wore for the first years. He scrabbled about in lawn dresses with lace collars, his neat black laced boots showing incongruously beneath the frilled hems.

He was in the drawing room at the back of the house playing with a toy Judith Mendoza had given him, a Punchinello head on a stick which jingled with bells. Beatrice was sitting at the piano, not playing but humming softly to herself, '. . . zim zim zim . . .' Lilith had slipped away for a moment to the kitchen to fetch Simeon a biscuit. She must have taken longer than she thought, for when she got back into the room she was just in time to see his ridiculous padded bottom in its napkins and skirts vanishing as he fell down the steps which led from the open French window to the garden. Beatrice, oblivious, still sat at the piano. Her heart in her mouth, Lilith flew across the room, the more terrified because of his silence – why didn't he cry out? Then she heard Chan-Tu's soothing voice.

'Ah, little fellow. Are you a bird, then, with wings? Or only a jumping bean, eh? A plump little bean.'

He glanced up as Lilith appeared on the top step, and clicked his tongue at the apprehension on her face. Simeon was sitting comfortably in his arms, with an intent, serious expression. Lilith saw that one plump hand was firmly holding Chan-Tu's pigtail.

'I catch him, Mrs Lilith, you see?' Chan-Tu beamed with satisfaction. 'I save.'

'Oh, you certainly did. Thank you, Chan-Tu.' The words seemed inadequate, and she ran down the steps and put her hand lightly on his arm. The man, both pleased and embarrassed, took a step back and bowed politely. There was silence, while Lilith waited, for he clearly had something to say.

'Please, Mrs Lilith, you let me hold for a little bit? We very good friends, you see.'

She laughed.

'Of course you can. Of course. Why didn't you ask me?'

He shook his head.

'Oh, no. Mr Joseph would think most unsuitable.'

'I'll talk to him.' She watched the man holding her son so tenderly, his face a mixture of pride and adoration. He glanced up and she saw the light in his eyes deaden as he looked behind her, and hostility take its place. Without turning, she knew that Beatrice was there. But why should Chan-Tu have reacted like that?

And then, of course, it became clear. Not for a moment had it occurred to her that Beatrice might have rescued Simeon: it was not within her power to do so. But Chan-Tu could not be expected to understand that. He must have been aware that Beatrice was not like other people, but her failure to save the child must seem to him like indifference. Lilith looked from the Chinese servant to her sister. She could not be disloyal to Beatrice.

'You do understand, Chan-Tu, that my sister did not realize the baby might hurt himself?'

He replied dutifully, 'Yes, Mrs Lilith,' but his tone was flat with disbelief. 'If you say.'

She went on, 'Babies are important to everyone, after all. It's just that Beatrice – is different. She loves Simeon, but she doesn't know how to look after little children.'

Gravely, Chan-Tu handed the child back to Lilith, and he clung affectionately to her neck. The manservant gave his customary deep bow and went off to the kitchens. It was, she thought, the first time they had ever held a conversation about anything other than household matters. And the Chinaman had said very little.

Cromer was only two miles to the west of them, over the windy golf-links, but she had put Simeon to bed before Joseph and Doris returned. It was past six, and the sun still shone. Tempted by the scent of lavender and the white tobacco plants she walked across the grass to the fountains, set in deep basins of brilliant blue mosaic. All around them fuchsia were in flower, their oriental blue-pink bells reflected in the water. She had felt happy all day but now, for no reason she could think of, the drops of water seemed to her like tears, and as she looked at them her own eyes filled. And then – as so often – she was weeping herself, almost soundlessly, as Beatrice did. And she wept more at that, because perhaps she was suffering from the same nameless affliction as her beautiful sister; perhaps she, too, would never be able to stop?

Conscious that someone was approaching over the grass, she tried to stem her tears, pressing the backs of her hands over her eyes in a childish gesture. Joseph must be home. Only it wasn't Joseph, but Liu Chan-Tu, his scarlet satin embroidered jacket blurred by her tears, his shallow black eyes concerned.

'I see you crying. What is wrong, please? I can help?'

'No, no, thank you. It's nothing, I don't know . . . I just can't stop.' She started a tremulous laugh but it changed to sobs before it left her throat, and she crossed her arms over her breasts and hugged herself as she attempted to control her breathing.

'Is best to cry, Mrs Lilith,' the oddly accented voice advised her. 'Is good to cry for baby.'

'Baby is lovely. He doesn't need my tears. I'm so silly.'

Her words were barely audible, and the Chinese servant, who reached only to her shoulder, looked at her with compassion. He said, hesitantly, 'I think . . . it is not for Master Simeon you cry. For the other baby. The little dead one.'

Lilith felt as if a hand had wrenched her heart round in her chest. Unable to speak, she stared at him, her eyes full of horrified appeal. *What do you mean?*

For months now Chan-Tu had waited for Joseph to tell this unhappy young wife of his what he had done, that September evening, without ever a word to her. It hurt him deeply, it offended his Chinese soul, to see the little grave he had dug still unmarked.

Chan-Tu had not been surprised that so tiny a baby had failed to live. He came from a society where there were always too many mouths to feed and too little money to care for those who could not ever be expected to fend for themselves. It had happened as it had happened, and the simple funeral – for he was himself a country man – seemed to him fitting and natural.

But though he had waited, the other obligations had not been fulfilled. Because he not informed Lilith, Joseph had spent scant time at the grave: he had caused flowering shrubs to be planted, but there was no memorial, no cut flowers, no headstone. Chan-Tu was unaware of the Jewish ritual which prescribed that a year must pass by before the headstone was raised. Nor did he recognize another sign of mourning which Joseph had regularly made upon the grave. So now he pressed his fingertips together in a gesture at once apologetic and pleading.

'It is not for me to tell you. But you are so thin, so sad. I think Master Joseph has not spoken of the second child. The one that came after Master Simeon. He lived' – he held up one finger – 'an hour only. And you were most ill, so you were not told. Only now too much time has gone by, you have a need to learn of this.'

'Where is he?' Lilith's voice was hoarse. 'What did they do with him?'

For answer, Liu Chan-Tu gestured with his head, further down the garden, for the Chinese do not point.

'Show me.'

It was hard to walk, her feet felt as though they were bound and weighted. But she followed Chan-Tu down the long garden, through the grassy alleys and shaded paths to where pear and apple trees were woven in walls of green and gold. She must have been this way a hundred times, so why had she never seen it before, this small, inconsequential hillock with shrubs planted head and foot, carefully covered with smooth turf. For a moment she even persuaded herself that it was not true, that this solemn little man at her side was lying to her for some purposes of his own. Then she saw, and it was all the proof she needed, the little heap of stones on the green grass that Joseph must have made, one at a time, in the immemorial gesture of Jewish mourning.

She sank to the ground and even Chan-Tu noticed how graceful she was, reminding him of the figures of the princess on willow-pattern plates, with her tapering hands and her coils of dark hair. She lay on the grass beside the grave, her head on the green mound, in an attitude of such abandoned grief that Chan-Tu felt his throat close.

In that hoarse, harsh voice she said, 'Go away.'

Obediently he went, and though he looked back many times, he left her there as she wished. He hurried to the house to go up to the baby's room, open the door and check that he was safely asleep. Then he went downstairs, past Beatrice sitting placidly in one of the wrought iron chairs in the shadow of the house, and back down the garden. Reaching the path nearest to the fruit-garden, but before he was in sight of his mistress, he squatted on the turf to wait, arms clasping his knees, the picture of patience.

He waited a long time, more than an hour, while the shadows of the sycamores slanted across the lawns and the fading rays of sunlight lit the windows of the house so it seemed on fire. He waited while Lilith's sobs subsided and she lay in utter silence across the hillock of grass, as though she could warm the little body beneath it. He squatted unmoving and listened to the sound of her voice as she sang to her baby, a childish tune he had never before heard, a lullaby that had become a lament:

'Cuckoo! Cherry-tree! Catch a bird and give him to me . . .'

Chapter 12

'What did you call him?'

She was standing in the hallway when Joseph
came into the house; he had the distinct impression
she had been there for a very long time, stiff and
still, her hands by her sides, her face bleak as her
voice. Joseph put a conciliatory hand on her arm
but let it drop at the feel of her unyielding flesh.
She might have been carved from stone. Slowly, to
gain time, he removed his Panama hat, held it and
his cane out for Chan-Tu to take as usual. No one
accepted them, and he glanced irritably to the place
where Chan-Tu always appeared, unsummoned,
only to find it empty. He put the hat and cane down
himself, his eyes still on Lilith.

Behind him, Doris came into the hall. She opened
her mouth to speak but seeing Lilith's face, changed
her mind and hurried away to the kitchen.

'Tell me my son's name. Or must I learn that, too,
from the servants?'

'You know, then.' He was conscious that he
sounded unfeeling, but he seemed unable to change
his tone.

'I know everything: I know nothing. *What did you
call him*?'

'Come and sit down.' He led the way into the
sitting room. She took half a dozen steps to the
threshold and waited. Joseph lifted his hands and
let them drop helplessly.

'I should have told you before. They all warned

me, your father especially. I waited too long, and it became harder and harder . . .'

Indifferent to his excuses she broke in sharply.

'For God's sake, tell me his name!'

'Judah. I called him Judah. There was so little time, he only lived a few minutes . . .' Joseph closed his eyes against the memory.

'Judah.' The name was foreign on her lips. 'Judah.' She had no image to which she could attach it. She whispered, 'What was he like? Joseph, what was my baby like?'

This time, she let him lead her into the room, sat on the edge of a chair. He sat beside her, elbows on his knees, his face buried in his hands.

'He was very small. Too small. He had no chance at all, he couldn't have survived. They didn't even know he was there. You were almost unconscious with the effort and the chloroform, Dr Craven said you knew nothing. We buried him in the garden, in a little pink . . .' He faltered, went on in a stronger voice. 'We buried him in the garden. Your father was present. We said the prayers, it was properly conducted. We neglected nothing.'

'Except to tell me.' Her words fell cold as clods on his hurt. He dropped his hands, palms upward on his knees. More clearly than words, that gesture showed his state, but she was in no condition to see it.

'I'm sorry. Lilith, I'm sorry. At first, it seemed the best thing to do. And then, it became the *only* thing to do. I felt I couldn't go through it all again.'

'But I go through it *all the time*. All the time, do you understand?' Lilith wasn't speaking in a whisper now, her voice was growing and growing so that it filled her head, filled the room. 'Every night I dream I've lost something precious, and I search and

226

search. And until this afternoon, I didn't know what I was looking *for*. I thought I was going mad. I was so frightened, I was becoming like Beatrice, crying for no reason . . .' She drew a deep, shuddering breath, 'And all the time, it was my baby I was searching for. It was Judah. And you could have told me; you should have told me. *Why didn't you tell me*?' She was shouting now, spitting the words at him, out of control, beyond caring. All she saw, before her open eyes, was the concealing grass clutching at her skirts as she fought her way through to the crumbling cliff. Only now she saw also what it was that rolled and fell to the flat beach and its death. She put her hands over her ears, to block out the sound of her own voice.

Joseph stared at her. In all his thirty-six years he had never been witness to such a scene and here he was, the object of this fury. He had often thought that Lilith reminded him of a wild creature, so dark, so quick and lithe in her movements, expressing feelings not with words but in more delicate ways, in the angle of her head, the turn of her body.

She was like a wild creature still, but one caught in a trap. She had become ugly in extremity, her voice a sharp weapon she was using against him, to open afresh his own unhealed wounds. He heard her cries, observed her distress, and yet he could not connect this outburst with what he alone had experienced that night in her bedroom, when his little son had briefly opened troubled eyes and found himself in an alien place.

Joseph would never forget the exhausted droop of those mauve lids, the heart-rending fragility of the tiny body lying in the open bureau drawer. He had not spoken of those moments to Lilith – or anyone

227

else – and so his emotion had turned inward and eaten into him: *his* son, *his* suffering.

Joseph was a man unused to unhappiness, in himself or in others. Like all loved only children, he had always been the centre of his world, sure of his place, pampered and protected. Nor had things been any different when he reached adulthood: his brief sojourn in Paris when he attempted to become an artist was the only time he had ever spent alone, and even then he did not subsist in an artist's atelier (as he always claimed) but boarded in a comfortable *pension*. All his adult life, he had prided himself on his individuality, his style, his independence. That was the illusion. The truth was that he lived hedged about with family and friends, ministered to by Liu Chan-Tu. He believed himself to be even-tempered, equable. And so he was – but only because he had never permitted anyone to intrude upon his heart.

Now, despite himself, the unthinkable had happened. Into his calm and ordered life had come such anguish as he could not have envisaged. He had tried to evade its clutches by refusing to think about its cause. But now he was face to face with Lilith's passionate pain, he could no longer pretend.

He said, striving to keep his voice down, 'There, there. Of course you're upset. Let me send for Dr Craven . . .' He was already moving towards the bell to summon Chan-Tu. She forestalled him, whirling past like a dervish, standing in his way.

'No. *No*! You just want me kept quiet, so you don't have to listen. But I'll make you listen, I'll make you hear!' She had to stop then, to draw breath, and found she had no words for what she wanted to tell him: that he had compounded her misery by keeping the baby's death from her. Maybe she had been dazed by chloroform, but somehow what happened had infiltrated her blurred brain. The terrible sense of loss she experienced in her dreams, the concealing grass, the crumbling cliff . . . if she had known, she could have mourned. As it was, she had been haunted by a spectre she could not name and the fear of her own madness.

And Joseph had let this happen, had by his silence willed it upon her. There was nothing she could say to mitigate her misery, and now he wanted to fetch doctors, he wanted her silenced. When he stepped forward, to reach the bell, his movement released her like a spring. She flung herself on him, hitting out, pummelling him, twisting away when he tried to grasp her arms, hurting her hands against him. She was in a frenzy, her blood roared in her ears, so she heard only faintly his cries of protest, saw as if under water his white astonished face.

Without warning she felt herself caught from behind, her arms pinned to her sides. She struggled fiercely, and felt herself lifted off the ground. She kicked out, the breath rasping in her throat, but whoever received the kicks remained unmoved by them. She writhed and fought, held in an implacable grip.

Suddenly the fight went out of her and she drooped like a broken marionette. Joseph was there, trying to lift her, but a warning voice spoke and he stood aside. Only then did she realize that it was Liu Chan-Tu who held her, and even in her turmoil she was amazed at the strength of that stooped figure, the hardness of his slight frame. He spoke again, so quietly only she could hear.

'If I let you go, you will be still. You will not beat my poor master any more.'

She responded to the unaccustomed authority in his tone, agreed wearily.

'No.'

He looked across at Joseph.

'Please, sir, to excuse us for a moment. If you will.'

Joseph, as surprised as Lilith by the Chinaman's authority, took himself off. Chan-Tu urged Lilith into a chair and seated himself by her side on a footstool, still holding her hand in his own dry, light grasp.

'I think you do not know my master as I do.' He sounded regretful about this. 'He is difficult to understand, even for me, and he has been in my care much of his life.' She was looking down at her hand, and noticed now that his own, holding it, had the loose yellowed skin of the elderly. It was strange: she had never before thought of Chan-Tu being any age at all. He was stroking her hand as he spoke, and unconsciously her breathing slowed to match his movements.

'Mr Joseph is not like you. He is frightened of his feelings. Do you understand? He has perhaps been too much alone, he believes he does not need other people. He cannot carry the weight of their troubles, they are a burden he does not want.' Still he was stroking her hand. 'You must not think he does not care about the baby who died. I watched his face down there by the pear trees.' They both looked out of the window, where fading day had drained all colour from the garden, filling it with shadows of lilac and grey.

Still the Chinaman stroked her hand, and she listened to his oddly-accented English, his stilted phrasing, as he spoke quietly to her: about the siblings he could now himself scarcely remember, the brother who had died because his mother's milk failed during a famine, the sister sold so the rest of the family might subsist on rice. A lifetime living in

230

England in luxury had not changed Liu Chan-Tu. He still had the mind of a peasant, and he knew no grief was so great time could not soothe it. 'You wait,' he urged Lilith, 'just let the days go by, and this will be gone from you. Perhaps it will be soon. Perhaps not. But it will happen.' He, who once had so yearned for his family in China he thought his soul would appear there before them, tried to give this sad young woman some of his serenity.

For many days afterwards he watched her carefully, appearing in the garden ostensibly to pick herbs, but in reality to check that she was not beside the little grave. If he saw her starting down the driveway alone he would hurry to accompany her himself, or send Doris after her, though what he feared he could not have said.

In any event, he could not watch her all the time, and he was marketing in Cromer the afternoon Lilith walked out of the house, turned left at the gate into the lane and followed it downhill. Past the cottages of grey cobblestones from the beach with their sloping roofs of dark red tiles, past the pair of gossiping women who smiled uncertainly at her set face, checking the greeting they had started to offer, past the half-dozen children released from the dame's school, too intent on prodding a dead vole with sticks to notice her.

She walked rapidly downhill, oblivious to the heat, until the lane joined the broad cobbled bulwark partly overhung by the cliff that served as a meeting place for the men of the village. Here the catch was boxed for sale in Cromer, the smaller fish sold to the village housewives, the boats overhauled and varnished during the winter months and the nets mended and maintained. It was deserted now except for an ancient hulk of a man called Kipper.

231

For a long time, Lilith had supposed he was so nick-named for the way he smelled, but Doris had recently discovered that a whole family of Kippers lived in Overstrand. As she passed, he sucked with toothless gums on his clay pipe and rumbled something she did not bother to decipher.

She went down the steep stone steps that led to the beach. There were three families with young children playing in the sand, all of whom Lilith knew, but she pretended not to notice them, keeping her head down under the floppy straw hat, striding down to the sea. The tide was far out, further than she had ever seen it, and still, wavelets rippling in almost without sound. To her right, a long way out, she could make out a dark hump in the water. It looked like an upended boat, and on an impulse she took off her shoes. She was already barelegged under her thin dress. Joseph deprecated this habit of hers of going without stockings in the heat. He laughed, without sounding at all amused, and called her a gypsy. She pulled a face, hearing his reproving voice when she had appeared at dinner one night recently without changing from her crêpe de soie afternooon dress: 'People who do not dress for dinner sink in their own estimation.'

The sea lapped warm round her ankles as she headed towards the boat and she could feel under her toes the coils of sand left by worms and shallow shells crunching beneath her weight. Behind her, the children were calling shrilly to each other, their voices fading as she neared the wreck. She could see now that it was the skeleton of a fishing boat, the remaining wooden ribs whitened by salt water and sun.

Just before she reached it she found to her sur-prise that between one step and another the sea reached to her thighs, though the boat itself was high out of the water: it must be resting on a sandbar. For the first time she wondered why it had not been pulled ashore. She hoisted her wet skirt higher and waded on. When she touched the battered hull it felt dry. She peered inside. One of the seats appeared intact, so she scrambled over what was left of the side and sat down. The bottom of the boat was gritted with the encrustation of years and tiny crabs scuttled away from her feet. She drew them up quickly on to the seat, circling her knees with her folded arms to make a rest for her chin.

She stared out to where a faint mist was drifting towards her, turning the sea the milky blue of Aunt Florence's Lalique bowl. Behind her, the children's shouts had become indistinguishable from the cries of sea birds, and from somewhere came a keening cry that reminded her of the curlew she had heard, that night on the Trouville sands. She gave a shiver that might have been recollection, or the tendrils of mist touching her skin, and when she licked her lips there was salt again, as she had tasted her tears. *Curlew shall not sing tonight.* She had wondered then how it had come about that she was married to Joseph. And now, nearly three years later, the question had not changed. Isolated physically from him in the skeletal boat, she acknowledged that they were isolated mentally also. Perhaps both of them had imagined they were getting someone else, someone who could provide what the other lacked and needed.

Three years ago, she had been too young and inexperienced to realize what it was in Joseph that both attracted and frightened her: the soft brutality she had detected in him in the greenhouse at Richmond, the subtle cruelty of his honeymoon behaviour. She did not fully understand now, but she had

233

Valentine Audry's down-to-earth advice behind her, and many things made sense that had been unclarified before: the Baron's scornful references that night on the yacht. 'Any woman married to Joseph Mendoza would have good cause to indulge in a little harmless pleasantry.' And their infrequent lovemaking which had always been so perfunctory, rousing in her cravings which remained unassuaged, so that afterwards she felt parched and dry, longing for something she had never had. And by her side Joseph rarely fell asleep, but lay silent, locked in thoughts he did not share with her.

They shared less and less. They had not shared the brief life of Judah, and though they both loved Simeon, he had not drawn them closer together. Rather, he had separated them, for since his birth Joseph almost never entered her room at night.

Lilith sat in a trance, lulled by the heat and the sound of water and the gentle rocking of the boat on the waves. The mist was on her now, blocking out the sun's rays, though it still shone on the flat beach behind her. It had become very quiet, the sea birds had flown and the families packed and gone, she could no longer hear children's voices. It must be late. She didn't care.

She sat motionless, staring into the pearly cloud, feeling its filaments flatten her hair and dampen her face. She was too heavy, too tired ever to move again. She must sit still, and then soon there would be nothing to hurt any more. She had only to wait for the silky sea, she could feel it around her ankles already.

She glanced down and realized with surprise that she must have been there a very long time. Ominous rills of water had deepened around the wreck and on the bottom of the vessel the mermaid's hair of

234

greenish-brown seaweed floated. When the water covered her feet it was warm and she welcomed it: not long now. Soon it had risen to the level of her seat. She felt no fear, though she could not swim. Afterwards she wondered what madness had kept her there so long, but at the time she was hypnotized by the wreathing mist, the blue glass sea.

'Mrs Mendoza, hey, Missus. What ails you?'

Her shoulder twitched in irritation and she turned to the shore. She was just able to make out through the mist a male figure at the water's edge.

'Get you here, or we'll have to send out for you!' Old Kipper was bellowing at the top of his lungs. She sighed and holding what remained of the gunwale, stepped over the side. The water reached her knees and she thought, I wish he'd left me alone. But with the next step she plunged into water almost to her throat: she had forgotten the sandbar on which the boat rested. The water was cloudy brown with sand and much colder than she had expected. She gasped and almost lost her footing, swallowed a mouthful of sea, spluttered and gasped. She tried to shout, but another wave coming in behind her almost knocked her down. Where had the waves come from, when it had been so calm? Even as she staggered forward she realized that to yell was useless: old Kipper clearly could not reach her in time.

With her hat still on her head – an absurdity that was only to strike her later – she tried to let herself float, using her arms the way she had seen swimmers do, like paddles. Another wave slapped her in the small of her back and shoved her forward, and then her foot felt sand again, and she was able to stagger a few steps.

Another yard, and she could walk properly, and

only then did she become conscious of her flimsy dress clinging to her body, outlining breasts and thighs. She must look indecent. Old Kipper was mopping his face with a grubby necksquare: she realized now that it was a warning about the swiftly incoming tide he had rumbled earlier when she passed him.

When she had almost reached him, she gasped, 'I'm sorry, Mr Kipper. I didn't mean to give you a fright.'

'Tis you should be frightened. I thought you lost and no mistake. That boat be ill-luck. Three men drowned there long since, no one will go near it now. Here.'

He started to pull off his jacket, which carried the whiff of live mussels, but she stopped him.

'Don't trouble, Mr Kipper. It's warm still, and I'll hurry home: I'll be dry before I get there.'

'Well,' he said doubtfully, 'if you're sure no 'arm's done . . .' But she was already walking up the beach.

She literally dragged herself up the lane, weighted down by her dripping dress. Her legs trembled from fright now that she was safe, the muscles aching as though she had been dancing too strenuously. It was tea-time, and the villagers were safely inside their cobbled cottages. Only one old lady sat shawled in her low doorway, staring with inquisitive eyes at the sodden young woman from London.

When she reached the house it was quiet, the garden deserted, the hallway empty. Doris must be giving Simeon his supper and had not missed her. She carried her shoes and walked upstairs barefoot, leaving damp imprints on the polished wood of the staircase. She paused at the deep window embrasure on the half-landing and glanced outside.

Below her, on the terrace in the angle of the house, Joseph sat at his wrought iron table: she could see his shoulders in a pale suit beneath the umbrella, head bent studiously over his work. To one side, and a little behind him, dressed all in cream with her sunshade protecting her pale skin, sat Beatrice. Her hands were folded in her lap, her feet crossed demurely at the ankle. Lilith knew she was thinking of nothing, simply existing, companionable as a white kitten, the pretty pet Joseph had always wanted.

Lilith looked at her husband and her sister, sitting so peacefully in the late afternoon sun, and experienced a wave of self-pity: they had not even noticed how long she had been gone, they had no thought for her. She saw that her dress was leaving a puddle on the stairs and went on up to her room. By the time she opened her door, her mind had cleared. It was her fault, not theirs, that she had risked drowning. She had behaved like a fool.

Drying herself after a hot bath, mechanically performing the actions for dressing in a pale chiffon blouse and skirt, she went over the afternoon's events, trying to make sense of them.

She would not have died, out there on the glassy water. Though she had deliberately sought the circumstances, even her deep unhappiness would not have been enough to carry her through the final desperate act. Life ran too fiercely in her to be denied, ran stronger than the current of that sluggish sea. Even if old Kipper had not called her at that moment, she would have climbed out of the boat and forced her way to the beach. But it was not for Joseph she would have done so. Simeon, Beatrice, her father – for them she had returned, not for her husband.

She had acknowledged, sitting there in the misty stillness, that nothing linked her to Joseph any more. Like a rope too thin for its task, the tie between them had frayed invisibly over the last months. It had never been strong, the strange relationship they had shared, based as it was on her ignorance, his aberration, their misapprehensions about each other.

Lilith tied her hair in a thick plait that fell over one shoulder. She twisted the end round and round her finger, the glossy curls warm and living, reassuring as the fur of an animal. She was not thinking about herself. The image of Joseph and Beatrice together on the terrace was etched on her mind with painful precision.

The summer seemed long to Lilith, each day endless. She did not sense it was happening, but during them she came to grips with the death of Simeon's twin and accepted what Chan-Tu had told her, that only one child had been intended. The other had been a promise unfulfilled. She went often to the little grave, always alone, and she, like Joseph, built a heap of small stones. And then one day in early August she did this and stood up and thought, *that part of me is finished now.*

Later that same day, she led Beatrice – who had been sitting, as she always did in the afternoons, beside Joseph as he worked on the terrace – up the lane to the ruins of the old church.

It had been a year since she last danced. Before the birth she had been too clumsy, and afterwards too preoccupied. But under Moura's instruction she had developed the habit of exercising every day, and the older woman had insisted that she must continue even if for only ten minutes at a time. Almost

238

without thinking, she had obeyed. Each morning, before she dressed, she lay on the floor stretching and reaching, tensing and relaxing. And all summer she had been walking out in the strong Norfolk air. She had been despondent, but her muscles and sinews and tendons did not know it.

Now she stepped on to the pale polished stones of the old nave, roofed only in ivy. She had not bothered with her white tunic, merely removing her skirt and blouse so she was wearing a camisole and petticoat tucked up round her waist to leave her legs bare, and her hair was twisted into a rough plait. She stood in a ray of sunshine that struck through the meshed leaves like a spotlight on a stage, and felt its warmth on the nape of her neck. She waited, breathing lightly, for the moment when the music in her head was irresistible, when she could no longer contain her impatience to be moving, leaping, weaving through the dappled shadows in a pattern only she could follow.

She had been afraid that childbirth would somehow have affected her movements, made her body different, but it did not fail her. She was a little stiff, that was all, her gestures lacked their customary effortless flow one into another, but time would cure that. She had never felt so light, so confident. The stones were smooth and warm to her bare feet as she whirled over them, and energy flooded through her as it had that day at Trouville when she ran along the boardwalk, confirming again that dancing for her was not a diversion but an imperative, reminding her that she ignored it at her peril.

As she danced, everything else fell away. Nothing mattered but the music in her mind and the movements it demanded. Nothing was real but her twisting torso, her strong supporting legs, her arms that stretched and her fingers that reached, the sweat that she wiped with her forearm, brushing the damp curls from her forehead. And when it was over, she was as drained, exhausted and triumphant as other women for whom the act of love has ended.

That night, she had Doris pack her clothes and Beatrice's, and she herself got their boxes from the attic. She was not going to risk telling Chan-Tu, much as she wanted to: his loyalty to Joseph would be strained too far. By ten o'clock they were finished. She went downstairs to fetch Beatrice up for the night, and felt her sister's start of surprise when she saw the luggage piled in her room. She hurried to explain.

'Bee, I've got to go back to London. I can't stay here with Joseph. But if I tell him, he won't let me go. So we'll leave quietly, in the morning.'

Lilith did not expect any reaction and certainly not the one she got. Beatrice of course did not speak. She ran over to the dressing case which lay open on the bed, and began to remove the contents. One by one she took out brushes and combs, spongebag and manicure set, flinging each one hard on to the bedspread until the case was empty. Then she rushed across the room and fell on her knees beside the nearest suitcase, wrenching it open and pulling out the dresses, hurling tissue paper everywhere in her haste, tossing garments haphazard on the floor. Her smoothly coiled hair had come loose from its tortoiseshell pins and hung round her face like satin curtains, so that she could not see what she was doing.

Lilith watched all this with amazement: she had never known Beatrice do anything so decisive and purposeful in her life. She crossed the room and laid a hand on Beatrice's slim shoulder, conscious of the delicate bones beneath the beaded evening dress.

'You want to stay.'

It was not a question. Beatrice put up a hand to sweep back her hair. She looked full at Lilith, who for the first time read entreaty in that soft blue gaze.

Lilith's hand quivered on her sister's shoulder. She should have seen this coming, after all. There was an inevitability about it. Beatrice, who all her life had gone only where Lilith led, who had taken steps only when Lilith pressed her, who had Lilith decide what she was to wear, what she liked to eat – of course she loved where Lilith had loved. She knew nothing else.

And if she loved, if Beatrice felt for Joseph more than she had ever felt before – and her unprecedented action suggested this was so – then it would be cruel to take her away. Lilith had wished often enough for Beatrice's happiness. She was not about to deny the request she understood her sister to be making.

And there was a more practical reason for letting her stay. Lilith was desperate now to get back to London by herself. She did not want Joseph to know, for he would surely prevent her, and Bee seemed capable of making enough fuss if she was forced to leave to attract even his notice.

Lilith leaned down and put her arms round Beatrice, and kissed her cheek.

'You stay,' she whispered. 'If that's what you want.' She had half-expected a reply, a response, but it was as though Beatrice had not heard. Back in her room, Lilith scrawled a note for Doris. 'Take care of Beatrice for me.' And added – she really did not know what put the idea into her mind – 'Watch she doesn't walk too near the cliff.'

Lilith got up at four o'clock. She had not slept, but turned over and over in her mind Bee's unprecedented behaviour. So determined, so sure of what she wanted. The way she had emptied her cases had been the first positive act Lilith had ever seen her perform. And all to stay with Joseph . . . but if she could do that, perhaps she was getting better? Lilith never thought of Bee as ill, though she knew others did. She would have to ask her father. Her mind skated round his reaction to Beatrice remaining with her brother-in-law. She could always be fetched back in a few days' time, but Lilith knew she could not cope with Bee and the baby on the journey if her sister was an unwilling traveller.

She moved silently about her room. She had decided to leave most of her things to be forwarded and take only a travelling bag and another for Simeon. When she was dressed she went to the nursery and woke him by stroking the top of his head. He opened his eyes in loving recognition and she put a hand softly over his mouth to stifle the crow of pleasure he always gave when he saw her. She picked him up, smelling warmly of sleep, changed and dressed him. She had already taken their bags downstairs, and she tiptoed down the second time with Simeon pressed against her chest so he would remain silent: she planned to nurse him in the Ladies' waiting room at the station. No one else would be there at this hour, but she imagined the expression on Joseph's face if she had suggested such a thing.

At the front door, she held Simeon against her breasts and wrapped round them both her creamy cashmere shawl, winding and knotting it so that he was strapped tightly to her in a makeshift sling. Then she opened the door, picked up a bag in either hand and edged carefully through.

Walking on the grass, so as not to crunch the gravel underfoot, she glanced behind at her prints dark on the dew and for a moment felt they were incriminating, as though a criminal had left them. She turned right and started to walk up the lane. The bags were heavier than she had anticipated, and Simeon's weight pulled the shawl tight across her shoulders. She had only been walking for ten minutes when she heard the sound she had been waiting for. She put down her bags gratefully as the horse and trap rounded a corner. Josh Gibbons always left Overstrand at this time on his way to Cromer. She had often heard him when she fed Simeon in the early hours.

The man drew his horse to a standstill as he reached her.

'Goin' away for a bit, 'M?'

She held up a hand to shield her eyes against the first low rays of sun, but she could read nothing into his expression.

'Would you take me to Cromer station with you? I have to get back to London urgently.'

He nodded noncommittally, and clambered down to take the cases. Then he handed her up beside him, awkward with her bundled baby. The trap started again slowly, and as the house was left behind she relaxed, listening to the creaking leather of the harness and the tuneless whistling of the man beside her. She liked Josh Gibbons, who had a toddler of his own, and felt half-inclined to talk to him, ask questions about his work at the local brewery. but then he might ask her why she had to travel so early. Better not.

243

When they reached the station he helped her down, and carried her bags on to the platform. She gave him a shilling.

'Thank you, Josh. Give my regards to Mrs Josh.'

He said, solemn as ever, 'Take care, now. Mind the babby.'

There was an hour to wait for the train, and when she had fed Simeon in front of the coal fire in the Ladies' room, she spent much of it walking up and down the platform between the hanging baskets of geraniums so lovingly watered, knowing they might come for her at any moment from the house. But the signals jerked with astounding suddenness in the silence, and the train appeared curving round the distant track, and she knew Joseph had not noticed her absence this time, either. She sat in the carriage, holding her son on her knees, waiting for the signal to lift for their departure, and thought, as she had done beside Judah's tiny grave, *that part of me is finished now.*

Chapter 13

Lilith took Simeon in a cab to Hans Place. It was still not midday, and she kept the leather curtain half-drawn as she sat staring at Joseph's empty house. She thought of it as his still, even after years of marriage, even though she held the key in her gloved hand. She sat so long, trying to summon up the will to get out, that the driver pulled the reins and the old cabhorse stamped until the vehicle shook. If she entered, then within a matter of hours Joseph would know where she was. It would be no escape at all, merely a futile gesture. Suddenly decisive, she said, 'I've changed my mind. I want Covent Garden, please. Henrietta Street.'

Toiling up the stairs she thought, *what if Moura isn't home*? But she was, wearing a bright kimono, hair in disarray, sleeping late after a long day: matinées on Wednesdays, Lilith had forgotten. She greeted Lilith warmly, and though she was momentarily taken aback at seeing the baby and the bags, kept her thoughts to herself as she urged her friend in, swept the sofa clear of discarded clothes and the toe-shoes she darned incessantly.

Lilith sat, clutching Simeon – who was beginning to squirm in her grasp, asking to be fed – staring round her at the little flat, the brilliantly coloured shawls on all the chairbacks, the paintings, the film of dust which she knew Moura never noticed. She looked up at the watching woman and said, with a sigh, 'Oh, I've missed being here.'

'And I've missed seeing you here. Take off your

coat and hat, and let me look at the baby.' Lilith held him out, but Moura shook her head.

'I'm not used to them, you know. Can I just gaze and make admiring noises?' Lilith laughed, the first time she had done so for many weeks.

She did not ask if she could stay, and Moura did not offer hospitality. But after they had drunk the smoky Matte tea with honey she prepared, and Lilith was feeding Simeon, she went into the cramped room where she put up the occasional guest, and began hauling out bundles and boxes, exclaiming over costumes she had not seen for months. She bundled up tutus and old programmes, made the narrow bed and spread it with a striped Mexican shawl. Then she produced a woven Moses basket in which she kept magazines, and showed it doubtfully to Lilith.

'Would that make a bed for Simeon? I know it would only do for a night or two, but it's clean.'

Lilith, who had been suckling the baby with her eyes fixed on her own problems and had not heard a word, looked first at the basket and then at the tidied room behind her friend, and her eyes glittered with tears.

'Thank you,' was all she could manage to say.

That night, when Moura got back from the theatre, she found Lilith sitting on the floor in the dark in front of the gasfire, her knees drawn up, her chin on her folded arms. Then for once she allowed curiosity and concern to assert themselves. Moura had never before asked Lilith a direct question about her personal life. Because she herself was normally reticent – she had surprised herself by telling Lilith so much at first meeting – she had too much tact to intrude on her friend's privacy.

Although she had often wondered about her relationship with Joseph Mendoza, although she found it strange that this young married woman should want to spend so many hours each week sweating away in a makeshift studio in Endell Street, she had never so much as suggested that she found Lilith's behaviour odd.

This time, it was different. Here was Lilith, obviously unhappy, the strain showing in her tensed shoulders, the stiff carriage of her head, the sallow tinge in her skin. So Moura poured them both a glass of cheap wine and observed, as she handed Lilith hers, 'You'd better tell me, you know. Maybe there's something I can do.'

She listened without interruption for a long time, watching Lilith's mobile face in the red light, and her expressive, flickering hands: when the words would not come, those tapering, back-bent fingers spoke instead.

'And then,' Lilith finished, 'when I was dancing in the old church, I felt quite different. I was another person; as if I'd been born again.' She looked up at Moura, her eyes dark with emotion. 'I had to get away from Joseph. It wasn't his fault that the baby died, but he made it hurt much worse. And he's changed, Moura, he's become so difficult, I don't know how to please him any more. Everything I do, anything I say – always, always wrong.'

'But Beatrice doesn't annoy him?'

Lilith's harried expression softened. 'How could Bee annoy anyone? Of course not, he's much better when she's there. She makes him calm, I think, the way she does me.'

Moura nodded, her eyes scanning Lilith's face for something, some anxiety she expected to find but could not see.

'And you. What about you? You're welcome to stay here as long as you want, but shouldn't you go to your family? To your father, or to your Aunt Florence? Or even to Joseph's aunt – what's her name, the one with the strange hand?'

'Aunt Judith. If I go to any of them, they'll push me back to Joseph. Oh, I know what they'll say. I can hear them. *Of course we understand, dear.*' Wickedly she mimicked Aunt Florence's tone. '*But a married woman belongs at her husband's side.*'

'Surely they'd understand that you're not happy,' Moura interjected.

'Yes, I'm sure they would. Only I don't think it'd make any difference to what they expect of me. Marriage isn't primarily about happiness, in their view, it's about duty and position at least as much.' She shook her head. 'If I go to any of them, I'd be back with Joseph within the week.'

Moura asked, 'And would that be so terrible?'

'No,' said Lilith flatly. 'I wouldn't die from it, if that's what you mean.' (She kept to herself the incident on the skeletal boat upon the glassy sea.) 'Only that isn't what I want, and it just won't do.'

Moura hesitated. 'You say Joseph has changed, become harsh and critical. You say he is happier with Beatrice.' She swirled the wine in her glass reflectively. 'But those alone don't sound to me like sufficient reason for leaving your husband, when you have a young baby. Are you not over-reacting? Perhaps . . .' she made an apologetic face '. . . perhaps in a month or two, you'll find things aren't so bad between you. It would be a shame to throw everything away without thinking it out properly. And from what you tell me of Joseph, he's an unforgiving man. If you hurt his pride by leaving him publicly, it may be that he would never take you back.'

Lilith asked abruptly, 'Were you happy with your husband?'

Moura stared at Lilith for a moment, wondering what had made her so aggressive. She answered quietly, 'Very happy.'

'How did you meet?'

'By chance. We were introduced at a diplomatic reception. A group of us from the theatre were putting on a musical interlude. Afterwards, we were invited to stay as guests.' She stopped, remembering how she had looked that night in her bell-shaped white tutu, hair coiled smoothly round her head, and how the nervous young man from the Foreign Office had asked if he might take her home.

'And when you married, he was the same person he had been before? You didn't discover things about him that you had not expected?'

'Well, of course, when you're married to someone you get to know them better than you've ever known anyone else . . .' She paused. 'What are you saying?'

Lilith lifted her hands and shoulders expressively.

'Joseph is all sharp edges. Nothing seems to be right for him.'

'A lot of men don't realize how hard it is to live with someone else, and it takes them a long time to get accustomed. You've only been together – how long is it – three years.'

Lilith shook her head.

'It's not that. He's the only man I've ever known, but even I am not so ignorant now as I was. Joseph is odd . . .' she glanced across at Moura, her long eyes flickering in embarrassment, ' . . . he wants things I can't . . . that I can't . . .'

Sudden comprehension came to Moura.

249

'You mean, in bed.'

Lilith nodded, and Moura let out her breath slowly.

'He looks at me sometimes,' Lilith went on, 'and he doesn't see me. He touches me as if I was someone else – I can't explain. But I know I must disappoint him, because he's always so unhappy, afterwards. He turns away and I feel him closed against me, cold. Cut off. As if it – his failure – is my fault.' She dropped her face on to her folded arms, and her muffled voice added, 'And perhaps it is. Perhaps it is. I just don't understand anything.'

Moura reached over and put her hand lightly on Lilith's hair, compassion in her touch.

'You must be tired. In the morning you'll feel better. We'll work something out, don't worry.'

When Lilith had closed her door and settled down with the baby beside her, Moura sat for a long time before she turned off the fire and went to her room.

In the morning, she was up earlier than usual and made breakfast, not normally a meal she bothered to eat. When they had finished she said to Lilith, 'Later, we'll leave Simeon with my mother, if that suits you, and go to Endell Street. The room hasn't been used for months, but it won't take long to clean it up. I want to see what you've been doing.'

Lilith agreed, relieved that the older woman had taken command, anxious as always to please Moura, determined to show her that the break in routine had not affected her dancing.

Endell Street looked shabby in the sunlight, dull and grey after the Norfolk garden and the clean beaches. The room above the stained glass factory smelled as always of chemicals and disuse. Moura went to get the gramophone stored in a locked cupboard while Lilith opened the windows wide to the street sounds and the pigeons strutting the windowsill with fanned tails. The two women did their warming-up exercises together, using the movements Lilith had adapted to suit herself, lying on the ground lifting and reaching, straining and relaxing. Only after an hour, when they were resting, did Moura ask with apparent casualness whether Lilith had practised during the summer. So Lilith told her about the exercises each morning, the nave of the ruined church with its floor of polished stone, and then jumped to her feet.

'Look,' she said, 'what I did there.'

She took up a position in the middle of the floor, arms held loosely, hands clasped, one foot behind the other. She breathed deeply, closing her eyes, summoning the music in her head, waiting for its commands and directions. Then she began to move.

It was a slow dance, quieter than her usual exuberant displays, and Moura knew that whatever music she heard was soft and sad. Lilith's arms and hands floated like weed on water, supple and pleading, the curve of her body infinitely tender.

And then the mood changed, and Moura was made aware just how much Lilith had matured. She had stripped away every superfluous gesture, subdued every flamboyant pose. Where before she had hinted, suggested, now she made stark statements. Moura had never thought her capable of such raw power: astonished, she saw in Lilith the fierce pride of possession and then the poignant pangs of loss. And she told Moura more about her life during the last months by her dancing than she had been able to put into words.

When she finished, sinking to the ground so gently she seemed almost to drift there, Moura stood without speaking for a long time, watching the still figure. She said, finally, 'I don't know everything that's been happening to you while you've been away, but I tell you this: it's made a real dancer of you.'

The two women spent hours discussing plans for Lilith: what theatres needed dancers, which directors might be approachable. Lilith objected that her lack of formal training would tell against her, but Moura was convinced she was good enough to overcome that.

'And if I do get work, what about Simeon?' Lilith looked across to where he sat, fist in mouth, staring around him and babbling cheerfully.

'You'll have to get work, my dear, until some sort of financial settlement is made. And you saw for yourself how happy he was with my mother. She meant what she said: at least for a few months, while he's so small, she'll be happy to cope with him for a few hours each day.' She gave Lilith a quick smile. 'And I daresay I could be persuaded to take care of him occasionally. If I'm not working, and if I am – I often see small babies sleep in the dressing rooms.'

Lilith listened with rising hope.

'You really think someone would employ me?'

'I'm sure of it. But you must be, too. Remember, what you do is unique, no one will have seen anything like it before. You must have confidence in yourself, if you're to succeed.' She crossed the room and sat on the sofa by Lilith's side, took her hand and held it between her own. She was not a woman who touched others spontaneously, and Lilith was aware how seriously she meant her words.

'I've seen other girls who were trained dancers,

who could have danced as you do, but they didn't have the brains to learn, to use their bodies so well. They did not put their whole life, their whole will, into their dancing. You *can* do that. If you do so, nothing will stop you.'

Lilith thought she was prepared, but the round of auditions on which she embarked was disheartening. Moura was well enough known for her recommendation to get Lilith seen, but none of the directors and producers who watched her were impressed. The best she was offered was a two months' tour of the provinces, which she had to turn down because of Simeon. The day she refused it, her father arrived back from Holland. That afternoon, she went to Sloane Square, taking Simeon with her.

Her father looked years younger, she thought; how long had it been since he had had such a rest? He had put on weight, and bustled around to find the present he had brought the baby, mislaid amongst his unpacked belongings. When he had given the child the carved wooden rattle with the bell inside, he looked at her properly.

'You're too thin,' he said sharply. 'What's that husband of yours been thinking of to let you run yourself down like this at such a time. You need to be taking things quietly. In fact,' he went on, peering at her over the tops of his glasses, 'I thought you were spending the whole summer in Norfolk. How long are you here for?'

She drew a deep breath.

'I came back three weeks ago. I'm not returning.'

'Well, I suppose Joseph'll be back in a month or so, won't he?'

'I don't know whether he will or not. I didn't ask him. Papa, I've left him.'

'I hear the words,' Samuel da Costa observed

253

mildly, 'but they don't make a deal of sense. You cannot stand there with that child to look after and seriously expect me to believe you have walked out on your marriage.'

Lilith was well aware that her father's mildness of manner was deceptive. She nerved herself to say, 'I'm not going back. Not ever.'

'You're a silly child who has no idea of life's realities. Of course you're going back.' He sighed impatiently as Lilith shook her head. 'Are you out of your mind? What on earth happened between you to bring this about? You'd best tell me.'

So once more she went through the story she had told Moura. Out of delicacy, and a kind of loyalty to Joseph, she forbore to add details that might have enlightened him still further. Samuel da Costa listened attentively, only interrupting once to ask, 'You mean, Joseph didn't tell you about the second baby until you had heard it from the Chinaman? That's almost unbelievable.' He thought for a moment. 'But not entirely. I'd warned him what would happen if he didn't talk to you.' He leaned forward in his chair, rubbing his fingers over his forehead in an anxious gesture she knew well. 'I should have told you myself. I offered to do so, but Joseph didn't want that. I was reluctant to interfere between you, but I see now I should have done so. Perhaps it would have prevented all this.'

'It wouldn't have made any difference in the end, Papa. It's not just one thing that's wrong between us. It's everything. We're like strangers. He doesn't want me, Papa, I can tell he doesn't. Maybe he did at first, but even then when I think back, I'm not sure. From the start things were strange, even in Trouville.'

Samuel da Costa said heavily, 'You didn't have to

254

take him. No one forced you. I seem to remember I told you I was far from anxious for you to marry.'

'I should have listened to you. Only I wanted him. I thought we would be happy. And I was, at first . . .' Her voice tailed away.

'You sound uncertain.'

'I wasn't then. I made a mistake.'

Her father held out his arms for Simeon, who went to him happily.

'And how has Joseph taken this? I can't believe he will relinquish his son easily.'

'I wrote telling him we were all right, but I didn't say where I was staying. So he couldn't reply. And,' she said defiantly, 'I haven't been near anyone else in the family, so no one knows.'

'A fine thing to greet me with when I get home. They must all think you've run off with someone.'

'There isn't anyone else,' she said simply, and her father nodded.

'Still, you can't have disappeared off the face of the earth. You'll have to tell Joseph where you are.'

'*No*. If I tell him, he'll come and take Simeon away.'

'You'll have to come to terms with the fact that eventually he may do so anyway. He has more rights than you, especially if he is the injured party in this. Where are you staying, by the way?'

She started to tell him, but he broke in, 'No, I don't want to know. If I don't, I can't tell anyone, can I? Are you safe, is Simeon being looked after properly?'

'You can see he is. I'm with a friend, a woman.'

'Jewish, is she, one of your married friends?' He looked surprised when Lilith shook her head. 'Well, my advice for the moment is keep quiet. The Mendozas must be going mad with worry. I'll talk to everyone and see what comes up. And in the meantime,' he fished in his wallet, 'in the meantime, how much money d'you have? Will this help?'

She took the proffered wad of notes gratefully. 'I'll continue your allowance,' he said, 'but I'd best pay it direct to you. You come to the house for a meal on Friday nights, you'll get it then. Now where's your sister? I don't imagine she's with you.'

'She's in Norfolk. I tried to bring her with me, but she wouldn't leave.' She explained how Beatrice had reacted, the way she had pulled her clothes from the suitcase. Samuel da Costa listened in amazement. 'I've never seen her behave in such a way,' Lilith finished. 'It's the first time I've known her to be positive about anything.'

He looked worried.

'I should go down and bring her back.'

'Maybe she won't go with you, either. She acted very strangely. And Doris will look after her. Beatrice is twenty-three, Papa. Perhaps she's getting better.'

'Perhaps.' Her father sounded doubtful. 'I'll see. At any rate, I think I should talk to Joseph.'

When Lilith left, he saw her to a cab and turned away before he could hear the address she gave. It was a sad business: he had never thought to see her alone like this, and with a child to support. For more than an hour, he sat in his study in the half-dark, trying to understand how their marriage had deteriorated so swiftly. There was more to it than she had told him, something she was not saying. She had always been determined, and he would be very surprised if she changed her mind. Still, time would tell.

* * *

Lilith drove away feeling more optimistic than she had for many days. She had scarcely expected her father to be so understanding. He had not insisted she stay at Sloane Square, as she had feared he would. And her allowance from him, supposed originally to be pin-money, would meet her obligations with Moura.

When she got home, Moura was waiting. She shouted her news while Lilith was still plodding up the stairs, Simeon in her arms.

'You've got a part! A part! One of the girls has broken her ankle and Frederick Jay says he'll take you!'

Lilith stood stock still on the landing, staring up at Moura's excited face, recalling the sharp, bird-like man who was the ballet master at the Drury Lane Theatre, and who had so rudely rejected her efforts when she went to him hoping for lessons. She said, convinced that Moura had forgotten, 'But he thought I was terrible. He said I was only fit to join a circus . . .'

'And who did he say that to?' Moura interrupted. 'As far as he was concerned, he didn't like Mrs Mendoza's modern dancing. Well, he's not going to get it. He's going to get a woman called Lilith, who's more than capable of doing simple dance routines.' She went on talking as Lilith came up the remaining stairs. 'He doesn't even want to audition you. He's taken my word you can do it, and you can. It'll never even cross his mind he's seen you before. You begin tomorrow. Rehearsal at eleven, and we'll take Simeon with us. Can you believe it?'

Lilith dumped the baby unceremoniously on the sofa and capered round the room, kicking up her legs in an improvised cancan, whirling Moura round with her until they collapsed on to the floor. When they had sobered, Moura added, 'You realize this is pantomime ballet? No chances to do your own steps, I'm afraid. But you'll be working at the Drury Lane Theatre, you'll get to know people: it's a start.'

Going next morning through the same stage door she had entered three years before, seeing the same wrinkled old man in his caretaker's cubicle, she could hardly contain her nervousness. Moura secured a corner of the cramped dressing room for Simeon's basket, and he lay contentedly watching the bustle around him as the girls of the ballet changed into practice clothes. Moura introduced Lilith, and explained she had no one to leave the baby with.

'I hope you don't mind,' Lilith added shyly, 'I'll try to stop him bothering you all.'

'He'll be no bother, love,' said a little blonde woman with a strong Lancashire accent. 'We're never all on at the same time, so you needn't worry when you're not here. Someone will look after him. Won't we, girls?'

They were as good as their word. Lilith found she had no cause for anxiety. She could leave Simeon awake or asleep, for the dancers handed him around between them like a chubby doll. At first he stared at them all solemnly, fist in mouth, but as he became used to them he would reach out to touch a bright feather or the glittering sequins on their costumes. Moura, watching him one evening in the arms of one of his admirers, observed, 'He'll never get over this, Lilith. He's destined to be a stage-door Johnny.'

'I can think of worse fates,' Lilith retorted.

The girls of the ballet were quite different from the young women she was accustomed to; worldly and pragmatic. Most of them lived from hand to mouth, never allowing themselves to think beyond the present engagement. At first, their bawdy stories had made her turn away in embarrassment, but after a while she almost ceased to notice them, though she was grateful that Simeon was not able to understand some of their less inhibited remarks. She thought of them collectively as a tough bunch, and it was only when she knew them far better that she realized how precarious their lives were, balanced like bright birds on a wire. She began to catch allusions she had not heard before, to notice that one girl was suddenly pale and drawn and kept her eyes averted from Simeon, while the others were concerned and attentive with her. Lilith listened, and discovered that behind the brash façade her companions presented were vulnerable girls no older – and in several cases two or three years younger – than herself. Because she was so evidently alone with a baby, they assumed she was single, that her wedding ring was no more than propriety demanded. They talked to her about their lives, of men whose interest quickly faded, of reputations tarnished by unsatisfactory indiscretions. She realized that Moura was different to the others: she used the pantomime work as part of her life only. She had her own home, small as it was, while these girls lived either with their parents in crowded homes or in boarding houses where the food was indifferent and the facilities worse. Lilith learned more about harsh realities in those weeks than she had done in all her twenty years, and she thought more than once of Valentine Audry, and the evening tie flung over the bedroom mirror, the man's shoe abandoned beside the bed. 'I stay with him because he pays the milliner.'

The pantomime that year was *Sleeping Beauty*, and Lilith was at various times a fairy, a serving maid and a courtier. She learnt the simple steps easily; they required a minimum of effort and concentration, and as her figure was so unspectacular, she was always in the back row anyway.

Frederick Jay, the ballet master, seemed satisfied with her. At any rate he made no comment on her progress, which Moura told her was tantamount to praise. She did her best never to catch his eye; she even tempered her movements, restricting the height of her kicks, endeavouring to curb herself so that she was adequate but inconspicuous. To her surprise, she even found herself beginning to like the spry, energetic little figure and admire his tireless energy. 'More flow,' he would cry, from his position in the centre aisles, watching his dancers go through their paces, 'more graceful, please.' And the girls would sigh and start again, sweating with effort, legs aching, complaining under their breath about their feet. Lilith found, to her amazement, that for the first time in her life her muscles were hurting. Moura explained it was caused by dancing in shoes with Louis heels, so that instead of balancing naturally on bare feet her pelvis was thrown forward, and the strong muscles of her back could not do their work.

It seemed a small price to pay for the excitement of being on a public stage at last. She was intoxicated for the first few performances by the intensity of her own emotions as she waited in the wings amongst the chorus for the curtains to rise, and the music to sound, and the first tentative steps that brought her finally into the limelights. It was an excitement that renewed itself with each performance, but faded away even while she was on stage. She spoke of it only to Moura, who said, as if surprised Lilith could not see something so evidently true, 'But don't you realize, it's because you're only part of the performance. And you're not dancing your own steps, just repeating those of other people. There's nothing individual in it, you're not achieving anything for yourself, are you?' She smiled. 'My poor little prima donna, you can do better than this. And you will, I promise you.'

They were sitting side by side in the dressing room, in front of the long mirror that ran the length of the far wall, where the girls put on their make-up. Now Lilith started taking the pins out of her hair.

'And what about you?' she asked. 'You can do better. Why don't you get depressed, doing this?'

Moura made a face in the mirror and put her head on one side, staring at herself. Then she took a powder puff and put a large, clown's dollop on the end of her nose.

'Because,' she said, in a mock-European accent, 'because, I am not like you. I haff not ze talent.' Suddenly sober, she wiped off the excess powder and went on, 'I haven't, that's all there is to it. I have to earn a living and I'm a good teacher. But I'm too old for classical ballet, and I haven't enough pupils to support me. And I accept this. I don't have ambition burning me up, I'm not stifling my creativity. Whereas you are.' She made a gesture of dismissal when Lilith started to argue. 'We both know it's true. You're special. You've got to hold on to that. By the way,' she added, with a typical rapid switch of topic, 'has Freddie told you the news? You're getting your name on the programmes from next week.' She winked at Lilith's reflection. 'Fame at last.'

* * *

261

A fortnight later, Lilith was hurrying home from rehearsal to Simeon. Now that she was working regularly she had engaged the sixteen-year-old daughter from the nearby Italian bakery to look after him, but she did not like to be out too long. It was nearly lunch time: if she hurried, she could take him out for a walk this afternoon. She was skirting the market, walking between the high warehouse walls when a vehicle beside her slowed to match her pace. Thinking she was being accosted – it had happened to her before in this area – she hurried on stern-faced. The cab kept beside her. She was aware that the rear window was being wound down and a familiar – and feminine – voice said in its customary abrupt tone:

'Get in, Lilith.'

Startled, she stopped dead, her mouth open in surprise. Accustomed to answering such summonses she had already taken a step forward before she came to her senses, and managed to say politely, 'Thank you, no. I'm on my way home,' and continued to walk quickly down the street. The motor puttered beside her while Judith Mendoza looked consideringly at the slight, hurrying figure of Joseph's wife. She sighed, and unconsciously cradled in her right hand the withered left, encased today in dark brown kid. She had grown to love this vivid girl, and had felt unexpectedly bereft when Joseph dragged her off to the wilds of Norfolk. Perhaps she had been too sharp with her. She gave an order, and the motor shot away, which made Lilith feel relieved and oddly disappointed. But when she turned the corner she found Judith standing there, her thin body more severe than ever in her dark suit.

'Please, I have something important I must discuss with you. Just for a moment.'

Lilith stopped walking. 'I won't talk about Joseph.'

'Nor will I . . .' – Judith Mendoza's tone was tart – 'though I've plenty to say on that score. Another time, perhaps. No. I want to make you a proposition.' She glanced round at the busy street behind her. 'We can't talk here.' She gestured towards the motor and Lilith opened the door for her. As the older woman got in she said, half in apology, half defiance, 'I can't take you to where I live.'

Judith settled herself and then observed, 'I should hope not, indeed. That's your own affair so far as I'm concerned: I'm not here to pry.' She leaned forward and tapped the glass separating her from the driver.

'Drive around for ten minutes, then bring us back here.'

They were in the Strand before she added, looking straight before her, 'I'm happy to see you looking so well. We've all been very anxious.' She turned to see Lilith. 'You could have come to me. At any time. I would not have turned you away.'

Lilith was touched, aware how hard it was for this difficult, lonely woman to express her feelings.

'You're very kind. But if I had, then Joseph would have known where I was.'

Judith's eyebrows went up.

'You think so? Yet I know where you are now, and be assured I have told no one, least of all my nephew.'

'How did you find me?'

For answer, Judith fished in her large handbag and brought out a theatre programme. 'My maid noticed a familiar name. Did you alter it for disguise, because I must say it wasn't very effective.'

Lilith smiled. 'No, it came like that from the

printer.' She took the programme and turned to the page listing the chorus. *Lili Mendoza*. 'It's in such small type, it never occurred to me anyone would see it.'

'You must be very pleased with yourself, nevertheless. And you're right to be.' She tapped the page with a gloved finger. 'It is an achievement. I wonder how you have managed, and with the child so small.' She paused, and then added, 'I came to see you, last evening.'

A delighted smile lit Lilith's face.

'Did you really? I hadn't thought anyone I knew would see me.' Suddenly anxious, she added, 'But you never go to pantomimes, I remember you only like serious plays.'

Judith watched her companion thoughtfully for a moment.

'I would have sat through more than a pantomime to see you, my dear Lilith. And I enjoyed it enormously, as it happened. You were splendid, though why they put you in the back row I cannot for the life of me imagine. And that, really, is why I wanted to talk to you. I remember how you danced that day at Florence's house, when Joseph was so disapproving. I've seen what you can really do. You don't belong in a pantomime, it's a waste of your time.'

Stung, Lilith retorted, 'It isn't what I would choose, but it's better than nothing. And I have no alternative. At least I'm doing this for myself.'

'I'm not criticizing you. Don't think that. I'm offering to help.' Lilith shook her head, but Judith went on, determined. 'If people saw you dance properly, as yourself, they would be astounded. I thought I would hire a hall where you could give a performance alone. I would pay for everything, and undertake to make sure that the right people attend: critics, people of influence. What do you say?'

Lilith shut her eyes.

'I must be dreaming. Pinch me.' She opened them again and caught Judith's good hand between both her own.

'It's a wonderful offer. But I can't possibly accept. For one thing, Joseph will hear of it.'

Judith brushed this objection aside. 'Nonsense. You *will* accept, and you cannot hide from Joseph for ever. I'll make sure he doesn't interfere. Now, how long would you need to rehearse? Three weeks? Four?'

Judith Mendoza had long ago decided that it was an intolerable intrusion to interfere in anyone else's life. She recalled with bitterness the quiet, angry little girl with the claw hand who had spent too much time on her own, kept out of sight by embarrassed parents. And when, much later, she had been given her one chance to lead her own life, her single offer of marriage, they had stepped in and refused, insisting that the risk of passing on her deformity to her children was too great. She had been young and impressionable, had listened and believed them. Though even then she had suspected it was their disgrace and shame they feared more than her own. By the time she discovered how unlikely it was that such misfortune could be inherited, it was too late. Over the years she had retreated more and more into herself, and few people had come as close as Lilith had done. Judith had often wondered why the two of them should get along so well, despite their obvious differences, and had come to the conclusion that it was because of them: Lilith was what she herself might have been. She saw in the girl's graceful movements an amelioration of her own ungainly ones; in her vivid, responsive features a youth she had not been permitted to enjoy. And Lilith in turn found the brusque, lonely woman was the only person to whom she could talk freely about Beatrice, the only person able to comprehend the implications of her predicament.

Judith had listened, and worried that the sister's mysterious ailment might somehow affect Lilith's future, as the shrivelled hand had blighted her own. For once, she had forgotten her determination not to interfere, had engineered the introduction to her nephew. It had seemed perfect, everyone had apparently been delighted. But the misgivings that had begun to whisper somewhere deep in her mind had become louder and louder as she became aware of Lilith's increasing tension, missed her verve and sparkle. And then, without warning, had come the news that Lilith had disappeared from Overstrand, had taken the baby and walked out on her husband, leaving behind her sister and a letter.

Judith had cursed herself: it was her fault, she should not have presumed to plan the girl's life for her. She had spoken to her brother and even she, spinster as she was, caught the uneasy suspicion that there was something strange about Joseph, something not to be spoken aloud. She wanted to right the wrong she had unwittingly done Lilith, reinstate her, make her a gift.

Then her maid had brought in the pantomime programme from the Drury Lane Theatre and she had seen the entry. *6th Fairy, Serving Maid, Lady of the Court – Lili Mendoza*. Scarcely knowing what she planned to say, she had ordered a cab and sat in it outside the theatre. She had waited all the previous day without seeing her, convinced that if she went in and announced herself, Lilith would evade her. By the time Lilith did appear, Judith had come to the conclusion that she was going to interfere just once more.

Lilith had been taken aback to see Judith in the street, and anxious to get home to Simeon. Surprised and flustered, she found herself swept along by the older woman's determination. Almost without realizing, she promised to visit her the following week to discuss it again. When she did so, it was to find that the Hampstead Town Hall had been hired for an afternoon. Judith had already written out the programme and leaflets she intended to distribute: she showed them to Lilith for approval.

'They'll be ready just in time. What do you think?'

Lilith looked at them in puzzlement.

'But you've put *Lili Mendoza*, as well. Why not my real name?'

'You can change it if you want to. But I think it looks right for a dancer. It's more memorable, too. And it's appropriate.' She raised her eyebrows. 'A new name for a new life?'

'All right,' said the new Lili. 'Why not?'

Chapter 14

The recital was a matinée, because of the evening performance at Drury Lane, and although they had tacked black material over the windows, the long room was still not really dark. On the platform Lili had arranged screens she and Moura had covered with inky blue velvet to create the illusion of evening.

Before it were rows of chairs. Looking at them, Lili could scarcely imagine them filled, but as the time grew nearer they were, more and more of them, until Moura appeared in the improvised dressing room to say, 'You won't believe it! Almost full!' as she smoothed her friend's tunic and tidied a lock of hair escaped from its ribbon. Lili nodded, too tense to speak. And then it was three-thirty and she was standing hidden behind the screens while the pianist Judith had engaged, a nervous Russian Jew named Leonid Gluzman who had lived in Hampstead for ten years and still spoke scarcely any English, had begun to play, and the buzz of conversation from the hall had faded and died.

Ravel's music filtered through the dim hall and after a minute or so a single spotlight played on the curtains, turning them purple. Very slowly, Lili came through the screens, without any display or drama, and walked – that extraordinary walk, from the hips, flowing and smooth – down to stand in it watching the pianist. As they had arranged, he played for several minutes while she stood absolutely immobile. He paused, and still she did not move, waiting until the notes had ceased.

After a moment, the Russian began to play again. As the opening bars sounded Lili turned her back on the watchers and began to run away from them, with the rapid little steps she always used. She was ahead of the music, anticipating the notes, coaxing, leading, oblivious to the rustle that had suddenly arisen in the hall behind her, the gasps and murmurs.

Lili was wearing her old practice tunic. It was the most comfortable and suitable garment she had, and she had been too busy between rehearsing, working and looking after Simeon to make anything new. Her legs and feet, as always, were bare. She had not planned this, but it had been years now since she danced in ballet shoes, and the thought had not even occurred to her.

But the audience did not know all this. As she moved the brief tunic parted, revealing the smooth flesh of her legs bare to the thigh, and there was a murmur of shocked surprise. When she raised her arms they gasped again, for the white garment was cut down to the waist, its soft folds almost disclosing the body beneath.

Her nakedness went far beyond anything even these sophisticated, worldly Londoners had seen before. *'Outrageous,'* some woman muttered, and her chair scraped loudly on the floor as she made an indignant exit, heedless of Judith Mendoza's furious glare.

On the stage, Lili did not notice. The audience, so important to her five minutes before, had ceased to be a group of critical individuals, had become instead a single entity somewhere out there. She was caught up in the music now, and the movements she made were unfamiliar to them. No ballet master had annotated these steps, no other dancer had ever interpreted them. They were her own, and there was no yardstick against which they could measure what she did.

Moura, sitting in an aisle seat towards the back of the hall, was aware of the uncertainty of the people around her. Their faces registered all sorts of emotions: disbelief, shock, amusement. As Lili leapt and swirled and spun before them, they sat stiff and unyielding, resisting her, defying her. Then, very gradually, the music and the mood changed. Lili's movements reminded Moura of lace: she wove them together, intricate stealthy steps of a forest creature, sinuous and subtle gestures. She became languorous and seductive, she swayed so slightly she scarcely stirred the air, and her observers could not help themselves, they began to respond to her sensory appeal, leaning forward in their seats as if to get nearer to her.

And as they sat there, even those who had only a few minutes before been hostile and horrified, found themselves increasingly fascinated by her flickering limbs. She no longer seemed to them brazen and half-naked, but natural and innocent. She communicated at a level beyond words, her body eloquent and expressive. Every gesture touched the blurred figures in that dim hall as if she were speaking a tongue strange to them but increasingly intelligible. She used it to tell them things they had never thought to hear, but recognized and acknowledged deep down. Every man and woman watching understood her, each in their own way, as if she were imparting a secret only they could comprehend. Her dancing brought absolute stillness. No one coughed, no one stirred.

When the music finished, she was at the left of the stage, her back against the deep blue screens.

She held a simple pose, head bent back and arms extended, abandoned by the music. She did not curtsey or smile, she did not seek their approbation or ask for their approval.

There was a moment's astonished hush before the applause broke out.

Lili did not know what she had expected. It had only gradually become apparent to her, as she sat in the improvised dressing room wrapped in her creamy cashmere shawl, a glass of cold milk in her hand, that the enthusiastic group crowded in to see her were mostly artists and musicians themselves. Judith Mendoza had always had an affinity with such people, and in her later years her considerable wealth had allowed her to become something of a patroness to them. They rewarded her by accepting her as she was. Eccentric themselves, not one of them ever made her feel in the least odd, and they went out of their way to praise this protégée of hers.

Behind them came Florence Hartsilver, folding Lili into her upholstered embrace, exclaiming over her success. She had brought a group of well-to-do women like herself, who prided themselves on being artistic and cultured. Clearly a little uncertain in makeshift surroundings, they stood together in their glossy furs, bunches of violets pinned to their collars, more used to the foyer of the Savoy or His Majesty's than to mingling with the performers.

Florence drew up a chair beside Lili.

'I'm so relieved to see you looking well,' she said, scanning the girl's face for signs of fatigue. 'And quite thrilled by your dancing. You really are exceptional, my dear.' She laid a jewelled hand on Lili's arm, cold against her flushed flesh. 'You must accept my apologies on behalf of Mrs Saltoun. She imagines

271

she has delicate sensibilities, and it seems you were a little too much for her.'

Lili gave her a solemn smile. She was exhausted, she did not want to talk. Florence rose.

'I'll let you rest, but you must promise to come and see me. Don't fear I shall try to get you together with Joseph. I have no contact with him at all.'

Only when everyone had left, and Moura had helped Lili dress again, did they go back into the main hall, where the midnight blue screens were already being dismantled. Lili held out her hand to the pianist, 'You played beautifully,' she said. 'Will you do so again?'

Gluzman bent from the waist and kissed her hand.

'You have only to ask,' he said, 'and I will do.' Judith Mendoza handed him an envelope. Behind her, Lili saw her father. Samuel da Costa was seated in the last row of chairs, still facing the empty stage. He got up as she ran towards him, holding out his arms, so that she did not notice until later how tired and drained he looked, like a man who has been ill for a long time. He clasped her very close, as he had not done since she was small.

'I could not believe it was you,' he said quietly. 'I did not recognize you. You were so different, up there on the stage. I had no idea you could dance like that. Surely, you did not learn *that* from Madame Cotin in the attic?'

'She was the start. Then it grew.'

He shook his head in disbelief.

'And I never realized. You must have worked so very hard, for it to appear so effortless.'

Lili turned.

'You must meet Moura Lemburg. She has been teaching me for a year now. I couldn't have done this without her.'

Samuel da Costa looked at the tall figure in her flowing gypsy clothes, at the dark patterned turban she wore wound round her hair. While Judith Mendoza took Lili's arm to walk out of the hall to their cabs, he drew Moura aside and spoke earnestly to her, quickly handing her his card.

Judith said, 'I invited several critics, but I didn't see one I recognized. I hope they were there.'

Lili shrugged.

'It was wonderful of you to do this for me. I don't care about critics.'

'Don't be so unworldly, Lili. I want to advance your career, bring your work before the public, and press notices are most important. Make sure you get all the papers tomorrow.'

The following day, just two papers carried reports of the recital. The *Daily Mail* printed a brief paragraph in which the writer admittedly referred to 'Lili Mendoza's exhibitionism'. *The Times* ballet critic had no such reservations. Lili and Moura sat on the living room floor, reading the review over and over again:

'Never before have I been permitted to witness so gifted a performer taking the first steps of her career. Her dancing follows no rules and conforms to no standards. She is an original. And that, I fear, may be a hindrance. It is not easy to accept the new. She interprets the music with movements that are not ballet, nor do they come from any distinguishable ethnic roots. She does not appear to care what her audience thinks of her. Lili Mendoza is captivating: it remains only to be seen whether the public accept or reject her.'

Lili dropped the paper on to her lap with a sigh, and Simeon seized it and tried to bite a large piece off the front page. Moura rescued it and read the review again.

'Does he like me, or not?' demanded Lili. 'I don't understand what he's saying.'

Moura looked up.

'It's only to be expected. What he writes is true: it isn't easy for people to see the value of something new. They expect a dancer on points. They anticipate pirouettes and *fouettés* and they don't get them from you. It's going to take a long time.'

Lili privately felt certain that she was being unduly pessimistic, but she held her peace. But even her absurd and boundless optimism began to fade as one week went by, then two and three, and still she performed once and sometimes twice a day the pedestrian routines of the pantomime. She was beginning to feel the strain of caring for Simeon in the small and inadequate flat. Washing was difficult in the ill-equipped room where Moura had an old galvanized bath, and though her hostess never uttered a word of complaint, Lili tried to confine the baby's drying clothes and napkins to her own room, but it was often impossible, and a heavily-laden airer would stand in front of the fire blocking the heat as she tried desperately to dry them.

Although she had had the minimum of help at Hans Place for Simeon, the novelty of doing everything for him had begun to wear off. He was taking more food now, and she had to feed herself: shopping and cooking had always been done for her, and it was a considerable effort to haul her purchases up the stairs. She had thought she liked to cook until it became a necessity, then she discovered she hated it. And to all this unaccustomed labour was added the theatre, and the relentless daily demands of working for her living.

Lili was nearly twenty-two, and although she had never considered it lavish at the time, the way she lived had not seemed to her different from anyone else's. It was only when she compared Hans Place with Moura's home, or the way the theatre dancers struggled to survive with her own protected past, that she realized just how easy her life had been. She did not regret the change: it seemed to her in many ways she was better off now than she had ever been. For the first time in her life, she made her own decisions. She thought of Valentine Audry. 'Sometimes, Lilith, a woman is better on her own. Not many people will tell you that.' And yet, perhaps the Frenchwoman did not believe what she professed, for she had stayed with the unsatisfactory Alain for the sake of appearances and the milliner.

Lili did not see that at last she was beginning to grow up. Moura was aware of the differences: when the younger woman first came to her for lessons, she had found her disarmingly ingenuous; when she knew her better, she thought Lilith was almost dangerously innocent. She was without pretensions or affectations, and her dancing was the same: there were no tricks, no artifice, no attempts to please. It was both a strength and a weakness. But since the summer in Norfolk when Simeon had been born, Moura had been aware of a change in Lili: she was more wary, more reticent, wiser. And now her precarious independence had underlined that change, made her cooler and more calculating. It even showed in her dancing, Moura observed, watching Lili one morning when they had gone to practise in the Endell Street room. Moura had suggested they give it up, to save the three shillings a week, but Lili had been adamant and taken the cost from her father's allowance. The hours of prac-tice were the only time when anxieties were lifted from her, when she could let her body do what it wanted, free from the necessity to keep in line or follow the steps. She was not aware how her movements had altered, become firmer, more controlled. It was as if, Moura reflected, Lili was able by some alchemy to transmute experience into action.

Soon after the recital Lili received a letter which Judith sent round to the theatre. It was from Joseph's parents: Nora asked if she and Solomon might be allowed to see the baby. Lili read it quickly then pushed it back into the envelope, and it was nearly a week before she replied. Determined that no one in the family should know where she was living, she suggested they visit the theatre before a performance.

She had chosen a time so early she knew none of the other girls would be there, so she would have the dressing room to herself. She had dressed Simeon with extra care that day but too late she noticed that he was growing out of his tailored pale blue coat, which she could scarcely fasten.

It was a difficult meeting. Nora and Solomon came into the room as if they had never been anywhere like it in their lives, their faces a mixture of excitement and apprehension. Lili had decided to be very formal, but when Nora burst into tears at the sight of Simeon she found herself putting her arms around the elderly woman and leading her to a chair.

'We've been so worried,' she sobbed, 'so worried about you both. Joseph won't tell us anything, we don't know what's going on.' She reached out and stroked Simeon's hair, and Solomon said, 'Won't you come home with us, Lilith? Surely this misunderstanding can all be sorted out?'

She heard the desperation and answered as calmly as she could, 'I don't think so. I can't ever go back to Joseph, and I have somewhere to live.'

'But, my dear,' Nora objected, dabbing the network of fine lines beneath her eyes with a handkerchief, 'how are you managing with the boy? He's getting so big, he needs a proper home.' She watched as Simeon wandered round the room, hauling himself up to the dressing tables, pulling experimentally at a tinselled headdress. 'Surely it really isn't suitable for him to be here?'

Lili flashed, 'He's well, as you can see, and very happy. It isn't what you're accustomed to, but he doesn't mind. And neither do I. And as soon as I can afford it, I'll have him properly looked after.'

Solomon looked pained.

'You needed something for the child, you should have asked us. Did you imagine we would refuse you?'

'Sol, she was afraid we would tell Joseph.' Nora turned to her. 'We love our son, and he was always very close to me. But I'm not such a fool as people seem to think. I can tell that something has gone very wrong between you two, and I am convinced the fault lies with Joseph.'

Solomon nodded agreement.

'We both feel the same, Lilith. Joseph hasn't confided in us, he's kept away and we have hardly heard a word from him these last weeks. We can see how hard you're trying. But is it quite respectable, to be doing this?' He looked round the cluttered dressing room. Lili looked too, and for the first time in all these weeks saw it as it really was: the stained floor, the mildewed mirror, the racks of shoddy finery hung carelessly away. At that moment the door opened and Jessie Wilson stuck her head round it, 'Won't be a minute, luv, I'm just off to get some fish,' she said and vanished.

Nora and Solomon exchanged a look and she

gathered up her bag, handing Lili the large parcel she carried.

'That's for Simeon. We'd better go, we can see you're busy. Will you bring him to Richmond soon? We won't have Joseph there, you needn't worry. But we must see more of you and the boy.'

Lili bent to Simeon to hide her face.

'I can't. You must see I can't come to Richmond.'

'Then you'll let us visit you, won't you? Won't you, Lilith?'

Lili had never heard such feeling in Nora's voice, and willed herself not to answer. If she gave in, if she let herself be drawn into the family, then in no time she would be back where she had been. And the very fact of their understanding strengthened her conviction that they knew something about Joseph they were not admitting: something that made them sympathetic towards her. But whatever it was, she had no doubt that eventually they would try to bring her together with Joseph again, if only for Simeon's sake.

So her silent refusal stretched out until Solomon shook his head at his wife, and Nora shut her eyes for a moment. They kissed Lili on the cheek, and Solomon swung the boy up in his arms so he chuckled, and set him down with a sigh. He ushered his wife out of the door and Lili heard her say uncertainly as they walked back down the dark corridor to the street, 'I suppose it's all very Bohemian, Sol.'

Only when they had gone did she find the wad of banknotes Joseph's father had left her, tucked into the handle of her dressing case. A more cynical woman might have wondered if he had given it to assuage his own suspicions about Joseph. Lili saw in it only generosity.

* * *

278

A month had passed since the recital. Then it was two. Lili abandoned any hope that it would lead to the offers she and Judith had wished for. The pantomime was due to end in a few weeks' time: she would have to find more work. She started reading the advertisements in *The Stage*. On Moura's advice she answered several but the brief auditions brought nothing. She was becoming dejected by her lack of success when she noticed a card in the window of the tobacconist at the far end of Castle Street.

When she announced she had taken a job dancing in a drinking club in the Strand, Moura's reaction was unexpectedly disapproving.

'I don't know if it's a good idea,' she said, her lips pursed with worry. 'Such places are not really respectable.'

Lili had never expected to hear such condemnation coming from Moura.

'I'm not being hired as a hostess, I'm the entertainment, that's all. Eleven o'clock and midnight, two dances of ten minutes each.'

'I don't think you realize,' said Moura, as if she had not spoken, 'the gulf between legitimate theatre and what you're proposing to do.'

'I thought you'd be pleased.' Lili's voice was flat.

'Don't misunderstand me. I'm impressed that you've tried. I just don't want you to be exploited. What are you to be paid?'

Lili flushed. 'The manager said we'd discuss that after the first performance, when he sees what the customers think of me.'

Moura frowned.

'But he said it'd be good money,' Lili added hastily. 'It means I'll have no financial problems *and* I can look after Simeon myself, when the pantomime finishes. I'll get a bit tired, that's the worst that can happen.'

She arrived for her first evening's work feeling apprehensive, despite her bravado to Moura. The place had looked dingy in the afternoon, and seedy. But at night it had a tawdry glitter; shaded lights glowed in the smoky atmosphere, and the three-piece orchestra played barely recognizable versions of music from New York's Tin Pan Alley.

The dressing room they had given her was a cubbyhole curtained off from the passage and cold: the oil-stove that warmed it smelled alarmingly. Lili changed hurriedly, wrapping the cashmere shawl round her shoulders in an effort to keep warm. There was nowhere to exercise and she shuddered at the thought of lying on the floor, finally compromising, by standing in the middle of the limited space to throw her arms wide, and swing her body from the waist, like a runner limbering up for a race.

She was wondering what to do next when a man's voice just beyond her curtain called, 'You're on, Lil.'

She stared at herself in the mirror with the single gaslight above it. She looked thin and pale with tiredness: she had already done a pantomime performance that evening. Quickly she dabbed on some rouge but the hectic flush was no improvement and she rubbed it off again. Then she made her way to the curtains that surrounded the minuscule stage and waited in dusty darkness for the first chords of her music. She had given the orchestra her sheet music, Ravel's *Le Poisson d'Or*, but they burlesqued it so she almost failed to recognize her opening. Angry, she got herself on to the stage and stood still for a moment, as she always did before a performance.

Immediately in front of the stage was a small dancefloor with the orchestra to one side, and then dozens of tables crowding the long room. Waiters deftly balancing trays moved among them, customers chatted and smoked. At the table nearest her a large group were talking and laughing.

When Lili came out from behind the curtains, her appearance caused a stir. The majority of the audience was male, and her appearance – the bare legs and feet, the heavy knot of dark hair – kept them quiet for the first minutes of her dance. There was scarcely enough room for her to move properly, but she quickly adjusted and pruned her gestures. The dance she had created for the piece was one she had been working on for some time; to match the distinctive music her actions were heavily stylized as she danced the part of a golden idol. One of the costume fitters at the Drury Lane Theatre had copied her white practice tunic in gold lamé after the club manager had remarked at their first meeting, taking the unlit but well-chewed cigar from his mouth: 'You'll give us something to look at, I expect.' The result had been more daring than she had anticipated. The tunic was simple but revealing when she moved. The gold lamé clung to her body and when she twisted it swirled away from her, the shiny stuff making the bare skin it disclosed seem even more naked in comparison. As she stamped and postured in the poses she had taken from Balinese temple dancers, she was conscious of the low, gravelled sound of masculine approval in the room.

Lili had never heard it before, that guttural growl from a group of men watching her voraciously. It had nothing to do with her dancing, it did not mean they were appreciating the intricate steps: it was an animal response. And it had an odd effect on her: it made her suddenly contemptuous of them, out there in the darkness where she could scarcely see them; it gave her a power she had only experienced briefly once before, when the bloated Baron Dabescat had sought her favours, suddenly humble, on his yacht that night in Trouville.

So she danced on, filled with an arrogance that was new to her, and it showed: in the tilt of her head, in the turn of her leg, in the proud carriage of her shoulders and the cool stare she gave back to her watchers. And the more scorn she showed them, the more they loved it, until the final moment when she stood as the music faded away, fingertips pressed together, indifferent to their response. And then they beat on the tables and yelled for more, as the curtains dropped and hid her from view.

As she made her way back to the cubbyhole that was her dressing room, the manager appeared. This time the cigar was lit, and his hand on her bare arm warm and clammy.

'That's got 'em going,' he announced. 'I never thought you'd do it so quick.'

She nodded. 'Thank you,' she said briefly, and brushed past him to reach for her cashmere shawl: the stone floors here made the building very cold.

'Yes,' he went on, 'they liked you. Come into my office tomorrow and we'll discuss that contract I mentioned.'

Lili was desperately tired. The pantomime that evening had not been particularly strenuous, but the effort of going out again so late, even though the distance was negligible, had been tremendous. But she was not tired enough to lose the advantage she had so suddenly gained: by tomorrow, in cold daylight, he would have forgotten, or reconsidered his response.

'I'd prefer to do it now, if you don't mind.'

He looked taken aback. 'I don't normally do business so late. But if you must . . .' He led the way to his office. It was only marginally larger than the room he had given her, almost entirely taken up with a desk piled high with papers. He seated himself behind it and waved her to a chair. Picking up a pen and pulling a piece of paper towards him, he scrawled for a moment and then said, 'I'd like to employ you for three months on the basis we arranged of two dances a night. And I'll pay you twenty-five shillings a week.'

Lili drew a deep breath.

'No.'

'No what? No you don't want the contract?'

'No to twenty-five shillings a week. I'm worth ten times that to you.'

He put the cigar between his teeth and tipped his chair back, putting his feet on the desk. He was wearing black patent evening shoes, and it occurred to Lili that no man had ever behaved so rudely in her presence. In the old days. But that was when she had been a lady. Evidently she was not one any longer. The thought made her even more determined.

'Two pounds, then,' he offered, 'and that's being generous.'

She looked at his insulting feet.

'Ten,' she said.

'Ten pounds a week? For a cabaret turn? You must be very new to this business, Miss Mendoza, if you think you rate that.'

'It's Mrs Mendoza, not Miss. And if I can do the

work successfully, what does it matter whether I'm new to it or not.'

He chewed his cigar thoughtfully, then swung his feet off the desk. He grinned at her, and she could see that he had enjoyed watching her.

'All right,' he said, 'I'll give you five guineas a week. And I tell you, that's two more than the top price I ever pay here. But if I find you're not going down well, we'll have to talk again.'

Lili nodded. She had not expected to get so much, and she did not want to make her elation apparent to him. 'Very well. I'll sign now.'

For the first few weeks her twice-nightly shows at the club were if anything more successful than the original had been. The three men in the orchestra had stopped burlesquing her music after that single occasion, and even suggested improvements to her. She could tell herself that the place became livelier just before her shows, as more patrons crowded in. The manager was delighted, and asked her to do an extra performance each evening but she refused, as the pantomime was still running.

She was becoming more and more tired by the punishing evenings. She could afford to take cabs to and from Moura's flat now, but even so she had to get herself out in the darkness, and Simeon seemed to wake earlier each morning. She felt she never got enough sleep, and this lowered her spirits. Nor did it help that still there was no word from Joseph.

At least she was able to visit Beatrice regularly, for she was back at Sloane Square. Lili saw – without really registering the fact – that her father looked drawn and white, and he seemed less patient than usual with Beatrice. It never occurred to her that he was growing old; still she saw him as he had been when she was seven and eight, fixed permanently in her mind as their protector. He had abandoned the majority of his practice to a recent partner, a much younger man, and even spoke of selling the Sloane Square house. She had not of course mentioned to him (or anyone else other than Moura) that she had a second job. She dared not imagine how such a revelation would be greeted.

One afternoon her father came into the sitting room that had been his wife's, where Lili and Beatrice were watching in companionable silence as Simeon played on the floor between them. It was a peaceful domestic scene: the two young women and the child amongst the pretty knick-knacks Bella had loved, the china cabinets, fans, sprays of feathers. Even the back of the piano was draped in China silk, plaited on to slender brass rods. Every mirror was swathed in a valance, or studded with tiny brass nails in a fleur-de-lis design. Samuel da Costa surveyed it all with a wistful expression. If only Bella could see this grandchild of hers.

He cleared his throat.

'Lilith, I have to tell you Joseph has been in touch with me.'

She turned her head towards him, and he noticed, as he always did now with his younger daughter, how expressive all her movements were. When they were little, it was on Beatrice his eye always lingered, and did still; but there was something about Lilith, a quality that had developed over the years, a conscious grace that was irresistible. He grunted to himself. He did not want to upset her.

'He has heard that you are working in some kind of club. Is that true?'

He hoped she would deny it, but she said quietly, 'Yes, Pa.'

'Then it is as bad as he says.'

'I dance there, that's all. It's well paid, and I'm free all day to take care of Simeon.'

'You didn't have to do such a thing. Am I not giving you enough money?'

'It's not that, Pa. I want to dance, that's the one thing I have, and no one else wants me at the moment. And besides, someone from one of the theatres may see me.'

Dr da Costa snorted.

'Fairy tales. Farradiddle. That's no way for you to behave. Dancing around for a lot of men in their cups. You'd best stop it straight away.'

Lili turned an obstinate face away from him.

'Don't you make faces at me, Miss,' he said sharply. 'Joseph has found out and clearly thinks no more of it than I do. He insists that if you do not act as he thinks proper, he'll demand that Simeon be looked after by someone fit to bring up a child.'

Lili said bitterly, 'Joseph is no more capable of looking after a child than of looking after a wife. He hasn't even attempted to get in touch to see Simeon.'

'That's as may be. He is the boy's father, and he has more rights than you do. Be careful, Lilith, or you may regret it.' He sat down heavily in the armchair beside her. 'It's you I'm thinking of, my dear. I don't believe he cares much what you do, to be honest. Certainly he's shown no sign that he does. But if he heard about this from someone else, he may feel bound to make a move at last.'

Lili sprang to her feet. The thoughts crowding her mind made movement essential. She paced the carpet, up and down in front of the windows, up and down.

'How could he take Simeon from me? He doesn't

know where I live, no one does. Not even you.' Her father nodded slowly.

'That's true. But there are ways. He could have you followed.'

Lili seized her hat and crammed it on her head, jabbing the pins in wildly.

'I can't stay here.' She caught Simeon up in her arms. 'We're going home.'

At the door, she glanced back. Her father remained slumped in his chair, and she knew she could not look to him in this. Beyond him, Beatrice was in profile, not looking at her. The silvery hair glinted in the lamplight, clear blue eyes were turned away. Lili knew, all the same, that she was listening.

She had been working at the club for nearly three months when the manager called her into his office as she passed the door on her way to her dressing room. She stood in the doorway. His feet were on the desk again.

'You'll be needing a new contract next week.'

'I know.'

'Well now, Lil, I think we'll have to think very carefully about that. I'd like to keep you on, of course . . .' he took the unlit cigar from between his teeth and inspected the end carefully, '. . . but it seems to me your, shall we say, novelty value has worn off.'

Lili stood a little straighter.

'What do you mean? They still cheer and shout for me.'

'I'm not denying it. But you're not bringing any more custom in, they're used to you. I consider two guineas a week would be nearer your value to me now.' Too upset to reply, she went on into her cubbyhole. The clarinettist, whose landlady provided meagrely for him, had been frying kippers again on the wire guard over her gas bracket. He spread newspapers to catch the drips, but the smell lingered for hours.

Lili sat down at the bare table where she kept her make-up and hairpins. Her shoulders were hunched, her hands clenched. She knew there was some truth in what the wretched man said: there had been less interest in her lately. People talked and drank as she danced, wandered in and out, spoke to people at neighbouring tables. They regarded her as they did the orchestra: secondary to the real business of the evening.

Somehow, she got through her two performances, managed to respond to the friendly chatter of the musicians during their break, dress again and escape gladly into the street, where a brisk wind whipping along the Strand finally dispelled the odour of kipper.

She turned her key in the lock of Moura's door. All she wanted was to get into her hard little bed in the narrow room where Simeon slept beside her, flushed in his miniature flannel nightshirt, black feathers of hair clinging damply to his head, his battered Punchinello on a stick tucked under one arm.

She had not expected Moura to be awake so late but she was standing by the window, staring out across the roofs. As she turned, Lili saw that she had been crying. She started to ask what was wrong, but Moura broke in.

'I'm so sorry,' she said, and Lili felt her scalp stiffen with fear. 'I'm so sorry, Lili. They've taken Simeon away.'

Chapter 15

'*You must be mad.*'

Lili thought she was shouting, but the words came out as a choked whisper.

'To send men – strangers – to snatch a small child from his bed. He must have been terrified. Could you not at least have come yourself? I can't believe you could be so cruel.'

Joseph had risen when she was shown into the gallery. Now he seated himself again, his face showing no reaction to her accusations, composed in the cool morning light. He rubbed the palms of his hands together in a way that Lili found she hated. When he spoke, it was so quietly she had to strain to hear.

'I was advised not to involve myself. I'm sorry if it distressed you. The intention was merely to recover Simeon in an expedient manner.'

His self-command seemed a deliberate affront to her over-wrought state.

'So it was expedient for two men to burst into my friend's home at midnight and carry off my son. That makes it all much more civilized.'

He appeared not to notice her sarcasm, but regarded her with an odd expression. If she had been more sensitive to his feelings, she might have seen pity in his eyes, but that would only have angered her further.

'Do sit down,' he said. 'You look exhausted.' He gestured towards a chair.

Lili ignored it. 'I look exhausted because I haven't

slept. No doubt you heard me ringing your doorbell in the middle of the night.'

'Ah, yes. I believe Chan-Tu did mention something this morning . . .'

'He said he had orders not to let me in. Orders!' She fairly spat the word at him. She did not add that the Chinese servant had promised her Simeon was safe, had shaken his head with sorrow over his master's unreasonable behaviour and whispered to her to come back to see the boy in the morning: she planned to go there as soon as she left the gallery, though she had no intention of informing Joseph.

'Naturally I have to protect Simeon's interests. And I can only do that by providing a safe environment for him.'

'And what do you suppose I was providing? I dance for my living, that's all. It hasn't changed me. I'm the same person. I am doing it for myself and my child, and you have no right to take him from me.'

Joseph contemplated his hands, which he had placed precisely on the polished desk. With an effort he kept them from clenching and raised his eyes to her face as if seeing for the first time the changes that the brief years of marriage had brought to her. He had chosen her because he wanted what she had in abundance: purity, candour, innocence. Qualities which he believed would endure, the very antithesis of the darkness he felt within himself, that so worried and perturbed him. He had felt a tender love for her, he sometimes thought. But she had changed.

He understood that it was his own behaviour which had brought this about. Purity and candour had been sullied by what he had taught her, innocence soiled by acts he had perpetrated. And he hated her for it, the cruelty and cynicism that were latent in his nature released by her failure to be what he wanted.

And now she had put herself beyond the pale, behaved in a way no decent Jewish woman would have contemplated. Not for one moment did it cross his mind that only an unworldly girl would be unable to comprehend his repugnance at what she was doing.

'It seems to me,' he began carefully, 'that I have every right. I understand you appear in some sort of drinking club. I am told you dance in an erotic manner ...' Lili made an involuntary movement refuting this, pushing away the idea, but he went on inexorably, '... performing half-naked night after night, and God knows what you do besides. You say you have to provide for yourself and the child. That is patent nonsense. I would have refused you nothing. You had only to ask – but you chose not to do so. You cannot defend your behaviour on any possible grounds. And you will also please remember ...' he got to his feet and stared intently into a display case of Japanese *cloisonné*, ' ... you will remember in future that your behaviour cannot but reflect on me. A man like me does not have a cabaret dancer for a wife. I have a reputation to safeguard.' He turned to her, his expression adding for him, *which you do not*.

Lili listened to him in stunned disbelief. Her father had been right: he did not care about her at all, only about his own standing in the eyes of others. She sat down, arranging the folds of her skirt carefully to give herself time to think.

She said slowly, 'I'm doing what I want for the first time in my life. It may not be much, but it's perfectly respectable, whatever you may imagine, and I'm not going to give it up. You say a man like

291

you does not have a dancer for a wife. I think you're right. I think we should divorce each other. And I must have Simeon back.'

Joseph's head went up, and the muscles in his jaw went rigid.

'No. You are my wife and nothing will change that. *You* deserted me. I am the injured party. And I will not add to the scandal you have already caused my family by involving myself in the process of a divorce.'

Lili heard the heavy, deadening words as if he were shovelling them on top of her, weighing her down.

She said, helplessly, 'But Joseph, if we feel our marriage is over, we must at least have a formal separation.'

He raised his eyebrows.

'And why must we? To assure ourselves that we have taken some step, no matter how unnecessary? Or to provide a nice little piece of tittle-tattle for our acquaintances? I think not.'

She put a hand up to cover her eyes, and he noticed with the appraising eye of the connoisseur the length of those tapering, back-bent fingers.

'I must have Simeon,' she repeated, 'I must.' Now the hands were moving as she struggled to express herself. 'I can't exist without him. And you don't want him, you know you don't. Let me take him now. Joseph, *give me my baby*.'

She had promised herself she would not plead with him, but all that was forgotten. She stretched out her arms towards him in unconscious supplication, and even as she did so, saw his mouth curve with distaste at the extravagant gesture, and let her arms fall limp. Her hands lay open on her lap, hopeless, and she felt something warm on them.

When she looked down, she saw that it was her tears. She had not even known she was crying.

Joseph fumbled in his pocket and held out a handkerchief. She took it and mopped at her eyes while he glanced away in embarrassment: he did not like to witness her distress.

It did not trouble him that he had caused it. To his mind, he had behaved impeccably. He was not at fault. He had done nothing: not raised a hand or even his voice to her. There had been no other women, he did not drink or gamble. What had she of which to complain? He admitted that perhaps he had after all done the wrong thing with the baby they had lost. He should have told her then and there. But he had thought it would be kinder to her to be left in ignorance; he had thought to spare her, by taking it all upon himself. And instead she had raved at him, attacked him like a wild thing, blaming him for her grief.

When she left the Overstrand house, they had found her note to Doris. For himself, nothing. After a day a letter had arrived, telling him she and the boy were well and staying with a friend. And that was all. Since then, he had heard that his parents and her father had seen them. He had not asked any questions. He was not interested in such answers as she might give him.

Joseph was now thirty-seven years of age, more than a little pompous and as rigid and unbending as he had ever been. Looking at Lilith now, her face ravaged by emotion, her hair caught up in a careless knot, clothes flung on anyhow, he wondered how he had ever come to embark on matrimony.

He chose not to remember, in the austere gallery among his prized exhibits, the unspeakable desires she had aroused that first day in the moist heat of the Richmond greenhouses. He was able with conscious effort to obliterate the times he had tried without success to lose himself in her boyish body. He expunged from his mind images of Lilith during their first months: dark eyes shadowed and alluring across the French hotel table; eloquent hands groping for words she could not convey without their aid; vivid face and quick movements unique in a room full of people who looked by comparison slow and senescent.

But try though he might, he could not submerge the way she had looked to him in the rainy light of the synagogue on the afternoon of their marriage, when he accidentally glimpsed her draped in the cashmere shawl, hooded, haunting. The daemon Lilith. He remembered that, remembered it all the way back to his childhood, where the old woman sat in her dim room, giving him scented sweets and talking in Ladino about Lilith, who inhabited the air and the wilderness, threatening children.

And now, perhaps, threatening his own child. He could not allow the boy to live in a squalid flat in Covent Garden, where he understood that the amenities and furnishings were only rudimentary. He would not tolerate Simeon growing up with a woman who chose to flaunt herself before other men, whether for their delectation or her own.

Joseph Mendoza was able to ignore the fact that he had been perfectly happy for Lilith to have the child when he assumed – as any man would – that she was living with her father back in Sloane Square. It was only when he said as much to his mother and she had looked anxious and murmured something about Lilith having become 'so very Bohemian' that his suspicions were aroused. His Aunt Judith clearly knew where Lilith was, but refused to tell him. It was only when his close friend and mentor Oscar Delal reported seeing her dance in a Strand drinking club that he had acted, spurred on by Oscar's evident disapproval.

He had discovered that she was not living in Sloane Square and, indeed, went there only once or twice a week. At second-hand (for he would not stoop to follow her himself) he learned how she and the boy lived. He had contemplated sending a solicitor's letter to demand Simeon's return but in the end decided Lilith would only move and hide again, necessitating further time and searches on his part. The law, his solicitor assured him, was on his side, and possession was nine points of it. Once he had the boy, it would be easy enough to dispute the case against a cabaret dancer.

And he had him now. So he was able to say, quite kindly, 'No, Lilith. There is no point in our arguing over this matter. You have not shown yourself to be a fit guardian for the boy.'

She noted, in a detached way, how still he sat as he delivered himself of that condemnatory sentence. Had he always been like this, and she had never noticed? Had he always been so stiff, so suppressed? She examined him as if she had never seen him before: the fine hair, thinning at the temples, the light eyes that seemed cold and distant, the narrow, over-precise mouth. Once he had seemed to her distinguished and sophisticated. Now she saw the same characteristics and read them differently. He appeared diminished and what she had seen as natural authority was a sharp, almost bullying manner he revealed more easily.

She did not know what to do next. Her anger had no effect upon him, nor her tears. So she stared at him and he, feeling her for the first time to be defenceless, found himself saying encouragingly, 'Eventually, if you establish a proper way of life, then I see no reason why Simeon cannot spend some of his time with you. Provided, of course, that he wishes to do so.'

Lili had begun to brighten at the first half of his speech, but something made her hesitate.

'A proper way of life?'

Joseph adjusted the knot of his tie.

'Naturally you will have to stop this dancing business.' He pulled down the front of his jacket. 'I thought I had made myself plain on that score a long time ago, after your exhibition at your aunt's house. But you chose to disobey me.'

'No,' she said wearily, 'I chose to ignore you. And now you want me to stop appearing at the club.'

All his good intentions evaporated at the insult.

'I want you to stop appearing *anywhere*. It is not respectable for a woman of your background. You're not some little chit from the suburbs.'

She said, with a sudden flash of comprehension, 'You were determined I should give it up, weren't you? You always hated the idea of my dancing, and you think you've finally found a way to put an end to it.' The scorn she felt for him lifted her to her feet. 'You threaten me with my own son. You tell me he can come to me if he wishes to, when we both know that you intend to tell him lies about me. He's so young, he *needs* me. Every child needs his mother. Simeon doesn't know or care what we feel about each other. He's a little animal still, he wants only to be cared for.' Agitation quivered in her tapering hands. 'Joseph. You can't take him from me.'

Joseph did not move a muscle.

'You should have thought of that before you crept out of my house like a thief, stealing my son away.'

My house, *my* son. Lili took an involuntary step back, to be further away from him. He was stubborn, unyielding. Despair poured through her so that she could not stand still, her limbs trembled with the weight of her anxiety. And yet nothing touched him.

Lili stared round at the carefully lit display cases, the great Chinese baluster vase on the marble pedestal, yellow and white flowers decorating its surface of transparent green floated over black. For a moment her fingers itched to hurl it to the ground, valuable as it was, to smash it to pieces: she could actually see herself doing it, hear the sharp, splintering, satisfying sounds of destruction.

She glanced back at Joseph. He was still watching her, his face inscrutable as ever. She shrugged her shoulders, an involuntary gesture, one her body made for her, revealing her anger, her frustration, her utter contempt for him.

Joseph read all this in the message delivered by her expressive body with the force of a cutting and unanswerable insult. He said nothing, but a cold hatred he had never experienced before for anyone twisted a fist between his ribs.

Lili turned abruptly and walked away from him across the discreet, colourless carpet to the door. The gallery assistant had tactfully absented himself and she fumbled with the handle, her habitual grace deserting her, clumsy as a child. Escaping at last into the clattering street, she hurried away from the gallery and her husband.

She realized now that what divided her from Joseph was not lack of love, or misunderstandings that had arisen between them, or even her evident inability to be whatever it was he wanted. It was simpler than any of these.

Once, during the first months together when she

had supposed herself to be happy, Joseph had showed her a jade figurine, an unusual purchase for him. 'Jade is the most courageous of all stones. It breaks, but does not bend.' There had been admiration in his voice.

She remembered her puzzled reply. 'But surely it is better to bend than to break?' Better to bow to the inevitable and survive than to struggle fruitlessly and die. Joseph had not even bothered to answer, clearly finding her naïveté too absurd to discuss.

The truth was, they were too foreign, too alien for each other. Their expectations, needs, responses were utterly different. And living together had merely accentuated the disparities. Lili had seen in happy marriages the partners gradually assume characteristics – almost the lineaments – of the other, as time blurred and fused them. It had not happened to her and Joseph. They remained two hostile elements. And if he was like the jade he so admired, cold and hard, then she was water, all movement, changeable, fluid.

Lili walked rapidly towards Park Lane, looking for a taxi-cab to hail. She thought that the way she and Joseph reacted to the gradual dissolution of their marriage reinforced the images she had of them. She had swung into intense activity, seeking physically to express the emotions Joseph rejected. And what had been in him a donnish, pedantic streak had hardened into obduracy.

She strode on with that prancing dancer's walk of hers, feet lifted high, shoulders back. She was quite unaware of the attention she caused, of the way women glanced at her at first with surprise at her unladylike carriage and speed, and then with envy. She was totally unconscious of the long stares men gave her, or the way they turned to watch her slender departing back, so unfashionable among the hour-glass silhouettes to which they were accustomed, so lithe and free. She did not even see them, absorbed in her thoughts and the release of action, hurrying to Hans Place and an hour or two with Simeon.

Joseph, for the moment, had won.

Samuel da Costa accompanied his daughter to seek legal advice.

'We don't want anything too formal at the moment,' he said. 'The man who handles my affairs – wills and so on – is knowledgeable and we get on well. He suggests we meet near his offices in Fleet Street and see if he thinks we have any kind of case.'

On the appointed afternoon Lili was late. It was a grey day, the streets smelled of smoke and rain and she caught a red and yellow varnished omnibus for the half-penny ride to keep dry. She got off at the Law Courts and crossed to Twinings Tea House where her father and the solicitor waited for her in a booth at the back.

'My dear, I'd like you to meet Woolf Lander. We've been talking about your problem.'

Lili held out her hand and looked gravely at the man who accepted it with an oddly tentative gesture. He had the slightly stooped shoulders of someone who spent many hours working at a desk, and the long face and narrow features of a man to whom the mind was more important than the body. His smile was surprisingly sweet, softening the severe expression.

While Dr da Costa ordered lemon tea, Woolf Lander remarked, 'I expect your father has told you

I don't specialize in divorce, though I have colleagues who do so, even though it's still a relatively restricted field: we like to move with the times.' He smiled again, and she noticed that his eyes behind the severe gold-rimmed spectacles were an almost childlike blue.

She said, ruefully, 'I don't think I need a specialist. Joseph says he will not consider divorce, or even a formal separation. He says I'm his wife and nothing will change that, ever.'

Lander looked at her carefully, and for the first time it occurred to her that he was quite young.

'Has he tried to persuade you to return to him?'

She was appalled at the idea.

'Oh, he wouldn't do that. You don't know Joseph.'

Lander nodded. He had already spoken at length to Samuel da Costa while they waited for her to arrive, and he knew rather more about the son-in-law than she supposed; he had, for instance, heard conjectures about Mendoza that the doctor had not voiced to her. He watched Lili sympathetically, seeing the way strain tightened the corners of her long, glowing eyes as she asked (with a shiver, though the tea-house was warm and airless), 'Can you get Simeon back for me?'

Woolf Lander paused for so long before replying that she sensed the answer before it came.

'I don't believe there's much hope at the moment. Your husband has everything on his side. If you were to give up the dancing, move back to Sloane Square with your father, be seen to be more ... what can I say ... more conventional, then I feel we would stand a chance.'

Dismay stopped her voice and stung her eyes; she could actually feel her limbs aching with it. Dumbly she shook her head.

Samuel da Costa caught her hand, the slender fingers lying unresisting in his.

'You're asking more than you realize, Lander. I've seen her. Not at this cabaret place – I myself don't like the idea of that. But she has something very rare, even I can tell it. I don't want her to stop dancing, it's asking too much.'

'Surely not.' The solicitor was clearly puzzled. 'She can always go back to it later, after all.'

Lili and Samuel looked at each other with sudden hope.

'Yes,' he went on. 'If in a year, say, we apply for custody under those conditions, then we would be in a far better position.'

Lili found her voice.

'Are you sure?'

'One cannot be sure of such things until they are accomplished.'

'So if I don't dance, I *might* get Simeon back. Or I might not. But I'm too old to lose a year now: I'll have lost my chance for good. I'll never be able to regain the lost ground.'

'Everything has to be paid for,' Woolf Lander laced his fingertips together in a precise gesture that reminded her for a fleeting moment of Joseph. She could tell he did not see her predicament as a serious one.

'I'll stop dancing at the drinking club.' It was a small enough sacrifice, especially after her salary cut.

He nodded in approval and took a leather-covered notebook from an inside pocket.

'Good. Your father and I both think we should formalize the arrangements between you and your husband. He is, after all, responsible for you. Formal

301

separation or not, he must look after your financial security.'

Lili put down the cup she had been lifting to her lips.

'But I'm going to get a job somewhere else. I'll try the theatres.'

The solicitor had been unscrewing the cap of his fountain pen. As he answered her, he absent-mindedly did it up again.

'I imagine your husband might well make it a condition of his allowance that you do not dance at all.'

'Has he the power to do that?' Samuel da Costa was incredulous. The other man frowned.

'Under the law as it stands at present, an unmarried mother is permitted to earn a living only if she gives up her child. Of course that does not apply to you' – he glanced at Lilith – 'but the fact is, it remains a man's world. Mendoza holds all the cards. Lilith deserted him, after all.'

'She could dance under an assumed name.'

Woolf Lander looked from father to daughter.

'These things always leak out after a time. And I must confess I see why the man would prefer his wife, estranged as she may be, to behave with decorum.' He tapped his teeth with his pen, prim as a parson.

Lili started to speak, but he held up his hand to stop her.

'Whatever you decide, I prefer you do not tell me. My business is to safeguard your financial future. You must live in some comfort and your own home before we can reasonably attempt to get Simeon back. And you must have proper access to visit him. That's really all that concerns me at present.'

When he had gathered up his notebook and gone,

Lili poured more tea. Samuel stirred his without noticing he had not put in any sugar.

'I'd like you to come home. You wouldn't be so alone. Beatrice . . .'

'I know, Pa.' She cut across his offer, sharper than she had intended. For once, her sister's soft presence was not what she needed. 'Thank you, but I think I'll stay where I am.'

'You'll miss the boy.' Still he stirred and stirred the pale liquid. Lili watched his mechanical movements. She was drained of all emotion. She felt nothing. A year. A year before she could even try to get Simeon back. A year in which he would grow, change, learn to speak, and all without her. What had she done?

A waiter, passing their booth, glanced curiously at the tired old man and the young woman who had been sitting there so long without speaking. He noted the droop of her head on that graceful neck, the long fingers pressed over her eyes. He hesitated, about to offer them another pot of tea, but decided against it.

The rain had stopped when they emerged from Twinings and pale sunlight slanting across Fleet Street emphasized the gilding on shop signs, defined the face of the clock above the jewellers. The air was clouded with petrol fumes from taximeter cabs and train smoke from Blackfriars drifted like tattered gauze across the sky.

Lili and Samuel stood bemused amongst the tide of people hurrying homeward, their voices lost in the uproar and clatter of vans, of drayhorses. He wanted to take her home in a cab, she preferred to walk. He drove away from her, an old man suddenly (she saw it as he climbed stiffly into the cab), aged

303

in an afternoon, worn out by sadness for her. She saw it, but still she felt nothing.

She walked mechanically through the throng, past the church of St Clement Danes on its island and towards the grey bulk of Somerset House. Somewhere she could hear military music playing a sound to put spring into the step, but she moved with the careful tread of an invalid. A small boy, darting in and out of the traffic collecting horse droppings to sell for fertilizer, almost fell in front of a horse-drawn omnibus. It swooped past him, and he scrambled up out of the gutter in front of her. She looked at him, dishevelled and barefoot, and it was all she could do not to burst into tears.

She could not tell what dangers might come to Simeon, without her there to watch over him. She had left Joseph and Overstrand because there was nothing for her there, no possibility of happiness. She had thought, as she danced that last afternoon on the old stones of the ruined church, that she would somehow make a life for herself and her little son. When she danced like that, anything seemed possible.

It had not occurred to her that she would lose Simeon: she had never thought Joseph wanted him. She could not go back – that train journey from Overstrand had been one way only – but perhaps, if she had anticipated this, she would not have taken so irrevocable a step.

She was in the Strand now, passing the shops full of pith helmets and spine pads, tropical drill and veld shirts, puttees and ammunition belts. Two old colonials, faces mottled from too much sun and too much brandy and soda, standing in mutual admiration of all these trappings of imperialism, parted to let her through, but she did not see them. She could only see Simeon's face. A year. A year to wait. A year before she would be told if Simeon would come back to her. A year to get through.

She found herself outside the drinking club and it was still barely six o'clock. The main door was not yet open and she had to knock on the back entrance for the surly cleaner to let her in. The semi-basement room was in half-darkness and as she walked through to the manager's office, it occurred to her that she had never before noticed the stifling smell of stale liquor. The door to Mr Lane's room was ajar but there was no sign of life anywhere. With a sigh she made her way to the curtained cubicle that served as her dressing room. She turned up the gas and lit the fire, illuminating the roughly painted walls and the piece of grubby carpet over the stone floor. She began to pack: cashmere shawl, gold tunic, the few sticks of theatrical make-up she now used.

'You look a bit low. Is something wrong?'

She turned with a start: she had not heard any footsteps. But it was only the clarinettist from the three-piece orchestra, carrying a parcel wrapped in newspaper. He held it out for her inspection with a rueful smile.

'I was hoping to cook my kippers over your gas. Didn't think you'd be here so early.'

She gazed at him without answering. His land-lady was an atrocious cook, she remembered, and he seemed always hungry. Embarrassed by her silence he said hesitantly, 'I've enough for two, if you're hungry . . .'

She shook her head.

'No. Thank you, Woody.' Everyone called him that: she had never even wondered what his name was. She had occasionally caught a glimpse of him, sitting at one of the tables watching her rehearse

early in the evening, and once or twice had found
flowers left in her cubicle – early snowdrops, a bunch
of wallflowers like rich velvet. Charmed by his
thoughtfulness, she had thanked him and forgotten.
She picked up the carpet bag in which she carried
her dancing equipment and he asked, 'Why are you
packing up? You're not leaving, are you?'

'I have to.'

'No one's been bothering you, have they? That
wretched little Lane said the other night . . .' he
broke off, embarrassed by his indiscretion.

'Nothing like that.' She managed an uncertain
laugh. 'The only thing Mr Lane's done to upset me
was cut my salary.'

'So that's why you're going: I don't blame you. But
it'll be dreary when you're gone.'

'You'll be able to cook your kippers, though.'

He looked down at the parcel he was still holding.

'I hate kippers, but they're cheap and filling, my
mother says.'

'And they smell terrible.'

'Terrible,' he agreed cheerfully. 'I suppose you
won't stay if I promise not to cook any more? I shall
miss your dancing.'

Lili picked up a towel and folded it. 'None of you
were very impressed when I started. I seem to
remember you played as if I were something from
the music-halls.'

Woody shuffled like a small boy and his face
flushed so that freckles stood out on the fair skin.
His hair was red and thick, and his smile revealed
an endearing gap between his front teeth. He smiled
now, and she could tell it was from nervousness.
'Well,' he said, 'we were fools, but it didn't take us
long to realize what you were doing. Lane's an idiot
to let you go.'

Lili's voice was bitter.

'He pays for someone to bring in the customers. They're used to me now, I'm just another turn. But that's not the only reason I'm going.' She sat down on the straight-backed wooden chair that was the only one in the room. 'I can't tell you everything, but it's all going wrong. I don't know what to do next, I just don't know.'

Woody took a step forward. His eyes were a warm brown, she noticed, full of concern and sympathy.

'I've always admired you so much, Miss . . . Lili. You could ask me to do anything, I'd be honoured to help.'

She was about to reply, to say there was no help he could possibly give her, when she realized that was not true. Her brain buzzed with words: with Joseph's charges, the solicitor's inquiries, her father's advice. It seemed as if she could barely understand what they were all saying, only that somehow they kept her from Simeon. She could not listen, not to counsel or criticism, she could not bear any more words.

Very slowly, like someone in a daze, Lili stretched out both hands to the young man with red hair. As she saw the surprise and then the excitement on his face as he came towards her, she thought how ridiculous that she could not remember his name.

Not that it mattered.

Chapter 16

She lay awake for a long time before she opened her eyes. In the first moments of consciousness she felt the warmth of Beatrice's sleeping body curved against hers, escaping again from night-time terrors. When she touched the hand that rested heavily on the dip of her waist – a man's hand, square and hot – she gave a start. And then recollection flooded in.

His room was in Lancaster Gate, at the top of three flights of narrow stairs covered with oilcloth and smelling of disinfectant. He had hurried her up them, anxious that the landlady should not open her door to check which of her tenants was returning. When they reached his room, and he had locked the door behind them, they had laughed, pleased with themselves. He had lit the table lamps and while he poured the wine he had insisted on buying on their way, she had looked round the room. It was almost painfully bare and clean. Rag rugs decorated the oilcloth which continued into the room, the washstand held a painted jug and bowl and towels hung on the wooden stand beside it. There was a table in the window with an embroidered runner, two upright chairs and an easy chair with machine-made lace arm rests tacked over the fabric. Several pictures decorated the walls, one of them a copy of an Impressionist scene she recognized, and a shelf crammed with books and sheet music. She had walked across to examine this and found it to be handwritten. When she asked him to play something for her, he had fitted his clarinet together and done so without looking at the music. Standing before the window, his back turned to her, he had lost himself in the music for so long that she had finished her glass of wine, stood, moved about the room, looked at the single bed with its clean sheets and neatly turned corners. She liked his playing, it was simple and restful; country music, shepherd's music. She removed her hat, thrusting the long pin through the velour, and then her jacket. Still he did not turn round. She took off her blouse, twisting her arms to reach the buttons all the way up the back, and her skirt. Wearing her camisole and petticoats she turned down the lamps until the room was almost in darkness. Then she walked across and stood directly behind him. Very deliberately, she laid her cheek against his back and put her arms around his waist.

He had placed the clarinet carefully on the table before he kissed her. His lips were soft, his cheek absurdly smooth against her own. He held her clumsily, in a great bear hug, and she touched his eyebrows, the broad cheekbones.

'I can feel your freckles,' she whispered, and he gave a little shout of laughter, and his fingers found the bare flesh of her shoulders. His arms slackened and he pushed her away from him so he could see her skin glimmering against the shadows.

'What . . .' he was stammering, 'what are you . . .'

She pressed one hand over his mouth, and with the other started to pull the knot of his tie. The starched collar creaked as she pushed at the studs, and she had to use both hands.

'Lili, you mustn't . . . we mustn't . . .'

She stood still, searching his face which was suffused with sudden colour even in the dim light.

'I haven't . . .' he said, 'not with anyone like you.'

'I'm just like everyone else,' she whispered, and swayed towards him. 'Just like everyone else.'

'No. No, you're not.' He struggled for the words to tell her of his lack of experience, his uncertainty, but the length of her body touching his was an argument he could not match. His hands felt huge, he didn't know what to do with them, or with his unwieldy limbs.

Lili leaned against his chest, breathing lightly. She did not need him to tell her that his only other experiments had been hasty and fumbling, with little pleasure given or received. He saw her as sophisticated, a woman of the world. If he could have watched her face at that moment, he would have found it expressing bleak amusement at the recollection of her own lovemaking with Joseph; so dry and quick, so lacking in tenderness or generosity.

She made a sound low in her throat, almost like a groan, and said, 'Come to bed.'

She moved back until she had the bed against her leg and dropped on to it, pulling him on top of her. He muttered, 'Sorry, I'm sorry,' and she laughed, pressing him closer, so that after a minute he became familiar with the feel of her beneath him, soft and strong at the same time, firm and yielding, infinitely exciting.

Lili lay in his clumsy embrace. She felt a cool detachment. She watched herself critically, taking his hand, guiding it to her breast, she heard his indrawn breath as he searched beneath the ribbon and lace, encountered the stiff centre against his palm. Calculated as a choreographer, she moved under his weight, circling her hips against his, encouraging the hardness that grew against his thigh. Like a woman administering medicine to herself for some ailment, she observed her own reactions, waited for some change to come upon her, some sign that the mixture was working.

Always, in bed with Joseph, she had been conscious that he had to block out the reality of her presence. He shut his eyes against her, as though to keep her at a distance, he did not want to see her face or acknowledge her own need. But this young man, with red hair and the gentle eyes of a puppy, was quite overcome by her. He kissed her shoulders, her hair. Again and again he returned to her mouth and she caught on his breath the flavour of the hot bread rings they had shared on the omnibus.

And gradually, she found herself responding to him. She held his face between her hands and tasted it with her tongue, taking the lobes of his ears between her teeth, feeling against her skin the flickering red-gold lashes. Emboldened by the openness of her liking for him, he began to explore the peaks and valleys of the body she was so freely offering. Cautiously, as though she might break, he touched her intimately. Carefully he caressed her, alert for a signal to warn him to stop. Only the signal never came. Instead, she murmured, 'Get undressed.'

He knelt astride her, hastily unbuttoning, possessed by an urgency so great he thought he would choke, his tongue huge in his dry mouth. Frantically he pushed down his trousers, his under-trousers, kicking them away from his ankles, forgetting that he still wore his shoes. He hurled himself on to her, gasping, like a man flinging himself into a stream. The limbs that entwined with his were cool and he was grateful for the assurance with which she moved, the brief whispered words as she told him when he pleased her.

He pulled up her long petticoat, and she raised herself slightly to help. The scent of her was like fruit, he thought hazily. He arched over her, pinning her to the bed. Her eyes recalled the wings of a tortoiseshell butterfly he had caught years before, a dark brown layered with endless colours. He rose and fell over her, and she echoed his rhythm, a silent song. Sensations and images jostled in his head, so brilliant, so intense, he could hold out no longer.

Conscious of his coming climax, Lili breathed, 'Be careful,' and he pulled himself apart from her at the last moment, the harsh sound bursting from his throat like another man's cry in his ears as he thrust against her thigh. Then he collapsed beside her, one arm locked across her body.

Lili lay in that bleak, clean room, her mind as calm and relaxed as her body, feeling his sticky warmth cooling on her skin, the spilled seed that did not endanger her.

It had been an odd experience. As always, Lili found it exceedingly difficult to analyse her feelings. She had chosen Woody simply because he was there when she was desperate, because he had been kind and interested at a moment when everything else had failed her. And she had been lucky, she realized that, lucky in his youth, his niceness, his appreciation of her. Because, her mind told her quite coldly, this coupling would have come about even if she had not liked him so much. She had not let herself think as they hurried towards his room just what it was she intended should happen, but nonetheless she had known, had decided upon it.

312

She had relied as usual upon her instincts. She had needed comfort and words were no use to her: Woolf Lander's well-meant attempts to bring order out of the chaos she had created, her father's efforts to assist her, had not helped. The child in her who had been so close to Beatrice could find consolation only in physical terms: the warmth of this man beside her, the feel of his arm across her hips, his thigh against her own – from these human things she could draw strength.

Lili was almost asleep when she heard Woody's voice.

'Oh, Lili.' He was confiding his new secret to her on the edge of sleep like a small boy. 'Oh, Lili, I do love you.'

She opened her eyes and stared at the ceiling. Suddenly the room closed around her, dark and stuffy. She could not breathe, stifled by a sense of responsibility, by unwelcome emotions where she had wanted nothing but action.

She remembered all this next morning, woken at dawn by birdsong from nearby Kensington Gardens. Only pigeons were to be heard at home in Covent Garden and the early morning market sounds were now so familiar they had long ceased to disturb.

Woody's last words had inexplicably worried her. She puzzled over them. She should be pleased. It proved that she had not misjudged him, or herself: she was, after all, loveable, despite Joseph's rejection. But she was possessed by a grave disquiet, so that she could no longer lie still. Furtively she moved his arm aside to ease herself out of bed.

The floor, even through the rag rug, felt cold. Shivering, she smoothed her petticoat, pulled up the chemise that had rumpled round her waist. She wanted to wash, but that must wait. Stealthily she crossed the floor to the chair where she had left her blouse and skirt. Stockings, shoes. Her corselet she folded small and stuffed into the carpet bag she had brought with her, containing the shawl and tunic she kept at the club. Coat. Hat.

At the door she paused. He was still fast asleep, breathing gently, face in the pillow. For a second she wondered if she should leave him a note, but that reminded her of leaving Overstrand, and she decided against it. He did not know her address, and she was not returning to the club: unless she chose, she need not see him again.

She turned the key in the lock, shut the door softly behind her and passed quietly down through the house. She held her breath opening the front door, fearful that the landlady would hear her. But nothing stirred, and then she was out in the pale morning with the sounds of milkmen and bakers' horses, hurrying towards town and Henrietta Street. It did not occur to her that she was escaping.

She had to wait for the omnibus, the horses trotting out of a light mist that draped the park. She went up the winding steps to the first of the open garden seats upstairs, and pulled the oilcloth apron over her skirt to keep dry. Holding the rail as the vehicle sped along the Bayswater Road, her body adjusting to the swing of the vehicle as naturally as a sailor's to his boat, her mood changed. Movement, as always, soothed her, and she felt the stiffness go out of her back.

The thought that she had behaved improperly for a married woman – albeit a separated one – did not cross her mind. She did not see what she had just done in terms of morality, of right and wrong. She had sought comfort as an animal might, or a child, yearning for physical warmth and proximity to keep out the fearful dark. And then, when morning came, anxious only to be gone, to be free and uncommitted.

They had reached the Tyburn Convent just before the Marble Arch when she found she knew his name after all. It was Woodford. Peter Woodford.

She had hoped to be back in Henrietta Street and her room before Moura woke, but as she ran up the last flight of stairs she heard movements and the rattle of china. Moura gave her a sharp glance but made no comment and Lili offered no explanation. They spoke briefly about the solicitor's depressing appraisal of the chances of retrieving Simeon while Lili heated water for a bath, then Moura left to give a ballet lesson in the West End.

Lying in the tin tub watching the reflections of water on the walls, Lili flexed her muscles in the warmth. She did not want to think. Last night she had done her best to shut out the world. She had used Woody as occasionally she had used Judith Mendoza's ether bottle, to blot out her anxiety and the despairing loneliness she had felt. It had worked, but too briefly, leaving her where she had been before. She could not stop her mind turning towards Hans Place. What was Simeon doing, was he happy, did he miss her? Her longing for him, the feel of his downy skin, his gurgling laugh, made her hollow inside. Doris and Chan-Tu took care of him between them, and both loved him. But not as she did. She became very still in the water. Before her open eyes she was seeing it again, the crumbling cliff and the concealing grass, experiencing afresh the bitter sadness the image always brought. She gave a little cry and sat upright so abruptly water splashed out on to the floor. She scrambled out, grabbed a towel and wrapped it round herself. She must go anywhere, so long as it was away from here. She must do anything, so long as she was moving.

She went to the room above the stained glass factory in Endell Street. And there, alone and in silence, she danced herself into exhaustion.

She could not take it in at first, but kept the letter open, stealing quick glances as though to catch it unawares. Finally she showed it to Moura, who was getting ready to go to the theatre. The older woman took it from her casually, propped it against her mirror and started to read as she bound her hair up in a long scarf. Her fingers stopped moving and she looked at Lili in the glass, her arms still in the air, an expression of utter amazement on her face.

'I don't believe it! Lili, I don't believe it!'

'Nor do I.'

'Have you ever heard of this man? He says he's an agent – did you approach him?'

'No, the whole thing is a complete mystery. But look,' she picked up the letter, 'he says he was given my name in New York by an English friend.'

Moura shook her head.

'I just don't know. And anyway, how did he get your address?'

'He didn't.' Lili held out the envelope. 'He wrote care of Judith Mendoza. I think it must be through someone who was at the recital. Maybe the ballet critic from *The Times*.' She started to smile, and then she couldn't restrain herself any longer, but jumped to her feet to twirl round and round in the middle of the room, arms flung wide with elation. 'New York,' she carolled at the top of her voice. 'I'll be dancing in New York.'

'Three months' engagement,' Moura read out, 'at the Shubert Brothers' theatre.' There was a wide smile of pleasure on her face. 'It's too good to be true.' She glanced back at the letter, then frowned. 'Hey, wait a minute. You'll have to find the fare yourself, Lili. It'll cost an arm and a leg to get there and back. Maybe it *is* too good to be true.'

Judith Mendoza thought differently.

'And about time,' she remarked with some acerbity when Lili showed her the letter. 'If they waited any longer, they'd be pushing you on stage in a wheelchair.' She looked up and Lili caught the satisfaction in her expression.

'So it *was* your doing.'

Judith pursed her lips and frowned.

'Nonsense. I may have talked about you occasionally. And I believe I did send a few copies of that *Times* dance review to one or two people I know. And why not?' she demanded with vigour. 'I spoke of your talent for your own good. I've no use for shrinking violets.' Her fierce expression softened and she asked anxiously, 'You will accept?'

Lili had been standing beside the mantelpiece. Now she crossed to Judith's chair and dropped to her knees beside it, putting her arm round the woman's angular shoulders, feeling her resistance to an unfamiliar gesture of affection.

'If you think I should.'

Judith smiled for the first time.

'If you don't, I shall have wasted a great deal of time and used up a considerable amount of goodwill.' She touched Lili's hair with a finger. 'I understand Louis Engels is something of a rough diamond but he's someone you can trust: he has a good reputation in the theatrical world. Now then . . .' As if embarrassed by her unwonted display of emotion, she turned to practicalities. 'I propose to purchase your ticket. No ...' she waved aside Lili's thanks, '... how else would you be able to make the journey, after all?' She picked up the letter. 'I see there's no mention of refunding you for the voyage. I'd like to come with you myself ...' she gave Lili a mischievous look, '... but I've sense enough to know I'm too old for such gallivanting. Still, it's quite impossible for you to cross the Atlantic alone.' She tapped the paper reflectively against her kid-covered left hand. Lili looked downcast.

'I'll be perfectly all right,' she protested, but she did not quite believe that. She knew no one who had even made the voyage, certainly not a woman. And if the hazards of the journey were not daunting enough, she would then have to face strangers in an unknown city. Perhaps after all she could not go. But to lose such an opportunity ...

Judith cut across her thoughts.

'Would the Lemburg girl go with you? I'd pay her fare too, of course.' She waved aside Lili's token protest. 'You can pay me back sometime, if you must, though I'd rather you didn't. I have too much money for my wants and you have too little for your needs. Now I suggest you write to Mr Engels telling him you accept.'

Lili caught hold of Judith's hand – the tiny, hidden one – and held it against her cheek for a moment. She had no words to thank Judith for her generosity and she knew that none were needed: the older woman's indrawn breath and long silence before she said briskly, 'Off you go now, straight home to write that letter,' were response enough.

The agent's reply, when at last it came, was satisfyingly detailed. She read it aloud as Moura dressed.

'The Shuberts are happy for me to perform my own dances,' she reported. 'And a contract is on its way for me to sign.' She stopped, then added carefully, 'He says he will reserve a room for my companion.' Moura listened as she put on her blouse. As always she was dressed in sombre colours, mole and charcoal, against which the silk scarves wound round her head gleamed. Now it was warmer, she wore open Greek sandals, and the effect was arresting and attractive.

Lili went on, hesitant, 'I don't like to ask. It sounds selfish, when you've so much to do here. But – will you come with me?' She paused, to see what effect her words had. Moura said nothing and she continued in a rush. 'Judith Mendoza will pay both our fares, and we could have my fee between us. Will you at least think about it?' Still, Moura went on mechanically fastening her buttons. Lili searched for something to sway her, finally offering the simple truth. 'It's so far, Moura. I'm afraid I won't be able to cope with it alone.'

Moura secured the high-necked blouse with a heavy gold pin and buckled a broad black belt to emphasize her narrow waist. Only then did she turn and grin at Lili.

'I defy you,' she said, 'to go without me.'

As the date of departure neared, Lili in particular became increasingly nervous. Moura had lived abroad for many years but it seemed unbelievable that she – who had never been further from London than Norfolk – should be crossing the Atlantic.

'I feel like Columbus,' she confided to Florence Hartsilver, the most experienced traveller she knew, 'only more frightened.' Her aunt forbore to point out that she and Nathan had never ventured beyond central Europe, gave her salts of bromide to combat seasickness and followed this unnerving gift by sending a provision hamper from Fortnum and Mason to the liner.

Their cabin was on F-deck ('Down among the lower barnacles,' as Moura observed), and most of the space was taken up by their cupboard trunks. The Fortnum's hamper, perched on top, caused considerable mirth.

'Which,' Lili inquired, 'am I supposed to consume first, the bromide or the pressed chicken?'

Dr da Costa, who together with Beatrice and Judith Mendoza, had accompanied the two women on the boat-train to Southampton to see them off, settled the question by opening a bottle of champagne to toast the travellers. Sipping it, Lili stood very close to Beatrice, as though to compensate for her defection. Her sister gave no indication of distress. A knock on the cabin-door brought a steward with a bouquet. There was no message on the card, which was printed with Joseph's name. Silenced by surprise, Lili put the flowers in water – the bath taps obligingly yielding a choice of fresh or sea – wondering what could have prompted him. She had of course told him about the Shuberts' theatre because of Simeon, and he had received the information without comment, so that she could not be sure he had heard. Perhaps the flowers meant he wished her good fortune, though that seemed unlikely. In the excitement of departure she forgot about them, until she found Beatrice fingering the blooms. Lili broke a stem off short and gave it to her; Beatrice regarded it with unnaturally wide eyes then, with a gesture of such violence the blossom might have been a reptile, she hurled it on to the floor. Very soon, Dr da Costa and Judith took her away.

The novelty of the crossing – the slow blue hours, the hat-pools and auctions – acted on Lili like a tranquillizing balm. But after the first days she would find, lying on her sunbed on the promenade deck, choosing from the interminable menus, listening to the orchestra in the wood-panelled ballroom, that her thoughts had drifted back to her sister's sudden, inexplicable rage. Perhaps it was not possible ever really to know anyone, however much one might love and be loved. The realization saddened her.

The two women arrived in New York full of anticipation and apprehension. Lili longed for rehearsals and stage jargon, and the possibility of acclaim. But when the ship's band played the 'Star-Spangled Banner' and the gangplank was up, and the crowd of relatives and friends waiting on the dock surged forward to embrace the passengers, she and Moura were overwhelmed by other people's excitement. They made their way through Quarantine and found themselves a taxi, subdued by the bustle, the busyness, the sheer size of the city.

Louis Engels had booked them into a brownstone on Ninth Avenue and they spent most of the first day at the windows of their rooms, fascinated by the unfamiliar scene below them: a long line of small boys clutching little flags in a temperance march, their boots laced high, their voices shrill; the fine-boned Italian woman with her small daughter who sat all day hopefully offering for sale their trays of carefully hand-made flowers; the young office-girls in their trim shirt-waists hurrying to their work as telephonists, bookkeepers, stenographers. They watched Hasidic Jews in dark overcoats and black hats carrying out mysterious transactions on the sidewalk and men going into Rudy Sohn's Barbershop opposite. When the door opened they caught glimpses of the reclining leather chairs and mirrors in massive wooden frames, the rows of shaving mugs displayed in cabinets and the advertisements on the walls: Antiseptilene, Damschinsky's Hair Dye. It seemed there were advertisements everywhere, on walls and the sides of vehicles, painted on trolley buses and proclaimed from every available corner, even suspended from the steps at the end of the street and painted beneath the stairtreads that led to the elevated trains which whizzed around the city: Sam Dannenbaum Cigars, Blaine D. Durant, Dentist, Boar's Head Tobacco, Ice-Cream Soda, Butterick Patterns, Snider's (Pure Food) Catsup.

Promptly at four, as he had promised, Mr Engels arrived to escort Lili to the theatre. He was a stubby man with a thick pepper and salt moustache and unruly hair. His striped suit of soft flannel was creased but clearly good. When Lili came down the stairs into the front parlour where he waited, he looked at her for a moment without saying anything, removing a case from his pocket. Then he put on severe, steel-rimmed spectacles to inspect her thoroughly from head to toe. She waited, eyebrows raised until, apparently satisfied, he nodded. She held out a hand.

'Mr Engels. Good afternoon.'

'Please, Louis. I like to be on close terms with my acts. Nice to meet you. Good journey?'

Lili nodded. 'Thank you, yes.' She introduced Moura, who had come into the room behind her, then Louis Engels said, 'If you two ladies are ready, we'll walk round to the theatre. And take a glass of tea, perhaps, on the way?'

They stopped at a small restaurant a few steps along the street. Their guide pushed open the plate glass door and shouted in Russian, '*Gospoda, Ya s'vami!*'

A stout man in a long white apron emerged from the back and hurried forward to embrace him. They talked excitedly, then the proprietor pulled out chairs for Lili and Moura.

'Tea?' he asked them. 'And you'd like a little something to eat, maybe?'

Louis Engels watched them enjoying cheesecake and remarked, apparently to the ceiling, 'What I always say, give me a woman who eats like a bird and gives out like a lion.'

Lili choked. She caught Moura's eye and started to laugh, putting down her fork and throwing back her head. The agent did not even smile. He watched the long line of her throat and the slender shoulders, the attenuated fingers pressed over her mouth.

'You dance as good as you laugh,' he observed, 'we're in business.'

The Shubert Brothers' theatre, the Winter Garden, proved to be on 44th Street, opposite the Astor Hotel. Lili and Moura exclaimed over the elaborate mosaics, quite failing to notice – until Louis Engels silently pointed – the bills pasted to the boards hanging outside. 'Opening this week. English dancing star Lili Mendoza.' To Lili's dazzled eyes, the words might have been blazoned in gold.

Perhaps she expected too much. In any event, nothing seemed to go right from the beginning. She had not realized that she was only the opening act, dancing to a 'cold' audience. She and Moura agreed they should have foreseen this, but it was less than she had hoped for. There was little time for rehearsal: the Shuberts wanted her to open almost immediately. The two she had seemed promising enough, but on the opening night it quickly became clear that the orchestra found her music excessively difficult. As if antagonistic to what she was doing, they performed with a leaden lethargy that loaded her legs with invisible chains. There seemed no link between what they played and the music she always heard in her head and the audience, sensing the discord, were aggressive as no audience had ever been before. For the first time she could remember, she hesitated as though the steps she knew so well had failed her. Once she stumbled and almost fell, and the murmur that began in the gallery spread swiftly through the auditorium. There were giggles from somewhere high up and several light little objects showered to the stage near Lili. She glanced down and saw that they were unshelled peanuts. She danced on, concentrating with every ounce of her being, willing the orchestra to play faster. And miraculously, they did, as if she was pulling them after her like so many ploughs.

When the dance finished, Lili was left as always holding a simple pose, alone before the deep blue curtains which she had insisted should be the only scenery. When the last notes had died, she bowed low to the tepid applause and walked off. The applause faded. She stood for a moment in the wings, between two painted backdrops. Then suddenly decisive, she ran back on to the stage, picked up a couple of the peanuts, shelled them and tossed the nuts nonchalantly in the air only to catch them in her open mouth.

There was a shout of approval from the audience.

This time, they really clapped, she had to return again and again to the stage. Afterwards, Louis Engels patted her on the shoulder with an avuncular gesture.

'Didn't think you had it in you, girl,' he said. 'You're a real little trouper.'

Lili glowed, and he started to hum a quick tune she didn't recognize. 'You know it?'

She shook her head, and he crooned the words to her:

'Oy, oy, oy, those Yiddishe eyes,
Eyes that could tell a diamond in the night ... You know it? Irving Berlin, a great man.' He pulled a chair forward by hooking a foot round the leg, sat down and proceeded to light a strong-smelling cheroot. 'You don't mind if I smoke in your dressing room?' Lili, who was sitting wrapped in her cashmere shawl, a towel round her throat, nodded: he clearly wanted to talk. Moura said warningly, 'Don't get cold. I'm going to buy some fruit before the second house. Remember you need to rest.'

When she had gone, Louis Engels puffed in silence while Lili lay down on the divan the management had provided at Moura's insistence, and covered herself with a heavy quilt. As always after she had danced, she was drained and empty, all her movements slow.

'You really worked out, huh?'

'Mmmm.'

'You handled them well out there. What went wrong in the beginning?'

'Maybe I chose music that was too difficult. It hasn't happened before.'

He grunted, squinting thoughtfully at a smoke ring.

'Not difficult. Classical is all.'

325

'Modern,' said Lili reprovingly.

He brushed the smoke ring and her correction aside with a casual hand.

'What matters? The musicians don't like, the audience don't like either. No need to hinder yourself like that. We'll find you new music. Something with a bit of bounce to it.'

Lili said doubtfully, 'I don't know. I'd have to think about it.'

'What's to think? You want to make it over here, you give 'em what they like.'

She closed her eyes. She needed to sleep, and wished Louis Engels would go away.

'I don't know what they like.'

He heard the weariness in her voice and got up.

'Maybe not. I do. Leave it all to me.'

Louis Engels exerted himself to show Lili and Moura what Americans wanted from entertainment. He played them hits from the past ten years: 'Meet Me in St Louis, Louis' and Harry von Tilzer's 'Bird in a Gilded Cage.' Together with his wife, a person even smaller and rounder than himself, he accompanied them to a ten-cent theatre on 116th and Lenox Avenue where they watched a one-reeler slapstick comedy and a young woman called Sophie Tucker singing Yiddish parodies in blackface. They listened to songs that men sang in their cups, and one of them Lili thought she would always remember, after hearing a whole tiny theatre singing it on the East Side, a song about a tart in the Klondike: 'But she died game, boys, let me tell, and had her boots on when she fell . . .' They heard Gershwin's blend of Yiddish, folk tunes and black melodies, and Irving Berlin's 'Sadie Salome': 'Don't do that dance, I tell you, Sadie, That's not a bus'ness for a lady.'

Lili responded to it all with delight. She loved the dash and vigour of the performers, the quick and witty music. But on stage herself, she could use none of it. She came from a different culture, she could not express herself through such music, however hard she tried. And she did try. She and Moura worked to unite her dancing with these sounds, but nothing caught alight, and Louis Engels shook his head dolefully over the results. One evening, when she had performed as usual to her original music, he brought a woman backstage with him after the second house.

'Lil, I'd like you to meet Leonie Samson. She works at the Follies as an assistant to Flo Ziegfeld. I thought we'd ask her for an opinion.'

Holding her glass of Matte tea, Lili nodded guardedly at the visitor. She was a big woman, with sleek hennaed hair, well-cut clothes and the poise that accompanies authority. But when she spoke, in the warm, rounded tones of Northern England, Lili and Moura exclaimed simultaneously. Miss Samson laughed at their expressions.

'I've been here for years,' she explained in answer to their eager questions. 'I sailed away from Manchester when I was eighteen and I'll never go back. I started as a dancer – chorus line only, I wasn't a feature girl – and when I got too mature for the stage . . .' she tapped her large and shapely rear, '. . . I moved into administration.' She turned to the agent. 'Lou and I've been friends a long time, he's found us some great acts. And now he's found you.' She seated herself on a hard chair, pulling it forward so she faced Lili. 'I gather he thinks you should change your routine, do something that's less difficult for people to understand.'

'I'm only thinking about her future,' Louis protested. 'It's her interests I've got at heart.'

Moura said quietly, 'You can't make a silk purse into a sow's ear,' and Leonie Samson gave a rich chuckle.

Lili, who had hardly spoken, said now, 'I have tried to do as Louis suggests. I've used the kind of music he wants, but it's all wrong for my movements, it just doesn't fit.'

'Tell me about your practising technique.' Lili recognized the professional speaking, and told her about the hours she spent doing her own exercises each morning, the afternoons spent polishing any part of the performance which needed attention.

Leonie Samson watched her carefully. Lili was lying on the divan and as she listened, the red-haired woman picked up one of the dancer's feet and held the heel in her hand. When Lili finished speaking, she nodded.

'Look,' she said to Louis, 'at these feet. I've never seen such beautiful insteps in my life. The girl's a *dancer*, Lou, an artist. You can't ask her to perform the way Fanny Brice does.'

The agent raised his eyebrows and his shoulders simultaneously.

'I'm asking this? I'm some kind of *meshuggeneh*? Of course she must dance the way she wants. All I'm asking . . .' he held out his hands in a gesture of impassioned pleading, '. . . all I'm asking is we should find some music that doesn't make people yawn. Something with a little more oomph is all I want. A bit of bite to it.'

Leonie Samson smoothed the fur collar of her jacket as she said to Lili – and it was a statement, not a question – 'You seem almost to be hiding a classical training: you've been taught ballet at some

328

time.' Lili nodded. 'And now it's something you absorb into your work: I think that's what makes it so striking.' She turned to Moura. 'I assume you do the choreography between you?'

'I make suggestions. It's really Lili's ideas.'

'The way you merge two styles is very effective. And you have an elegant classical line – that's the ballet training coming through.' She patted Lili's foot. 'But I'm afraid you'll never make it as a hoofer. It'd be like harnessing a racehorse to a milk float, Lou, you must see that.' She smiled at Lili. 'He's a nice man,' she added, 'but don't let him bully you. You know best.'

Louis Engels frowned at her.

'I bring you here for professional advice,' he grumbled, 'and what do I get but a thumbs down. I want to be told I'm wrong, I ask my wife.'

'I haven't done, Lou. Now . . .' she tapped one expensively shod foot thoughtfully on the ground, ' . . . maybe you could compromise a little, both of you. The ideal answer would be to get music written especially but it'd take too long, you're unknown here and anyway it would be expensive.' She paused. 'You do realize, don't you, that if you want to achieve real artistic success – and I'm not talking about popularity, or money, now – then you must find music that is quite unique to you, to your personality and your dancing. Something that marks you out from everyone else. Your movements are totally original, but right now you're matching them to someone else's imagination. The result is very effective – though I do see Lou's point about popular appeal. Only you'll find in time that you're limited by even the best composer.' She took a silver case from her bag and lit a cigarette. 'If you are to exploit

329

your gift, everything must be moulded around it. You must have music written especially.'

There was a silence, then Moura said impulsively, 'You're right. I don't know why I didn't see that myself, it's so obvious when you say it.' Her face was bright with enthusiasm. 'We'll find someone, Lili, someone you can work with, create music just for you.'

Lili was sitting up, the creamy cashmere shawl fallen from her shoulders.

'Would a composer really do that? For me? I can't believe it.'

Leonie Samson blew a cigarette ring and studied it.

'Unless I'm very much mistaken. Your difficulty is going to be finding the right musician. And the right style. And I'm not the person to help you there, I'm afraid, my field is revue.'

Lou Engels shifted impatiently.

'It's a great idea, Lee, great. Only it doesn't help right now.'

Leonie Samson shook her head at him. 'I'm just coming to that. Lili, why don't you leave the Ravel in – for the moment, anyway – but maybe start with something more popular.'

Lili, her mind full of brilliant possibilities she had never before considered, answered absently, 'Like what?'

'It needs to be something most people know, something they can go away humming. But it must be distinctive – nothing you would hear anywhere else ...' She snapped her fingers. 'I have it. *Peer Gynt*. That marvellous "Dance of the Trolls". She hummed a few bars. 'You can't say it isn't classical, but everyone knows it and it's memorable. And it gives you a lot of scope to create something special.'

330

Lili and Moura looked at each other. Louis Engels took the unlit cigar from his mouth.

'Sure,' he bubbled. 'Sure. I can just see it. Lots of throbbing chords, very moody – wonderful. Think you can do it, Lil?'

She hesitated. 'I should think . . .'

"Course you can. No problem.'

Leonie Samson said, 'I don't want to railroad you. but it could be very effective, don't you agree?' She appealed to Moura, who nodded.

'It's up to Lili, of course, but I like the idea.'

'Don't let yourself be rushed into anything. Take your time.' Leonie rose and linked her arm affectionately through the agent's. 'Come on now, Lou, and let the girl rest.'

It took less than a week for Lili and Moura to work up a routine to match Grieg's fierce music. When Lili danced it first at the early performance the following Saturday, she 'brought the house down' as Louis Engels remarked with proprietorial pride. During the days that followed, more and more seats were sold and by the next Saturday there was standing room only.

Nonetheless, when at the end of the third week Engels sent her a letter enclosing a cheque for two hundred and fifty dollars, she looked at it with a stricken face. It was about half what she had been led to expect. Attached to it was a typed list headed 'Expenses and Taxes', deducted by the theatre. When she queried it with him he showed her the contract she had signed, accepting such deductions. Moura said, 'It's an outrage. The theatre has been full all week.'

'Sure it has. But every other act pays these fees, and I guess you must too.'

'I still don't see . . .' Moura began, but Lili interrupted, 'Don't, Moura. It won't do any good. And really I don't care about the money: I'd have accepted this even if I'd known about the taxes. And something will turn up, don't worry.'

'Maybe it did already.' Louis Engels fished a letter out of his inside pocket and tossed it on to Lili's lap. 'Came today.'

Lili turned it over, saw the unfamiliar crest on the heavy linen envelope. She hooked her thumb under the flap and tore it open. In an elegant Italian hand she read:

'Dear Miss Mendoza, I have heard from a close friend about the dances you are presently performing. I felt I must write to ask if you would consider appearing privately at a social function. In three weeks I celebrate my birthday. We are holding a large party and would be most happy if you could dance for us that evening. Yours most sincerely, Frieda Warburg.'

Lili handed the letter to the agent, who studied the flowing, assured signature with interest.

'Do you know her?' she asked.

'Who doesn't. She's only the daughter of the most famous Jew in New York, and wife to one of the richest. Her father is Jacob Schiff, a financial wizard who made a fortune out of railways. Took her to Europe, chaperoned to the hilt, and she slipped the leash and fell in love with the son of one of Germany's biggest bankers. They say father objected furiously but finally gave in.' He gave a rasping chuckle. 'To those who have, more shall be given, eh? I'll get in touch with her next week. Arrange a fee. A handsome one.' He copied the telephone number carefully into his pocket book. 'You do realize,' he added, squinting over the page, 'what this could mean, don't you? Felix Warburg is one of the country's great collectors. He's musical, too, on the board of the Metropolitan Opera House, and the New York Symphony Orchestra. He knows every artist and musician worth a dime. Make a hit with him and his old lady, your troubles are over.'

Walking away from the drab, brown-painted office with its fluted glass door which Louis Engels shared with two other agents – neither of whom ever appeared to work – Lili said thoughtfully, 'I'm going to think carefully about the Warburg evening. I'm not happy with the new music, whatever Leonie Samson says. Not for people who know what they're seeing.'

Moura slowed her pace.

'You know what I think about it: I'm sure you're right. The sort of guests Frieda Warburg invites will be travelled, cosmopolitan – they'll have seen it all. You'll need to be very good to please them.'

Lili gave a little skip.

'I'll ask if I can use the theatre to rehearse. There's a new movement I've been wanting to try – look . . .' She lifted her skirt so Moura could see her feet, and right there, in the middle of the street, started to dance. Moura caught her arm.

'*Lili*, you idiot, people are looking at you!'

'Of course they are. Who cares?' But she allowed Moura to lead her along the sidewalk. They walked arm in arm for a while, relishing the street bustle around them, the harsh jabber of immigrant voices, the clatter of electric vehicles.

'I'm so glad you came with me,' Lili said impulsively, 'I'd have been so lonely without you.'

Moura squeezed her arm.

'I've been waiting for a moment to tell you . . . I had a telegraph after you'd gone out this morning.

My mother's had a slight stroke. I'm going to the steamship company now to arrange a passage home as soon as possible.'

Lili stopped walking.

'But that's terrible – you shouldn't have waited to tell me such a thing! Your mother, how is she?'

Moura fished the telegraph out of her handbag.

'Hard to know from this, but she's suffered some paralysis on her left side. They say she will probably recover the use of all her muscles, but it will take time. She doesn't want me to go back, she says she can wait till I'm ready, but of course I'll go. There's no one else to really take care of her.'

'I'll come with you! We'll get the first boat!'

'You really would, wouldn't you?' Even through her anxiety, Moura was filled with tenderness at her friend's generosity. 'No, professionals don't break their contracts. And anyway, what would you do back in London? Far better you stay here and work. Will you be all right, alone?'

Lili brushed that aside.

'Of course I will – and you're right, I suppose. Then how can I help?' Her face brightened. 'I'll give you all the money I have, and I'll get an advance from Lou for the Warburg evening.'

They talked of Moura's plans for the journey as they waited for a trolley bus that would take them to the steamship office. Moura remarked, 'I'll have a day or so before I sail. Maybe longer. Time to help you work up a routine for the Warburg party. Louis said you had to make a hit with them. Have you any more ideas?'

Lili did not answer for so long that Moura turned to see if she had heard. And stared, arrested by the sudden hardness and determination on her friend's face.

'Oh yes,' said Lili, watching the approach of the trolley, gaudy with posters advertising Onyx silk hosiery and the *Ladies' Home Journal*. 'Yes. I know exactly what I must do.'

Chapter 17

1109 Fifth Avenue was a daunting five-storied mansion built in grey stone and a style Lili later learned was François Premier. At the time the ornate façade – balconies and towers, double glass doors framed in bronze with Gothic decorations – and the huge entrance hall awash with liveried footmen, made her believe for a moment the cab had deposited her in error at an hotel.

She gave her name to the servant who opened the door, and he summoned a man in black tails who took the small case she carried.

'Mrs Warburg asked me to show you to the bedroom where you can change and rest, Miss Mendoza.' His tone was deferential, his accent unmistakeable: she might have guessed the Warburgs would have an English butler. He led her through a hallway as high and forbidding as a cathedral, past tapestried rooms filled with chattering guests, up a curving staircase, walls encrusted with oil paintings. The room into which he showed her was vast, shadowed with screens. She noted gratefully that a fire burned in the marble fireplace.

'I shall return for you in a half-hour, if that is convenient, to escort you downstairs.' He paused. 'Do you require one of the maids to help you change?' His tone made it clear that it would have been proper for her to bring her own. She shook her head, and the door closed discreetly behind him.

She scrambled out of her clothes, put on the tunic

she had brought with her and wrapped herself in the cashmere shawl. Then she decided against any of the formal chairs and sat on the floor in front of the fire to make up her eyes with bistre as Valentine Audry had taught her, lengthening and shading them. When she had finished, she walked round the room, examining the furniture and pictures, the enamel and silver-backed brushes and mirrors set out on the dressing table, the spray of fresh gardenias laid elegantly across the bedside table. She stared at that for a long time. More than all the luxury of the house, it seemed to her a symbol of opulence; that they could afford to let flowers die rather than display them in water.

There were still more than fifteen minutes to wait. Opening the door, she listened to music and conversation from the rooms below. Then she heard something else. Gathering the shawl round her shoulders, she followed the heavily carved oak staircase up another flight. As she ascended, the noise grew louder; children's voices and a loud buzzing. The fourth floor, when she reached it, was obviously the children's domain. The rooms here were smaller, the walls no longer richly gilded but papered with tea roses. Two small boys burst out of the doorway, stopped short when they saw Lili.

'Hullo,' she said. 'You sound as if you're having a good time.'

The smaller boy, who was wearing a sailor suit with a pleated skirt, stared at her balefully, but the older one said politely, 'We're playing with our 'lectric train set. You can see it if you like.'

'Yes,' she said. 'Please.'

Very self-possessed, the child walked across to her and took her hand, leading the way into the room

337

they had just left. The buzzing was louder here, and she saw that it came from the miniature locomotive drawing four carriages behind it, running on rails which serpentined on into the next room.

'That's wonderful,' she said admiringly. The children looked pleased.

'I'll ask Papa to show you the goods yard, shall I?' queried the boy who was still holding her hand, and tugged her towards the further room. Intrigued, she followed, to see a man in evening dress kneeling on the floor with his back to her, playing with the train.

'Now then, Carola,' he said to the girl who was helping him, 'take this one back – no, back – and we shall see what we shall see.' The girl looked up at Lili and the kneeling man followed her glance. Catching sight of Lili he made a little grimace, suddenly boyish despite the heavy moustache he wore.

'You must forgive me if I don't get up. As you see, I'm responsible for deliveries and we've had a breakdown.' His words were heavily accented, and Lili remembered that Frieda Schiff had fallen in love with a German banker.

'Don't worry, Mr Warburg,' she said. 'Anyway, I'm not a guest. I'm Lili Mendoza. Your wife asked me to dance tonight.'

He brushed back a quiff of dark hair.

'Ah, I remember. I'm pleased to meet you. I'll be with you in a moment.'

'No, I don't want to interrupt. I heard the train and I was curious, so I came up. Your butler will be looking for me in a minute.'

The man asked, 'Carola, what's the time?' When she told him, he pantomimed horror to make the children laugh. 'I've got to go, *kinder*.' He got to his feet. 'Your mother will never forgive me if I miss this lady's performance.' He came towards Lili, smoothing the creases from his trousers. 'You won't tell Frieda I was here, will you? She would be most cross. But I don't care for the small change of conversation. And as you see, my children are wonderful company.'

Lili heard his words with a pang, the boy's hand warm in her own. This man had – she glanced round the room at the other children – four sons and a daughter, all of whom he clearly adored. She had only Simeon, and she had somehow separated herself even from him. She looked down at the child by her side and Felix Warburg caught the longing in her eyes.

'Do you like children, Miss Mendoza?'

'I was thinking of my own son. Of Simeon. He's only two years old.' She saw his surprise and explained, with a smile, 'It's Mrs Mendoza really. The Miss is a stage name.' She bent down. 'Thank you,' she said to the boy, 'for letting me see your train. May I look at it again, sometime?'

As they went downstairs, the banker remarked, 'So you're from London. Do you like our city?'

Lili said fervently, 'It's incredible. Nothing is the way I imagined. Only of course I've only had time for the area round the theatre.'

'You must see something of the country before you go.'

Just as she was about to answer they reached the first floor.

'I'd better go and wait in my room,' said Lili.

'Not at all, I'll take you down myself. Have you everything you need?'

'I'll just get my music.'

339

As they walked down the last flight of stairs, Lili remarked, 'I've heard a lot about your family, especially your father-in-law. He's very famous.'

'He's a formidable man. He can trace his family tree back to the fourteenth century.' He lowered his voice confidentially. 'He swore his daughter would never live in Germany with a flashy young man like me. So – I left Hamburg.'

On the ground floor, the noise of the party was overwhelming. Felix Warburg led the way through a conservatory with mullioned windows, the trailing plants skilfully lit from beneath. 'Yes,' he went on, thoughtfully, 'everything is relative except relatives and they, alas, are constant. Now, you wait here while I get my wife.'

The woman to whom he introduced Lili a few moments later scarcely reached to his shoulder. Her eyes were direct, her mouth firm, and Lili noticed how slim her wrists were: the delicate bones of a young girl overlaid with soft pillows of white flesh. Four ropes of magnificent pearls cascaded down her bosom to below her waist, so that Lili wondered how she held her neck so straight under the weight.

Frieda Warburg looked at Lili with an odd expression on her face, seeing the slender body wrapped in the cashmere shawl, the hair bound back simply with a red silk ribbon. Self-consciously she touched her own hair, coiled in artful whorls by her maid and held with diamond pins.

'You'll be dancing in the music room,' she said. 'Normally, our entertainments are string quartets and soprano solos.' She glanced at her husband. 'You'll be a lovely surprise for everybody, won't she, Felix?'

'They'll be more surprised if we don't put our skates on. Did you tell Herbert our dancer's here?'

'He'll be in directly.' She turned to Lili. 'Victor Herbert is *the* bandleader. He does all the society functions. I'm sure you'll get on well with him.' She paused as a man hurried into the conservatory, a harassed expression on his face. 'Mr Herbert, I'd like you to meet Miss Mendoza.'

The bandleader was visibly relieved.

'Thank goodness you're here, I've been worrying about the music.' He said to Frieda Warburg, more than a touch of petulance in his voice, 'We really needed a rehearsal, you know. Such a rush.'

Lili held out the sheets of music she carried.

'I've got a dozen copies. I hope that's enough.'

'I could have done with another six. But I suppose we'll have to manage.' He accepted the music and glanced through it, apparently bemused.

'You're going to dance to *this*?'

'Of course.'

'Richard Strauss isn't easy to play without rehearsal, you know. My boys play dance music, not *Lieder*. And have you brought a singer with you?'

Lili said patiently, 'I don't need a singer. *I'm* the words.' Frieda and Felix Warburg glanced at each other and she slipped her arm through his.

'Come along, Felix, you've spent long enough away from our guests this evening.'

With a dry little smile to Lili, he was drawn back to the thronged room she could see beyond the conservatory. The bandleader watched her wonderment as she looked about her: a real little provincial. Lili neither knew nor cared what he thought of her, enraptured by the fairy lights strung round the plants, by the arbour of trees hung with artificial

341

fruit in which live nightingales sang. She had removed the cashmere shawl and wore only her tunic. Apart from its colour – the deep soft red of a peony – he thought it looked a rag, hanging flatly round her like a couple of limp scarves, without so much as a belt to relieve it.

'Perhaps,' he suggested desperately, flipping through the music, 'you might prefer us to play something else. If you like the Strauss family so much, how about "The Blue Danube"? I understand that's very popular with dancers.'

'No,' said Lili.

He sighed, glancing back over his shoulder at the richly dressed crowd in the great drawing room, the women gorgeous in their jewels and embroidery, then back to Lili.

'They won't know what to make of music like this,' he warned her. Or you either, he added privately to himself.

Felix Warburg waited until everyone was seated on the gilt chairs in his vast music room beneath the staccato glitter of crystal chandeliers. Then he nodded towards the footmen who were handling the lighting. The chandeliers were extinguished and the limelights Miss Mendoza had insisted must be used were trained on the improvised stage, which was backed with the deep indigo blue screens brought from the theatre. The limes caught the Botticelli in the background and gleamed strangely on the ornate pipes of the rare Aeolian organ. He had to admit the effect was magnificent. He introduced the unknown dancer from England, and she came quietly through the velvet screens, without any drama but with an amazing walk, lithe as a leopard, that he had quite failed to notice before. Standing in the grandiose setting, in the room punctuated by Gothic statues, waiting silently for her music, she appeared slight and oddly pathetic, with her bare legs and feet, the dark crimson of her dress eclipsing the lustrous hair. Victor Herbert caught the eye of his first violinist and imperceptibly shrugged: it was not his business.

He lifted his baton and glanced towards Lili. 'Wait,' she had asked him, 'until you think you've waited too long.' He counted slowly to ten, dropped the baton and the music began. The first song was quiet, full of hope, a song of youth and spring. Lili's first movements trembled with anticipation, her arms bearing those hands like fragile flowers. Tentatively she moved across the stage, hesitantly she took tiny running steps that grew increasingly confident. *Tomorrow*, the words whispered in her head, *tomorrow, the sun will shine again* . . .

The music curved and grew, and her movements matched it, smooth and serene. *And to the broad shore, blue with waves* . . . her limbs floated on water.

She had been tired before she began to dance. She had slept badly, and her back had felt stiff and painful. Unaccustomed to even the slightest physical disability, this had worried her, and she had not been at her best for the evening performance at the Winter Garden. But unaccountably, all her discomfort had fallen away, tossed aside as easily as the old cashmere shawl: she hardly felt her body at all. Power flooded through her with the realization that tonight she could not make a wrong move.

When the Strauss songs ended, Lili had still used only the most restrained gestures. Everything had

343

been slow. The audience were rigid even in the darkness, she could sense their indifference. She willed herself to relax, as the orchestra rustled and readied themselves for the central part of her dance.

She had chosen a piece by a young Russian composer, newly written for Diaghilev's ballet company. Leonid Gluzman, the Russian pianist who had accompanied her Hampstead performance, had sent her Stravinsky's sheet music and she had scanned it with an interest that turned rapidly to excitement.

The first sounds filtered through the darkened music room, establishing a mood, silencing the whispers. The music painted a dark landscape where nothing stirred.

And then suddenly Lili was moving, flinging herself into the waiting space. The short tunic that had hung round her in flat folds became part of her, liquescent, brilliant in the focus of light, so that with her streaming hair she flickered in the watchers' eyes: she heard the collective indrawn breath at the length of burnished thigh exposed by her leaps and spins.

This was no society performance and she knew it. These rich people expected something pretty and easy on the eye, conventional and traditional. They were used to ballet dancers who turned out their feet, plump young women with decorous gauze skirts and silk-sheathed legs. From somewhere she caught the sound of a woman's scornful laugh but tried to ignore it, to concentrate her attention on the music, always a step before it, luring it on.

A few moments before, she had appeared shy, even timid. Not any more. There was nothing submissive in her, nothing gentle, nothing tamed.

Flaunting a hard, muscular beauty she made her body a challenge, a weapon to attack, subdue and subjugate.

Lili could still sense the antagonism out there beyond the lights, she could feel enmity cold in the air. She singled out a man in the audience, near the front, a tall figure whose face was no more than a dark blur over the gleam of his shirtfront. She did not know who he was and she did not care. She danced for him alone, disregarding everyone else, careless of what they thought. The ferocity vanished from her movements: she made herself beguiling, irresistible, utterly persuasive.

The music changed. A deep note throbbed in the bass, insistent, vibrant: Lili writhed and glittered on the stage. The dark red tunic emphasized the colour of her lips, the golden skin tempting as ripe fruit. But underneath her softness was something hard and reckless, utterly determined.

As she danced, the chiffon slipped from her left shoulder and caught on her upper arm. When she dropped her hands it fell even further, so that it impeded her movements. Only fractionally, she hesitated. Smoothly, without missing a beat, she slipped her arm free of the constricting cloth so that her shoulder was bared. For half a dozen steps the fine material clung to her damp skin, then as she turned it slid down to her waist.

She was moving in profile and for a moment she seemed – the strong line of her throat, the shallow globe of her breast framed in crimson fabric, the long shadowed eyes – like the proud figurehead of some ancient Phoenician vessel, sailing across the stage.

The silence was audible – and then shocked surprise rippled through the audience. Lili never noticed. All her being was focused on that dim figure in the third row, the only person in the room. She danced for him like no woman he had ever seen before, establishing an intimacy so great his breathing became shallow, his body hard with desire for her, conscious of the mute promise she was making him.

And slowly, as she had known they would be, those other, hostile watchers were drawn in, caught by that primitive, sexual thread she was weaving. She could see, even in the darkness beyond the lights, how their posture had changed; no longer sitting formally, conscious of themselves, they were leaning forward eagerly, craning towards her. At the back, people had risen the better to see, and moved nearer.

The music was carrying her now, she was dancing as she had never danced before, every gesture full of strength and grace. She had never been so sure of herself, so confident: the possibility of failure, of disaster, simply did not occur to her. She danced as she lived, without a mask to protect herself, without compromise. And so she could not have said, afterwards, whether it was by design or by accident that the chiffon slipped from her other shoulder and left her almost naked, revealing the tapering, smoothly furrowed back, the muscled waist, the strong dancer's loins. It seemed quite natural that this should happen and so she did not falter for a moment. And the audience accepted her nudity as proof of her trust in them, as a gift she had made. They sensed in her the wildness, the spirit that was able to give everything and retain nothing, to abandon dignity and formality and all the careful posturing that holds most people together.

And in doing so, she did not lose but gained: gained control over their eyes and their minds, so that they sighed when she wished, drew breath when she permitted. And then, when she had them, when she knew she could not be denied, when she loved them all – she let them go. The last note sounded, faded, disappeared. And Lili vanished behind the velvet screens.

The audience was on its feet, applauding wildly, shouting for her to return. She stood behind the screens, wiping the sweat off her back with a towel, drying her face and her damp armpits. In the music room the frenzy was building up, the cheers and shouts drowning the attempts of the band to play them out. She dropped the towel and wrapped herself in the cashmere shawl. Then she walked slowly through the screens to stand before them.

She did not curtsey or smile, only stood quite still to receive the adulation she deserved. Flowers torn from the great display vases were flung at her feet. Victor Herbert, baton in hand, caught her eye. Another dance? his expression signalled. She shook her head slightly. She wasn't tired, energy surged through her limbs, she could dance on tables until morning. But her sense of theatre forbade it: she must leave them not sated but hungry for more.

She began to move away from them, walking backwards. Just as she was about to step behind the dark velvet screen at her back something hit her sharply on the cheek. She thought it must be a badly aimed flower and ignored it. This time she shut out the applause. One of the Warburg footmen brought her a chair but she waved it away, sitting as Moura

347

had taught her, flat on the floor, her back against the wall, her limbs slack and loose, her eyes closed.

'Good heavens, you're bleeding!'

Frieda Warburg was at her side, all concern.

'Get me a damp cloth, quick,' and a footman scurried away. Lili put up a hand, to her cheekbone, brought it away wet and red.

'Something hit me, I thought it was a flower.'

'Can I get you anything?'

'Water. Please.'

They brought her champagne. She sipped it once and left it. Frieda Warburg held the iced cloth to her cheek, keeping away the people who refused to leave the room, but clustered eagerly around the stage, waiting to see her again.

'You were unbelievable. I've never seen anyone dance like that.'

Felix Warburg added, 'Yes, you were wonderful. Wonderful. Quite fantastic. Ben was right, your dancing is unique.'

'Benjamin is the friend who saw you and suggested you should dance for us,' explained Frieda Warburg. 'He's here somewhere.' She glanced up at her husband. 'How are we going to get her away? They're wild to see her again.'

The English butler appeared at her shoulder.

'I think, Madam, the most discreet course would be to take her up the servants' stairs to her room.' He turned to Lili, deferential as ever. 'May I assist you, Miss Mendoza?'

Between them they ushered her, huddled in the cashmere shawl, up the narrow backstairs, through a heavy door and into the main part of the house again. When they reached her room, Frieda Warburg said, 'You must rest. Then we'd very much like you to join us for a while, if you feel able. We're all so anxious to talk to you.'

Lili was grateful to be left alone in the shadowy room. The lights had not been turned on, firelight gleamed on brocades and polished wood. It was quiet, she could hear only the faintest music from below, where the band was playing again: she recognized an Irving Berlin melody that Louis Engels was always humming. With a sigh, she crossed the room to the fire. She would lie down on the bed, but not for a moment. She was too elated, too full of nervous energy. Although she sensed the onset of that marvellous lassitude that came sometimes after dancing, it had not yet overtaken her. She was feather-light, unable to keep still. She wanted to savour her achievement – the shouts of acclaim, the audience on their feet – talk about it to someone who understood: if only Moura were here.

She stretched up both arms about her head and gripped the high marble mantelshelf, staring into the fire. Perhaps it was the thought of Moura, but for no apparent reason she was seized suddenly by a pang of loneliness harsh as a blow. She remembered something Judith Mendoza had said once, half to herself, in a voice so bitter it had scarcely sounded like her own: 'No one is so lonely as a childless woman.' Lili pressed a hand to her belly. But she was not childless, there was Simeon, far away. The richly decorated room afforded her no pleasure, for she saw instead a bleak and empty landscape, long grasses concealing a crumbling cliff . . .

With a choking sound she turned from the fire, stumbling, almost falling over the folds of the cashmere shawl. She wanted Simeon, she wanted Beatrice, she wanted someone to hold against that

349

fearful image of loss. She could not stay alone for another minute. She ran across the dark room and wrenched at the handle of the door, flung it open, started down the stairs.

The man walking up was taller than she, dark-complexioned, solid and distinguished in his formal evening clothes. He glanced up at her standing so distraught at the top of the stairs and said calmly, 'Whatever is wrong? You look as though you have seen a ghost.'

She stood still, clutching the shawl around herself, conscious under his stare that beneath it she wore only the remnants of the chiffon tunic. She was suddenly too tired to speak, too tired to care, to think. Evidently the man saw this because he added, speaking slowly as though either he thought she was too far gone to understand him otherwise, or because English was not his first language and did not come easily to him, 'You should not be out here. Let me escort you back to your room. I understood you were to rest.'

She shivered violently. 'No. Oh, no.'

He was standing beside her now. 'You are cold,' he said and put an arm round her waist. The gesture was so assertive, so confident, that she was not surprised by it. Without meaning to do so, she found she was leaning against him, so grateful was she for the physical contact. He was – how old – in his forties, perhaps. His body felt broad and substantial, he smelled pleasantly of tobacco. She laid her head against his shoulder and he tightened his hold. Her legs were still quivering with the effort of dancing, and she sagged slightly. He was carrying a shallow glass of champagne and he said, 'Here,' and handed it to her. Before she realized what he was doing, he picked her up in his arms, walked into the bedroom and kicked the door shut behind him.

He set her down beside the fire, and straightened up with a grimace.

'I'm too old for these capers, and you're heavier than you look.'

She did not reply.

'It's excellent champagne. I'd drink it if I were you.'

'I can't. If I drink alcohol after dancing, it makes me dizzy.'

'Drink it anyway.'

She seated herself on a low tapestry stool before the fire and sipped.

'Who are you?'

He took a chair from which he could see her face.

'Schaeffer. Benjamin Schaeffer. I'm a friend of Felix originally, in Germany, but now of both. I saw you dance when you first arrived at the Winter Garden. When Frieda was planning this evening, I suggested she should engage you.' He gave her a slow smile. 'I had no idea that you would give such a performance. You created quite a sensation with that dance of yours: no one can talk of anything else.' He was near enough to put a hand under her chin and turn her head, to get a better view of the cut on her cheekbone. He examined it for a moment with professional interest. Perhaps he was a doctor. 'I'm sorry about that.'

'It was not your fault.'

He said, seriously, 'But it was. I caused it myself.'

'I didn't think a flower could draw blood.' She was beginning to feel better already.

'But it wasn't a flower, it . . .' He stopped, and fished in an inner pocket for something which he dropped into a dish on a side table. 'I picked it up afterwards,' he said apologetically, 'and I should never have thrown it in the first place. It seemed an irresistible gesture at the time, to fling it at your feet. Don't forget to take it before you leave, will you?'

'No.' She sipped the drink again. She habitually drank so little, it was already having an effect, she could feel bubbles rising through her skin.

'Frieda said you were intending to rest. You do not appear to have done so.'

She opened her eyes wide in alarm. He was going to go, to leave her alone with her thoughts.

'Stay. Please stay.'

He put his head on one side as if trying to decide whether she meant this, and she noticed how his thick brows formed a single dark stroke across his forehead. His eyes were deepset, the skin beneath puckered and drawn: she thought he looked as though he did not sleep enough. He was far from good-looking, with a heavy chin, a nose that thrust forward aggressively. It was a dominating face, decided, authoritative. He could not be more different from Joseph; she sensed there were no self-doubts here, no hesitations, no anomalies, and his assurance was more potent than any aphrodisiac. That, and the penetrating gaze with which he was regarding her. She pulled the shawl closer, despite the fire. He asked, his voice a low rumble, 'You are still cold?'

She heard his question, but it was another that she answered, one unspoken and yet perfectly understood between them.

'Yes.'

He was close enough to lean forward and very lightly lay his lips against the cut on her cheekbone.

'You could have a scar for a long time. I think I am bound to make some restitution.'

She put up her right hand and laid it against his face, the skin bristly to her palm. They looked at each other, evidently liking what they found. Lili's eyes, elongated and exaggerated by the bistre shadow, gleamed in the half-light. He murmured, half to himself, 'When you were on that stage I wanted you. My God, how I wanted you.'

She gave a shiver – of apprehension, of ardour, she didn't know – and pressed herself to his chest. He felt bulky and burly, a bulwark against the desolate cliff-edge of her imaginings. He gripped her shoulders hard and she could feel the steady thud of his heart. This physical intimacy did not surprise or disturb her. She wanted it: she would be what Joseph had so unjustly thought her. This man was not forcing her against her will but acceding to her wishes.

He took the glass from her hand and pulled so that she slid off the stool and knelt beside him. He pushed aside the cashmere shawl and she caught her breath, putting up her free hand in an instinctive gesture to cover her bare breasts. He caught her hand in his. There was amusement in his voice, but beneath it the deep note of desire.

'You did not mind me looking at you when you danced for me. May I not look at you now?'

She wanted to explain to him that on stage she was another being, free of all constraints, only the words evaded her, and then it was too late for words. He dipped a finger in the champagne and very delicately touched it to the tip of each breast. She gave a little gasp, *What are you doing*, but for answer he guided her between his knees, holding her fast, and began to smoothe the warm liquid over her, massaging her shoulders, her back, her waist, his hands slipping down to caress her hips. And all the time he watched her, watched her, assessing her reactions, endeavouring to rouse her. She felt a surge of triumph: he did not turn her away from him as Joseph always did, he wanted to see her face, he found her valuable.

'My lovely little dancer.'

She had not imagined the words. He was murmuring them, to her and himself, over and over. She closed her eyes in a daze of delight, the excitement that still had not left her after the performance flooding through her as he stroked. She put her hands against his chest and he caught hold of them, putting her arms behind her back and pinioning her wrists with one hand. He kissed her mouth – the first time – and she felt his tongue seeking her own. She did not know how to respond: Joseph had never kissed her like this. His rare kisses, so tentative and brief, had left her unmoved. But this man demanded more than passive acquiescence, drawing her tongue between his own lips, tasting her, testing her. It was no prelude but a penetration in itself, a rhythmic imitation of another insertion and withdrawal, kindling in her such immensity of feeling she thought she would have collapsed if she had not been strained so closely against him.

After a long time he relinquished her mouth and she drew a shuddering breath. But he gave her no time to collect herself.

'I'll make you a carpet of flowers,' he whispered, and as she wondered what on earth he was talking about, began covering her neck and shoulders with small, close kisses so sweet she wanted him to go on for ever. His mouth moved from the base of her throat to the soft, spicy tufts of hair in her armpit even while she protested, knowing that she had been sweating after her dance, and had not bathed; he rubbed his face against her, revelling in her perfume. Then he bent his head, black in the dim light against her skin, and she experienced a fierce little shock that curled the soles of her feet as his tongue circled her flesh. He licked the wine from her breasts; long, slow, broad strokes of his searching tongue stiffening her nipples as she struggled to free herself. But he still had her wrists caught behind her back, and there was no evading him as his head sank lower and he kissed her navel, licking her, lipping her, nipping the invisible skin-hairs with the lightest possible touch. Lower still, and he touched between her thighs, through the divided skirt of silk chiffon that was still caught round her hips, the film of material no protection against his avid assault, that tender, terrible tongue, the tyranny he was exerting over her. The surface of her skin tightened and she made a sound deep in her throat.

He stopped what he was doing, raised his head.

'Do you want to go on? We don't have much time.'

She leaned back, releasing herself from his grip and standing in one swift movement, pulling him after her, reaching up to put both arms round his neck. When she kissed him, he tasted of wine, and herself. She left his mouth to cover his face with a flurry of delicate eyelash kisses as he fumbled with his clothing, hissing with impatience as a button refused to yield, and she could sense his mounting

355

agitation. He caught her to him, guiding her bare feet on to his own, the leather of his patent evening shoes smooth beneath her skin. She put her hand down to her tunic, to get rid of the impeding material, but he stopped her with a whispered, 'No. Leave it. It'll be safer.' (She recalled Valentine Audry, that husky, worldly voice in the Trouville hotel room: 'strained through a silk handkerchief.') He locked his arm under her knee and she curved her leg easily around his waist.

'Like an Indian temple girl,' he whispered. 'Lovely.'

His body hair fuzzed the inside of her thigh. Deliberately she again brushed over that unprotected part of him smooth and promising. He lifted her, settling her into position, the silk chiffon grainy as it slid against her secret skin. He let out a groan of satisfaction as he guided her body on to his own, his hands supporting her buttocks. He murmured, 'Not too heavy after all,' and she laughed, tucking her head against his shoulder. But the high collar he wore was harsh to her cheek and she pushed herself up, to rest in the hollow of his neck. The faint scent of tobacco she had noticed earlier had changed: she could smell lemony cologne and something else, something pungent and heady that rasped the breath in her throat.

He reacted to the change in her breathing by holding her so fiercely he hurt her, so that she wanted to cry out, but she could not make a sound. And she found he was stirring deep inside her, the stalk of the dark flower filling her, fulfilling her, ripening in the moist heat between them, making her think of the hothouse at Richmond where green things flourished in damp air, rich and sweet and fertile. Then he began to move, and all thought fled before feeling.

At the last moment he changed position, turning his head, burying her face against his to stifle the bird-cries she had begun to utter as the sensations that had been building, building all the time she was dancing coalesced and shivered down the length of her body. In that blinding instant she tightened her grip, all her muscles tensing to a single point – and then her bones and nerves liquefied with pleasure.

For a long minute he stayed absolutely still inside her, giving her the hard core of himself, honouring her with his body until she ceased to vibrate against him and relaxed to become a soft weight in his arms. He took a couple of steps, still with her wound about him, so she could rest her back against the wall. He held her more firmly, squeezing her buttocks together, and pushed into her, gently at first, slowly, so each stroke made her quiver in anticipation of the next while he looked down, watching his own actions, exciting himself with his own potency. Lili closed her eyes, sensations sweeping through her as she felt him stirring, swelling, hidden and disturbing, a power she could not, would not, deny. Faster and faster, suddenly imperative, he drove himself home in her. And when he, in his turn, tensed and stiffened, waiting for that moment when everything would be expunged, wiped out, erased, leaving him in white silence, he pressed his lips to her bare shoulder and the muffled words he called out were in no language she understood.

Unmoving, they stayed locked together as if to prolong what had already been lost. At last he sighed and pulled back to look at her. Then he

357

kissed her again, his mouth soft now on hers, sated,
all demands met. Reluctantly, she loosed herself
and slid from him to the ground like a pile of silk.
Looking down at her, he straightened his clothing,
buttoning himself, pulling taut his waistcoat,
adjusting the gold and lapis links in the silk shirt.
He smoothed his hair back with the heels of his
hands.

'Am I respectable?'

'Scarcely.'

He laughed, the first time she had heard him do
so.

'And you. Are you comfortable down there,
Liebling?'

She reached up a lazy arm, and he caught her
hand, kissing the palm.

'My God, you smell good.'

'It's the dancing. I get very hot.'

'I know what it is, and I like it.' He shot his cuff
with a businesslike gesture; he wore his watch on
his wrist in the modern manner. 'It's nearly midnight. I'll go down first. Don't be too long. And don't
forget what I put in the dish.' He gestured with his
head towards the occasional table where he had
deposited whatever it was that had cut her cheek.

With his hand on the door, Benjamin Schaeffer
turned to look at her, coiled on the carpet, as if
seeking to imprint on his memory the curve of her
cheek, the soft indolence of her sprawled limbs.

When he had gone, she yawned and stretched,
savouring the moment voluptuously. Her craving,
compelling body was satisfied, her mind quiet. He
had not asked for what she could not give; he had
not spoken of love, of possession, of permanence. He
had taken just as much as she had to offer. And in

358

return he had shielded her, however briefly, from the desolation of which she was so afraid.

Half an hour later she appeared downstairs in a silver dress, caught at one side with sulphur coloured roses. She saw him immediately through the throng which pressed about her, offering congratulations, clamouring to be introduced. He was with a group of people: perhaps one of them was his wife. She caught his eye and they exchanged an enigmatic glance. He bowed, but made no move towards her. As she turned to speak to someone at her side, her face vivid and responsive, he saw, gleaming in the shadowy hollow between her breasts, the platinum chain fine as thread, the feline figures of Art Nouveau nymphs woven by René Lalique into an endless linked dance.

She was to wear it often. But she carried the faint diamond-shaped scar on her cheekbone for the rest of her life.

Chapter 18

'*Gottenyu!* – I don't understand! You stand there and tell me no! You look at me so pretty and then put me in this *mish-mosh* . . .' Louis Engels's voice took on the note of hysteria.

Lili watched him in the glass as she meticulously brushed her lashes free from powder. She forbore to point out that she was actually seated: he looked as though he might have a fit at any moment.

Patiently she explained again.

'Louis, listen. I'm not a Ziegfeld girl: I don't take off my clothes to order. What happened at the Warburgs' just happened. I didn't plan it, but it came out of that dance, at that moment.'

'So it comes out of *another* dance, at *another* moment. What matters, so long as you do what the audience are waiting for you to do? You've got a nice shape, they like to see it, and they'll pay.' He waved the paper in his hand. 'Look how they'll pay. I can't stand to turn down this kind of money, girl. It hurts me. It goes against my nature.'

She lifted her hands, palms upward. 'It goes against *my* nature to dance to popular music in a suggestive manner. I'm not a vaudeville act. I won't turn myself into a common showgirl.'

The agent looked at her with an expression of utter disgust.

'So help me, I never thought to hear a woman speak like that about other performers. You think because they take off their clothes they take off their feelings and their decency at the same time? It doesn't occur to you they might have to earn to keep other people – a whole family maybe – and if that entails showing a bit of skin, still they do it. They're professionals.' He paused for breath and continued with deep sarcasm. 'But for you it's different. You dance so wonderful, when you drop your skirts it's artistic impulse. What's so special about you that you can dispose of other people like they were rubbish?'

Lili endured this outburst. When he had finished, she muttered, abashed, 'You're right. I'm sorry, Lou. I didn't mean to be insulting.'

'Then oblige me, please, by giving this contract some real consideration. Don't turn it down without any thought. OK, for the Shuberts you were a gimmick, something to fill in between seasons.' He caught her expression and shrugged. 'So I didn't tell you. You want I should hurt your feelings? That was just revue – a marriage of burlesque and vaudeville, no more than that. But *these* people . . .' he wagged the paper he held, '. . . they're offering to build a whole evening round you. And you talk to me about suggestive!' He sat down, patting his stomach with an anxious hand. 'I go on like this, I give myself heartburn.'

Lili slowly laid down the hairbrush she had been holding.

'Did you say they'd really make me the centre of the show?'

'Absolutely. Guaranteed. They want to open with a troupe of Russian dancers, and you get the whole of the second half of the bill.'

'And did you say they only want me to take my clothes off right at the end?'

'*Nearly* at the end. Everything very tasteful, very
. . .' he made a rocking motion with his left hand,
'. . . very understated. And you must on no account
lose your tunic at every performance.'

She stared at him.

'Now *I* don't understand. You've just been telling
me that's what they want.'

'Sure it's what they *want*. But you can't be as
risqué on a stage as you can in a private house. And
this is New York, remember, there's a strong Puri-
tan streak in society here you wouldn't find in Paris,
for instance. They say you see bare bosoms at the
Folies Bergère, even if it's only a fleeting glimpse.
Right here, just before you arrived, our police chief
insisted chorus girls at the Winter Garden cover
their knees. It's one of the reasons the Shuberts
didn't fight to keep you with them.'

Lili was bewildered.

'Then what do you expect me to do?'

Louis Engels waved his cigar expansively.

'You deliberately strip night after night, they'll
get you for corrupting public morals. But if it only
happens say, two times out of three, and if it's
accidental, like, the way it was at the Warburgs',
and if no one is quite sure if it happened the night
before – then you'll get away with it.' He was still
looking at her reflection, gauging her reaction. 'And
while you're considering, bear in mind the amount
they're offering. It's not what Anna Held gets, and I
hear that little French lady Deslys is coming to New
York next year for four thousand dollars a week.
But it's a small fortune just the same. Enough to
live well and put a lot away. Enough . . .' he weighed
his words, '. . . to buy a nice house when you get

back to London, have that boy of yours with you again.'

Lili ran her hands down her thighs. They were narrow and smoothly muscled: nothing to be ashamed of there. What did it matter, after all, if she did deliberately what until now had been unpremeditated. To an audience it made no difference whether she planned to show herself near-naked, or it happened by accident: the effect would be the same. And if, after all, she danced to music that was more easily accessible, surely she was only doing what was necessary to ensure that she worked. And made enough money to have a home and Simeon with her.

She found herself wondering how Aunt Florence or her father would react. Or Judith, or her parents-in-law . . . but that was idiotic, to allow her actions to be dictated by others. She had done that before, and the result had been a disastrous marriage. She asked herself what Moura would say, recalling the doubt her Polish friend had expressed over her dancing in the Strand drinking club. And yet at the same time, the Henrietta Street rooms were crammed with pictures and statues of Moura, half-clothed when she had posed as a model for her artist friends. For a fleeting second, the warning the solicitor Woolf Lander had given about Joseph crossed her mind: 'Behave with decorum.' She dismissed it immediately: Joseph would not learn of it. She did not think Moura would disapprove, and she did not care for the opinion of anyone else.

She held out a hand.

'Give me the contract, Lou. And a pen.'

* * *

Lili opened at the Eden Museum Theatre a month later, in March 1909. For once she had been unable to prevail upon the management to provide indigo velvet backcloths. Instead, they had turned the stage into an oriental harem. Red and purple gauze hung from the flies, gold bead curtains swayed with every movement. For the first time she was supported by a troupe, young men who spent the first half of the evening performing energetic Russian dances, playing guitars and mandolins. When Lili made her entrance she was as always alone, the simplicity of her movements exaggerated by what had gone before. She danced to *Scheherazade*, Rimsky-Korsakov's overwhelmingly sweet and languorous music. She was an irresistible princess, a beauty veiled in harem robes. As her dance became more impassioned, smoke began to drift across the stage, pumped by an over-enthusiastic stagehand until the evening when she could barely be discerned through it. 'Like a tug coming up the East River on a bad night,' Louis Engels remarked rudely. Evidently the critics had been on a clear night then, the manager had retorted, offering him an excellent and unprecedented cheroot.

If the audiences were enthusiastic – crowding the theatre nightly, roaring their approval, forcing her to take curtain call after curtain call, filling her dressing room with flowers and mobbing her when she appeared outside the theatre – the newspapers were no less laudatory.

'The Girl with the Midnight Eyes', the Brooklyn *Eagle* called her, and the name stuck: the theatre splashed great banners across her posters confirming the title. The *New York Journal* wrote excitedly that 'Not since La Belle Otero have we seen such a performer. Lili Mendoza is superb, captivating. When she moves, the boards glitter beneath her feet.' She was described as 'dark and serpentine,' as 'infinitely voluptuous. Sensual,' declared *Truth*, 'sensational and sleek as a panther, she has taken audiences by storm.'

At first bemused, later intoxicated, Lili was forced to move from her hotel in order to preserve any privacy at all. Felix Warburg had suggested she look at an apartment that was available in the new Dakota Building on the north corner of 72nd Street and Central Park West. Frieda had objected.

'Felix, it's so far north it might as well *be* in Dakota. She can't live out there.'

'And why not? Fifth Avenue isn't the only socially acceptable address on earth, you know.'

So Frieda accompanied Lili, and the two women giggled over the gods and dragons ornamenting the iron railings outside the carriage drive.

'It's like a mad German Renaissance palace,' Frieda had remarked. 'No wonder Felix likes it so. And you'll have a wonderful view of Central Park.'

'That's about all I will have,' Lili had replied, gazing round the vast room in which they were standing. 'It's a good thing it's carpeted, because I don't think I can afford furniture.'

'We'll lend you whatever you need. I've two houses full, you have only to choose.'

Lili said slowly, 'You are very generous. Thank you.'

Frieda Warburg had smiled, trying to keep the anxiety out of her eyes. She and Felix felt oddly responsible for this strange young woman. It had been in their house, after all, that she had given the provocative performance that had launched her into the public eye. The Warburgs saw that the powerful dancing was by now less important to the audiences than the possibility of her scandalous nudity. And they understood that beneath Lili's confidence lay anxieties of which they knew nothing. Frieda especially was sorry for her: separated from a difficult husband, kept apart from her son. She thought of her own close family and wondered how Lili could bear to be so much alone. When Moura Lemburg wrote that she would not be able to return to New York for some months as her mother showed few signs of recovery, Frieda encouraged Lili to employ a housekeeper and a companion, a girl who would help her dress and be available to escort her around the city, to and from the theatre.

With money to spend and a public to please, Louis Engels urged Lili to buy expensive clothes, and Frieda Warburg offered to take her to her own dressmakers and furriers. But Lili refused. Until now, her clothes had all been those chosen for the other woman she used to be – Joseph Mendoza's wife. Everything had been beautiful, but formal and constrained. She was determined now to dress in the stylized garments she had for so long admired on Moura Lemburg.

So she found dressmakers who devised at her direction simple things devoid of the ribbons, flounces and furbelows of fashion: flowing dresses in pale greys and creams, woollen cloaks edged with fur. They were like armour, these clothes, utterly discreet, demure as those of any nun. Voluminous, they no more than hinted at the long lines of the body beneath. Where other women exposed ample expanses of bosom and back, Lili insisted that necklines be filled in with opaque net. It did not occur to her that it was an odd sense of modesty which allowed her to dance near-naked before hundreds of people but would not permit so much as a glimpse of flesh off stage.

The shoes she had made for her at this time were of the softest available leather, little boots that did not constrict her feet. And she refused to wear any of the hats that had been brought to America pinned so carefully round the sides of her hatbox. She gave away the great cartwheels loaded down with fruit and flowers, feathers, ribbons and dead birds. She no longer wore her hair high on her head but kept it tied loosely off her face as she did when she danced.

'You look like a gypsy,' Louis Engels said, not without admiration. 'But your public seem to like it.'

They liked it so much that they began to emulate it. An article in *Vogue* photographed her at home, surrounded by great bowls of lilies, wearing Greek sandals and a silk scarf bound round her hair like a Pre-Raphaelite painting: young New York women started adopting the 'Lili Look' as enthusiastically as a few years before their elder sisters had worn Alice-blue in imitation of the President's daughter.

It was after this that she began to experience a backlash from her first impact. A few newspapers started to criticize her. 'A bid for sensual approval,' declared the *New York Sun*. And another, 'this display of limbs and lungs should be prohibited . . . it will only cause agitation and unrest among the spectators.' A third considered that 'this young woman dances like Delilah and with the same intent – to inflame those who observe her.' And yet another

367

considered her performance 'grossly indecent, suggestive of vice'.

Louis Engels hid these reviews from Lili, estimating rightly that they would only add to her popular appeal, and anxious not to upset her. He was well aware that the curious innocence she showed on stage, her obvious unself-consciousness, was one of her greatest assets, to be preserved as long as possible.

Well before her three-month run at the Eden Museum Theatre was due to finish, the management had offered Louis Engels another contract at a substantial increase. Lili agonized over it for twenty-four hours before accepting. It would entail staying in America a further six months: she would have no chance to see Simeon even if Joseph were to relent. And it would be the longest separation she and Beatrice had ever experienced.

Against that, she had to set the success she was enjoying, the chance to consolidate her achievement. Even so, there were drawbacks she had not envisaged. With this renewed contract, the theatre had pressed her to include more modern music, had even proposed that she try the *valse chaloupée*, the athletic and suggestive 'Apache' dance that Mistinguett had introduced in Paris the previous year to an enraptured Moulin Rouge. Even Louis Engels had drawn the line at that, pointing out that anyway she would need a partner. Relieved, Lili had found herself agreeing instead to use popular melodies. Perhaps it was the result of the time she had now spent in America, perhaps her attitude had changed, but she found it surprisingly easy to adapt and alter her routine to fit. She had also been persuaded for several numbers to abandon her filmy tunic for a more theatrical garment – something she had never imagined she would do. They had designed for her a sumptuous costume with a fantastic crested head-dress so that she appeared on stage like an irides-cent bird, a flutter of feathers and flesh that had the audience standing on their seats.

Lili had become slickly professional, to the delight of Engels and the management. Only she knew that any technically proficient dancer could do what she was doing now; the individuality, the thing that set her apart from anyone else, was being insidiously eroded.

She would have worried about this more, but by now her off stage hours were almost entirely given over to outside engagements. She was invited to dance privately at functions and parties – when she always performed the Strauss and Stravinsky that had caused such a sensation at Frieda Warburg's party – besieged with requests to open galas and fêtes, charity bazaars and ballrooms. Anyone but Lili would have become vain under the torrent of adoration, but a lifetime of self-doubt was not to be overcome in a few weeks.

So it was with some surprise that she found herself taken up by society – one of the attractions of New York drawing rooms. She intrigued everyone she met, for success had fired her with energy. She was dazzling in her vitality. Everything was accel-erated – her words, her laughter, her movements: she walked in a rustle of silks, impatient and rapid.

Lili was now twenty-two. She stood five foot six inches, but held herself so straight, the small head tilted on the strong neck, that she appeared taller. Childbirth had matured the articulate artiste's body, constant gruelling exercise had fined it down

369

so that she was pliant and lissome, barely curvaceous enough for the taste of the times, so slender she could achieve the effects she wanted on stage.

And her Persian prince's eyes, that had so fascinated Joseph Mendoza, were more arresting than ever. They dominated her face, lustrous beneath the skilfully shadowed lids, knowing and mysterious. Lili, so artless and ingenuous as a girl, appeared a woman of poise and style.

But beneath the elegant exterior, she had scarcely changed. She was by now a consummate actress, well able to behave in public with an ease and confidence she did not feel. For even in the face of success, Lili was still assailed by uncertainties. The doubts and anxieties that had always driven her pursued her still. She felt herself to be neither lovely nor loveable and sought endless reassurance that she was both. Night after night, the child who thought her pale blonde sister was prettier than herself, who had experienced the loss of her mother as rejection, and the young woman who recognized that her husband did not really want her, offered herself upon an empty stage to a vast, unseen audience. *Take me. Love me.*

And there were times when all the tumult and applause were not enough. She would sit in her dressing room while the girl fussed around with flowers and cold milk, a towel across her shoulders beneath the cashmere shawl, legs planted apart like an old woman's, hands on knees, head hanging heavy as a boxer after a hard bout. And she would wait in vain for the sensation of stillness after effort that was for her the greatest reward.

After a night like that, she came to understand she would be assailed by longings for her little son, with his feathery tendrils of dark hair and his plump hands. She would see behind her open eyes the crumbling cliff, the concealing grass, experience again the terrible despair for that unknown baby.

Then it became imperative that she should not be alone. The one person she really wanted was Beatrice, the silvery soothing presence, the physical closeness from childhood. But Beatrice was an ocean away, so Lili turned instead to many people, to the parties to which she was invited by Mrs Pembroke Jones or the Cornelius Vanderbilts, leaving in the early hours to sleep through the morning until rehearsal time.

Sometimes she would find Benjamin Schaeffer waiting unannounced after a performance to take her to dinner. He always chose noisy cafés on the Lower East Side – Schreiber's on Canal Street for Yiddish playwrights and actors, Goodman and Levine's on East Broadway for the young poets. Once it was the Monopole at Second Avenue and Ninth Street where he had seen Leon Trotsky in the flesh, another time the Café Royale on Second Avenue and Twelfth Street, where for a dime each and a nickel tip they had coffee cake and glasses of tea among philosophers and writers in an atmosphere of steam and cigarette smoke and sweet gypsy music. Or they would eat delicacies from Eastern Europe – borscht and salt-beef – in vast eating rooms where portions were generous and talk was loud and patrons read the Yiddish papers (*Morgen Zhurnal* and *Jewish Daily Forward*), going down the classified advertisements from want ads to matrimonials, arguing about politics, poetry, poverty. Afterwards they would walk through the one and a half square miles bounded by the Bowery and

Third Avenue, Catherine Street, 14th Street and the East River; the cramped, crammed heart of New York Jewry where six-year-old waifs peddled matches and elevated trains rocketed above rows of narrow shops selling goods that had never been new. Once, on impulse, they went into one of the city's many nickelodeons and for five cents sat amongst European immigrants munching fruit, cracking nuts and greeting with noisy approval the silent, flickering movie shorts. Afterwards, Schaeffer would leave her with a brotherly hug, and she would lean against the door when he had gone, her mind full of images.

More rarely, he would write to her: she never knew when to expect one of his brief, ardent notes. Or arrive at the apartment like a man on his way to a station, hurried and preoccupied, too impatient for polite preliminaries. She did not ask about his life away from her, she did not want to hear. If he was married, he never spoke of his family. She still was not aware what he did for a living. They talked – if they did so at all – of themselves and each other, of childhood memories, of music that moved them, of meals they had eaten. The relationship existed on a physical level that entirely suited Lili.

Once or twice she glimpsed him, when she dined at the homes of Mrs Stuyvesant Fish or the Hermann Oelrichs. His name might be mentioned by someone at a fashionable restaurant, at Sherry's or Delmonico's, but she deliberately avoided hearing what was said, concentrating on the person to whom she was speaking, dazzling them with her attention. She paid her way by being decorative and unusual, a fascinating young woman unencumbered by a husband, bringing the glitter of her success to people whose own glitter was that of money. Before long, she carried also the more doubtful glow of notoriety.

When the second contract ended, the theatre released Lili for two weeks in order to undertake a limited tour of Boston, Chicago and Cincinnati. Well-publicized, the show predictably sold out weeks beforehand. She travelled with Jane Martin, the nineteen-year-old dresser, and James Elroy, a sensible man in his late twenties Louis Engels had persuaded her to hire. His tasks were to organize the productions, overseeing the clearing of the stages before Lili's appearances, and the setting in place of her dark velvet screens. After the first engagement in Boston it was decided he would journey ahead to anticipate any problems. Two hours later, Lili and Jane Martin followed him to the station. Louis Engels drove with them in the cab: he was returning to New York.

The performances the previous night had been a resounding success, and as they reached the station Jane Martin leaned forward excitedly.

'There's a lot of people cheering, Miss Lili. They're waiting for you.'

Two dozen or so young men had appropriated a luggage trolley from a porter and were busily engaged tying ribbons to its metal struts. The moment the cab stopped half a dozen hands opened the door.

'It's a triumphal exit,' announced the youth who handed Lili out. 'If we can't make you stay, the least we can do is ensure you remember us for a little while.' He gestured to his lapel and she noticed all of them were wearing bunches of lily-of-the-valley.

'You are very kind,' she said, laughing. 'What a pretty idea.'

'We'd like to carry you shoulder high, but I guess you wouldn't like that?'

'I would not. What if you dropped me?' She pantomimed fear, putting a hand to her throat and widening her eyes.

'So we propose to draw you to the train in state.' He was drowned by the shouts of his companions.

'Come on, Lili, climb up. Climb up!'

She glanced back nervously.

'Louis?'

'Go ahead, gal. Have yourself a party.'

Eager hands caught hers and pushed her on to the trolley among the fluttering ribbons. Someone produced a ukelele and followed by Jane Martin and Louis Engels, they proceeded to escort Lili across the station concourse, past the smiling bystanders and over to the platforms. The ticket collector tipped his cap, called her by name and insisted that she sign his cigarette packet for him before he would open the iron gates to let them through. Once on the platform, where the train was already filling up, the youths started to run, towing the trolley, some running beside it. Lili held on, riding the rickety vehicle like a bucking horse, glad she was as usual hatless.

They stopped at a first class carriage at the front of the train, and two of the boys took the bags into the carriage.

'You've plenty of time,' said her self-appointed guardian. 'There's ten minutes before it leaves.'

The carriage they had selected held three passengers, and glancing in Lili saw without interest that two of the men, conservatively dressed, were reading newspapers while a third was watching the riotous scene outside in which she was involved. Lili's escort swung himself up the iron steps on to the observation platform. A couple of cases were passed to him, and he carried them into the compartment and stowed them on the netting racks, returning to the platform to hand Lili up. He followed her into the compartment, opened the window so she could speak to the youths clustered round outside. They had assembled themselves into a circle, and now started to sing, barbershop style, 'You're the girl, the girl that I adore, you are my lilee and my rose . . .'

Lili, framed in the window, laughed with pleasure at their high spirits. Jane Martin, standing behind the boys, looked as though she wished she were invisible. Lili waved to her impishly, so the girl was forced to wave back in response, thoroughly self-conscious. Still laughing, Lili turned from the window to encounter the remote gaze of the two men who had emerged from behind their papers. They must be city men, she decided, and clearly neither knew nor cared who she was. The third occupant of the carriage, though, was a florid figure wearing a herringbone suit, his hair oiled flat against his head. As she sat down opposite him, he took out a cigar and cut off the end preparatory to lighting up.

Lili scarcely noticed, busy with her belongings, but her young admirer, standing at the carriage door, spoke with civility.

'Sir. Please do not light that cigar in the presence of a lady.'

The man raised his eyes to the slight shape of the boy in the doorway. There was a moment in which no one moved, frozen like the jerky black and white figures on the cinematograph screen. Then the man grunted and proceeded to strike a leisurely match. He held the flame against the cigar's end, puffing deliberately, still staring at the youth.

'Sir, I asked you politely. I must insist you refrain from smoking. Do you know who this lady is?'

'Lili Mendoza.' The man's voice was mocking. 'She's Lili Mendoza. And by all accounts, a lady she ain't. Takes off her clothes, don't she, for anyone to see.' He stretched out his legs comfortably, and gave Lili an appraising look. 'Might be worth payin' for, at that.'

Lili picked up the bag from the seat beside her and said quietly to the youth in the doorway, 'Would you find me another compartment, please?' She started to rise but before she could do so the young man had reached into the carriage and grasped the smoker by his necktie. The older man half-rose and caught the youth's hands in his own, pulling him forward. Smaller and lighter, Lili's self-appointed defender punched him hard in the gut so the man grunted again, this time from pain. But he did not loose his hold. By now he was on his feet, and Lili saw that he was bigger than she had thought, six foot and more. He gave the youth a violent push, so that he staggered out of the carriage door, past the feet of the two seated men who had not yet had time to react: she was aware of their startled expressions, their instinctive recoil. Then the boy slammed hard against the corridor window, the back of his head striking the glass with a sickening soft thud and to her horror Lili saw his eyes turn up in his head so the whites showed as he crumpled on useless legs and slid slowly down the wall to the ground. The big man failed in his fury to understand that the youth was unconscious and hurled himself forward towards his victim, but by now the other two occupants of the carriage were on their feet, grasping his shoulders and upper arms to hold him, yelling at him to stop.

Lili was up too, pushing past the shouting men, struggling through to reach the boy on the ground. She stepped over his legs and crouched beside him. His eyes were half-open, his breathing stertorous: he was clearly in a bad way. She knew she should not move him. Tentatively she touched his hair, and her seeking fingers encountered warm wetness and came away stained red. She gasped with shock and glanced up. An attendant in uniform was coming through the door beside the observation platform and she called,

'Get a doctor. *Quick*. There's someone unconscious here.'

The attendant turned to obey, and she could see him pushing through the crowd that had materialized from nowhere, drawn by the commotion. In the carriage where she had been sitting, the two men had by now restrained the cigar-smoker, who was seated on the edge of a seat, head in hands. One of the men came out of the carriage. He could not shut the door because the boy's feet were in the way. He asked in a low voice, 'How does he seem to you?' and she shook her head.

'I don't know. He's bleeding heavily and . . .' she checked his wrist again, '. . . his pulse is irregular.' She stared anxiously at the boy's face. He was very young, his skin pale, his mouth slightly open beneath the narrow blond moustache so carefully cultivated: he could not be more than eighteen. As

377

she looked down at him, she saw an ominous little pool forming beneath his right ear, coating the dusty train floor with its brightness.

She heard Jane Martin's voice behind her, 'Oh Miss Lili, are you hurt?' and snapped, 'Of course not,' hearing the guilt sharp in her voice. It was her fault this boy was lying here, her fault this whole horrible little episode had taken place. He had tried to defend her honour. For what that was worth. Crouched there on the floor beside him, heedless of the dirt and discomfort, holding his limp hand in her own, she scarcely noticed the press of chattering people, the policeman who had arrived to survey the scene. Or the photographer who had set up his tripod on the platform to await her descent.

The young man was unconscious for three days and when he regained his senses had no recollection at all of the incident. Within two weeks the case was heard at a local court and the cigar-smoker convicted for a month.

But newspaper coverage of the case was out of all proportion to its importance or the seriousness of the crime: Lili's name was enough to ensure that. It had started with front page pictures of her on the platform, one cheek streaked with blood, hair tousled. And it went on for days. She was followed everywhere by reporters and was amazed to read comments she had never made, phrases taken out of context. 'Lili's Lover Laid Low', read one headline, and while she seethed at the imputation, there was nothing to be done. Lawyers assured her that protests would merely provide more fuel for her detractors. When she wanted to visit the injured boy in hospital, Louis Engels dissuaded her. 'Why give 'em more cause for scandal?' So instead she went to his family to apologize for her unwitting part in their son's accident. She spent an hour with them in their home in a Boston suburb, leaving them money towards hospital fees – and found yet another photographer lying in wait for her when she left: more pictures, more headlines.

'There's nothing you can do,' Louis reasoned. 'Scandal is what they feed on, and there's nothing newspapers love better than discovering it about someone successful. And if the person involved is a pretty woman, then it makes an even tastier morsel to fill their pages.' He paused and added drily, 'The theatre, however, is ecstatic at the publicity.'

Lili was in his office, just returned from Boston. Too fraught by recent events to sit still, she paced the room as Louis talked, so he had to swivel his chair to keep her in view. She was tired, eyes burning, her tightly drawn hair accentuating amber skin. He had always thought her a pretty woman, but now he saw as if for the first time that strong line of the muscular throat, the smooth, almost Oriental eyelids, the curve of her cheek. Even like this, anxious and distraught, her face and body had an arrogant elegance. Louis glanced down at his pudgy hands, the corpulent belly bursting from his waistcoat buttons: hard to believe he and she were fashioned by the same god. He reached out and caught her hand as she passed him, holding those slender, back-bent fingers, feeling her hand hard in his, not soft as a woman's should be. He said slowly, 'There are two kinds of women, Lili. Those that everyone talks about – and the kind that nobody does. Which would you rather be?'

'That boy might have died.' Her tone was sombre.

'Might. But he didn't. And you didn't ask him to take your part. Be reasonable, girl. Whatever you do, they'll write about it now. It's part of the price you pay for success.'

Lili pulled her hand from his and went to the door. With her hand on the knob she turned.

'I know you're right, Lou. But maybe the price is too high. And maybe it isn't the success I want. I always said I wouldn't be a showgirl, and I remember how furious you were with me. But all the same, people come to see me now from curiosity, not because of the way I dance. What that man said about me in the train is true – I take off my clothes for anyone to see. And what does that make me?'

Louis Engels sighed and shook his head. Lili closed the door.

She thought she would eventually have forgotten that incident. After all, the youth had recovered completely, and in time the newspapers lost interest. It certainly made no difference to her acceptability in the drawing rooms of New York, and the Eden Museum Theatre was pressing Louis Engels to consider extending her contract until the end of the year.

Over the summer Lili had become accustomed to walking in Central Park for an hour in the afternoons before going to the theatre and the first performance. She found it hard to believe the eight hundred acres in the middle of Manhattan had been rocky wilderness less than forty years before: now there were carriage roads and bridle paths, tangled woodland walks, a miniature zoo with monkeys and birds and on summer afternoons concerts would be held where hundreds of people gathered, sitting on benches and the grass to listen. Jane Martin usually accompanied her, but one day in late May when the girl had time off, Lili went alone.

She used the 72nd Street entrance, passed through the wisteria-hung pergola and down the steps. She crossed the quiet road to the lake, following the path north. At the mooring post, one of the swan boats was tied, waiting for passengers. The flat, narrow vessel carried three long slatted wooden seats, and a great white metal swan spread its wings in the stern. It was a muggy afternoon and as she paid the boatman her ten cents she noticed the only other passengers were a couple of women with three children. The boat had already begun to steer away from the bank when a man hailed it and sprang nimbly across the widening strip of water to jump aboard. The boatman sighed at his carelessness but accepted his money, and Lili noticed without interest that the passenger – a man in his late twenties – wore a distinctive cap, with a long peak.

The ride was a delight, and she gave herself up to the pleasure of sun on her face, the rocking movement of the light skiff, the sound of water and children's voices.

Children's voices. It had been months since she saw Simeon. His progress was reported to her in regular letters from Aunt Florence and Judith Mendoza. 'He has two more teeth. Yesterday Doris brought him round for tea, and he sat up at table like a little gentleman.' Doris reported more prosaically, in her rounded schoolgirl hand. 'Mr Mendoza said I was to buy summer clothes. I went like you did to Debenham and Freebody. Spent nearly ten guineas on little trousis and blouses. Simeon looks so handsome now, you would be proud.'

381

Lili carried the letters round with her, as she did a leather-framed photograph of the child. It was not enough, but better than nothing. She had accepted this enforced separation as the cost of her freedom, but that did not make it easier. Still, she got through the days without grieving too much until something small, like the children in the boat, brought back with piercing clarity her longing for her small son.

She stepped off the boat at the end of the ride, and walked back the way she had come, over the low curve of Calvert Vaux's bridge. She paused for a moment, shading her eyes to look across the bright water at the couples in their rowing boats, the women lying back against the leather cushions, the men with their jackets off and their sleeves rolled up. She loved this energetic city where the people had welcomed her. The bad moments – the trouble in Boston, the newspaper stories – were no more than minor irritations in retrospect. Just the same, she would not renew the contract. She must go home to Simeon.

She was concerned too, about her father. Like so many doctors, he refused to acknowledge his own ill-health. The years of unremitting work had taken their toll and she knew – though not from him – that he was growing frail. His rare letters to her were always shaky and occasionally illegible. The last one had been in a stronger hand, as he told her of his plans to visit the family in Egypt. Everyone was trying to prevent him, he wrote, Florence was furious. But he had set his mind on it. This would be his last visit, he knew that. The harsh London winter had made his bones ache, he needed an Eastern sun to warm him now. He was employing a companion, a young man who would assist him and take care of everything. He would be away for three months, no more. It had been arranged that Beatrice should go to Florence and Nathan Hartsilver, but then Joseph had offered to take her to Overstrand with Simeon for a few weeks. 'Strange,' he wrote, 'she responded so positively to this idea. Most unlike her, as you know. When I told her I preferred her to go to Portman House, she beat on the wall with her bare hands. In the end, of course, I gave in.' Here the writing wavered. 'I hope I did the right thing.'

Thinking of the letter, Lili gripped the low parapet of the bridge with her gloved hands. Beatrice. She could think of Simeon, if with pain. But she shut Beatrice out of her mind, afraid to admit to herself how cruel she was, to leave for so long the flawed and fragile woman who for all their lives had moved always in her wake. Her sister. Her shadow.

Reluctantly, Lili turned from the bridge to make her way to 72nd Street and a cab for the theatre. She quite failed to see the man in the peaked cap who had been patiently following her the whole afternoon.

Two days later she went to Benjamin Altman's recently completed department store on the northeast corner of Fifth Avenue and 34th Street. She like the Renaissance palace its founder had constructed, with the dolphin fountain at the entrance and the eighth-floor art gallery. That was in fact her destination, to buy a small painting as a gift for Louis Engels and his wife to celebrate a wedding anniversary.

She had been in the gallery for perhaps ten minutes, and had narrowed her choice to a couple of charming Dutch-style interiors in gilt frames. She was standing in front of them trying to make up her mind when something made her twist her head. The man who stood perhaps ten feet away to her left, apparently examining a bronze cat, was unremarkable and unknown to her. She was already turning away to speak to the salesman who was awaiting her decision when the man moved and she saw in his hand a distinctive cap with a long peak. She had seen it somewhere before. The salesman approached and spoke, and it dropped out of her mind.

The purchase completed, she went down to the lower floors. She was in no hurry, and wandered through to the furnishing fabric department for nothing more than the pleasure of looking at the designs and rich materials so lavishly displayed on wooden pedestals. As she examined stylized wallpapers and matching curtains in one of the Art Nouveau designs from the Silver Studio in London, a voice beside her piped, 'Miss Mendoza?'

The speaker was less than four foot high, a messenger boy in the store's livery, a pillbox on the side of his head. He held a letter in his hand, and a single red rose, which he presented with every formality.

'Thank you.' She was amused. 'How did you know who I was?'

The boy pointed behind him.

'The gentleman asked me to say that, Ma'am.'

They both looked, but no one was there. Lili drew off a glove and opened the letter, assuming it was from one of her admirers: she had received plenty of missives over the last months, declaring undying love. This one used the same phrases. 'I have watched you on the stage night after night ... your eyes have met mine across the lights, and I know what might be between us . . . you have my heart, and you must give me yours in return.' She scanned the page with growing concern. This letter was different. The writing disturbed her, the strokes falling haphazard, without direction, so thick they bit deep into the paper like black scars. With a jolt, she read the second half of the page.

'For weeks now I have followed you everywhere. I am with you when you leave your apartment, with you when you leave the theatre. When you ride on the swan boat, I sit behind you. You do not enter a cab without my knowing. No one visits your apartment without passing me. There is nothing I do not see. And when you sleep, I watch.'

Lili dropped the paper with a shudder. It was ridiculous to be upset by such a thing. He made no threats, it was probably not even true. But the idea that she was under the surveillance of an unknown watcher was horrible. The messenger boy thought she had dropped it in error and bent to retrieve it for her. She waved it away and then common sense asserted itself. She should tell someone about this, someone in authority. Louis would know what to do.

Louis Engels read it and patted her shoulder. Sure, he'd seen stuff like this before. An over-excited admirer was all, a guy had overstepped the boundaries of polite behaviour.

Lili eyed the letter in his hand, refusing to touch it as though the paper were contaminated.

'"And when you sleep, I watch." That's terrifying, Lou. Does he really mean it, that he can see when I'm asleep? It's so frightening.'

'Don't be silly, Lil. You're in your own apartment, the drapes are drawn, who can see if you don't want them to?' He drew on his cigar and thought for a moment. 'Why don't I have a word with the managing agents about security arrangements. And I think I'll do the same at the theatre. No sense in taking chances.'

Lili shook her head doubtfully.

'I don't know. I'd prefer to tell the police about it.'

'Oh sure.' Louis had an impressive line in sarcasm. 'Sure. You get letters every day of your life from people think you're wonderful. What makes this guy any different? So he's a little more imaginative. But he makes no threats, he doesn't want you to send him money . . . no, the police won't be interested. I'll take care of it.' He patted her knee. 'Leave it to Lou.'

An extra commissionaire duly appeared in the opulent foyer of the Dakota Building, and doormen at the Eden Museum Theatre made extra checks on fire-doors and stage-door entrants. Louis himself started to accompany Lili home on evenings when she was not going out straight from the theatre.

After two weeks, Lili had almost dismissed the letter as the work of a crank. Until the morning when Jane Martin brought in her breakfast on a tray and with it the morning's post. The fifth letter she opened had a handprinted envelope and the paper was in her hands before she recognized the heavy black lettering and flung it away from her unread. She summoned Jane, who picked it up from the floor and read it aloud. This time, the message was more hysterical.

'"If you do not agree to see me,"' Jane read out in a flat voice, '"I shall do something desperate."'

'Is that all he says?' Lili demanded.

Jane turned the paper over, perplexed.

'There's no signature, no name. What does he

386

want you to do? How could you answer, even if you wanted to?'

Lili pushed the breakfast tray aside.

'I don't know. But I'll feel safer at the theatre. And I'd better telephone Louis.'

At the second house that night, a large bunch of roses was delivered without a card. Jane Martin put them in water and stood them on the floor where Lili could see them when she came back to the dressing room, one of the ten or so bouquets she had received that evening. A little later, sitting swathed in the cashmere shawl, Lili asked Jane who the flowers were from. The girl read out the names, most of which were known to Lili. When she came to the roses she said, 'I don't know who these are from . . .' and then stopped short. The two women stared at each other, the same thought in both their minds. When Louis Engels knocked and entered, he found them both waiting to leave. Lili told him what had happened, pointing to the flowers. Louis nodded, then explained what he wanted them to do.

Ten minutes later he hurried the two women out of the theatre, to the unavoidable press of fans. On this occasion, Lili was as usual besieged by people who wanted to touch her, to obtain her autograph, to ask her for money. Usually she smiled, smiled, shook hands and gracefully signed the proffered pieces of paper. This time she kept her head down, her hair and face partly concealed by the cashmere shawl, and spoke to no one. Louis had organized the young 'Russians' whose spirited dancing preceded her own as the first part of the performance, and ten of them had linked muscular arms to make a cordon to get the two women through the throng. When they reached the waiting Cadillac at the kerb, Louis barked to the driver, who obediently extinguished the interior lights and was ready to accelerate away even before the door was closed.

'Nothing happened after all.' The speaker was Lili. She helped Jane Martin unwind the cashmere shawl from her shoulders and smiled. 'You didn't mind?'

'Not if it helped, Miss Lili. You look strange in my coat, though.'

The two women, dressed in each other's garments, were quiet for the rest of the journey. As they approached 72nd Street, Louis said, 'Put the shawl on again, Jane. Just in case.'

'You don't really think he'll be there, do you?' the girl appealed to him, nervous.

'I'm sure he won't. But it seems sensible to take no chances. No one in the crowd recognized Lili in that hat of yours, and if anything happens you're to pull the shawl down so he can see you're not the person he thinks.' Louis craned to see the eccentric turrets of the Dakota Building coming up on their left, and cursed softly: the great iron gates of the drive were closed. As the Cadillac halted the commissionaire, alerted by the horn, started across the gravelled driveway to open them. But the man who suddenly appeared from the shadow of the wall was quicker. He stepped in front of the motor, his back to the gates. In the headlights his face was a white mask with blank black eyes. He called Lili's name once in a voice hoarse with despair, put the barrel of the short gun he carried into his mouth and blew off the back of his head.

Chapter 19

'Look, look! Oh, can I go near them? Can I?'

Laughing, Lili let herself be towed along by an excited Simeon, knicker-bockered legs twinkling in his haste. They were in the Botanic Gardens at Regent's Park to watch the children's summer carnival. Liu Chan-Tu followed them carrying Simeon's coat and a hamper containing their lunch, which he would serve with every formality on the grass, his face seamed with satisfaction at seeing Mrs Mendoza united with her son again.

The four-year-old stood still in wonder, his mouth half-open, his eyes sparkling, as he took in the procession that was forming in the open air outside the many-windowed Palm Hall. Sturdy ponies were harnessed to low broughams, the entire ensemble garlanded with streamers of ribbons, flowers and sprays of greenery: even the spokes of the wheels had been lovingly decorated. The children wore flowers too, garlands of them wound round their waists and across their shoulders, bound into their hair and stuck into their caps. Simeon squeaked with excitement as a palomino pony with blooms tucked into his harness proceeded to eat the streamers of the large satin bow hanging from one twitching ear. A boy of about eleven pulled it away and some of the flowers fell to the ground. Simeon slipped his hand from his mother's and ran forward to help gather them up again. The boy spoke a few words and, red-faced with anticipation, Simeon ran back to her side.

'He says I can go with him, Mama. Oh please, do let me!'

A woman stepped forward.

'We'd be happy to take your boy with us. I'll be walking beside them and it's only for a half-mile. He'll be back in no time.'

Lili thanked the woman, and helped Simeon into a seat. Beaming, he waved to her with the odd little stiff-armed movement of very young children as the procession moved off. She watched until he was out of sight, then saw that Chan-Tu was hastening after the brougham in which Simeon sat, determined not to let the boy out of his sight.

Waiting for him to return she wandered amongst medicinal and water plants, gazing in through steamy glass at oranges and lemons crusting miniature bushes, at curious flowers perched locust-like on slender stems, at creepers that hung from high vaulted roofs, fine as a woman's hair – a giantess' hair – moon pale as her sister's. Beatrice. Ever since Lili had returned from New York, she had been amazed by her sister. She was still living in Hans Place, sleeping in Lili's room and looked after by Doris who, kind as she was, could not quite disguise a faint aversion for the beautiful woman with the blank face she felt had somehow taken her mistress' place. Beatrice looked well, though Lili thought her waist painfully small in the crêpe dress: no bigger than a child's. When she said (using words that last time had provoked a frenzied response), 'I'm back, Bee, I'm back,' her sister had met her eyes for a drawn-out moment before her gaze had moved on to the window. Wiser this time, Lili had gone on talking, to Doris and to Simeon. The little boy had some of Joseph's reserve, had watched her for the first ten minutes, right thumb in mouth, his left hand holding the lobe of his left ear in a characteristic pose he had always used for comfort, or falling asleep. Then he had made his arms wide, holding up his face for a kiss. She had held him then, tears standing in her eyes, giving in to the impulse to squeeze his sturdy little body against her own, sharply aware of how much she had missed him. She had pressed her face into his warm hair and when she had looked up, Beatrice was watching them both, her expression indecipherable as ever. Doris had tactfully left the room and Beatrice, as if taking her lead from the child, had moved across to Lili, standing beside her docile as a doll. Lili had risen, still holding Simeon's hand in hers, and put her other arm round Beatrice's shoulders. And then suddenly, incredibly, Beatrice was hugging her: Beatrice, who never showed joy, clinging as if she would never let go.

Lili could not believe the difference in her: she wished Samuel da Costa had been home, to discuss the change, but he was still in Egypt and even intended to stay longer than the proposed three months. Beatrice still did not speak – though this as always was not necessary between the two women, whose understanding of each other had not been impaired by Lili's absence – but she nonetheless took part in conversations now, watching the speaker's face intently as a lip-reader trying to decipher a new language.

It was as though for the first time in her life, Beatrice was really aware of other people. Lili remembered her father telling her many years ago,

'Beatrice thinks only you are real.' She had known it to be true. Her sister had treated human beings as if they were inanimate objects, of no more interest to her than a chair.

Lili made a point of visiting Hans Place occasionally during the day, when she knew Joseph would be absent. Following Woolf Lander's legal advice and her own instincts, she had no wish for a confrontation with Joseph. He had finally and reluctantly agreed that she could have Simeon with her twice a week, on Wednesday and Friday afternoons when Liu Chan-Tu brought him to the house she now occupied in Half Moon Street. But if, Joseph had warned, she started appearing in public in England, he would have to reconsider his permission.

This still meant that without going to Knightsbridge, she would not see Beatrice until her father returned home: an intolerable situation. So it happened that one afternoon she and Beatrice were sitting in the drawing room while Simeon played with his farm animals, when they heard the key turn in the lock and Joseph's voice in the hall. Lili was watching Simeon, who jumped to his feet to greet his father, when a small sound made her glance towards Beatrice whose pale face was not impassive as it had been a moment before, but lit with eagerness.

In the act of rising, Lili had stopped transfixed. So it was true, then, what she had felt and feared when she left Beatrice behind her in Overstrand that summer morning: her sister loved Joseph, and it was this unprecedented emotion which had brought about the change in her.

And then the door had opened and Joseph had entered. Lili had forced herself to speak calmly and exchange a few sentences before she could escape. Walking home, she found she could not bear the implications of her discovery. They were in each other's company a good deal, those two. Whatever malice she ascribed to Joseph, she could not believe he would love Beatrice in any way but as a brother. Then she had come to an abrupt halt in the middle of a crowded pavement so that people had bumped into her.

She had been walking past Hyde Park on the railing side, had moved across so she could hold on to them, so urgently did she need support, horror-struck at the possibility that here existed a love more strange and disturbing even than the relation-ship she had had with Joseph. Whatever that had been, they were man and wife. But Beatrice was defenceless as a child, needing protection. Lili had leaned against the railings. It had started to rain but she didn't notice, unaware of the drops that clung to her hair and the fur edging of her hooded cloak, unaware of the glances she attracted from passers-by, standing there beneath a gaslight, star-ing into her thoughts, her gloved hands clenched. An elderly woman stopped and touched her arm.

'Are you all right? Is something the matter?'

Lili looked down at the woman's hand on her sleeve, then up at the speaker. She shook her head.

'No, it's just . . . I just realized something. Thank you.'

She had started to walk towards the house in Half Moon Street, appalled by the realization that Joseph, for whom she felt such violent antipathy, was now responsible for the happiness of the two people in the world she loved most.

* * *

393

All this went through her mind now, as she watched the curious swaying creepers in the Botanic Gardens. With a sigh she turned away towards a white iron bench, to await Simeon. A woman was walking past her, parading a tiny toy dog, of the sort which had become increasingly fashionable. This one was a Chihuahua, a hairless, skinny creature with mournful eyes. Lili stood back to let them pass, quite failing to see that a second dog trotted behind. An agonized squealing informed her that she had trodden on the creature. She disliked these over-bred dogs intensely, but she couldn't bear to think she had hurt it: the dog was crouched on the ground emitting a horrible noise, while its owner, making very similar sounds, pressed a beringed hand to a heaving bosom. The second dog, meanwhile, ran in frantic circles so that its leash wound round Lili's legs: the whole scene rapidly became ridiculous as Lili tried without success to free herself so that she could attend to the wounded animal, and its mate yapped frantically round her ankles. The noise was appalling, people were stopping to watch, one or two tried to intervene. A man picked up the injured dog, while Lili apologized profusely, pink in the face from confusion, still inextricably entwined with the other wretched creature. A second man said, in a mercifully low voice, 'Hold still. I saw what happened, it wasn't your fault,' caught up the dog and walked round her to release the leash. Lili thanked him and hurried across to the woman, whose glare could have been no less malevolent had Lili attacked her baby.

'I'm so sorry, but I didn't see your dog ... he's so small. Is he all right?'

The woman was holding the injured animal now,

its right foreleg – no thicker than Lili's finger – seemed to be bleeding slightly.

'How *could* you? How could you be so careless? My poor Chi-Chi, someone must take us to a veterinarian. And you . . .' she favoured Lili with another basilisk stare, '. . . will be kind enough to meet his fee.'

'I will, of course.' Lili was by now quivering with annoyance. She fumbled in her bag, handed the woman a calling card. 'Please have the bill sent to me. I hope the dog recovers quickly.'

'No thanks to you if he does,' was the snappish reply. Lili started to move away, conscious suddenly of the number of interested onlookers the exchange was attracting. The woman shrilled something after her, and then a man's voice – it sounded like the one who had untangled her from the leash – spoke.

'Madam, I assure you it wasn't the lady's fault but a genuine accident. I saw it all. You mustn't blame her, she simply didn't notice your pet.'

Lili was close enough to hear the woman's reply. In a quite different tone, suddenly affable and surprisingly coy, she said, 'Why, Mr Falconer, isn't it? Well, if you say it was an accident, then of course you must be right. How kind of you to involve yourself in my little trouble!'

Amazed, Lili glanced back, to see the woman beaming up at a tall figure in a lichen corduroy suit, the sort of clothes usually worn in the country, topped with a soft-brimmed hat. He was examining the injured paw now, reassuring the woman, who continued to smile beatifically at him.

'. . . such *great* admirers of your work, Mr Falconer, both of us . . .'

Lili wondered vaguely who he could be: the name

was familiar, but she was too flustered by events to place it. She hesitated, wondering whether to interrupt the woman's flow of words to thank him, but then heard Simeon calling her name as he hurried towards her, his hand firmly grasped by Chan-Tu. With the child's excited chatter, the incident passed out of her head.

As it did from that of the tall man in the suit of lichen corduroy, who had on his mind a matter so weighty it was by now giving him a very bad headache. With difficulty he detached himself from the voluble woman and her unattractive animal and continued on his way.

The Botanic Gardens were usually a deserted enough spot on a mid-week afternoon, provided one missed the musical promenades, but today the place was thronged with children, whom he liked well enough but knew nothing about, and their voices shrilled through his brain so that the soothing benefits of the place – the customary calm, the green gloom – were quite lost. He waited to see if the children, their attendants and their ponies were about to depart, and when it became apparent that some sort of prizegiving was to take place, he took himself off.

He walked for a while along the path that cut through the centre of the park, enjoying the shade of ancient elms, then his eye was taken by a particularly pleasing composition: a slope of grass leading to a stretch of water, beyond it one of the park's white stucco Nash villas set against a backdrop of flowering chestnuts. He sat down, the better to appreciate it, and after ten minutes or so the wine he had taken at luncheon combined with the heat and his headache to suggest that he lean his back against a useful stump, fold his arms, tip his hat over his face and concentrate on his thoughts with his eyes closed.

When he awoke, it was to hear a child's voice singing. His thoughts had clearly done him good, because the sound no longer grated but rather charmed him. It wasn't a tune he knew – something foreign, he fancied, that somehow brought to mind orange groves and minarets – and when he opened his eyes he saw that a group of three people had seated themselves further below him on the slope. One was the singing child, absurd in his sailor suit. A little behind him sat a most curious figure so that for a moment Falconer took him to be in fancy dress until he turned and his features revealed him as the genuine article. A Chinaman in a red silk coat and baggy black trousers, with a narrow drooping moustache, was a most unlikely inhabitant of this impeccably English landscape. Yet there he was, and clearly very comfortable in it.

The third person was a woman, executing on the grass – and in bare feet – a dance for the child. Unless he was much mistaken, it was the woman who'd tripped on the wretched dog an hour before; he'd been rather taken then by the fact that she wore no hat, and her heavy hair was bound back by a narrow ribbon. He shifted a little, and thought to himself that she moved well. No, by God, she moved beautifully, she was like a swallow, swooping and turning in her pale dress, utterly free yet trailing the child's melody with her. It struck him that she was almost like a musical instrument herself, so perfectly did she transmit the melody to him. She must be a professional dancer, surely: no amateur would move with such control. He screwed up his

eyes against the sun and looked at her more carefully, and then he was sure he was right: the taut
body, shoulders a touch muscular for her torso, was
that of a highly trained athlete. Who could she be?
The only name he could remember was that Isadora
Duncan. She danced barefoot, but he understood she
favoured a Greek classicism which did not appeal to
his taste. This woman's movements owed nothing to
any school he recognized, though there was something of the Orient in the way she held her arms
with those expressive hands. He'd ask his wife,
when he got home, she followed that kind of thing
with more interest than he.

Falconer withdrew his gaze and turned his mind
back to his own very considerable problem, but his
thoughts were interrupted when the child stopped
singing and he and the Chinaman both applauded
enthusiastically. Glancing towards them, he saw
that the woman was standing quite still, without
any attempt at a curtsey, accepting their applause
as of right, knowing she had earned it. He smiled to
himself, liking the quiet arrogance she displayed,
the lack of humility. She knew what she was worth.
That, combined with the dark hair and eyes, made
him think she was not English: an English woman
would have blushed and bobbed.

It came to him suddenly: Lili Mendoza. Of course,
that's who it was. He'd been reading about her only
the other day in the *Tatler*, and her photograph had
appeared in the *Sketch*. She had broken a contract
to appear in New York following a man's death in
her apartment, was that it? Apparently she had
decided she would never dance in public again. After
what he'd just seen, that would be a pity. But now
he thought of it, there'd been another scandal, two

men fighting over her. She was clearly no more than a trollop. But that conclusion was oddly at variance with the clarity of her dancing. And he had been struck by the dignity with which she had comported herself when that woman had been screaming at her. Nothing provocative there, even while he'd been unwinding the dog's leash from her skirt: she had turned upon him a distracted gaze, soft and sombre. Hard to believe anything discreditable about a woman who could look at you like that. Still, there was no smoke without a fire.

Falconer reached into his pocket for his pipe and the leather pouch in which he kept the mild tobacco sent over especially from Amsterdam. Concentrating on filling and tamping and lighting, he did not notice that the group below him had gathered themselves up and were now nearly upon him, the woman holding the boy's hand and looking down into his eyes with an expression of such tenderness that he felt a lump in his throat. If only he and his wife had had a child. How different life would have been for them.

He had not meant to stare, but Lili felt his gaze and glanced incuriously across at the long figure in the corduroy suit lolling on the grass. When she realized it was the man who had rescued her earlier, she halted. The woman with the dogs had acknowledged him with some excitement: 'Why, Mr Falconer.' But Lili still could not identify him. Holding Simeon's hand in hers, she crossed the slope towards him.

'I owe you my thanks,' she said simply, when she was about ten feet away. 'You were very kind.' She had meant to say something else, but his eyes met hers and she could only think, how blue they are, they must be blue right back inside his head.

He got to his feet. She may be no lady, but that was hardly an excuse for ungentlemanly behaviour. He removed his hat and in an unthinking gesture ran a hand through the dark blond hair streaked with silver which he wore over-long, due more to a reluctance to spend time at the barber than to vanity.

'It was nothing,' he said, 'I would have done the same for anyone.' Damn it, that sounded rude. But she did not seem discomposed as she inclined her head and moved off, very correct and formal, another being entirely from that sinuous dancer he had observed with such astonished pleasure. He watched the odd little party walk away beneath the elms, the woman and the child utterly absorbed in each other, the attentive Chinaman a few steps behind.

He seated himself on the tree-stump to smoke his pipe and continue his meditations, but for some reason it had become hard to concentrate. Quite soon, he stood up. He would catch the next train home to Bath.

Charles Falconer had the face of an adventurer, the morals of a church dignitary and the strong and clever hands of the musician he was. He had become a minor public figure by the time he was in his late thirties, much admired for the quality of his music – huge canvases of audible colour on which he painted the infinite variety of England's countryside as no one had before. In a country where social boundaries had never been so distinct, so separate, he crossed them with ease. He was able, charming, urbane. He had not made enough money to be arrogant, nor so little as to be bitter. An indefatigable worker, he had scant interest in maintaining an active social life, though the combination of his exceptional talent and excellent manners made him welcome among the rich and great, but it would have bothered him not at all had they forgotten him entirely. Such a possibility was unlikely, to say the least. He was tall – well over six foot – with a beak of a nose that only a man of his height could have supported without embarrassment. The extraordinary eyes of piercing blue that had struck Lili so forcibly were lit with intelligence beneath brows that gave a sardonic tilt to the upper half of his face, hinting at something raffish and sybaritic that was apparently at odds with his character. He wore a moustache heavy enough to balance the determined square jaw and partly obscure his mouth. And this, had one been able to see it, would have revealed him to be a profoundly unhappy man.

He had been born to a middle-class family with no musical interest beyond acquiring sufficient skill to play the piano which stood, covered with a velvet runner and several well-used pieces by Bach, Mozart and Handel, in one room of the shabby gentleman's residence on the outskirts of Bath. His father was a solicitor, a grumpy man with unlikely habits for a member of so conventional a profession. He would frequently refuse to speak to his family for weeks on end, shutting himself in his study (a room he kept always locked) and often sleeping there. Only much later did the family learn of his involvement with another woman.

Cecily Falconer put up with his behaviour for several years. When she could stand it no longer, she abandoned her husband and sought refuge with her father-in-law. The serene old man was an archdeacon in the city, attached to the Palace of Wells, and he radiated goodness and a love of God so strongly that the small Charles thought of him always as being illumined by a halo of light like the pictures in religious books. Old Falconer could not begin to comprehend his son's behaviour, and while he willingly protected his daughter-in-law from it, at no time did he utter any condemnation. He never had, believing that young people should be allowed to grow as naturally as plants. In his son's case, this had possibly contributed to an unfortunate outcome. But in Charles he had his justification.

Cecily Falconer, née Harrington, had no family within reach. Her father had followed the family tradition of service to their country, going out to India with his regiment. Like so many of the Harringtons, he had met a violent death, in his case at Rawal Pindi, leaving a widow – mercifully in England at the time – and two small daughters to whom he had never been more than a portrait of a handsome, high-nosed, ever-young officer in the uniform of an adjutant with Prince Albert's Somersetshire Light Infantry. Neither of his daughters resembled him in looks or temperament. But Charles, as his mother frequently remarked, might have been a reincarnation of his grandfather.

Except for the music. That gift was his alone and had come, Grandfather Falconer often said, straight from God. He employed the best teacher he could find for the piano and later, when that was mastered, Charles moved on to the violin and, by the time he was seven, the clarinet also. For hour after hour, throughout his childhood, he would practise one or other instrument, and it seemed to him his grandfather was always there, listening intently, nodding like the metronome, encouraging him by his loving presence, as a gardener will nurture promising seedlings. Even when Cecily died – too young, in her late thirties, the final tragedy in a life beset by misfortune – Charles was protected by his grandfather from the worst of his grief, sustained by his love and faith. The two became even closer. They understood each other perfectly and were always together: walking through the town, attending concerts, shopping. People smiled to see them together, hand in hand, the small boy's face upturned to the old man.

John Falconer had meantime married, predictably, the woman with whom he had for many years deceived his wife. He was happy enough to leave his son in his father's care. Charles's relationship with him became easier as the years went by until, in his twenties, he found it possible to be cordial to the taciturn man who had fathered him, but who had given so little of himself.

When Falconer was seventeen, his passionate affair with music won him a scholarship to an eminent Oxford college. There, too, he was happy, revelling in the opportunities to expand his limited horizons, striding to and from his lodgings with his short gown flapping from his shoulders, those far-seeing traveller's eyes of his fixed on sights well beyond his immediate destination. He had begun to look by now like an adventurer – his Harrington legacy – but his were voyages not of the body but of the imagination. He was full of dreams in those days, dreams of what he would achieve, of the music he would create, was already creating.

In the five years after graduating he played with one or two good orchestras and began to publish short pieces. At first, his grandfather paid for the printing (one of the few indulgences he allowed himself). Then a music publisher decided to invest in him, gave £100 advance – a fortune to Falconer – and let him have his head. The result, two years later, was *Symphony of a Green Country*, and it set the music world alight with excitement at its breadth and beauty. His music lauded England, its downlands and dales, forests and foaming seas. And through it all ran recollections of tunes from childhood, part of the country folklore, echoes of melodies old as the landscape itself.

Despite his success now as a composer – and increasingly as a conductor – for a long time he did not earn enough to maintain his own establishment. Not until he was thirty-one did he marry and then he chose a distant cousin on his mother's side, a delightful creature with transparent skin and innocent eyes. Within a year she was expecting their first child but could not carry it to term. The second she lost also, and after the fourth attempt her health failed her. By the time she was thirty, Beth Falconer was an invalid spending much of her time upon a chaise longue in the conservatory in the house Grandfather Falconer had left them in Bath. She suffered from headaches and attacks of faintness. Charles worked in a nearby room, where she could hear the piano, and always sought her comments and criticisms, for they were very close. Only sometimes, coming home after a trip to London to work with an orchestra on a new piece, perhaps, he would stand in the doorway of his own house and his nostrils would tighten at the indefinable odour of illness he so hated, compounded of close air and the flowers of camphor she took steeped in hot water to stimulate her heart. He was always particularly tender towards her on such occasions, gripped by guilt that he had unwittingly caused her suffering, for who else was to blame? There were times when he detested his own potency, for it was his never-to-be-born children which had ruined her health.

By now, Charles and Beth Falconer had become man and wife virtually in name only, both of them terrified by her weakness and the awful results their lovemaking had already had on their lives. Near celibacy suited Beth. She was a religious woman, and if things had turned out differently, she had often thought she would have liked the measured tranquillity of the cloistered life. She loved Charles deeply, but it seemed to her now that she loved him with more than her body: she loved him with all her soul.

She scarcely missed their former physical intimacy, illness draining her of desire. She was grateful to Charles for his abstinence and lacked sufficient imagination to comprehend just what such deprivation might mean to him. And he would not for his life have let her guess the depths of his despair. He had always taken care of Beth and he would continue to do so, and this included protecting her from himself.

Charles Falconer sometimes had the bizarre feeling that he was two entirely different people. One was the kind and considerate husband who would on no account force himself upon an ailing wife. And the other was the man whose face he saw daily in his shaving-glass, with the far-seeing eyes and hooked nose of one born to conquest, to impose his will upon others, the man with the sardonic eyebrows which gave him the look of a pleasure-loving hedonist. For months at a time the first man was uppermost, sensible and sensitive. But every so often that second man demanded recognition, and then Falconer suffered bitterly from his self-imposed celibacy.

For never, in his married life, had he betrayed his wife. His religious convictions would alone have been enough to prevent any infidelity, however brief. But beyond that he had the memory of how his mother had suffered from his father's perfidiousness. He would not see Beth endure that, whatever the cost to himself.

So in his mid-thirties, in the prime of his life, Falconer poured all his passion and pain into his work. On long evenings when he could have lifted his head and howled like a dog at the moon from sexual frustration, he sat at his piano and wrote music that seared the heart.

By the time he was in his early forties, he and Beth had lived for more than ten years as brother and sister. As his fame steadily grew, he met many women who clearly wished to improve upon first acquaintance, but he treated them all with the quiet courtesy that he showed everyone, man or woman, young or old. He never allowed himself to be approached, he seemed proof against them. It was understood that he was deeply in love with his wife. And while this was true, no one realized that trapped beneath the smooth and polished exterior lay something they would rather not see, a raw desperation that lacerated his spirit.

Falconer lived like a man suspended over a crevasse: if he allowed himself a single move in the wrong direction, he knew he would be lost. At the same time, he acknowledged that he did some of his best work when most tormented, and the irony of this never ceased to amaze him, that so rich a stream could flow from such sterile ground. He often thought he would rather not have had success, it had cost him too dear. But it had come anyway: there was even talk of a knighthood soon. He had only just learned that three hours ago, over luncheon at Verrey's in Regent Street, where a Private Secretary had booked their table, questioned him discreetly and intimated that only his assent was required ... When they parted, Falconer had decided not to go home immediately, as he had earlier intended. He needed to turn over in his mind the implications of acceptance. He had neither wanted nor sought such recognition and his impulse was to refuse. He did not think he liked the idea of becoming a member of the establishment, he felt the honour to be more of a penalty than a distinction. On the other hand, he knew how much it would mean to Beth, how it would gratify her to know his talents were recognized. And he would be a fool to deny that it would aid his worldly prosperity.

Falconer strode up Regent Street, oblivious to the graceful curves of All Saints Church on the corner of Langham Place, to the stately porticoes of Portland Place. Unseeing, he crossed the handsome Nash terrace of Park Crescent, heading for Regent's Park, seeking instinctively a green and quiet place where he could collect his thoughts. Pausing on a hunched bridge over a stagnant pool, marsh flowers

at its edge reminded him of a favourite spot he had
not visited for years. He would go there, just for an
hour. He turned and followed the path that would
lead him to the Botanic Gardens.

And to Lili.

Chapter 20

Hands on hips, Moura stood in the doorway, foot tapping in time to the music, eyes narrowed in concern.

The attic was a good practice room and one of the main reasons Lili had bought the house in Half Moon Street. Then it had been a maid's bedroom, containing a broken iron bedstead and a washstand. Lili had it painted white and the wooden floor sanded pale, the same colour as the long *barre* that now ran along the far wall.

Lili was leaning against it now, hands behind her back, eyes closed, absolutely still as she absorbed the sounds issuing from the phonograph. She was not dancing: so far as Moura knew, she had never danced in this room, nor in any other since her return to England.

Moura blew out her breath in a sigh. In her stillness, Lili seemed to her like a bird trapped under a net, unable to release her energy. She could not bear waste of any sort, and the waste of talent least of all. She did not see how – day after day, week after week – Lili could deny herself the pleasure and relief she found in her dancing.

She understood that Lili was, before everything, a performer. What had started out as a childish need to be appreciated had become a consuming passion. The love affair with her public had deepened into the overwhelming emotion of her life. Whether she knew it or not, the older woman reflected, the adulation, the applause, was a drug without which Lili could not survive for long.

Moura wished she could have seen Lili on stage during the months in New York when she had the city literally at her feet. She could imagine, though, the fire in those performances, the emotional giving across the footlights to that dark mass of waiting people. It was incredible that she should voluntarily reject it all. Moura knew about the unhappy man who had killed himself in front of her limousine that night – the ostensible reason for Lili's sudden retirement. But she thought it must be something more than that. Perhaps there had been a relationship in New York that had turned sour? But Lili was not usually secretive: over their years together, she had confided in Moura. Who knew, for instance, about the episode with the clarinettist and the enigmatic Schaeffer in New York?

Moura had accepted these revelations as they were given; as a sort of confession, and had found them more sad than wicked, revealing as they did a side of Lili that was strangely immature. Watching Lili now, the scarf round her head striking white against the dark hair, it occurred to her that this perplexing woman found it easy to offer everything to an audience, yet hard to accept that love on a personal level was also a matter of giving herself totally, but to one person only. Perhaps, thought Moura with a flash of insight, perhaps love would always elude Lili.

As though she felt the other woman's thoughts, Lili opened her eyes.

'What's wrong? You look as if you lost a shilling and found sixpence.'

Moura smiled, an oblique little grimace.

'No. I lost a star and found – well, what *have* I found? You're like a racehorse without a track. You can't mean to go on like this, surely? You've been back in England for months now, you've turned down offers from every theatre management in London. What are you waiting for?'

Lili stood up, shaking her feet, loosening the ankles, the calf muscles.

'I told you. I told the newspapers. I'll never dance in public again.'

Moura glanced outside the door to see if either of the servants were around, then kicked it shut. She sat down on the floor.

'I'm not suggesting you should accept any of the offers you've had. Only you *cannot* waste everything you've done because of what happened in New York.'

Lili was looking at her with a horrified look on her face.

'You're not to speak of it. *Please.*'

'I must. *You* must. Lili, for five months I've kept quiet. For five months I've watched you shutting your mind to everything but Beatrice and the boy. You make sure there is no single moment when you're not busy. But you cannot go on like this: you must face facts, and see that it wasn't your fault. There was nothing you could have done for that man. You have to understand that you did not cause his death.'

Lili rested her back against the wall, hands behind her waist.

'But I did. I did cause it. You didn't see what happened that night, did you? You didn't see his face and the blood, you didn't see what was spattered over the railings. . . .'

Moura waited patiently until Lili was finished.

'You never told me everything, from the beginning. Why not tell me now? Start with the first letter.'

Lili drew a shuddering breath.

'You don't want to hear.'

'Yes, I do. I want to hear because it might help you.'

So Lili described all the events that had led up to the man's suicide: how he had followed her, the letters, the fear, the flowers. In a flat voice she told how he had never signed his letters nor given any address. 'If he'd done that, Louis said we could have sent the police round, got help to him before he . . .'

Moura said gently, 'He's not the first man to kill himself over a woman he could never have, and he won't be the last.'

'At the inquest they said he was twenty-six years old, and the only support of his widowed mother. She sat there all through, staring straight ahead of her, looking as if she couldn't believe it.' There were tears in Lili's voice.

'You mustn't blame yourself.'

'How can I not? You read the articles in the newspapers, you saw them. Night after night, they wrote, I deliberately provoked lustful thoughts with my dancing.'

Moura shook her head.

'Nonsense. One idiot of a critic, that's all. But we both know you mustn't do a . . .' she hesitated for a fraction of a second, '. . . a sensational act again. You have to go back to your *real* routines, the ones you worked so hard to perfect.'

'Easy to say. But you know very well I never got anywhere doing those dances: they weren't what people wanted.' She traced a circle on the dusty floor

412

with her toe. 'They're not going to book me at Dalys or the Empire or the Gaiety dancing to Strauss and Ravel.'

'Do you remember,' Moura said thoughtfully after a moment, 'what Leonie Samson said, about having music written specially for you? I think we should find someone who could do that.'

Lili paused in the act of pulling round her shoulders the creamy cashmere shawl she kept draped on the end of the *barre*: Moura recognized the familiar, comfort-seeking gesture. Then with abrupt, jerky movements she slammed the window down and closed the phonograph.

'I told you,' she said with finality. 'I'm never going to dance in public again. So what's the point?'

Moura got up and opened the door.

'Then why,' she asked, her tone very quiet, 'why, my dear, do you spend so much time in this room?'

Lili stared round the room in which she had tried to re-create the Sloane Square attic where Madame Cotin had taught two little girls the rudiments of ballet.

'Because,' she admitted reluctantly, 'I can't bear to stay away.'

The Wigmore Hall was far from full despite Judith Mendoza's best efforts. Her protégé Leonid Gluzman, the Russian *émigré* pianist who had accompanied Lili's appearance at Hampstead Town Hall three years before, was playing Stravinsky. Sitting beside Moura in the centre of the hall, Lili reflected that his performance was remarkable. She knew from Judith that it was only his frail health that had denied Gluzman a more successful career: he was unable to stand up to the rigours of continual

413

concerts or the touring involved. His talent was attested by the number of other musicians whose faces Lili recognized among the audience.

Beside her, Moura wondered whether his playing would inspire Lili to dance again. She glanced surreptitiously at the younger woman, but she seemed utterly serene, wrapped in her grey hooded cloak, hands palm up in her lap. Odd, Moura reflected, how someone so elegant unconsciously adopted the pose of a peasant. Lili worked with her body — like farmers, or fishermen — and when she relaxed it was as they did, without thinking or caring how she looked. Moura had seen old Italian women sit like that, outside their houses, legs planted firmly on the ground, tranquil as black cats in the afternoon sun.

When the concert was over the two women walked across to Judith Mendoza, who peered anxiously at Lili as she kissed her.

'I've hardly set eyes on you since you got back to London. You turn down my invitations, lock yourself away in that attic of yours for hours on end. You're avoiding me.'

Lili linked her arm affectionately through Judith's and patted her hand, the little claw fist expensively encased in suede. Not for the first time, Judith thought that Lili was the only person to whom her deformity mattered not at all, and the familiar guilt gripped her: if only she could undo some of the unhappiness for which she felt so responsible. She went on, concern sharpening her tone, 'You're very quiet. Too quiet. Are you brooding?'

Lili shook her head but did not answer the question. Judith and Moura exchanged a meaningful

414

glance: they were more than worried by the melancholy in her face, increasingly noticeable ever since her return from New York, the withdrawn and guarded state so uncharacteristic of a woman by nature vivid and spontaneous: it was as though a light had been extinguished.

'Come and speak to Leonid,' Judith urged, leading the way across to the pianist. He was standing beside the Steinway, a coat draped round his shoulders, talking excitedly to two men. As the women approached, they turned politely and the Russian beamed.

'Dear ladies,' he exclaimed in his formal fractured English, stepping forward and grasping Lili's hand and Moura's in his own. 'Dear ladies, how good of you to grace my evening.'

They assured him – and meant it – that he had been superb, and he glowed at their praise.

'Allow me to introduce my friends,' he said, and the men at his side turned politely. 'Miss Mendoza, Lili, Moura – may I present John Hale and Charles Falconer?'

It was only Judith – always the bystander, never the participant, and therefore all the more observant – who perceived that this was not the first meeting for Lili and the tall man in the black velvet jacket rather too informal for the occasion. He was regarding Lili with bewildered recognition followed by something else that passed across that brigand's face too swiftly for Judith to recognize. Lili, for her part, seemed as if she had been poleaxed: what was wrong with the girl? Then Judith, too, looked at those arresting eyes, set square as chunks of aquamarine, and thought wryly that any woman would have to be made of stone to remain indifferent to such a man. She could not know that Lili was furious with herself for failing to recognize the composer of music she both admired and loved, discomfited by her lack of awareness and the recollection that he had seen her in the park doing that ridiculous childish dance for Simeon. Another woman would have flushed; Lili spread her long, back-bent fingers in a gesture that said, clearer than words, *what must you think of me*?

There was a moment of tension between the two of them so tangible that Lili felt it as a finger stroking the back of her neck. Then he took an involuntary step back from her like a man moving away from a source of unnecessary heat, averting his head slightly so that Judith could no longer see his expression.

At her side, Moura murmured something in a low, urgent voice. Judith listened carefully. After a moment she nodded.

'You will dine with me,' Leonid Gluzman was saying, his open arms inviting them all. 'It will give me so much happiness.'

Judith demurred, protesting that they did not really want her, but allowed herself to be persuaded and it was decided they would walk to dining rooms in Cavendish Square. Judith passed through the glass doors of the Hall into Wigmore Street and beckoned with an imperious finger as Falconer emerged.

'Young man, there's something I should like to put to you.'

With his customary good manners, Falconer shortened his long stride to walk beside her, head bent slightly to hear.

* * *

416

At dinner, in the long room where maroon and gilt walls were covered with drawings and autographs of artists, opera singers and actors, Lili and Charles Falconer were seated at opposite ends of the table. When the first course arrived, it proved to be fat spears of asparagus soaked in butter, which Lili had not ordered, but she would not spoil Leonid's party by sending the plate back. The others started eating with some delight, for the dish was still an extravagant rarity. She had eaten it once before, at Trouville, while Joseph had told her that Julius Caesar loved asparagus, and Louis XIV insisted on a year-round supply from hotbeds. Then Joseph's voice had changed subtly as he described how asparagus produced male and female flowers on different plants.

'But just occasionally,' he had said, 'it puts forth hermaphrodite blossoms.' He had paused for a moment. 'It is said to be an aphrodisiac – scarcely surprising, considering its shape.' He had pushed the delicate spears about on his plate. 'Boy soprano asparagus, do you suppose?' She had not known what to say and recalled the little shudder his words had evoked. She had not finished that plate of asparagus, much as she had liked the taste. Now she set down her fork, leaving the vegetable untouched, a wave of despondency breaking over her without warning.

In America, she had escaped from Joseph. Not distance but success had freed her as nothing else could have done. Then she had come home because of that pointless suicide, and she still could not overcome the jerky horror of the figure trapped in the headlights, staring at her with blank black eyes. And now her success was soured, she did not want it, she would not reach out to take what was being offered her by London theatres: how could she perform if that death had been caused by her dancing? At the same time she felt obscurely that Joseph counted it a victory for himself. He seemed to believe that she had taken his threat to heart, when he had told her she would never see Simeon again if she persisted with the stage: his expression on the rare occasions when they saw each other told her as much.

The man on her left said something to her, she didn't catch the words. She turned to him with a bright smile – a professional smile – and he, not recognizing the performer's gift of pleasing, talked happily on, unaware that though her dark eyes were fixed on his face, her thoughts were elsewhere.

And across the table, distanced from the convivial talk, Charles Falconer also sat in silence, his mind far away, worrying about Beth and the faint fever she had been running when he left home that morning. She was well looked after, but he must get back before midnight. He pulled out his grandfather's gold half-hunter and tried to look at it unobtrusively in the palm of his hand. When he glanced up, the Mendoza woman was watching him with those long eyes of hers, that made him think, as her dancing had, of countries where sand was hot to the touch and strange fruits hung on glossy trees.

The older woman – Judith – most surprisingly had asked him to write music for her young relative. He had been politely noncommittal. He did not generally take such commissions, he was anyway very busy, he would think about it. He did not tell her that he had already spent hours at the piano where he composed, attempting to recapture the atmosphere Lili had evoked with such nonchalant ease on the park grass. It had so far evaded him, that elusive, Eastern quality she had. Perhaps it was too foreign for him, and he too English to interpret it. He wondered what she was thinking, eyeing him like a little sphinx across the table. He returned her look, noting the way one hand held the wrist of the other, tapering fingers curving back at the tips like exotic flowers. She had a disturbing intensity, he decided, with her dark liquid eyes and that feeling she gave him of being perpetually poised for movement, a wild creature in the company of domesticated herbivores. She was probably a neurotic. He made up his mind on the spur of the moment that he would refuse Judith Mendoza's request.

Lili had, in fact, been wondering why Falconer looked so sad. She had thought at first it was the black coat that made her think this, but when she considered the matter she decided it was the set of his mouth beneath his moustache, the slight sideways curve of his lips as if he were suppressing something that hurt him. The rest of his face made a very different statement: those far-seeing eyes, the hooked nose, belonged in portraits she had seen when the tutor Florence Hartsilver employed had taken her round London galleries, and she had gazed in uncertain admiration at high commissioners, imperialists and governors of distant lands, magnificent in tropical suits, gold braid and their own importance. She found it extremely difficult to realize that this was the composer of the masterly and moving *Symphony of a Green Country*.

She would have liked to talk to him, but he

appeared so aloof she was intimidated. Like everyone else, she decided ruefully, he had doubtless heard all the lurid stories about her. She was well aware of the censure she had attracted, particularly among the more conservative sections of society, and on the whole managed to remain indifferent to it. Occasionally, though, she was brought face to face with the realization that people relished the scandal; it caused far more interest in England than her dancing had ever done. Falconer did not appear to be interested at all. There was nothing on his face when he looked at her but a kind of polite boredom and an anxiety which kept him glancing at his watch. Very soon, before dessert was served, he excused himself, clapped Leonid Gluzman on the shoulder, bowed to the ladies and bounded up the steps of the dining rooms into the foyer like a man with an assignation.

In the spring of 1910, Joseph informed Lilith (he was the only person now who so addressed her) that he would be taking Simeon to Overstrand for a long summer. He proposed, he added, to take Beatrice also, since it appeared that Dr da Costa would not be home for some weeks at least. Lili received the stilted letter by the breakfast mail: by eleven o'clock she was in Hans Place with Beatrice. She could not stop Joseph taking his son if he wished, but she would not let Beatrice go if there was the slightest hint from her sister that she was being coerced.

She knelt on the floor by her sister's chair.

'Bee, Joseph says he is taking you to the house at Overstrand. Do you want that? You can stay with me – I *want* you to stay with me. There is no need to go, if you don't like the idea.'

Beatrice looked down at Lili's hand holding hers and stroked the narrow fingers tenderly. There was, Lili thought, an imperceptible nod of her head.

'You want to go with Joseph?'

The hand tightened on her own, and in its soft pressure Lili read affirmation.

'All right then.' She was still doubtful. 'If you're sure.' She did not often wish that Beatrice was like other people, that she could speak, but now she would have given anything to be convinced she read her sister right. Even when they had packed and gone, and Liu Chan-Tu had cleaned and closed the house and followed them, she still worried. Perhaps she should see how things were in Overstrand? She convinced herself she must go. And then, decision made, she could not face it, could not make that journey beneath the low sky, nor endure the sight of the little mound of green beneath the pear trees. She could not go back to that painful place and she could not forget it: after Simeon and Beatrice had been gone a week, the memories came back, and night after night she woke drenched with sweat, teeth clenched in terror and eyes wide, seeing again the concealing corn, the crumbling cliff and something falling, falling . . .

Judith Mendoza grew increasingly concerned about her. She attempted to enlist Florence Hartsilver's help, but the aunt viewed Lili's withdrawal with some relief: at any rate she would not be shaming the family any further. Florence expected everyone in her circle to behave according to her own high standard of propriety. She was by nature kindly, but so conventional that she appeared intolerant. She had been horrified by the reports of Lili's American 'exhibitions' as she referred to them, and had spent anxious hours trying to persuade Samuel da Costa to bring the girl home. He and Nathan had infuriated her, refusing to see how badly Lili's actions reflected on them all.

Judith Mendoza, on the other hand, had long ago learned that appearances mattered to other people, not to her. She had been forced by her deformity beyond the bounds of 'acceptable' behaviour; the life of a single, ageing woman in affluent married circles was less than congenial. She never forgot that marriage had been forbidden by her parents in case any child inherited her 'blemish', and she had always known that it was the censure of others they feared. So she had fashioned a life for herself where status was less important than sympathy. Among the Bohemian group of artists and musicians she befriended, she was regarded as a generous eccentric. Among Florence's friends, she remained, for all her money and intelligence, an object of pity.

Judith identified with Lili in a way that she had with no other being in all her life. Though her logical mind might mock, telling her that never, under any circumstances, would she have had Lili's talent or looks, still the girl was everything she had ever dreamt of being. Even now, with Lili so downcast, Judith envied her the swift and graceful movements, the warmth that made it possible for the younger woman to hold the claw hand from which everyone else drew back.

And because she was practical, she decided it was up to her to remedy the situation. She tried to interest Charles Falconer in writing music for Lili, sure that such stimulus would provoke her into dancing once more. When he refused (a polite little note delivered by hand regretting his inability to undertake the commission), she set herself to think again. This time, she consulted Moura, who had ideas of her own.

When Moura first suggested the trip Lili had not taken her seriously.

'You'll have a wonderful time. You don't want me with you.'

Moura had said, uncharacteristically aggressive, 'I wouldn't have asked you if that was the case. You know I hate travelling alone, and this is a long journey. Besides, you've never been to Europe: it'd be a wonderful experience for both of us.'

Lili shook her head.

'You're going to Spain to work. I'd just be hanging about theatres.'

Moura made a grimace.

'I am going as last-minute stand-in for a dancer with an injured tendon, with a company I don't know and a director I worked with years ago.' She did not add, *And I only accepted because I wanted to get you away from here.* Instead, she said, 'And I could do with your support.' She paused, and when Lili showed no signs of acquiescing, she said, pointedly, 'As you had mine when you went to New York.'

'Ah,' said Lili. And after a moment, 'Where will you be going, exactly?'

'All over, Barcelona. Toledo. Zaragoza. Granada . . .'

Lili giggled. 'All right, you can stop. The answer's yes. Of course.'

It had been surprisingly cold all across France, and after they left Biarritz they faced the prospect of a night sitting up in a carriage with quilted footwarmers their only luxury. In pale moonlight the train ran across the high bare Sierras and early dawn revealed the desolate tawny plateau of Aragon. It was midday before they reached Zaragoza, and nothing had ever tasted better than the goats' milk and pastries on which they lunched at a café in the old town, in a sunny square beneath the Gothic cathedral. Moura and Lili stared fascinated at the women in their bright skirts and scarves, the men in short black velvet breeches, slashed to reveal coloured inserts, worn over white stockings and topped with slash-sleeved jackets.

Afterwards they took an old-fashioned diligence to the Calle de Don Jaime Primero, where the English touring company with whom Moura was to dance were appearing at the Teatro Principal. It was siesta time, pantomimed the ancient woman who was painstakingly rubbing the dark wood panelling, pillowing her cheek in a gnarled hand. They would be back – she circled a forefinger – in three hours.

Florence Hartsilver and Judith Mendoza had already warned them that they must on no account stay in second class hotels, where sanitary arrangements were sure to be abominable. Even in some good establishments, Florence had added, the bedroom equipment would be inadequate for the most moderate requirements. So it was in some trepidation that they booked themselves into the largest hotel they could find – no more than a big house by European standards – and unpacked their clothes.

'I hope we don't need any of this stuff,' Lili observed, putting on a shelf the medical cornucopia Judith had insisted they take: Hoffman's drops and quinine pills for feverish attacks, rhubarb and tincture of opium.

'This is still a very primitive country.' Moura was leaning out of their window, staring across the flat red roofs. 'Did you see the women begging by the station, the flies on the babies' eyes?'

'Judith said nothing should ever be given to children, but that little boy in the ticket office looked so hungry. I don't think I'll ever get used to them.'

Lili found, over the next weeks, that the beggars of Spain were impossible to avoid. She spent most evenings in the theatre, for performances continued until midnight with very long intervals, but when Moura rehearsed during the day, Lili would walk around whichever town they were in. And always it was the same. In Barcelona they clustered around her as she stood amongst the flowers of the Rambla de las Flores, and followed her through to the bird market, where songbirds hung in rough wooden cages so small they could never stretch their wings. They chased behind the electric trams, and waited beneath the double avenue of plane trees that moved in the warm Libyan wind. When she and Moura, along with the dance troupe, took the train that ran beside the sea, they stopped at numerous fishing villages along the coast and children and ragged women appeared instantly, hands outstretched.

At Tarragona, they paused long enough to sit at a platform café, the sun hot on their shoulders as they looked across at houses built of stones from Roman ruins. Lili stared beyond the tiers of tiled roofs to the sea – a shimmer of turquoise streaked with lilac. The girl from the café came out of the shade bringing pale wine mixed with Seltzer water. She wore a dark skirt and a white blouse, a white scarf bound

425

round her head. As she placed a glass on the table Moura glanced up – and looked again. She touched Lili's arm wordlessly and made a movement with her head. Lili, turning slightly towards the girl as she dealt with the wine bottles, found a face which might have been her own reflection, so like Lili did she look: the same long, liquid eyes, the same matt skin and straight nose. She smiled at Lili, clearly noticing no resemblance herself, distracted by the elegant clothes, the patina of style that Lili had acquired. Watching her hands, Lili saw with a sense of relief that these, at least, were quite different: stubby, with the short fingers of a worker and gaudy gold rings.

Before they had finished their wine, the guard came to tell them they would be leaving in five minutes. The train steamed away from the groves of aloes which fringed the sandy beach; it never occurred to Lili that centuries before, her own forebears had come to Tarragona across that brilliant sea.

By the time they reached Toledo she learned to say *anda*, go away, but the small boys to whom she addressed herself ignored her completely, and mobbed her through the narrow, irregular streets of the ancient city. In Granada, with its hedges of laurel and myrtle brought by the Moors, Lili walked through the Plaza de los Campos to the Teatro de Isabel la Catolica where Moura was dancing, and there beggars even followed her into shops, and clustered round her when she tried to order the chocolate with whipped cream which she had discovered was Spain's favourite drink: she thankfully parted with all her coppers in order to be left unmolested by the children for a short time.

It was in Granada that she learned the art galleries were usually quiet for much of the day. She started looking at pictures and began to understand the history of this powerful land where she felt herself so inexplicably at home. She discovered the ravishing Infantas of Velázquez and Goya's vivid portraits, the anguished saints and sinners of El Greco.

But it was not until the troupe reached Sevilla that Lili found her own past.

Chapter 21

Afterwards, she thought it could only have been chance that led her towards the Cathedral that particular morning. She had dutifully visited other cathedrals as they passed through each city, and although she could appreciate the magnificence she found them oppressive, with their marble floors and shrouded shrines containing holy relics – the mummified fingers, the shrivelled skin, the painted box no larger than a dog kennel into which the body of some minor saint had been carefully crammed. She would look in admiration at a silver gilt candelabrum taller than a room, and then realize that the carved figures which formed its base were not angels, as she had thought, but sinister skeletons with leathery bat wings. Or the ring of some long-dead queen would attract her, with its strange, baroque stones and then she would shudder to see they were set in the eye sockets of a golden skull.

She had been wandering in the Parque María Luisa, scented with tangerine trees, and returned to the city centre through the palmed walks of Las Delicias beside the Guadalquivir river. She reached the Torre del Oro, the gold Moorish tower, and turned up beside a high-walled building, meaning to go to the Cathedral. As she did so, a flock of filthy children erupted on the grass in front of her, hands outstretched, their handsome gypsy faces intent and determined. By now accustomed to losing these battles, Lili opened her purse, but even when she had given every piece of change she had, they still pursued her. Ahead of her, two women turned into the tall building on her left and she followed them through wooden doors into a dim arched place which seemed to be the entrance to a museum or an art gallery.

Not until she had paid and entered did she realize she was in a baroque almshouse: a plaque on the wall informed her it was La Caridad, whose brotherhood had for centuries collected and buried the bodies of men executed in the city. Alarmed at the echoes of old horrors, she hurriedly looked for an exit, but before she found it, a death mask in a glass box made her gasp. In the next room, two huge paintings of the Triumph of Death dominated the walls: the bishop in his coffin devoured by worms was bad enough, but the skeleton in armour was a chilling comment. She actually started to run, to get away, and if it had not been for the elderly caretaker who called a warning, she would have run right past the Murillos. As it was, she spent the next hour discovering virgins and cherubs overflowing with life and colour, woven of light and shadow. The urchins in his streets could have been the very ones who had earlier pursued her, their faces alive and promising, and the adoring virgins stared at their babies with a burning tenderness.

Lili was standing enraptured before a picture of Rebecca at the Well, thinking that it looked different from the others, almost oriental in its treatment, when the caretaker came to her side to explain that it was lunch time, they would open again in the evening, in the cool of the day. Reluctantly she tore her gaze from the painting, took three steps, turned for a last look. The caretaker, elderly and brown in the monks' robe of the Caridad brotherhood, said, 'You like Murillo. He is the painter of Sevilla, as El Greco is that of Toledo, and Goya of Madrid.'

'I've never seen anything like them. They're so alive.'

'He painted what he saw, the people in the streets. You can visit his house, if you wish.'

'In Sevilla?'

'Until he died in 1682, he lived at 7, Plaza de Alfaro. It is in the Juderia, the Jews' quarter: you will be interested.'

So that afternoon Lili found her way to the old Jewish area of Santa Cruz, a labyrinth of narrow streets inherited from the Moors. Like the rest of Sevilla, the brush of the whitewasher – *brocha del blanqueador* – was constantly at work here also, and every garden wall was laden with vines and wrought iron lanterns. Windows were hidden behind spiked iron grilles, but passing open doorways hung with curtains Lili caught the murmur of voices and water, and once a stringed instrument played a fragment of melody that reminded her of Beatrice.

Along the noisy, smelly cobbled streets she came upon antique shops, their gas-lit interiors glinting gold and brown, scented with leather and age. On makeshift stalls second-hand clothes lay in bright heaps, cotton, lace and satins bundled together. The next stall would be a mass of apricots, lemons, and fruits that were strange to her. She bought a peach and ate it as she walked, the juice running down her fingers. Pausing to fumble in her bag for a handkerchief, she found herself outside a building different from those around it, with a door of greenish beaten brass and coloured glass in the barred windows. Then she noticed the inscription over the door and read the Hebrew: of course, a synagogue. She glanced at her watch: it was already four o'clock on Friday afternoon, time for the evening service. Thoughtfully, she took a headscarf from her bag and tied it round her hair. Then she went up the two steps, pushed the door and for the second time that day found herself in a dim stone-floored hallway.

She looked round her: a flight of stairs must lead to the women's gallery, but she felt too nervous to walk in alone among strangers. While she was debating what to do, the street door opened again to admit a group of people. Two men in dark suits carrying prayer shawls in velvet bags over their shoulders, and a woman following a pace behind them. They all glanced at her inquiringly and she said, nervously in English, 'I wondered if I might attend your service?'

The woman stepped forward. She was plump, well dressed, exuding the air of a prosperous matriarch. She must be the wife of the older man, the mother of the younger. Lili liked at once the warm smile and the discreet gold gewellery. The woman held out a hand.

'I am Rita Senior.' Her English was oddly inflected but good. She gestured to the men. 'My husband and my son also.'

Lili introduced herself, adding, 'You are very kind.'

'Not so, it is our duty to make you welcome. Come, please.'

Leaving the men, she led the way up the flight of stone stairs, and through a doorway into the ladies' gallery. It was narrow, divided from the main hall by oblong windows supported on columns. Seating herself, Lili could see that the synagogue was higher than it appeared from outside, domed in cedar wood. There were wooden benches, and at the back a curtained enclosure where they must keep the Ark of the Law, containing the written word of God. The synagogue was divided into sections by walls with arches – again supported on pillars, striped in blue and gold – which echoed the minarets on the Moorish Tower of Gold she had seen that morning. She noticed that the walls were covered with coloured mosaics picked out in gilt; even the curves of the arches were emphasized and detailed.

Lili had never been in a synagogue like this: the whole building was imbued with Islamic culture so deeply that – but for the benches and the hidden Ark – it might have been a mosque. Only no mosque would have those shawled figures swaying forward and back as they prayed, lost to the world. No mosque would echo to the sound of swift cantillation as the men uttered in deep voices the biblical words, phrases emphasized by musical intonation handed down by oral tradition, musical motifs and rhythms prescribed centuries before.

Beside Señora Senior, among the demurely shawled and veiled women, Lili listened to the patterns of prayer. Gradually, lulled by familiarity, her mind began to wander: Simeon, Beatrice, her father – all the little anxieties and apprehensions crowded in. Until her attention was drawn back to the scene beneath her. The Reader was speaking in sonorous tones one of Lili's favourite verses:

'Thou createst day and night, causest light to recede before darkness and darkness before light. Thou causest the day to pass away, and the night to

432

advance, and divided the day from the night. "The Lord of Hosts is His name." Blessed art Thou, O Lord, who bringest on the evening.'

The next psalm began. It was one she had heard often, though here she could scarcely follow it, the melody was so full of unexpected notes. But then so much here was new to her: the way the scrolls of the Law were enclosed not in an elaborate marble and wooden Ark as in Bevis Marks, but in a richly curtained enclosure; the bright barleysugar colours of the pillars, the ornate cloths ornamenting the walls.

Under cover of the activity of the main hall below them, where the men were gathering at the reading desk, she leaned across to Señora Senior.

'Everything sounds different here,' she whispered. 'The music is wonderful, but I hardly recognize it.' The older woman smiled, and asked her which synagogue she attended, and established the girl's background. A little later she laid on Lili's arm a plump hand laden with rings.

'You must come to my house. On the Sabbath evening. I will give you the address.'

Late on the Saturday afternoon, Lili made her way to the address Rita Senior had written down for her. The pony-trap deposited her in a narrow street just beyond the Plaza de Alfaro, before a forbidding iron-studded door set in a high wall. It was the first home Lili had been into during her weeks in Spain, and she found that the unpretentious exteriors hid unsuspected luxury. Rita took her through a small vestibule, separated from a patio by a *cancela*, a heavy grating. The inner court was open to the sky built, Rita explained, to the pattern of Moorish

433

houses, and flanked left and right by an arcade. In one corner a staircase ascended to the upper floor and Lili could see glass covered galleries overlooking the court. Rita told her how in the winter, the upper floor became the family dwelling.

'In summer we live in the patio and the rooms which open off it. We have five children, two of them married, and my uncle lives with us also. We are thirteen people in this house, and still there are rooms we scarcely use.'

She led Lili across the court. Striped awnings protected it from the sun, and rugs were laid over the marble floor. Lili had never imagined such a house. In the heavy foliage bright birds whistled, and among the plants and flowers were placed sofas, pianos, tables. Mirrors decorated the inner walls, and coloured lamps hung ready to be lit at dusk.

On the far side of the court, in the shade, a troupe of small children stood solemnly round the chair of the elderly woman who was addressing them, so engrossed that they did not hear the approach of Rita Senior and her guest, who stood quietly until the story was finished. Then Lili was introduced, 'My aunt Señora Luria,' and, with equal formality, to the children, some of whom were grandchildren, Rita proudly explained, others the children of her sisters. Prompted, they all greeted Lili in turn and in English. Amazed, she said, 'I did not expect to understand you!' and they giggled, turning their dark, smiling little faces to her, so that she experienced that familiar surge of melancholy at the thought of Simeon so far away.

Rita Senior explained, 'We have family in London. In the old days, we used to visit often, but now not so much. Still, we have many visitors from England,

and it would not be courteous to forget their language.'

Señora Luria peered at Lili through a lorgnette. She commented, querulous, 'Mendoza, you say? I don't remember any Mendozas.'

Lili took a step towards her.

'Before I married, I used to be da Costa. My father is a doctor – Samuel. I know the family came from Spain a long time ago, but now some are in Holland and the rest in Cairo.'

'And your husband's family?'

Lili hesitated, then decided against superfluous explanations. She merely said, 'From Baghdad, but all the old people who were there are gone now, and my parents-in-law live in London.'

The old lady patted the chair beside her with an impatient hand.

'Sit, sit. Tell me all about them.'

Beside her, Rita Senior said quietly in Lili's ear, 'It would be a kindness, if you have the patience. My aunt's eyesight is so bad she cannot read, and she loves to recall people she has known: it is one of the few pleasures left to her.'

But Lili had already smiled at the old lady and taken that frail hand in her own and begun to talk to her in a low voice. Rita Senior watched for a moment, then nodded to herself and left them alone together.

Old Señora Luria reminisced to Lili until she had exhausted her memories and fallen into a light doze. Getting up quietly, Lili found the courtyard deserted. She followed her nose, and discovered her hostess in a stone-floored kitchen, an apron over her festive dress. She looked round appreciatively at the

435

old-fashioned copper for heating water, marble-topped tables for rolling pastry, kitchen utensils hanging in ordered rows from hooks above the massive wall-oven, exotic vegetables piled in wicker baskets. The source of the spicy, aromatic aroma that led her here stood ready in a dim pantry: circular bread rolls sprinkled with sesame seeds, little cakes of transparent pastry stuffed with nuts and dates. There was rosewater in the air, and almond oil, and a plump Spanish girl with a kerchief on her head was stirring what looked like black treacle in a saucepan.

'What are you cooking? It looks wonderful.'

Rita Senior, hands floured to the elbow, beamed at her.

'Carola is making *ouk* – that's a syrup with pomegranate juice and dark sugar for flavouring vegetables. We are going to eat these ...' she gestured at the board in front of her, '... little pastries we call *pastales*, stuffed with ground beef, allspice and fried pine kernels.' As she spoke she was moulding the *pastales*, her hands working so swiftly Lili could hardly see how she formed the intricate edging which sealed the pastry cases. 'And there will be stuffed aubergines with oregano and cheese, and afterwards *gereybes*, very delicate short-bread biscuits like small bracelets fastened with a split almond.' She glanced up from her work. 'But you should know all these things – you are Sephardi yourself.'

Lili said slowly, 'My mother died when Beatrice and I were small.' The older woman made a sound of sympathy. 'My father preferred such food, but housekeepers couldn't always manage it. And my

Aunt Florence – his sister – her husband is Ashkenazi, from Germany, so their meals are mostly to his taste. We had some Eastern dishes – *houmous, takhina* – nothing like this.'

'That must have been very sad for you – the loss of your mother.'

Lili traced a pattern in the flour with a tip of a finger.

'It's hard to miss what you cannot remember.' Always inarticulate in the face of strong emotion, Lili could not find words to explain to this kind listener that she had never been able to forget it was her fault Bella had died, that she had not been good nor loveable enough, that she had failed. She did not understand herself how much her personality had been influenced by that first experience of grief, how so much of what she did even now – particularly on stage – was seeking the love and approval of which she had been deprived.

Rita Senior watched those eloquent, agitated fingers and divined something of this. Attempting to change Lili's mood she asked, 'But your husband? Doesn't he like Sephardi cooking?'

'Joseph's mother didn't care to cook, and he preferred European dishes, so . . .'

Rita Senior noticed the past tense but was too tactful to comment. Instead, she set the plate of finished *pastales* aside.

'Here,' she said, 'put on an apron. I'll show you how to make *kibbes*.'

The table beneath the striped awning at the edge of the courtyard was laid with linen and silver, and Lili thought there must be twenty people present, while behind them a smaller table took the children.

The meal was long and leisurely, enlivened with conversation mostly in Spanish and occasional songs in Hebrew. The *kibbes* – slender pastry cases which Lili had moulded on her finger and filled with minced lamb – were highly praised, and the sun had set before they finished the last date cake, the final roasted almond.

The sky had darkened and Lili noticed that all the lamps had been extinguished. The courtyard smelled of night-scented flowers and foliage damp from watering. Lili was sitting beside Rita's husband Israel, and now he beckoned one of the smaller children over and whispered something to him. Meanwhile, Rita had brought to the table the *Habdaláh* candle with two wicks and a spice-box like a silver fish resting on its fins. She placed a goblet and a bottle of wine before her husband and all the men made sure their heads were covered as the family celebrated the Sabbath evening service.

The boy solemnly took the holder containing the long candle and Rita Senior lit it, murmuring 'Blessed are You, Lord our God, King of the Universe, Creator of the light of the fire,' and as she held her hands over the flame, everyone watched the interplay of shadow and light between the Sabbath and weekdays – the *Habdaláh*. The double wicks flamed into a bright torch and by its light Israel poured wine into the goblet and blessed it, then set it aside. He made the blessing for the smelling of spices, opened the silver fish and put it to his nostrils before passing it to Lili to inhale the timeless perfume of coriander and cloves, refreshers of the soul.

He spoke in Hebrew words Lili had often heard,

but which seemed more meaningful than ever in this Spanish courtyard beneath the stars:

'The day is past like the shadow of a palm-tree . . . O hear my voice and reject it not: open the closed gate for me, for my head is filled with dew and my locks with the drops of the night . . . I cry unto Thee, grant me redemption, in the twilight, in the evening of the day, in the black night.'

The wine that night was smooth on her tongue when Israel drank from the goblet and passed it round the table for all to sip. She watched Rita pour a few drops into a dish and turn to the boy who still stood beside her. She touched her index finger to the wine then brushed her fingertip over his eyebrows. When she saw Lili watching, she explained, 'It symbolizes the wish for wisdom and enlightenment,' and reached across the table to repeat the gesture on Lili's face, the liquid cool on her skin. Then she extinguished the double candle in the last of the wine.

The lamps around the courtyard were lit again, and two or three cigars, and the children were released from the constraints of polite society and disappeared. Conversation grew desultory and flagged, and the diners stood reluctantly to wish each other a good week. Rita and Israel escorted guests to the door and the family drifted away. Lili thought it time she took her leave. And then she heard the singing.

It was the children. They were sitting on the far side of the courtyard, under the lanterns, the smaller ones on the laps of the older girls, and one or two were asleep already, thumbs in mouths. The rest were singing so softly no one else had heard them, singing for their own pleasure a song in

Hebrew, a song she could swear she had never heard and yet somehow knew. She stood there in the shadows, beneath an awning, and watched the children's faces in the lamplight; only days before she had seen a group posed just like this painted by Murillo.

A boy was singing alone now in a pure voice that swooped and swung across the illuminated space like a bird at evening, full of little trills and sudden sad cadences that shivered the skin on her arms and caught at her heart with an inexplicable emotion: Spain was in the song, and somewhere hotter and more foreign – Turkey, perhaps, or Egypt. There was joy in it and delight, and a yearning note repeated over and over, expressing such longing that it was too much almost to bear.

Lili glanced round at the glass covered arcade where they had eaten. The table was deserted, everyone had gone. For the moment she was alone with the children. She was wearing an ankle-length dress of pale grey and beneath it, as often in summer, she was barelegged. She slipped off her soft leather shoes and moved across towards the lamplight and the children. The marble was warm beneath her feet, and the air so moist her dress clung to her in flat folds. The children were watching her and the boy, with only the briefest pause, continued to sing as Lili started to dance.

She danced as the courtyard darkened around them and the lamps burned brighter; she danced for the attentive children and for herself; she danced because that music was not to be resisted. And when the children had repeated the song twice, and the boy's voice had at last fallen silent, and Lili had as always stopped with her arms at her sides, in a pose

440

of complete simplicity, there was the sound of a pair of hands clapping from the gallery above.

They all looked up – the children expectant, Lili embarrassed – to see an elderly man she had vaguely noticed somewhere at the table during dinner. She took a step back, into the shadows, furious at having been seen by an adult. She found her shoes and slipped them on, smoothed her hair self-consciously and went to thank the children.

'You sang beautifully,' she said, and the boy who had sung solo stood up politely.

'You dance beautifully. My sister would like to dance like you.' He paused, inquisitiveness getting the better of politeness. 'Are you a real dancer?'

'I used to be. Not any more.'

'Why not?' The boy was too young to be tactful.

'Oh, something spoiled it for me, and I just stopped.' She added, to change the subject, 'What was the song called?'

'It is the song at midnight.' The elderly man had crossed the courtyard so quietly in his indoor shoes they had not heard him. The boy ran to his side.

'Uncle Manassah taught it to us,' he said proudly, as the man slipped an affectionate arm across his shoulders. 'It's a very old song. Older than him, even.'

Uncle Manassah smiled at Lili.

'Older than all of us put together. It was the midnight vigil of the Watchers of Dawn, a mystic brotherhood of sixteenth-century Jews. They were celebrating the moment when the Holy One enters the Garden of Eden.'

Lili listened in fascination, all embarrassment gone.

'I never heard it before – is it well-known?'

'On the contrary. It was quite neglected.' He held out his hand to another child. 'One moment, please. I must take these children to their parents, it's more than bedtime. Have you a minute to wait for me?'

When he returned, Lili was sitting on the wide stone wall surrounding a pool where plump goldfish flickered, attracted by the lamps. He pulled up a chair beside her and she saw he was older than she had thought. His eyes were a bright greenish brown, far younger than the rest of his face which was seamed and lined with concentration.

Lili's voice was eager.

'Please go on about the music.'

Manassah Luria laced his fingers across his stomach and contemplated her tranquilly.

'My niece told me you were interested in synagogue music. I expected a middle-aged lady with religious mania and a dozen empty notebooks.'

Lili giggled.

'Until Friday night, I hadn't really thought about it,' she confessed. 'I mean, we always went to synagogue on the Sabbath, to Bevis Marks in the City. Only recently, I've been less often.' She offered no explanation of this lapse and he only nodded. 'And then I came across your synagogue by accident and went in on impulse. At first, I thought it was just the same as in London – and it is, really, I understand the pattern of service, and most of the psalms I've known for years.' She stopped speaking, and he watched those attenuated fingers groping for the words she wanted. 'I heard something in the melodies that I never noticed before. It reminds me – no, it's like something I once knew, years ago . . .' She held out her hand palm upward, with an expressive little shrug. 'Am I making any sense?'

442

'Some.' He leaned back in his chair. 'I take it your interest in music stems from your dancing?'

Taken aback, she said defensively, 'I used to dance. I don't any more.'

'Why? Are you ill?'

She stared at him, and he noticed her eyes were lustrous in the lamplight: truth showed in the eyes.

'No. I stopped for . . . private reasons.'

'And you danced to what sort of music, may I ask?'

She thought that in someone else, such curiosity would be offensive. In this courteous, civilized man it seemed no more than kindly interest.

'At first,' she said, 'it was to real composers.' He lifted his eyebrows and she elaborated. 'Rimsky-Korsakov. Richard Strauss. Stravinsky. They were what I liked. Then I suppose there were pressures – people wanted me to use something easier, popular music. So I did. But I was never happy about it.'

'Pressures. Then you were not an amateur.'

'No. In England, I had little success. More in America.'

He brought himself back into an upright position.

'My interest, you understand, is purely academic. But even I know that a dancer does not go on for ever. What are you – twenty-three, twenty-four? You cannot have too many years before you in which to change your mind and dance again.'

Lili's head came up sharply, shocked as much by the perception of his remark as its personal nature. He saw her reaction and added, mildly, 'Don't be offended. I was merely making an observation.'

Lili half-turned away from him, trailed her fingers in the dark water to hide her face: she still could not bring herself to discuss what had happened outside the Dakota Building (the fear, the

443

flowers, the blank black eyes, the muffled shot). And without doing so, how to explain why she refused to dance again? Instead she asked, to turn the conversation, 'You are a musician, then?'

'As a young man, I learned my father's trade. He made musical instruments – violins, cellos. He was most successful, with workshops here in Sevilla. I began to interest myself in the history of music – purely for relaxation, as a hobby, you understand.' He spread his hands, self-deprecating. 'As time went by it became an obsession. It took over my life. Not only the music fascinated me, but the instruments with which they made it, those people of the Bible.'

'They used the *shofar*, didn't they? The ram's horn.'

'The *shofar* was primarily a martial instrument for war-cries. It produces only two tones – the third and second harmonics – and only approximately at that. But you're right – no other instrument has survived so long in the same form. We had no way of reproducing the music of those times so that it sounded as it did then.'

'Had? You mean we have a way now?'

Manassah Luria rubbed his hands together meditatively, 'What time are you expected back at your hotel?'

'Late.' Lili laughed. 'My companion – the woman I'm travelling with – is dancing tonight, and the performances go on so long.' She paused. She could actually see the questions passing across his face, and had an odd impulse to unburden herself to him, to explain – about Joseph, and Simeon, and Beatrice. But this time he controlled his curiosity. He said, instead, 'If you are really interested in the music of the Bible, you might care to see some of my

444

work.' His voice was casual but Lili sensed it was deliberately deceptive, and it was as much to please him as out of interest that she said, 'I should like that very much.'

He got to his feet.

'Well, then, come to my workroom and I will show you *my* children.'

His room was on the upper storey. One window looked on to the gallery that ran round the inner court, the other was a long rectangle opening to the dusky street, shutters partly folded back. The floor was polished wood and in the half-light she could make out strange shapes everywhere: leaning against the walls, lying on the floor, on the high work table, propped in every corner. For one eerie moment she wondered if they were indeed children, for there was an extraordinary atmosphere in the room, a waiting. Then he turned up the light and she realized with relief that they were instruments: she recognized cellos and harps. She looked again, and saw that they were curiously shaped and carved like no instruments she had ever seen.

Manassah Luria lifted from a workbench two linked silver pipes, each twelve inches long with four fingerholes. He put them both to his lips and played a note, and then another, piercing and wild, while the left-hand pipe sounded a lower, droning accompaniment. He held them out to show Lili with a diffidence that was belied by the enthusiasm when he spoke.

'We believe from a Hittite relief and from pipes found in the royal cemeteries of Ur that the origin of pipes such as these lies within the Semitic world. The Hebrew name for them was *halil* and they were

445

played exclusively by women, on holy days in the era of the Second Temple.'

Lili took the instrument with reverent hands, and held it while he routed in a drawer for a velvet drawstring bag. He drew out what she thought at first were castanets. They, too, were silver and strangely shaped, almost hemispheric, with broad rims and a small central boss-like handle. He took one in either hand, holding them vertically, and clashed them horizontally with the clear, cool sound of bells.

'Cymbals like these were played in the court of King David by the musician Asaph. They were ritual instruments; the Hebrew word *selslim* was translated as *cymbala*. We know from Isidore of Sevilla that Jewish Sephardi women played them in the seventh century, though a smaller, cup-shaped medieval version.' He stopped. 'Am I boring you?' And smiled at Lili's breathless denial. 'Well, then, what else can I show you?' He put the cymbals down on his table. 'The combination of cymbal and drum is an ancient one and this' he moved across the room, 'was the frame drum of ancient Israel, the *tof.*' He picked up a small circular drum, its two heads covered with taut skins. 'The word was translated as timbrel. It was an instrument of the people, and it accompanied their songs as its descendants do today. Oriental Sephardi women, and those of the Yemen, play it even now. Here.' He held it out to Lili, who had put down the pipes and crossed the room to him. He showed her how to hold it beneath her arm. 'Beat it with the flat of your hand, striking each head alternately.'

She did so, cautiously at first, then faster and faster, producing a soft throbbing.

'It sounds like something purring. It's wonderful.'

'The timbrel has always been a woman's instrument in the Near East.' Manassah Luria knew his subject so well, it was as if he was speaking of yesterday, Lili thought. 'It has connections with the moon goddess of Ur and it travelled to Egypt in the wake of the slave-girl trade. Among the Jews, Miriam the prophetess took a timbrel in her hand and the women followed her with them in a dance. And when Ferdinand and Isabella ordered the Expulsion from Spain in 1492, we know that two hundred thousand Jews left the land they loved for a thousand years, and went accompanied by timbrels to meet an unknown future.'

Lili placed her hand flat over the skin to still the last notes.

'That's incredible. But I don't understand. You said these were ancient instruments – are they from museums?'

The old man smiled.

'I told you, they are my children. They are my life's work.'

'You *made* them?'

'Who else?' He reached out to the drum. 'See, you can strike the skin with fingers or closed knuckles to change the sound.'

She examined the timbrel. It was of wood, one head smaller than the other to produce a different pitch, the head itself painted in a geometric pattern. There was a fine cord attached so the player could sling it round her neck, and the single stick was a curve of carved wood. 'But if they no longer existed, how could you know how they should be made?'

Manassah Luria perched on the side of his worktable.

'I have a hundred sources. Scattered, inaccessible, incomplete. Pictures on ancient mosaics and descriptions from forgotten texts. Manuscripts so old they fall apart at a touch contain pictures. Engravings on vases found on historic sites, and tombstones. The seals of primitive rings, and the depictions on Hebrew coins. Excavations at Ashdod and Akhzir revealed incense-burners decorated with the woodwind and string instruments of ancient Israel. Numerous musical occasions are described in the Bible, and a whole array of instruments are mentioned. On a Purim jug dating back to medieval times I found an etching of the double pipes, and embroidered on a fragment of silk carpet the cymbals. But on an ivory plaque from the Canaanite city of Megiddo I found this.' He reached behind him for something wrapped in black cloth and drew out an object that Lili thought must be the most beautiful she had ever seen. It was of wood, curved and polished and heart-shaped, gleaming dark with age and care. Manassah tucked it beneath his arm, the small body pressed against him, and rippled his right hand across the nine horizontally-strung strings, the notes faint as wind in trees. 'When I had made it, I discovered another representation, on the walls of an Egyptian tomb, the same hand-held lyre played by a Hebrew musician. The resonator is of wood and the original would have used animal horn for the arms. We know the strings were thin, as I have made these, so the pitch is higher than the contemporary harp. When they accompanied dancing and needed more staccato and greater volume, they used a plectrum. To damp the strings, the left hand is used. And these, also, were instruments for women. They were played to stimulate prophetic inspiration and to calm troubled minds. Listen.' He started to play, and the room could have dissolved for all she cared, and nothing mattered but those plangent notes filtered back down the centuries.

When he was done, and the poignant music no longer stirred the air, he raised his head from the instrument and saw the look in her eyes.

'You like it?'

She nodded, beyond words.

'Good.' He laid the lyre on the table beside him and gave it a little pat. Watching him, she understood now the sense of waiting in this room: the instruments anticipating the man's hand upon them. Suddenly brisk, Manassah Luria asked, 'Have you much to occupy you here in Sevilla?'

She laughed.

'Almost nothing. The art galleries and walking. The theatre in the evening, to watch Moura.'

He hesitated, almost decided not to speak, changed his mind.

'You could come here. If you wish. If you would like to. I could teach you what it has taken me a lifetime to learn.'

Now it was Lili's turn to stare.

'Why would you do that?'

He made a rocking motion with his hand, a very Eastern gesture, at the same time drawing down the corners of his mouth and raising his eyebrows. It was so droll and so explicit that Lili understood exactly: he was an old man, he loved to speak of this consuming passion, he enjoyed her company. All this he conveyed without words, as Lili did herself with such ease. She could have flung her arms round his neck and kissed him. Instead, she held out a hand, and he took it in both his own, a light, dry touch.

'Come back tomorrow,' he said. 'I will be here.'

Moura's troupe were staying in Sevilla for six weeks, their last and longest booking. For the five that remained, Lili went day after day to the narrow street beyond the Plaza de Alfaro, and the grey-haired man who was opening to her a whole new world.

Manassah Luria had told Lili he was fascinated by the history of music, and even then he was speaking less than the truth. His passion for the sounds of the past obscured the present so that he had found no time for the ordinary pursuits of young men. He had forgotten to marry as he frequently forgot to eat, not because he lacked the appetite but there was so much to do. He was always in a hurry, in those years, always rushing to see some marvellous new discovery that would perhaps throw fresh light on his work. When, in 1896, nine-hundred-year-old manuscripts were discovered in the store-room – the *Geniza* – of an old synagogue in Cairo, Manassah Luria was one of the first to help sort the treasury of records that brought to life once more a Jewish community in medieval Egypt, and he did not remember to go home for almost three years. His family became accustomed to his increasingly eccentric ways, for they were proud of his scholarship, and for many years now he had lived happily with Rita and Israel Senior, honoured by them and adored by his numerous small relatives.

His interest in the music and the instruments with which it was made went side by side. When he saw Lili dancing so absorbed and unself-conscious on the patio that night, she had moved him for more reasons than he could name. That she pleased his eye was obvious enough, for what old man does not like looking at a pretty woman? He had been standing quietly in the gallery for a long time, smoking and listening to the children, and he had seen Rita's young guest hovering in the shadows like a moth in her grey dress, had watched as the music – *his* music – had lured her out into the light. And then she had begun to dance, and the cigarette had burned down unheeded to his fingers as he watched. It was as if one of those ancient figures over which he had pored for hours, etched on pottery, drawn upon the wall of a burial chamber, a figurine moulded in terracotta at the beginning of known time, had come to life: an Israelite princess, perhaps, a slave-girl, moving with a slow, sensual, sure grace like no woman he had ever seen.

When she had told him, later, that she was a dancer, when he discovered that for some reason of her own she had given it up, an idea had come to him. He knew the value of patience, and so he contented himself with teaching her what he knew. She proved a willing pupil and the two of them found a whole afternoon would pass in the blink of an eye as they talked of the history of Jewish music.

He explained the Yemenite tradition, one of the oldest, with their music influenced by Negro tribes, by Ethiopian and Indian music, and the Babylonian, with its input of Islamic tradition. He told her how the music of Persian Jews, sweet with sadness and mystical exaltation, had spread to Afghanistan and Bukhara. He detailed the Ashkenazi tradition,

451

seamed with song from Poland and Russia, Germany and French Rhineland and the Slavonic countries. In Morocco and the Atlas Mountains, he said, the sound was impregnated with Berber elements.

But what intrigued Lili most was the music of Sephardi Jewry. Manassah Luria spread out for her the brilliant tapestry that encompassed those first Jewish settlers in Iberia, who had left the Holy Land of Palestine to go to the end of the known world. Not content with the music only, he explained to her the history of the Jews in Spain, told how the country had once been called 'another Athens' for the physicians, scholars, musicians and diplomats who flourished there. He told how the country was the cradle of Jewish mysticism, touched on the teachings of the *Kabbalah*, the movement of profound and mystical faith rooted in the pre-Middle Ages: the formulas and invocations, the hidden names of God.

He read to her the Hebrew poetry of Spain, choosing what he thought would appeal most. He knew the poets of the golden age, like Samuel the Prince, who for twenty years commanded the Muslim armies of Granada and wrote lyrical, epic accounts of his campaigns. He translated for her the secular Hebrew poetry born in the courts of Jewish grandees, princes and administrators; wine songs and meditative poems, shaped by the stylized and powerful Arabic verse and the influence of Andalusia. But most of all, she loved the ecstatic hymns written by mystics, and the love songs. He showed her books in Ladino, fifteenth-century Castilian Spanish profusely sprinkled with Hebrew, Arabic, Turkish and Greek, written in rabbinic cursive script. Tracing the words lightly with a finger, he

452

translated for her so that Lili gradually discovered her inheritance.

Several times she accompanied him to the synagogue to hear traditional melody, the throbbing repetition of Oriental chant and the pure emotional expressiveness of Persia. Afterwards, as they walked, the elderly Spaniard would tuck her arm beneath his own and explain how secular Spanish music – Castilian hymns and folksong – had all been incorporated over the centuries with existing Jewish music to create a rare legacy. Once, listening to an evening service while the sky outside deepened towards nightfall, the cantor had sung his prayer of lamentation with such feeling that she had wept – who so rarely cried – and a woman seated behind her had leaned forward and said something in Spanish. Seeing her incomprehension, she had repeated it in English: 'The most beautiful thing we can experience is the mysterious.'

Lili was quiet that evening as Manassah Luria walked her back towards the hotel. She answered him absently, lapsed into long silences. He asked, with his now-familiar inquisitiveness, 'You are tired?'

She shook her head.

'I think you are, more than you realize. You have worked hard, these weeks. I have pupils all the time, you know, but few so apt as yourself.'

Lili turned to him with a smile for the compliment.

'I like to work,' she remarked.

'Then why have you stopped the work that is important to you? A man can die if he has nothing to do.'

'I've got plenty to do. There's my son, and my

453

sister needs me . . .' Lili stopped. *And they were both with Joseph*, her mind finished the sentence.

Manassah's arched eyebrows gave the lie to his murmured, 'of course.' In a long life he had seen much, and he knew a troubled heart when he met one. He liked this picturesque girl from London with her dark beauty, she reminded him of an ancient mosaic he had seen once in Toledo, a fragment of blue and gold paving found by workmen below the old Synagogue del Transito but older by far: the likeness of a young woman, black hair bound back by a filet, a Semitic profile, obviously engaged in some ritual dance.

He said, apparently thinking of something else, 'It is a sad fact that none of my instruments has ever been played in public except to small audiences. To other scholars, to musicians. I take them all over the world, as you know, and use them in my lectures. And quite often, they are played to informed members of the public. But the music they produce is so specialized, one could not expect them to have popular appeal.'

Lili thought of those instruments the first time she had encountered them, waiting only to be played.

'That's not true,' she protested, 'I'm sure people would be fascinated, if only they once heard them.'

'I've often considered it,' Manassah Luria admitted, 'but as I see it, the problem is getting a theatre interested in putting on such music. To have one evening, or two, would be pointless. The musicians would probably have to face empty houses. And of course, that is not the way these instruments were meant to be heard. They were, after all, made to accompany dancers.'

They had almost reached the Calle de Tetuan, where Moura was appearing in the Teatro de San Fernando. As they turned the corner they saw that the theatres had closed and the wide avenue beneath the double line of heavy trees was filled with people, chattering and gesticulating.

Lili watched them, reduced again to silence. They had clearly had a wonderful evening, she could see animation in their faces. Once, people had flocked to see her dance, had left looking like that. She felt a pang of that same envy she had experienced all those years ago in Aunt Florence's drawing room, when Nellie Melba had sung Mimi's aria and held her audience in thrall.

At her side, Manassah Luria spoke softly as though to himself, and it was only afterwards that she wondered how he could so exactly have divined her feelings.

'To possess a gift and yet deny it is to throw away a kingdom,' he said.

Chapter 22

It was four-fifteen in the morning when Charles
Falconer woke, his back and shoulders stiff and cold.
He sat up with a groan of disbelief at himself: it had
been years since he had fallen asleep over the piano
like that, his manuscript scattered about him. When
he was a student, with little order in his life, work
had mattered more to him than food or sleep and he
had often happily sacrificed both to the infinitely
greater pleasure of seeing the pile of pages grow
beneath his pen. He bent to retrieve those that had
fallen to the floor last night: it must have been two
o'clock before he had finished and he felt terrible.
He rasped a hand across his chin. But in those days,
he thought wryly, the novelty had carried him
through and youth preserved him from haggard
mornings. He'd better go upstairs, for Beth woke
early and her first act was to call a good morning to
his adjoining room.

Yawning, he stood and worked the broad muscles
across his shoulders: he needed a brisk walk before
breakfast. He turned down the gaslight – there was
no electricity yet in the house – drew the curtains
and opened the French window to the early morning
mist hinting of autumn; chrysanthemums and late
roses, the last of the crab apples and sawn wood.

He waited, listening not so much for the first
tentative birdsong as for the music which always
flooded his mind at such moments; the music of still,
green places, the music of his England. But this

time, the notes that cascaded in his head were different, evoking an Eastern landscape of pale sand and polished rock, primitive and harsh: an unyielding desert which once had yielded up an awesome god to beget the oldest religion of them all.

And he'd done it, by heaven. Finished it last night. In a flash of panic he snatched up the last pages to reassure himself he had not dreamt it. There it was, the incredible melody he had magicked out of those fragments of ancient tunes Manassah Luria had sent from Spain, carefully written down as suitable for the biblical instruments he had made. Flipping through them that first time when Leonid Gluzman had approached him, Falconer had asked, bemused, 'Why come to me? If Lili Mendoza wants a concerto to accompany a new dance sequence, surely you would do it better? This is your heritage, not mine.'

Gluzman had shrugged.

'If I only could. But I am an interpreter, not a composer. You could make something grow here, I know it.'

Falconer had stared again at the handwritten pages, the brief inconclusive scraps from an alien culture. But behind his eyes, he saw Lili dancing in Regent's Park, remembered how he had struggled to capture the atmosphere she had conjured up.

A few weeks later the instruments themselves had arrived, boxed and wrapped like babies in soft cloths against the boat journey. As always when Falconer thought of the cymbals, the timbrels, the slender pipes and above all the hand-held lyres, he wanted to shout aloud: their beauty, their simplicity, the craftsmanship and the sounds that could be conjured from them, like nothing he had ever imagined. They were the reason he had agreed to write this music for Lili Mendoza, they had obliterated all his doubts about involving himself in any way with the neurotic young woman.

When she and Moura Lemburg had shown him how they should be played, when Gluzman had assembled one or two friends and Falconer had realized just what a trained musician could achieve on them, he had been seized by excitement so he could scarcely speak.

It had been far from easy. He had started by attempting to understand the music but it had proved so foreign to him that he could not 'hear' it. He was struggling over a copy of the earliest notated document in the history of Jewish music – a chant from the Middle Ages, a religious hymn composed as an elaboration of the biblical readings from the sixth century – when he mentioned his problem to Gluzman. The Jewish pianist told him that melodies of equally ancient origin survived still in usage and that had been the key. Lili had taken Falconer several times to Bevis Marks synagogue where he sat at the back amongst the men, wearing a borrowed prayer shawl over his corduroy suit, his soft-brimmed hat at its customary rakish tilt. He listened to many services, stirred and fascinated by what he heard, and afterwards Lili would repeat to him what she had learned from Manassah Luria.

But Falconer was composing dance music for the first time and he had one thing more to learn. It was Moura who proposed that Lili allow Falconer to watch her work. At first she protested: without the music, she was only struggling with basic ideas, nothing was ready for exhibition. But Moura insisted: 'how can he understand you through explanations, through words?'

Lili had reluctantly conceded and Charles Falconer was allowed into the studio at the top of the Half Moon Street house, leaning against the wall with folded arms, his unlit pipe clenched between his teeth. After a while Lili almost ceased to be conscious of his presence as, either alone or with Moura, she sought to create – and re-create – the images Manassah Luria had shown her. Until Spain, she had thought that her dancing was her own. She had learned this was not so. An inborn skill, it had belonged to many before her: it had come to her down the years, through racial memory. She struggled now to make herself a medium for those dancers of the past, so they could speak again through her body, and she concentrated at first on minuscule detail: the whole would come later. She developed movements more stylized and angular than any she had used before, her head and limbs frequently in profile to the audience, so she would appear two-dimensional, a figure from one of Manassah's fragments of pottery. He had made her show him how she held her fingers when she danced, in an odd variation of the classic ballet position, an almost double-jointed pose, first and second fingers held close, then a gap, then third and fourth together. She had no idea why she did this, it seemed to come naturally to her. The old man had nodded slowly and told her hands like that had been carved by the Canaanites for their moon god in pre-Jewish times. The priestly hands of Judaism ('May the Lord bless you and keep you') were always held in this position, with the fingers held two and two. Depicted on antique gold Torah crowns, on hanging lamps, on ancient manuscripts, those hands were as old as man's idea of God. So now, more consciously, Lili stretched her back-bent fingers in this characteristic position.

Watching her at work, Charles Falconer discovered that the movement of a dancer's body was food for his own gift: even the sight of Lili and Moura at rest fuelled his imagination. One morning he opened the piano and played for them the section he had been working on. Lili listened to it twice, then got to her feet in one smooth flow of movement. It occurred to him she was like a flame. There were times when she flickered so slightly it seemed she would go out: she had been like that at dinner after Leonid Gluzman's recital. But now, responding to his notes, her radiance lit the whole room as she tried a series of steps. He played the fragment again and she said, 'I can't get it – is the tempo right?'

He repeated it. Faster, then slower. 'Is that what you want?'

She shook her head, danced once more without the music. He caught her pace and altered the rhythm to extend the pauses. This time, it worked perfectly, and he saw how to mould the music round her.

That marked the beginning of their collaboration and a profound change in the direction of his work. Lili showed Charles Falconer how her dancing echoed the long and sprawling tradition of her religion and her people. She could not have put it into words, could not possibly have made vocal the forces that impelled her. But her body spoke for her. Falconer found to his astonishment that Lili's dance imagination was like a poet's, it spoke so clearly, and like a poet she was able without embarrassment to disclose innermost feelings. It seemed to him

460

sometimes that the slightest gesture, the smallest detail, was a revelation of intense truth.

For her part, Lili understood that she had discovered what she had always been searching for. The music Charles Falconer was fashioning for her from the ancient Hebrew melodies was fresh-found treasure. It gleamed like gold: new harmonies, new expressions, new sound colours. And slowly, painstakingly, day by day, dancer and composer felt their way into this expressive language, her movements and his music fusing, each enriching the other.

The work absorbed them both. Lili thought of nothing else. She saw Beatrice, she played with Simeon, with part of her attention. In the middle of a sentence, of a game with the child, she would lapse into silence, her eyes fixed, lost in thought, as behind her eyes the leaping figures she had always seen spun endlessly.

Falconer, too, became uncharacteristically taciturn as the music grew in him. Gravid with the emotional weight of its gestation, he worked long hours and lost weight. Beth Falconer watched him anxiously. She had never seen him like this, so preoccupied and distant. She told herself his work was demanding, sensed more than that. Patient and uncomplaining, she did not protest when he spent long weeks in London and shut himself away with those peculiar instruments when he was home. She would hear the thrumming of the lyre if she woke in the night: it infiltrated her dreams, its soft, insistent presence like a lovely woman in her house. And like a lovely woman, it seemed to draw her husband away from her. Sensible in the mornings, she told herself she was foolish even to permit such thoughts. Only it was easier to imagine Charles fascinated by a hand-held lyre than to picture him working with Lili Mendoza. True, she had only ever seen a photograph or two of the dancer, but even badly reproduced in some magazine, those long eyes had glowed on the page. 'The Girl with the Midnight Eyes', they called her, and Beth remembered scandalous stories of her behaviour. Presumably Charles did also, but he seemed not to care. She chided herself for uncharitable thoughts towards someone unknown to her, and waited for him to complete this commission.

In the room below, her husband shut the window and reflected that he had run it close. It was already late in September and Lili's act had been booked for a three-month season from 1 November: October would have to be a month of intense rehearsal if the musicians were to be ready. He had been more than a little surprised when André Charlot had approached them for the Alhambra, though he should have realized word of their collaboration would get out. He himself always attracted public curiosity however assiduously he tried to avoid it, and as for Lili ... It was she, of course, who interested Charlot. The Alhambra was an unlikely setting for his kind of music. Huge, fashionable, the whole of London gathered there for elaborate ballets and shows featuring the biggest names in European variety, from glittering society in four-guinea boxes to the working class enjoying a night on the town on one-shilling benches in the pit. But if it was unlikely, it would nevertheless be critical. This new piece was a gamble for him: he had ventured into foreign country, he did not want to be seen to lose his way.

Turning to go upstairs, he passed the low table on

which some of Manassah Luria's instruments still lay after his work last night. He would put them in their boxes after breakfast. Without thinking he reached out to caress the honey wood of the lyre, ran his fingers lightly forward and back across the strings for the sheer pleasure of its sweet response. Lili had told him the other day how King David had hung his lyre on a tree so the wind might play it. His mouth curved into a rare smile beneath the moustache. That had charmed him as – despite himself – so much about Lili charmed him now. In the first days of working with her he had been wary. At that point, it had been the instruments which intrigued him, not the dancer: he saw her as the price he had to pay for the privilege of working with Manassah Luria's creations.

Lili had made him inexplicably nervous. Her quickness, her sudden flashes of gaiety, her lightning changes of mood to sombre stillness: he could actually see melancholy sweep over her as clearly as wind ruffling water. And then, before he had accustomed himself, she would be all movement again. A difficult woman. It had been a relief to go home to Beth, so diffident, so gentle.

Then he had arrived unexpectedly one afternoon with an idea he wanted to try for her. She had been standing in the doorway, waving goodbye to her small son who was walking sedately towards Knightsbridge, his hand clasped firmly in the Chinaman's. Before Lili noticed Falconer's presence he had watched her arm fall to her side: she had looked utterly bereft. She had seen Falconer in the next moment and visibly pulled herself together.

Another time, when he had found her particularly bewildering as she rehearsed, he had been grateful

463

when a woman came into the attic studio. Normally no one entered when they were working, but this time Lili was evidently delighted. She had put her arms round the silvery blonde, and talked quietly to her in a voice he had never heard her use, vibrant with tenderness. The woman had not spoken, but laid her head for a moment on Lili's shoulder in a touching, childish gesture before she went.

Afterwards Lili had said, 'Beatrice is my sister. We'll be apart for a while – she's going to my husband's house in Norfolk.'

He had been surprised both at the close relationship – they seemed utterly unalike – and at her phrase 'my husband's house'. He felt that she was more relaxed after her sister's brief visit as if soothed by her presence. Then Leonid Gluzman had told him about the circumstances of the separation from Joseph Mendoza and Falconer had begun to see Lili as a woman with an emotional life and sorrows of her own, not just the bright, brittle creation of gossip columns. So that when she asked one day about his wife, he found he was able to talk about Beth as he had talked to no one else, and Lili had sat on the studio floor, her arms round her knees, and listened intently, and when he spoke of the babies they had hoped to have, her fingers had curled in sympathy.

Falconer told himself his feelings towards Lili were protective and paternal, for she was little more than half his age. He could not deny that he was conscious of her presence in every note of the music he had just written, the image of the articulate dancer's body constantly in his head, a leitmotif to which he always returned. Nothing had passed between them that was not proper and seemly. Nothing he had not told Beth.

In her bedroom, Beth Falconer caught the ripple of lyre music and pulled the covers higher, suddenly chilled. Introspective and ill, she divined instinctively, long before he did himself, the unsought and unwelcome emotions that would beset her husband and threaten her peace of mind.

The Alhambra dominated Leicester Square like an enormous Oriental palace, hundreds of multi-coloured lights gleaming through the rain. Walking away from it after a late rehearsal, pushing her way past the crowds jostling on the pavements, Lili was soaked in minutes. When she was almost at Piccadilly it became so torrential that she turned aside into the foyer of the Criterion to shelter. Perhaps they would be able to get her a cab.

Because of the downpour, Charles Falconer had decided to dine there before catching the late train home to Bath for the weekend. He came out of the Smoking Room with a sealed envelope and, seeing Lili, hesitated. His immediate instinct was to go before she noticed him but even as he took a step back their eyes met. She, taken aback, so exactly mirrored his own reaction that he smiled instead and invited her to join him.

'Your wife is expecting you.' Lili looked anxious. 'She will have a meal waiting.'

'I'm always too late, so usually I eat on the train. But tonight I had some work to finish, so . . .' He glanced round at the orchid Art Nouveau lights of the restaurant, the marble and the gilt. 'It's a touch more civilized than railway cuisine.'

Lili did not want to hurt his feelings. She felt in

465

an odd way she knew him too well now to refuse, but not well enough to be able to relax in his company.

'Thank you. That would be very nice.'

She could think of nothing else to say, tired from a long day of rehearsal. She was half-sorry she had accepted, wanting nothing more than to get home and change out of her damp clothes. Besides, she was as usual hatless and the women in the foyer were faultlessly formal. She felt her hair: the rain had made it curl outrageously. Round Falconer's neck, over his soft corduroy suit, he wore a long muffler of Liberty silk in greens and blues. She touched it with a forefinger.

'Could I borrow this? I look too untidy for their restaurant as I am.'

Astonished, he handed it over without a word. In the Ladies' Room she rubbed her hair with a towel, folded the muffler into a narrow band and bound it round her head, the ends falling over her shoulders: she looked theatrical, but that suited her.

It was only as she walked ahead of Falconer into the restaurant with its long mirrors and the gold mosaic ceiling and heard the low buzz that greeted their passage through the tables that she realized it was the first time she had done her hair like this since New York. The Lili look had become so familiar there, and was so copied, that dropping it had seemed a good way of passing unnoticed back in London.

When they were seated Falconer remarked, 'Your reputation appears to have preceded you. And you haven't even opened in the West End yet. Now, what shall we have? Barbel or bloaters? Ptarmigan or teal? Scorzonera or truffles?'

She stared at the menu she was holding, unable to read it because her hands were shaking.

'Why did you have to say that? If I embarrass you, then I'll go.'

He looked at her across the table, head tilted back slightly, eyes half-closed as if challenging her. Then suddenly he relaxed, changed position, and she noticed again that his eyes were the intense blue of aquamarines.

'I apologize. You really don't like the publicity you receive, do you?'

She put down the menu and leaned her elbows on the table, putting her fingers together. He watched the way the tips did not meet but sprayed away like flowers. She said resignedly, 'Sometimes any public notice is better than none. In New York I wanted people to come and see me dance, so at first I suppose I encouraged it. I mean, I didn't choose my style of clothes to attract attention, but because they felt comfortable and I was happy in them. Then when I realized people were talking about them and even adopting them, I was pleased.' She gave him a brief smile. 'Flattered, I suppose. But the other things – the fight on the train, the man who killed himself outside the apartment – they were horrible.' The fingers opened and spread on the table before her, helpless to express her distress. 'And I know the people who come to the theatre because of that kind of publicity don't really want to see my dancing. They just want to see this outrageous woman.'

'And it didn't bother you to dance without your clothes.'

She searched his face, to see if he was being facetious or prurient: she was used enough to both responses. Finding neither, she indicated the dark

467

blue dress she wore, far simpler than that of any other woman in the restaurant, with no decoration but the fine platinum chain that vanished below the discreet neckline.

'The first time it happened was an accident: I didn't think about it, it seemed so unimportant. I'd never appear like that in a room, among people I knew. On a stage it's different. I can't explain – it's as though my body was a costume I'd put on, something extra like a coating of greasepaint and powder over my own self.' The expressive hands hovered over her body, protecting herself from prying eyes. She ended simply, 'So I really couldn't understand why everyone made such a fuss.'

The waiter arrived, and the business of ordering took some time. While they waited for their first course, Falconer asked if she was satisfied with the rehearsals. Lili's face lit up.

'Just to be on a stage again – it's marvellous. And the music sounds even better than I had imagined.'

'And than I had hoped,' he agreed. 'But I was wondering – can you have the lighting changed?'

She was puzzled.

'A different colour, you mean?'

'No. I was in the stalls earlier today, to make sure I could hear the pipes properly – I'd moved the players round – and when I watched you, I thought that the footlights probably suit other acts here, when the stage is full of people. But you need something that follows you round the stage. You lose half the impact you could be making.'

'Lights don't move. We could use limes . . .'

'No, but couldn't a spotlight or two be mounted above the stage where they would be hidden by the curtains? On a cross-bar?'

468

'And have a man positioned up there to direct the light!' She was delighted with the idea. 'The cross-bar would have to be strongly made – a sort of platform, and then we could kill the footlights altogether, at the end maybe.'

'Let's go into it on Monday.' He paused. 'I won't be in till late. You talk it over with the stage manager. Look.' He reached into one of his capacious, country-man's pockets, fished out a notebook and a pen, rapidly sketched his idea on the page. 'Show him this. He'll have to work out something a bit more sophisticated but that shouldn't be difficult.'

Lili watched his hand move rapidly over the paper as he sketched. The white cuff of his shirt lay on the tablecloth, his strong capable fingers held the black pen. As he moved the cuff slid back to show the surprisingly narrow wrist and the fine blond hairs on his forearm. She heard him say, 'That just about does it. I imagine we'll have to get permissions and so forth . . .'

What was he talking about? She could only see the tiny blond hairs glittering against brown skin. Mesmerized, she nodded.

'. . . no reason they couldn't complete it in a couple of days. Plenty of time for rehearsal, anyway.' He held the drawing out. She looked down at it. What was the matter with her? She could feel the back of her dress clinging to her as if damp: surely the rain had not got through her coat. The breath caught tight in her chest, though she had not been hurry-ing. He was still offering the piece of paper. Slowly she took it from him as if uncertain what to do with it, holding it carefully by one corner. He asked her a question but she could not answer, could not bring herself to look at the firm face with its high-bridged nose, the eyes like blue gems, the unhappy mouth.

She stared at the white cuff, the brown wrist with its blond hairs. Falconer was speaking, but while she heard the words, their meaning eluded her. Like someone drunk or hallucinated on opium, consciousness had narrowed down to the wrists, the hands, the voice of the man sitting opposite her.

For one week, for two, Lili hid from Charles Falconer any indication that she harboured feelings for him other than those of an amicable working relationship. She was professional, friendly, busy. When she was not practising either in the empty theatre or the studio-attic in Half Moon Street, she spent her time with Simeon. He and Doris, with two or three staff, were by themselves in Hans Place, for Joseph was still in Overstrand with Beatrice. So it was easy for her to see the child for hours at a stretch, to sit in the darkened night-nursery beside his bed. A rare pleasure, the last, and one she cherished, seeing the solid little figure beneath the bedclothes, thumb in mouth, eyes glazing contentedly as he slotted himself into sleep, the podgy fingers clasping her own relaxing as his breathing deepened, the warm curly smell of his neck as she bent to kiss him. At such moments she did not know whether to long for all those other times when she had not been there to sit so, or praise God that she had these moments. Sometimes, she did both.

Lili's delight at being so much with Simeon spilled over into everything else she did. It combined with the excitement of feeling the sequences for the Alhambra coming to fruition to make her believe that all her life had been shaping towards the night

470

when she would perform in public the dance created only for her.

Moura, the shrewd observer, noted Lili's wide, expansive, happy gestures and remembered how she had seen in the past the physical effects after she had been near Joseph. She always returned with not only her expression but her body tense, muscles contracted and tight, rigidly repressed in the presence of that critical, censorious man.

The Polish woman was sitting in the theatre one morning, a notepad on her lap, timing Lili's finale. The dancer was alone on the bare, unlit stage without curtains or orchestra, going over and over the same steps, absorbed in the drudgery of rehearsal. Moura was aware of people coming into the auditorium, closing the heavy door, waiting in the half-darkness. Lili must have been conscious of them too, from the stage, but gave no sign. A man spoke and Charles Falconer answered in that low, slightly hesitant voice which gave such weight to everything he said, as though he thought most carefully before responding. On the stage, Lili did not falter, did not miss a step nor lose her timing. But her whole body turned slightly towards that voice as a plant bends towards the light. And in the stalls, Moura exhaled softly: so that's how it was.

Seeing them together later, she decided that – at any rate for the moment – there was nothing to understand between them: no glances, no words said with extra meaning. Perhaps there never would be. Charles Falconer's impeccable morals were a source of irritated admiration in the Bohemian world from which so many of his friends were drawn. In the first years of Beth's illness, it had been generally felt he was so deeply in love with her that he

471

naturally could not look at another woman. But as the years mounted up, other opinions were voiced. Perhaps Falconer really did not care for women, despised them even – certainly his cool indifference to even the prettiest of them suggested this. Moura, though, did not believe it, knowing from her own experience that for anyone who truly loved, there could be no substitution. And Falconer's face – the mobile lips that curved so sadly down, the strong sensual features – it was a complex face, but never an unfeeling one. She had said as much to Lili soon after he had started watching them work at the house in Half Moon Street, and Lili had looked at her in surprise.

'But it's easy to understand him,' she had said. 'Just listen to his music. *That's* what he is – the way he behaves is just something on top.'

Watching the two of them discussing the last movement, Moura thought again, as she often had before, that Lili had no decorous mask with which to protect herself. She showed every emotion – she was doing so now, her face glowing with feeling as she gesticulated. It was what made her the artist she was. And Falconer had the same gift, he was able to give a clear and ringing voice to passions that found a response in everyone who heard his music. Maybe his circumstances had imposed a mask upon him, so that he appeared aloof, remote. But beneath it, he was like Lili.

Moura went off to buy some fruit, unaccountably apprehensive.

On the last Monday in October, Lili received two letters. The first she read carefully and then folded and put back into its envelope, tucking it out of

472

sight at the back of a drawer: she did not need to read it again, she would remember every word. It came from her father's solicitor, Woolf Lander, and told her that her husband's solicitors, acting on his instructions, had again confirmed that their client would not countenance releasing her from their marriage. Nor, at present, would he permit Simeon to return to her.

Lili wished her father would come home, so she could talk to him. The second letter had told her of his decision to remain in Egypt until the spring. 'I cannot face winter in London,' he wrote. 'I am staying in the family house on the Nile. I sit much of the day on a terrace among marble pillars watching the water-traffic and drinking Turkish coffee. I feel better than I have in years. My only concern is Beatrice's welfare and Joseph assures me she is well.'

She finished the Matte tea sweetened with honey and the fruit which was all she ate at breakfast and went to the Alhambra. The cleaning women let her in without comment, she changed into her practice tunic and went on to the unlit stage.

Alone in the dimness she eddied over the boards in agony of mind. She would never be free of Joseph, she was sure of it. He did not want her, he would not release her. And Simeon was his also, to keep from her if he so wished. The letter from Lander had stated it clearly: if she appeared on the stage in London, Joseph would not consent to the child living in her care.

She knew she could not acquiesce. For a husband to expect obedience from his wife was one thing, to exact it after separation was unsupportable. She stared across the proscenium into the empty stalls

473

and galleries, imagining them full of people. If she gave this up, what had she left? She might be allowed to have Simeon. Or perhaps Joseph would find another excuse to refuse.

Somewhere outside she heard a door open and slam, then footsteps backstage. It must be ten o'clock. She went back to her dressing room and lay down until the musicians were ready. She tried to relax but anxiety had taken a grip of her body so she could not keep still. The rehearsal went badly: for once she was unable to concentrate and afterwards Moura said rather than asked, 'You've heard from Joseph.'

'He won't let me have Simeon.'

Moura shook her head. That they had both expected it was no consolation.

'Get dressed,' she said, 'and we'll have lunch in the park.'

As they walked back from St James's it started to rain, huge drops that soaked them both in minutes. A cruising cab picked them up and took Moura to the Bond Street studio where she held her Monday class, then cut through the back streets to Leicester Square for Lili's afternoon rehearsal. On the corner of Savile Row the cabbie swore at the sight of a horse-drawn delivery van which had lost a wheel and slewed round to block their entrance to Vigo Street, and after five minutes Lili could have done the same. It had turned cold and she had left Half Moon Street at such speed she had forgotten to put on one of her flowing wool capes over her dress of cream frieze and the material was unpleasantly clammy. She took off one of her soft leather boots with a grimace, the sole was soaking.

A tap at the window made her look up and she

felt herself flush as she opened the door. Charles Falconer climbed in.

'Don't say anything,' she warned him. He took in her state and laughed.

'Oh dear,' he said, 'oh dear. You do rather make a habit of this.' A look of concern crossed his face.

'You look terribly cold. There should be a rug somewhere.'

'It's dirty.'

'So it is. Never mind.'

Without any warning, he put an arm round her shoulders. He had never touched her before. For a moment she leaned away from him, towards the far door: it meant nothing, it was only to keep her warm. The cab lurched and she was jerked sideways. She fell against him, and buried her face in his coat, feeling the bumpy texture of corduroy against her lips. Blotting out everything.

Above her, Charles Falconer sat as if petrified. He put a hesitant hand on the wet curling hair that was all he could see of Lili.

'Look at me.' He spoke quietly, she did not stir.

'You must look at me,' he insisted, 'I must know.'

With a sigh she sat upright, leaned back against the worn leather seat. She did as he wished, and the last trace of amusement vanished from his eyes as he read her expression. He took his arm from her shoulders, horrified and touched at the same time. Neither by word nor deed had he indicated his awakening interest in her. And never for a single moment had it occurred to him that she might reciprocate his feelings. She was so young – hardly more than a girl. There were no words to express the pride and dismay her silent declaration roused in him, so that he did not feel middle-aged, nor married. Tenderly, like a man holding a little animal, he cupped his hands round her pale face under the mass of hair and kissed her. For a moment his mouth on hers was light, a tentative brushing of warm lips. Then he felt her stir against him, strain upwards into his embrace and he could not help himself, crushing her against him in a joyful despair that he had never known, unable to be tender any more.

And then the cab grated to a halt.

He hurried away from the Alhambra at four o'clock as if the place were on fire. He was not needed the next day and had told Beth to expect him for a long weekend. Heaven knew he needed it, he had been working not only on the piece for Lili but on another symphony that had grown out of the hours he had spent listening in the synagogue. It was religious music, which he had never been drawn to write. Only he had a taste now for the sounds of those Eastern countries where Christianity had been born and he planned a triumphal paean like nothing that had been heard before.

On the train he tried to think about it but all the time Lili was on his mind. Not intrusively, trespassing where she was not wanted, but lightly, as if answering an unspoken invitation. He did not see her face before his eyes, as people are said to do in novels, but as he stared out of the window at the night rushing by, occasionally lit briefly by a village, an isolated house, a small station, it seemed to him that Lili was dancing on the outside of the glass, with those effortless, languorous movements that so beguiled him.

The lined manuscript paper lay unnoticed on his

476

lap as he chided himself. Such thoughts were a betrayal of his love for Beth. Disloyal. But he had never been that, would never knowingly hurt the wife who had lost her health and was now losing her youth also. They were both growing older. He had peered at his reflection when he went to the lavatory on the train, swaying this way and that as the coach rattled and bumped and in the mildewed mirror under the harsh little light there had been lines he did not recognize, deep grooves down the corners of his mouth he did not remember seeing. He had stood there a long time, holding the sides of the basin for support, staring at himself. Where has it gone, so fast? What had he done with all that vigorous youth, the boundless energy he had once taken for granted? Was this him, this man in his forties, the skin of his eyelids dark and drawn with tiredness, the downturned mouth that spoke of greater unhappiness than he ever admitted?

And if this was him, then how could Lili respond as she had in that taxi-cab caught in traffic in Vigo Street? He squeezed his eyes close against the vision of her clinging to him, supple and svelte, allure in her long eyes, a promise on her mouth.

He splashed his face with cold water and returned to his seat. And back in the old house with Beth, sitting over the long wood dining table, speaking of what he had done that week, of friends who had asked them to visit next day, he convinced himself that the moment had meant nothing to either of them, had been merely an impulse, a caprice.

Only when he lay awake, sharply aware of the pillow beneath his head, the prickly blanket touching his arm, the fierce little night-sounds of hunter and hunted in the garden, did he admit that after all these years he wanted a woman as he had never desired one before. It seemed easy, in retrospect, all the times he thought it had been hard to resist such temptations as had been offered him by other women; he had even been proud of himself for turning away from them, loving Beth as he did. But those other women had not buried their faces against his chest as if he was all they needed in the world; they had not looked at him with mesmeric eyes in whose haunting depths he seemed to swim.

This time, it was different, he was not sure he could resist. It would not just be Lili he was rejecting, he would be turning his back on youth itself, on all the loveliness, the restlessness and the wanting he had not felt those twenty years, condemning himself to the sterility of his middle years, his ailing wife, his half-empty heart.

Falconer thumped his pillow, puzzled and angry at himself. He did not understand Lili, he was not sure he approved of her, and he could not free himself from the image of her: those slender thighs, the slightly too-muscular shoulders, the curve of her body that was like a passionate sigh . . . He sat up, drank a glass of water.

And in the next room, Beth listened to his restless movements and wondered why, in all their conversation, he had never once mentioned Lili Mendoza.

'I'm too old for you. You must realize that. I'm forty-three. Almost twice your age.'

He was speaking in a low, hurried voice, a conspirator's voice, afraid someone might hear them. She had been lying on the chaise longue in her dressing room after the final full rehearsal – they opened the day after tomorrow – and had supposed she was the last person in the theatre. He had walked past her door without pausing, but she had glimpsed his reflection in the large mirror and called his name. He would not enter, standing stiffly in the doorway; she could feel him strung tighter than piano wire.

She swung her feet to the ground and got up in a single sweeping movement, the cashmere shawl floating round her. She took the four paces it needed to reach him and put a finger against his lips.

'It doesn't matter. I love you. Nothing matters.'

He caught hold of her hand, the exaggeratedly curved fingers.

'I don't know how any of this happened. It's absurd. Ridiculous. This isn't the way I behave, Lili. I'm a decent man with a wife I love, and who loves me. I don't know why I'm standing here talking to you like this.'

He gave a harsh little laugh that came out as a groan, bent his head and held her hand over his eyes, shutting out the world as she had done against his green corduroy coat. Lili looked down at the dark blond hair streaked with silver and his gesture touched her so profoundly it was as if he had thumped her beneath her ribs, bringing a huge ache she had to fill.

'We wouldn't hurt your wife. Only let me love you. Please.' She couldn't keep the desperation out of her voice. 'Please.'

He heard the appeal and raised his head, striving to make her understand.

'I've never deceived her. In all the years, not once.' His face was gaunt with the thought of deception.

'But Charles,' she realized she had never spoken his name before. 'Beth need never know. It's just between ourselves. I only want a little of you, I'd not ask you to leave her, I know you would never do that. But can't we be together sometimes, even for an hour or two?' She was struggling now, trying to make him see she would make no real demands. 'It wouldn't hurt Beth, it couldn't, if you were just a little happier. I wouldn't be taking anything from her, or alter all the years you've had together.'

He shook his head, his face stiff with sadness.

'It's no good, Lili. I can't parcel my feelings up and give out little bits here and other bits there. It wouldn't be fair to Beth, and it wouldn't be fair to you. We'd have to keep everything hidden, like a crime, we'd have to be secretive and careful and not let anyone know. That would be demeaning to both of us.'

She burst out, 'But I don't care who knows! I don't care what happens to me, if only you love me.'

Falconer took a step back. Nearer the door, away from her.

'It would be bad enough for me, but far worse for you. We live in a society which considers sexual indulgence outside marriage to be a terrible sin, and worse for a woman. You are still married, separated or not. Such a person cannot expect to be treated with ordinary respect. Unless of course she is very rich . . .' he gave a tight little smile, 'in which case everyone pretends the situation does not exist.'

He did not add the other words that were in his mind: that for his wife it would be worst of all, a public pillory before the eyes of the world. Better than most he understood the suffering of a woman whose husband was unfaithful, who had lived for years with his mother's broken heart.

Lili could hardly believe what she was hearing.

She had never felt for anyone the overwhelming emotion that Charles Falconer roused in her. All the many men who had paid court to her, attempted so assiduously to woo her – not one of them had meant anything. Beside Charles Falconer, that escapade with the clarinettist had been childish. Beside Charles Falconer, the brief episode in New York had been fantasy. Only this was real, something she could hold on to, something that would not fail her. She must not let him go. And if she had to keep her love a secret, if she had to whisper what she wanted to shout aloud, then it would be a small sacrifice.

It was pointless to talk, futile to repeat that she would never hurt his wife, that she would never bring more pain to a woman who had lost her babies as she had lost Judah. There was only one language left to her, and she used it now.

She opened the cashmere shawl like creamy wings and reached up to put her arms round Charles Falconer's neck, holding him against her naked body. He stood absolutely rigid in her embrace, as if he would put her arms away from him, step back, go. He intended to, he was about to – and then he could not help looking down at her, at her flesh fragrant as a pomegranate, and his control broke. He knelt and put his arms around her and pressed his face against the skin of her waist, and she wrapped her wings about his shoulders.

They remained very still, until Lili reached over his shoulder to push the door shut and turn the key. She whispered, 'Your clothes,' and had to do it for him, he was fumbling so, unbuttoning his jacket, pushing it from his shoulders, undoing his shirt, helping him struggle out of his braces, his trousers.

They lay down together on the floor, on the spread cashmere shawl. He did not know which of his senses was more ravished. Beneath his breast she was coral and rose. Under his thighs she was garnet and gold. To his skin she was silk and silver, to his lips honey, to his nostrils cinnamon, then musk.

The banging on the door was loud and frantic, forcing them apart to stare at each other in shocked bewilderment, hearing the voice of the theatre doorman.

'Miss Mendoza! Miss Mendoza! There's a message for you. From Norfolk. It's very urgent!'

Chapter 23

'It might be too cold now for the terrace,' Joseph mused aloud as he spread a wafer thin slice of bread with marmalade. Chan-Tu cut bread to perfection, buttering each slice first so that it did not crumble. The Chinaman moved forward unobtrusively to pour more coffee. Beatrice's cup was empty but she did not glance at him. Joseph nodded, and he refilled hers also.

The day was deceptive. Sun streamed through the window, so bright it dazzled the eyes, but there was little warmth in it. By noon it would be pleasant, but the heat of summer had long gone, and only the sea – in which Joseph never swam – retained the benefit of hours of sunshine.

Picking up his *Daily Telegraph*, Joseph glanced at Beatrice with his customary critical detachment. She looked particularly well this morning in her pale frock; since Doris was still in London with Simeon, they had brought in a local girl to help her dress and do her hair. He leaned forward and pulled her jacket straight. Even when he touched her, she did not look at him but continued to stare out of the window, a faint smile curving the corners of her mouth into contentment. He patted her velvety cheek as he rose.

'You must go and walk in the sun. In the water garden.'

The words were unnecessary since that was what

Beatrice did every morning. Like Lili, he had accustomed himself to speaking without any expectation of an answer. She gave no sign that she had heard. But in half an hour, he would see her down there, among the bronze storks and the water lilies, walking up and down, up and down. Still, she seemed happy enough. He stopped thinking about her and went up to his study: he was engaged on yet another book and there was much to be done.

Only when he had gone did Beatrice transfer her gaze to the door through which he had left, watching it with her cool blue stare in the confident expectation that soon he would come back to her. When Chan-Tu came through it to clear the table she blinked, but that was all, and he thought to himself, as he had often before, that she watched for Mister Joseph as that dog watched for her.

The dog in question lay just behind her chair. It was a white Pekingese given her by Joseph, who had chosen it with the care he accorded all his purchases. It was female, but only just; he had not wanted an animal that might breed. Although its name was Ping it never answered to it and rarely left Beatrice's side. No one could understand her attraction for it, for she never appeared to touch it, nor even to know its name.

Chan-Tu, who might have been expected to like the dog, in fact loathed it: in his mind Pekingese were Chinese Imperial animals, belonging to courts and high officials, and he still resented the rich too much to tolerate their playthings. Once, Joseph had caught him aiming a sly kick at its backside and had protested. After that, Chan-Tu let Doris feed it, or the gardener. If neither did so, he let it go hungry, as its former masters had let his people starve. He also, and secretly, thought the animal to be enchanted, ever since he had been locking up the Overstrand house late one night and had come upon Beatrice in her white nightdress, pale hair pouring down her back, standing at a downstairs window watching Ping on the lawn outside, dancing on her hind legs in the moonlight. It had been an eerie sight, confirming what he felt about Beatrice, who had somehow usurped Miss Lili in Joseph's affections, who had not even tried to save little Simeon when he fell down the steps. Chan-Tu had afterwards avoided both Beatrice and the dog more pointedly than ever.

He ignored her now, clearing the table with his back to her. When he left the room, she was still in her chair, useless as a puppet.

He did not see her again for two hours. He had been at the far end of the garden, collecting potatoes when it started to rain, and he was hurrying up towards the house. Coming through the green and gold wall of enmeshed pear and apple trees, Beatrice moved silently across in front of him without any acknowledgement of his presence, passing the small smooth hillock with its neat shrubs and the inscribed stone without a glance.

Chan-Tu stared after her, his mouth under its black waxed moustache tight with hatred. It was raining heavily now, and the woman wore only a thin coat; she appeared unaware of the water that already plastered down her hair and dripped from her clothes. Let her get wet, then. He turned back towards the house, and as he reached Judah's tiny grave, put down his basket and pressed his finger-tips together in obeisance.

* * *

485

The drenching Beatrice received before they brought her in made her so ill that Dr Craven was called out at two in the morning to attend to her fever. The quinine he prescribed lowered her temperature but afterwards she had shown signs of greater disturbance than Joseph had ever seen in her. She had appeared almost tormented, starting to her feet with her hands clapped over her ears, shaking her head frantically from side to side. For the first time in the years he had known her, Joseph began to comprehend the depths of his sister-in-law's strangeness. He wished Samuel da Costa was not in Egypt and called Dr Craven in again, who explained to them that ringing in the ears was a side-effect of quinine and the probable cause of her distress, though Joseph doubted whether she understood.

He hated to see Beatrice like this, her hair flat and lifeless, her skin blotched by her cold so that she appeared worse than plain. In her agitation she had torn the skin round her nails, making her pretty hands ugly. In the past it had soothed him to have her near but he was aggravated by her continual faint sniffing and went to elaborate lengths to avoid her. It did not occur to him that she sat for hours watching the door through which he might finally appear; only that her eyes were red-rimmed and puffy.

He wondered whether he should take her back to London, which was his inclination, and return her to Sloane Square. But she was here at her father's suggestion: Samuel wanted her to have the benefit of sea air before winter set in, for she always improved after staying at Overstrand, physically and mentally. Besides, the journey to London would lose him two days' work, not to mention the inconvenience.

He decided to let things remain as they were, but he grew increasingly irritable. Beatrice's silvery presence had always seemed to him delightful, the antithesis of Lilith's continual movement. Now it grated on him, he found her tongueless and apathetic, the face that had once pleased him with its serene expression merely vacant.

He had always thought of Beatrice as he did his porcelain: exquisite, fragile, requiring only his admiration. When he left the gallery, he did not think of his pieces left in the dark. When he shut the door on Beatrice, he did not concern himself with her feelings, for he did not ascribe any to her. Lilith's adoration of her sister had prevented her from ever telling him about that almost-forgotten day when their father had interrupted their game in the miniature garden with news of Bella's death, and Beatrice had stopped singing, robbed for ever of words. She had not referred to the times she had rocked Beatrice out of tantrums into tranquillity: 'There, there, bay-bee . . .' And Joseph, a heavy sleeper, had never woken in the night to hear the tearing sobs of the woman who was still an unhappy child.

Beatrice did not divine Joseph's displeasure since her self-isolation was too great for her to comprehend even the humanity of another person, let alone their emotions. She only knew that Joseph was not near her, that his voice, which had always been quiet to her, was sharp, that his eyes were cold. Like an animal, she sensed his antagonism, read anger in his abrupt movements and reacted as a dog does, the skin prickling on her neck. She became, if possible, even more still, like a hunted creature pressed into undergrowth. She could not help it: that was her nature.

Nor could Joseph help his reactions, which were not passive at all. As Beatrice fell day by day into the role of victim, so his manner towards her was more and more harsh. Another man might have responded with kindness to her evident distress, but it roused in Joseph the cruelty of the weak. He could not restrain the ferocity she roused in him now, any more than he had been able to control himself years before, when Lilith had fallen on the sands at Trouville during their honeymoon and he had used her as violently as he was able.

He did not recognize what he felt for Beatrice as the same emotion he had experienced then. His background, his image of himself, protected him from acknowledging that this, also, stemmed from unsatisfied desire. And he masked it with hard words. Forced into his sister-in-law's company for meals – for the sake of the staff, he could not eat dinner in his study – he had to speak to her. In the past it had pleased him to talk uninterrupted for he believed she listened to him: he had spoken of his work, of pictures, of the things that interested him. Now he contented himself with making perfunctory remarks and escaped from the room at the first opportunity.

One day, three weeks after she had walked mindlessly in the rain, she came up to his study, something she had not done since her illness. He used to like her to sit near him, he had believed it helped his work. She seated herself on her usual chair with low velvet covered arms. For a few minutes there was silence, then he heard the Pekingese snuffling along the bottom of the door. As if in response, Beatrice sniffed. Joseph said, without looking up, 'Not now, Beatrice. I'm busy.'

She did not appear to hear him. He raised his head, said again, louder this time, 'I prefer to be alone this afternoon. Please go downstairs.'

She had been gazing out of the window. She turned her head and he saw the pure profile outlined against the glass, the smooth hair. She looked her old self. For a moment he relented. Perhaps, after all, he had been harder on her than she deserved. He returned his attention to his papers and for a few minutes there was peace. He turned a page. He wrote. And then, just as his thoughts were flowing again, Beatrice coughed and coughed, unable to stop.

Joseph laid down his pen. Without looking up he said, '*Go.*'

It was a voice Beatrice had never heard. She did not know the words for the disdain and disgust it held, no one had spoken to her like that before: she sat as though riveted to the chair. Joseph got up and crossed the room towards her. He took hold of her upper arm, grasping the soft flesh in a grip that hurt, lifted her out of the chair and propelled her towards the door, releasing her with such force that she half-ran, half-fell and caught hold of the handle to save herself.

She stood with her back to him, clutching it with both hands, her breathing loud and uneven. Her head was bent, the nape of her neck absurdly slender, too frail to support the mass of pale hair.

'I don't care what you do.' He had spent enough time with her to feel the question she was mutely

489

asking. 'Go wherever you like. Do whatever you choose. But leave me alone.'

Obedient now, she pulled open the door, closed it quietly behind her. Joseph picked up his pen again and stared at the pages before him. He could hear her in the hallway, she must be standing just outside the door like a child who has been scolded. He heard her sniff and his shoulders twitched irritably. Then the sound ceased and after a few minutes he forgot her, absorbed in his work.

Beatrice went into her bedroom. Lilith's room. She ignored the wide bed with its feather eiderdown and underlay and made for the dark corner between wardrobe and wall, crouching down away from everything, arms round her knees. Eyes wide and unseeing, she rocked herself forward and back, forward and back.

She stayed there a long time. No one came to her. Lilith did not come, to put consoling arms around her and murmur baby words. Doris did not come, to speak briskly and tell her what to do. Her father did not come, to soothe her forehead with his physician's fingers. No one came. No one.

She stood up eventually and her movements were more jerky than usual, disjointed. She went down the stairs holding the rail, putting her left foot forward on each step as a child does. In the dining room Chan-Tu was laying the table for dinner and glanced up as she passed stiffly by. He noted without pity the paper-white face, the fixed blue gaze: she looked queer, he thought, but it was no business of his. He went on with his task.

Beatrice went through to the kitchen. There was always someone there willing to smile at her, give her a drink: the daily woman, the local girl who looked after her, the gardener. But the long room was deserted. She stared with equal blankness at everything: the blue paper that turned at the window, dark with the bodies of flies, the muslin-covered glass bottle on the sill in which a blackish-brown leech speckled with yellow twisted convulsively above the water, a sure sign – though it meant nothing to Beatrice – of impending storm.

She opened the scullery door, just in case, and found four young pullets, hung for ten days by the cook. She stared in fascination at the white slits of eyes, the curled claws, unable to understand what they were doing, dangling from ceiling hooks. She reached up and touched one. It swung heavily and brushed against her face, the feathers soft, bringing with it a dense, dreadful smell. She pushed it away more vigorously and a drop of blood trembled at the tip of its gaping beak.

Only it wasn't blood, but scarlet wax, fruit of miniature apple trees on a lawn of green velvet in a lilliputian garden. She started to hum beneath her breath, the tune of the song she had been singing that day her father had come into the nursery and shattered her safe childhood world. The words she heard only in her head: *Cuckoo, cherry-tree, catch a bird and give him to me.*

Still humming, she opened the door that led from the scullery into the flagged courtyard. She crossed on to the grass and started towards the far end of the garden. Then she halted. Perhaps she remembered Lilith's repeated warnings about the land beyond the wicker gate, where the cliff crumbled down to the sea. She turned and instead followed the drive to the road.

Before she reached it, Ping bounded down the

morning room steps and trotted along the gravel to her side, pleased at the prospect of a walk. When it reached Beatrice the animal halted, one foreleg raised, head tilted inquiringly, listening. Beatrice did not appear to see it and walked on with the rigid gait of a somnabulist. The dog growled softly and backed away from her. It whimpered, and the hair on its back ruffled dark in fear.

Beatrice passed out of the gate and turned left into the Louds. When she reached the fishermen's cottages a couple of gossiping women said their good-days and, receiving no acknowledgement, watched her erratic progress and glanced meaningfully at each other. A tiny boy still in skirts held out a chubby hand as she passed close by the doorstep where he played and wailed as she brushed heedlessly by him. A pony and trap halted behind her, the driver shouting at her to take care, but she took no notice and one of the Kipper grandsons, a tousled lad of eleven, had to run out and tug her dress to get her to the side of the narrow road.

The Louds ran steeply downhill now until it reached the cobbled bulwark where old Kipper had sat day after day in almost all weathers for the twenty years he had not worked. The fishing boats were not due for two hours and the beach was deserted. Old Kipper had died the month before, so there was no one to see Beatrice go down the lichened steps one at a time and toil across the sand, her skirt dragging unheeded through the rotting weeds. The sun hung low and red, the air was ominous with the coming storm.

Without a backward look, her face tranquil and untroubled, Beatrice walked into the water.

Chapter 24

Lili caught the next train for Cromer, the seven
o'clock. Falconer took her to Liverpool Street in a
cab, holding her hand all the way.

She refused to let him accompany her.

'Let me follow you down then. In the morning.'

She had shaken her head.

'No. The family will be there tomorrow. And I
must see her alone.' She had turned away from him,
huddled into her wool cloak, her face pinched and
thin. He had stood helpless; there was nothing he
could say or do. In the end he had touched her
shoulder briefly and gone, closing the compartment
door in the hope that no one would intrude on her.
He had waited on the platform for the flag, the
whistle, the surge of steam, but she did not notice
the train begin to move, or see him first walking
then running beside her carriage window.

She accomplished the change at Norwich mechanically, waited for the Cromer train on a cold platform, oblivious to the porter's attempts to make her
go into the Ladies' Room with its coal fire and water-
colours of the Fens. Joseph was at Cromer station,
the collar of his black Russian Astrakhan coat
pulled high, lips tightly compressed and skin sallow
in the weak lights of the station entrance. They
must have spoken, but she could not recall what
was said. Chan-Tu tucked the rug tenderly round
her feet ('You must be tired, lady') and drove them
the two miles across the golf-links to Overstrand,

the road potholed and puddled from last night's storm.

She had somehow expected the house to be dark, but it was brilliantly lit, every uncurtained window shining. She glanced up at her old bedroom to the right of the front door: that alone was in darkness, the curtains firmly pulled, shutters fast.

A girl she did not know took Joseph's hat and Chan-Tu tried to help her remove her cloak but she would not let him. Joseph said something to her which she did not hear for she was already hurrying up the stairs, along the corridor. Outside her room she stopped. Without letting herself think she opened the door and stepped inside. An elderly woman rose from a chair, bobbed politely and asked a question. She waited for an answer but when she received none, she went away.

Lili noticed neither her presence nor her absence. She had eyes only for the bed and the figure upon it, draped in a sheet, so flat and small on that wide space it looked like a child's. Someone had laid a single white flower beside the head. Like Ophelia, she thought.

But when she slowly pulled back the sheet it was not Ophelia she saw. It was not even Beatrice. The face was rosy in the light of the gas globe, open eyes glaring wide and empty. The lips were unnaturally red, drawn back from the teeth and partly obscured by fine froth. More bubbled from the nostrils, the long hair was matted to the head in dank ropes.

Lili dropped the sheet with a shudder. This grotesque thing was not her sister. She said aloud, 'But that's not Beatrice.'

'Yes.'

Joseph was in the room, standing on the far side

494

of the bed. He said, 'I warned you not to look at her. No one has been allowed to touch her yet.' He added in an attempt at consolation, 'She'll look better when . . .'

'*But it's not Beatrice.* There's been some mistake, it's not her. It's not her, it's not her, *it's not her.*' She heard the hysteria in her voice as if it were someone else's but was powerless to control it. Everything in the room became very small and far away and there wasn't any air. Her wrist hurt terribly so that she had to draw breath and look down at it and Joseph was holding it so tightly her veins stood out blue. It was only when she stopped she realized she had been screaming the words.

'It's not Beatrice.' A whimper.

'It is. Lilith, it is. Look.' His voice was quiet. He drew back the sheet, showing her the gold chain round the corded throat that her father had placed there, the dress she recognized. She reached out to one of the clenched hands, the skin wrinkled and sodden, pouchy to her touch. She bent closer, undeterred by the thin, rank smell which made Joseph say sharply, fastidious, 'Lilith, *don't*,' but she took no notice, carefully prising open Beatrice's poor, moist fingers. It was seaweed she was clutching, still wet in her palm, shining bright jewel green.

Lili's legs gave way and she sank down beside the bed, her sister's fingers still tight in her own. During the endless hours on the train, she had envisaged Beatrice walking into the sea, her face calm, her movements tranquil. How else could it have been, for this was her choice. She had thought painfully of the day she herself had sat in that barnacled hulk, while the same glassy Lalique sea lapped round her ankles. She had waited for it to overtake

495

her, had anticipated the rising tide. But the sea had not claimed her: life ran too strong in her for that.

But her beautiful Beatrice was different. She had no will, no apparent motivation, and the waves had been too much for her to resist. Or so Lili had thought.

The piece of emerald weed clenched in her sister's hand told a different story. Now Lili imagined with horrible precision how Beatrice must have grasped desperately for anything to catch hold of to save herself; throwing her arms above her head, groping, clutching; sinking beneath the water, rising and disappearing from the surface, each gasping breath drawing more liquid into her lungs, struggling until she was exhausted, until her mouth sank below the level of the sea, until she was unconscious. Until she was dead.

'How did they find her?' She did not recognize her own voice.

'After the storm, on the beach. The Kipper boy found her when he went out with a friend to fish by lantern light. He'd seen her in the Louds earlier – several people had – acting strangely.' Joseph took out a handkerchief and dabbed his eyes. 'Poor Beatrice, she was always strange.'

'I thought she was so happy, here with you.'

He did not look at her: she had the distinct impression there was something he had decided not to reveal.

'So did I. It must have been – an impulse.'

Lili's mind had just registered something.

'You mean that she was on the beach, in the dark, by herself?'

Joseph's sorrow manifested itself in quick anger.

'For God's sake, she didn't know! She was dead.'

'Beatrice hated the dark. It made her cry.' She was crying now, herself, weeping for the first time in all the slow hours, tears falling on to her hands and Beatrice's blanched fingers. She was filled with guilt: she should never have let Beatrice go away from her, then this would not have happened. And fear: the recurring image of loss that had haunted her for so long – the crumbling cliff, the concealing grass, something falling to the flat beach hundreds of feet below while she howled her despair – had been realized.

When she could speak again she asked, dreading the answer, 'What will happen to her now?'

Joseph blew his nose.

'We can't wait for your father to get back to England. I'm sorry. She must be buried as soon as possible. We take her to London in the morning for the funeral. There's nowhere here a Jewish woman can lie. Your aunt and uncle are taking care of the arrangements; I imagine it will be the Nuevo.'

Lili nodded. Of course, that was where her mother was buried. When she was old enough to ask such questions, her father had told her Bella lay beneath flowering cherry trees in an orchard, had let her envisage beauty where little existed, for when she saw the cemetery in the Mile End Road it had been black and white and grey, the cherry orchard long since cut down, the stones in their neat straight lines lying flat after Sephardi custom. They had done that first in Spain and Portugal, her father explained, for stability in marshy ground. And besides, the grave was only a temporary resting place.

Tomorrow she would have to stand there again and say the last prayers for Beatrice. Women were

497

traditionally kept from the graveside but she would go, she would not leave her sister alone until it was all over. Her sister. Her shadow. Her self. Very gently, Lili laid Beatrice's hand back on the bed and pulled the white sheet across her face, her actions as careful as if she were tucking a child down to sleep.

She insisted on spending what remained of the night beside her, half-sitting, half-lying in an armchair. Beatrice, who had meant more to her than anyone on earth, had left her. Beatrice, the golden thread woven through the fabric of her life, was gone. A link had broken, separating Lili from everything that had been before: her childhood, her past. Sitting there in the bedroom where she had given birth to one child and death to the other, she remembered two little girls hiding amongst the scented clothes in her mother's wardrobe; the colours of the stained glass window reflected on the floor as Beatrice danced; the miniature garden with its velvet lawn. And under it all, constantly reiterated, she heard the words from a Spanish courtyard: 'I cry unto thee, grant me redemption, in the twilight, in the evening of the day, in the black night.'

He kept his back half-turned to her as he spoke, so she could not tell from his expression what he was about to say.

'I've been thinking. All this – has upset me. And I can imagine what it has done to you. It has made me realize how very brief our lives are. No time to waste in regrets.' He paused, uncharacteristically lost for words, while she waited politely, watching the garden beyond him, the slope down to the enmeshed pear and apple trees. 'We have a son to bring up. I thought perhaps – you might return to me.'

She heard him with less surprise than she would have expected: the last twelve hours had been so extraordinary, and she was so exhausted, all her normal reactions were dulled.

'We need not – live as man and wife, if you prefer that. But we could at least be in the same house, could we not? We seemed happy enough once. We might perhaps be so again.'

She did not stir. He added, 'Lilith, please. I confess, my life looks very bleak at this moment.' He dabbed his eyes again with his handkerchief, and his hands shook visibly. 'I have missed you more than I can say.'

She was touched by his pleading: she had never heard him say such a thing before. She glanced round the room, in the house she had never expected to enter again, and when she looked back at him it was with pity. He had coped single-handed with this tragedy, he had not failed Beatrice or herself. All night he had stayed up also, and several times she had woken from a half-doze to find him sitting in the chair beside the door, head in hands, suffering as she was.

She thought briefly of Charles Falconer, and as quickly dismissed him. Whatever there was between them it would not include marriage; it might perhaps prove as fleeting as her other relationships. She no longer trusted her instincts where men were concerned. Only for Beatrice – she flinched at the thought – and for Simeon was her constancy unquestionable. And if she returned to Joseph, she would have Simeon again.

She said, trying the sound of the words, swallowing her doubts, 'I suppose . . . perhaps we could try, at least. If you want to.'

'I do, I do want to.' He came towards her and took her hand between his own, his face lit with pleasure, so that he looked as she remembered him when they first met at Richmond: the artist, the croquet expert, elegant in white shirt and trousers. 'I can't tell you what it means to me, what a relief it is to hear you say that.' He seemed to have heard her answer as a positive assent. 'Perhaps at least something good will have come of this sad business, if we are reconciled.'

Lili wondered at herself, at the unexpected sensation of relief, of something settled. The good side of marriage, she thought, the security, the certainty, the safety of being part of a family. And then an ironical little voice added, in the heavily accented English of Valentine Audry, 'Sometimes a woman is better off alone, Lilith. Not many people will tell you that.'

'We won't mention it yet, of course,' Joseph was saying. 'This isn't the time to be speaking of ourselves. But it will certainly put paid to any unpleasant rumours.'

Lili had been putting on her gloves, smoothing the kid over her fingers. Now she stopped.

'Unpleasant rumours. What d'you mean?'

A nerve twitched at the corner of his mouth. He shook his head.

'You know how people are.' He glanced away from her as Chan-Tu appeared in the doorway. 'The motors are ready. Time to go.'

* * *

After the funeral mourners were invited to the Meal of Consolation. Because of Samuel da Costa's absence – it would be three weeks at least before his return – this was at Hans Place. Lili was astonished at the number of people who attended, as she had been by those at the cemetery: she had not realized how many people knew Beatrice and loved her. The Hartsilvers were there, of course, Judith Mendoza, Joseph's parents and members of his family. But she had not anticipated that so many friends of her father would be there, and even his patients.

It was three o'clock before everyone had gone and Lili was alone in the drawing room. She could hear Simeon's voice in the nursery, and Chan-Tu busied himself clearing glasses. She might have stepped back three years, but for the mirrors draped in dark cloth in deference to death.

When Joseph came back she said, 'I must go in a minute. I need to sleep.'

He looked put out.

'I thought you were returning here.'

'Well, yes. But it will take me some time.' He was rushing her. 'I can't think about all that now.'

'Of course not.' He was all concern. 'Do whatever seems best. We'll make our plans in a few days' time.' He helped her on with her jacket. 'Now you must rest. Do you need something to help you sleep – a tisane?'

'No. I've only got' – she glanced at the watch she wore pinned to her blouse – 'two hours at most. Then I have to be at the theatre.'

'Don't be ridiculous, Lilith.'

He spoke with all the old authoritarianism, sure he alone was right.

She buttoned her jacket slowly. When she answered, she kept her voice deliberately mild.

'I don't think it's ridiculous. I have work to do.'

'You cannot possibly go on to a stage tonight.'

'I am not ill. I have not broken my legs. There is no reason why I cannot fulfil my commitment.'

'There is *every* reason. Not least of them, you have agreed to live as my wife again. You are well aware of my opinions. Naturally I expect you to give up this pastime of yours. I had not even imagined it was necessary to spell that out to you.'

She knew that voice of his, the voice he had used in the gallery that day when he told her she could not have Simeon back. She strove to keep herself calm: this was no time for argument. She took a deep breath.

'You don't understand. This is my opening night. A lot of people depend on me for their living: I can't fail them. Whatever my situation, however I feel inside, I am able to dance. And I will.'

'You can dance, after these two days?' He almost spat the words at her. 'You can dance, when you have just buried your sister?' He put a hand to his black tie, wrenching loose the knot. 'You don't care for anyone. You have no feelings, or you would have a little respect now.'

'How dare you say that. How dare you?' She kept her voice low, she didn't want Simeon to catch them quarrelling.

'You evidently have none,' he went on, 'for the dead or for yourself, or you would not cavort as you do, for all the world to see.'

'You've never seen me on a stage, so how do you know?' The retort was childish, but she could not keep it back.

'I don't need to. I know you.' He smiled, humourless. 'And I know what people say about you. No smoke without a fire, eh?'

Lili had heard enough. She moved swiftly to the door, stopped on a thought.

'Why in God's name did you ask me to come back to you?' She blinked down at the doorhandle in her hand. 'I don't believe you wanted me back at all.' She turned, scrutinizing the spare, unyielding figure of her husband as if she could wrest the answer from him. 'You couldn't, not if this is how you think of me. You were just afraid there might be talk. Gossip.' As she uttered the words, the truth of them became obvious. 'It'll be in the afternoon papers, about Beatrice. They'll print that she was at Overstrand with you, and I was not there. That's what you're frightened of.' She paused, added forlornly, 'Though I don't know why.'

Joseph did not answer. Unmoving, he stood there. Unbending, unreadable. Nothing touched him. He cared only for himself, he saw everything from his standpoint, even Beatrice's death: not once had he spoken of how she felt, how she had behaved, why she might have taken such a step.

Beside her, on a marble table, stood a Chinese baluster vase, the match of the one Joseph had in the gallery, its yellow and white flowers gleaming, so valuable that Simeon was allowed in this room only on special occasions. She reached up and took hold of it, balanced it for a moment between the palms of her hands. She caught Joseph's involuntary movement, hastily checked. He could not believe she would dare. She promised herself to remember the apprehension in his eyes.

It appeared to Joseph, in that moment, that she

was not the woman he knew at all, the mother of his child. She was Lilith, belonging to the night, with that mane of dark hair, the eyes that burned so fiercely from her pale face. Lilith, who haunted the air and the wilderness and was dangerous to children. And himself.

She was still watching him as she opened her hands and let the vase drop on the polished parquet. It seemed to fall in slow motion, turning, spinning, the exquisite surface of transparent green floated over black catching the light. Then the splintering, shivering smash and the slivers of porcelain spraying up in all directions.

'You go to hell,' she said.

The audience was audibly amused by the small orchestra which filed into the pit. Murmurs of surprise greeted the linked silver pipes, the ritual cymbals, the two-headed drums, astonishment was accorded the curved heart-shaped lyres. When Charles Falconer strode briskly out to his place on the rostrum, intimidatingly tall in evening dress, grey-streaked hair tossed back, high-nosed profile intent, a wag yelled from the gallery, 'Forgotten some of 'em, 'aven't yer, Charlie?' and humour ripped through the packed theatre. He took no notice, bowed to them all with a smile, turned to his orchestra and rapped sharply on the brass rail of his stand for silence.

For a long, calculated space he waited. His stance was menacing, feet apart, shoulders bunched. Then he raised both arms high, baton in hand. Absolutely still he stood, outlined against the heavy red curtains. Very delicately the arms came down, the baton pointed to a musician holding a pair of silver cymbals. He struck them once and the note that slid into the silence was cool as water. Another, and another, faster now as Falconer brought in the other percussionists, striking strident as marching feet. Falconer pointed the baton again and an incredible sound tore the air, a deep sustained blast that echoed off the walls, an ancient war-cry to freeze the blood. Again the great curved ram's horn trumpet was blown, the player straining visibly with the effort, cheeks distended. At the third blast of the *shofar*, the curtains parted.

Six men stood in line on the barely-lit stage, legs astride, backs to the audience, facing the velvety backcloth depicting night sky. They were dark-skinned against the brief kilts of linked metal they wore and the buckles of their breastplates, their hair was concealed by curious helmets fitted as smoothly to their heads as silver scalps.

The *shofar* sounded a sustained, quavering note as a seventh figure was glimpsed through gilded Moorish arches, helmeted in the half-light, and the line of men dropped to one knee heads bowed. A single light followed the cloaked shape across the stage, emphasizing the flowing, feline walk, the arrogant angle of the head.

In the orchestra pit Charles Falconer brought both arms down violently, swooping over the orchestra like a wave. The cellos and the great bass drum – which were the only concession he had made to the twentieth century – muttered dark threats, the row of kneeling men rose in perfect unison and moved forward, menacing and male, to engulf the cloaked figure. The stage went black.

In the glow of his rostrum light, Falconer nodded down at the orchestra. Eyebrows raised, mouth open as if about to sing, he cued them in. The baton slashed down, a swift chopping stroke. *Now*. The first timbrel-player beat a staccato roll on the taut hide and the others followed at intervals, creating a mood of stretched tension that was intensified as the lights gradually came up.

The front of the stage was occupied by the males in a semi-circle, backs again turned to the auditorium. Balanced high above their heads, on their outstretched hands, was a hieratic figure in white, symbol of a sacred order. The head was encased in silver and the arms held level with the shoulders, while the eyes were masked by the backs of the hands.

Timbrels sounded, cymbals clashed, the *shofar* bayed. With a simultaneous movement the men hurled the still shape up into the air, then stepped aside as the audience gasped. Only when she was on the stage, running backwards with swift little steps, tearing off the helmet to release a stream of dark hair, did they recognize Lili.

She wore a tunic of fabric so fine it both veiled and revealed the long lines of her body, the material gleaming with the pearly phosphorescence of fish-scales, weighted down with dozens of tiny silver discs attached to the hem, copied from the tunics of the High Priests of Judaism's remote past, in the time of the Flood.

At a movement of Falconer's baton, a phrase was repeated and Lili came forward, a beat before the melody as always, tempting, enticing, luring it on. At first, the audience muttered and rustled, eager to be outraged and scandalized, but they were hushed by Falconer's foreign, fierce notes, piercing and plaintive, bringing strange sound-waves out of the past. They recognized that he had forged music rich with the legacy of sorrow, hinting at fable and fantasy, harking back to a heritage of poetry and psalm.

The silver pipes were tremulous and haunting and it did not matter that the watchers knew nothing of the history behind that music and Lili's movements. She so perfectly expressed them that they could easily read the exultant whirlings of women after battle, the soaring joy of human love, the mystical expression of divine inspiration.

Sometimes the six youths were with her, lying prostrate on the edge of the stage as she danced solo; moving as a block, a single entity, a tribe dominated by the woman in white. More often she was alone in the dark blue space, her movements by turns savage and sensuous, imbued with excitement and the incredible muscular weight of an athlete. And there was something else, something that caught and clung to the imagination, half-forgotten, half-remembered, powerful and pagan.

Lili perfected her trade that night. She danced her grief and her passions and her loves; everything she had ever done poured into her movements. She danced for the husband she had rejected and the men she had known, and the conductor in the darkened orchestra pit below who had proved that love has many faces. She danced for the son who was withheld from her and for the child she had lost. And more than all of these she danced for Beatrice, for the sister who had been her other self, whose mute beauty so mysteriously fed her spirit: she danced for Beatrice's death.

The last passage of her performance was unaccompanied save for the plucking of a single lyre.

Charles Falconer turned down his rostrum lamp so that nothing should distract from the rapt figure on the stage bathed in the moving light, the swinging lyre of her back as she turned echoing the curve of the instrument.

Musicians and audience alike were utterly absorbed as Lili, with movements so slow she seemed to swim through water, lingeringly evoked lamentation and longing, so that tears stood in their eyes. She stretched up to defy a cruel god, every line in her body spelling grief; she sank to the ground veiled in her hair and women wept in burning cities. And for one whole breathless minute after she had ceased to move, and waited as always quite simply, arms held slightly behind her body as though she had been running, the tintinnabulating metal plates attached to her floating tunic chimed one against the other with the sweet hollow sound of drowned bells.

Charles Falconer waited for an hour and a half to see her alone. On stage, where she had beckoned him after the first curtain-calls, he had bowed and smiled and kissed her hand, and accepted the bouquets she offered him – he had not thought there were so many flowers in London in November – piling them before the footlights so he could take other tributes as they were thrust up to her. In the end, they had lowered the curtain while the audience were still cheering and shouting and stamping their feet, for it seemed they would never stop.

He had hoped to speak to her then, but it was just as bad backstage. He was cornered by *The Times* – he didn't think he had ever seen a music critic backstage before – who wanted details of the instruments and the music, and the man from the *Manchester Guardian* pumped his hand vigorously and could say only, 'What an evening, sir. *What* an evening!' Lili herself was invisible, hedged in behind a mass of admirers, posing for a photographer, signing programmes; he could hear her excited laughter.

He had gone to Beth, who had travelled specially from Somerset for the night. She kissed him proudly, and if a shadow of anxiety brushed her face when he said he would follow her to the hotel in half an hour, she did her best to hide it.

The narrow stone corridors that made up the back of the Alhambra were deserted as he made his way through them to Lili's dressing room. It was brightly lit, full of flowers and messages, but no Lili. Moura, who came in carrying yet more bouquets, had not seen her.

She was not in the props room, nor in the Green Room. He went up to Costumes but the two elderly women who were just leaving, chattering down the stairs with their bags of knitting, thought she must already have left.

In the end, in desperation, he went backstage, though he could not imagine why she would be there. He picked his way through stored flats, curtains and coils of rope and miscellaneous wires of behind-the-scenes paraphernalia. A couple of stagehands passed on their way out with cheerful goodnights. It was very quiet as he reached the side of the stage, but not completely: he might have known.

Lili was sitting on the dim stage, on bare boards, her back resting against one of her blue screens. She still wore her tunic, the old cashmere shawl was thrown round her shoulders and she had bound her sweat-damp hair in a white towel. She sat utterly relaxed as he had seen her do after rehearsal; muscles loose, legs spread wide, hands on her thighs, head back. And she was singing, softly, a song she had hummed for him once, learned in America, that men sang in their cups.

Falconer stood watching. This was the one thing Lili truly wanted. This communication, this gift she made of herself to an unseen audience was for her the single certainty.

The death of Beatrice had given him time to think. He was human enough to regret what might have been between himself and this vivid creature, mature enough to recognize that whatever he, or any man, gave to Lili, it would never be enough. For a month or two – a year perhaps – it would suffice, give her the illusion of contentment. But however desperately she wanted to love, she would not find in any single human being the reassurance she so desperately sought. Fulfilment for her was out there on the stage, emptied and exhausted, alone under the lights.

Falconer turned silently and went away. Lili never heard him. Facing the half-open curtains, the rows of waiting seats in the darkened theatre beyond, she was still singing. Not under her breath any more, but louder and louder, the *risqué* little song about a tart in the Klondike, and she was singing it about herself:

> 'But she died game, boys,
> Let me tell,
> And had her boots on
> When she fell,
> So what the hell, boys,
> What the hell!'